AUTHOR OF THE SERIES "A WOMAN OF ENTITLEMENT"

PORTION

BY **MARY ANN KERR**

THINK
WELL
BOOKS

thinkwellbooks.com

Eden's Portion

All Scripture is taken verbatim from the King James Version (public domain).

Published in part by Thinkwell Books, Portland, Oregon. The views or opinions of the author are not necessarily those of Thinkwell Books. Learn more at *thinkwellbooks.com*.

Design and cover illustration by Andrew Morgan Kerr
Learn more at andrewmorgankerr.com.
Copyediting by Dori Harrell
doriharrell.wix.com/breakoutediting

Published and printed in the United States of America
ISBN: 978-0-9891681-6-8
Fiction, Historical, Christian

BOOKS BY MARY ANN KERR

A WOMAN OF ENTITLEMENT SERIES:

Book One
LIBERTY'S INHERITANCE

Book Two
LIBERTY'S LAND

Book Three
LIBERTY'S HERITAGE

CAITLIN'S FIRE

TORY'S FATHER

EDEN'S PORTION

DEDICATION

I dedicate this book first and foremost to
God the Father; Jesus, the Son; and to the Holy Spirit,
who is our comforter and the One
who points us to God and Jesus!

I also dedicate this book to
Rosie, Rebecca, and Shari
the most wonderful daughters-in-law
any woman could wish for.
How you each do bless me

ᴀCKNOWLEDGMENTS

EDEN'S PORTION is another story that unfolded day by day. I continually give God all the praise and glory for giving me the ability to write stories beyond my own abilities. I look back on some of the things I've written and think, *Where did that come from?* My soul delights when I realize the Author of creativity is granting me storytelling ability. I cannot think from day to day what I will write. I just sit down and begin typing. It's crazy, but it seems to work!

A huge blessing to me is hearing from readers about how much they enjoyed the story or how something in the story inspired them and drew them closer in their personal relationship with God. I pray that happens.

Eden's Portion begins a few months after *Caitlin's Fire* ends. There are a few references to the previous book, as Kirk and Caitlin make an appearance toward the end of *Eden's Portion*. Beloved characters such as Liberty, Matthew, Elijah, Abigail, Diego, and Conchita are players in the story, as well as some new faces.

Donny Miller has been hired onto the Bannisters' Rancho. He makes a debut in *Eden's Portion*, but plays a major role in my next book...yet unnamed. Which reminds me.

Many of you voted for the naming of this book. I had *Eden's Portion* and *Sunrise Canyon* as the choices. Although many of you voted for *Sunrise Canyon*, *Eden's Portion* won hands down! It actually fits in line with the names *Caitlin's Fire*, *Tory's Father*, and now, *Eden's Portion*. The next book title will be something with *Cadence* in it.

I finished writing book number eight in November. It's time, I reckon, to begin a new story.

Becoming an author has been quite a journey. I am enjoying the writing portion, but marketing is another story. If you enjoy the stories, please tell your friends about them. Word of mouth is the best seller. And please leave reviews on Amazon.There are many I'd like to thank who have encouraged me to continue writing or have prayed for me.

I lived, my four years of high school, with the Rev. Allan Thompson family. Their daughters became sisters, Donna Rau, I haven't seen for years, but Beverly Geerdes and Barbara Guthrie—I thank you for your love and especially for your walk with the Lord. Thank you for your encouragement and being the special women you are.

Christmas 2015 is just over as I write these acknowledgments, and I loved the time spent with Stephen, in Spokane. David and Rosie, Peter and Rebecca, and Andrew and Shari...what fun to spend a week together! You all bless me. I am so grateful we love each other, have great times together, and that you all love the Lord. How fun that we had so much snow and could go sledding through the orchard!

A big thanks goes to Dori Harrell at Breakout Editing. She does such an awesome job of editing and has become a friend. Andrew, my youngest son, does the covers for the books, and every one of them is an eye-catching stunner. I thank you so much and am very grateful for all your help with my website as well.

I thank Allan and Karen Thomlinson, who are big fans and supporters of my writing. Craig and Karen Lange and Earl and Arlene Engle, Phil and I both treasure your friendship, enjoying our times of fellowship together.

Allen Wagner, Kerry Woitt, and Mitch Johnson, brothers-in-law who've lost their wives, my sisters, I thank you for your encouraging words and being part of my reader base...I love you!

Thank you to my husband, Phil. He's become a reader and is, at this moment, reading *Tory's Father*. He is such a blessing and a gift to me from God. Thank you for your love and patience as I get so engrossed in writing that I forget the time.

A special thanks to all my readers. May God's anointing be on your heads, and may the God of intimate love and compassion be your constant companion.

mak

List of Characters

ᴅ̄ᴇᴀᴛʜ

Death can wield a wicked blow
It's meant to bring us low.
It takes a loved one far from us
To a place we cannot go.

We say out loud "They're better off"
And heaven's our reward.
We know it's true and yet we weep.
What's left is memories stored.

The recollection of times we've shared
The love we had for them,
It bottles up and makes us choke.
We can never touch again.

We cry and mourn and hurt inside
For the loss we must endure,
For the pain of death and loneliness
In truth, there is no cure.

In saying that, my eyes look up
And suddenly realize hope.
There is the One who comforts us
Who, indeed, will help us cope.

As time goes on the pain's still there
But we find it daily, lessen.
The clamor we felt, the hurt and loss
Has dulled the pain's impression.

We sense God's love enveloping us
One day we find we sing,
"Oh death, where is thy victory?
Oh death, where is thy sting?"

MARY ANN KERR

PROLOGUE

In the secret places doth he murder the innocent:
his eyes are privily set against the poor.

PSALM 10:8b

MR. AND MRS. CHANDLER TOOK THEIR COATS from Francis
Harding. They laughed at Theo's jest as they descended the steps of their
friends' house. The two couples stood talking as the Chandlers waited for
the Hardings' stableman to bring around their carriage. The couple
hosting the party, Francis and Theodore Harding, were close friends of
Eldon and Camilla Chandler.

"Eldon Chandler, you drive carefully now, you hear?" Francis
Harding admonished as she waggled her finger at him.

"You don't have to worry—I will," he replied. "Camilla will be sure
to make me." He chuckled, and his wife laughed along with him.

"It was a lovely evening." Camilla donned her wrap as she spoke.
"And, I do make him drive carefully. He'd rather be on a horse than take
a carriage. He wants to drive the carriage as fast as he would ride his
horse." She smiled at her hostess. "But believe me. I don't let him."

Theodore Harding said, "At least there's a full moon, and you'll be
guided by it. Thank you for coming. We always enjoy your company, and
we certainly couldn't do without your jests, Eldon. My sides are sore from
laughing about that last one. Looks like your carriage is here."

"Thank you for having us," Camilla said as Eldon helped her up to the open carriage seat. "We had a lovely time. Good-bye now," she called out as they started off down the long drive to the main road. The night was beautiful with nearly a full moon. Stars twinkled in the inky blackness. The air had cooled, although the day had been unseasonably hot.

Camilla pulled her wrap closer around her neck as she turned to listen to her husband.

"Eden was out with that young whippersnapper again last night, wasn't she?" Eldon asked. "I know we haven't talked about it much, my dear, but do you like the Kerrigans' son? I simply can't see what Eden sees in him."

"Oh, I can see what she *sees* in him," Camilla replied. "He's quite a handsome, strapping young man. The problem arises when he opens his mouth. He seems to be quite open minded, and because of that, everything else has fallen out of it." She laughed at her own jest, but her husband's eyebrows creased to a frown.

"That's the rub, isn't it?" Eldon sighed. "He seems as brainless as his father."

"What do you think about Caleb?" Camilla asked. "He seems personable enough. He's a hard worker, and Eden enjoys his friendship."

"He's nice enough, but I don't care for his mother. She seems almost syrupy, doesn't she?" He turned to look at his wife with a rueful smile.

"Eldon, watch out!" Camilla yelled, seeing a body lying in the road.

Eldon pulled hard on the reins, and the carriage came to a halt.

He drew out his gun once he descended the carriage. They'd had no robberies in the area as far as he knew, but a man couldn't be too careful. All the sudden a shot rang out, and he clutched at his shoulder as Camilla screamed his name. Another, and he knew no more.

Sobbing, Camilla grabbed for the rifle. Another shot sounded.

The funeral was over. Everyone left the graveside to attend the reception, except Eden Rose Chandler. She stood at her parents' graves, mourning them, tears running down her cheeks. *How could this have happened? Who in the world wanted them dead? Why...why...why?* Questions with no answers bubbled up within her. She'd had no sleep for the past two nights as questions and remorse haunted her. The sky was seamless—no cloud marred its perfection. The warm weather was here to stay. The early June sun beat down on Eden's honey-blonde hair, pulled back into a severe chignon and held in place by a diamond-studded onyx comb.

She wiped at her tears with an impatient hand as soft gusts of wind pulled at her hair, whipping a few strands around her face. She'd talked with Buck, but he had no answers.

Sheriff Buck Rawlins of Napa could find no suspects, no evidence except the two dead bodies. He'd told her again this day that he couldn't find the shooter or shooters, no shell casings, no hoofprints. He was at his wit's end to find the perpetrators of this heinous crime. Eldon and Camilla Chandler had been a couple of his closest friends, and he mourned them almost as deeply as she did.

Caleb McHaney and Taylor Kerrigan had both wanted to stay and console her, but she'd sent the young men packing with a few curt words.

Her neighbor, Liberty Bannister, wanted to talk with her, but the press of people at the funeral had come between them. Many had driven miles and miles to attend the funeral of Eldon and Camilla Chandler. The couple had been stanchions in Napa society, well-known in San Francisco and beyond.

Eden stood now a lone figure, heartsick and grief stricken. "Oh, how I wish I hadn't yelled at you before you went to the Hardings' party. How shall I ever forgive myself?" Eden spoke to the two dirt mounds in the ground as if her parents could still hear. She fell to her knees and bowed over in grief as she cried tears of remorse and sorrow.

"Father, Mother, please forgive me. Oh, how I wish I could do so many things over. I knew you didn't want me seeing Taylor, and I reckon you worried about my relationship with Caleb. It was mean of me not to tell you Caleb and I were just friends. It was horrid of me to go on seeing Taylor simply to cause you worry." Tears of grief and remorse cut deep into the young woman's soul.

Her parents were dead, and the bitter truth was…she had no one.

CHAPTER I

But the meek shall inherit the earth;
and shall delight themselves in the abundance of peace.

PSALM 37:11

DRESSED ALL IN BLACK, EDEN ROSE CHANDLER strode out
the front door, slamming it shut behind her. She crossed the wide porch
and descended the steps with a determined stride, her mouth set in anger.

Flowers cascaded from pots lining both sides of the steps, which
usually gave her pleasure, but she didn't see them as she made her way to
the stable.

The day was gorgeous. Fluffy clouds hung low on the horizon, but
overhead the azure expanse was swept clean by the slightest breeze that
brought relief from the unaccustomed heat.

Eden saw none of it, her eyes misted by tears she brushed angrily away.

Reaching the stable, she heard a soft whicker of recognition from her
palomino stallion as he turned his head toward her. She opened his stall,
and he pawed at the straw under his hooves as he seemed to beg for her
touch. She grabbed his face and for a moment lay her cheek against his
as she smoothed his forehead.Slipping the bit into Spanner's mouth,
Eden realized he sensed her anger. He shook his head, prancing

sideways. Eden tried to soothe him, yet she herself seethed with uncontrollable anger.

She threw a blanket over his golden withers, the same golden color as her hair, and yanked the heavy material to smooth it. She lifted a beautifully tooled leather saddle off its stand, settling it comfortably on his back, buckling the hardware with shaking fingers as she thought about what had just taken place.

How can this happen to me? To have a man come here and take over as if he owned the place? Reckon he does own the place. Why in the world would Mother and Father do this to me? How could that lawyer stand there and nearly grin as he told me that a stranger now owns half of Sunrise Ranch? How could my father have left this to someone I've never even known to exist? How?

Eden stepped onto the railing of the stall and slipped her left boot into the stirrup. Once astride, she pulled gently on the reins, and Spanner stepped back out of the stall, ready for a good ride.

Once they left the dimness of the stable, Eden kicked her horse's flanks, and they were off. Sailing right over the corral fence with the ease of a jumper, Spanner, who had never been stopped by a hedge or fence, carried his mistress down the lane toward the foothills of Napa, California. Tears rained down her cheeks as the shock of finding her parents had deeded half the ranch to a complete stranger hit her in the gut.

Eden rode Spanner faster than she'd ever ridden before. The tears dried on her cheeks as the wind blew them away. She noticed the brilliance of the day but thought of nothing except the sheer pleasure of skimming over the ground. It was one of the reasons she saddled up. She knew when she stopped, the current affairs of her life would come crashing back in, so instead she concentrated on riding and didn't stop until she reached her favorite spot.

Arriving at the very top of a hill, she pulled Spanner to a quick halt. The vista overlooking Sunrise Canyon was spectacular. She had a clear view of everything from here in all four directions, and each held a calming, peaceful scene.

Eden dismounted and walked Spanner around to cool him off. He was lathered and breathing heavily. She knew she shouldn't have ridden him so hard on such a warm day and decided to remove his saddle. Reaching into a saddlebag, her hand fished around for a couple brushes.

She slipped her fingers under the straps and brushed Spanner's coat to help cool him.

When she finished, she rubbed her hands on some grass to clean them a bit and then on her Levi denims. She sat on the soft grass, wrapping her arms around her bent knees. She pulled at a blade of grass and stuck it into her mouth, chewing on the end of it while she mulled over what the lawyer had told her that morning.

The lawyer, a Mr. Hancock from San Rafael, had knocked on the door about ten o'clock. The housekeeper, Mrs. Dorothy Jenkins, better known as Dottie, told Eden she'd ushered Mr. Hancock into the parlor. Mrs. Jenkins also said she hadn't wanted to bother Eden until Gio joined her in the parlor. Mrs. Jenkins sent Dolly, one of the maids, to fetch him from the office, which was a in a wing off the stable. Eden's father had added the wing, which included a guest suite as well as a large office, to keep all the business materials together. Giovanni Coletti was foreman of Sunrise Ranch. Mrs. Jenkins told Eden once Gio was present, she'd sent Dolly to fetch her.

Once everyone was gathered in the parlor, the lawyer, Mr. Hancock, shared the terms of the last Will and Testament of Theodore and Camilla Chandler.

Tears began to stream down her face. She'd buried her parents only a couple days earlier. Having been an only child, she'd been extremely close to her mother and had nearly idolized her father. *How could Papa have done this to me? He never said a word, not a single word! Who is this Adam Brown anyway? Who killed my parents? Why? Why? Why?*

After Mr. Hancock had related his information, he'd left. Eden, stunned, had turned to Gio and asked if it was true…was it some kind of sick jest? His cheeks had reddened, and he told her that her papa had apprised him of his intentions after her parents had returned from their trip to Virginia last year. Gio told her he'd tried to talk her papa out of it, but his mind was made up. He'd gone down to San Rafael to see Mr. Hancock because he was the family lawyer and also a personal friend of Theo's. Gio told her that her father had met some man on the train and, for some reason of his own, wrote him into his will.

Eden sat and pondered the stipulation. If she remained at the ranch for the next five years, she would inherit half the property and had the option of buying this man, Adam Brown, out. Mr. Brown had to live in the house for the next five years and could buy her out. Each would inherit the same.

She thought about that stipulation again. They *could*, after said five years, buy each other out if they came to an agreement. She wrenched off her Stetson and pulled the remaining pins out of her hair impatiently. It had loosened after her ride, and she'd lost some pins. Her honey-blonde hair fell to her waist, and she wrapped it around and around until she had a fat bun once again. She thrust the few pins back into it, stood up, jammed on her Stetson, and grabbed Spanner's reins.

Think I'll ride over to the Bannisters' and tell Liberty what has happened. I need to get my emotions under control, but I cannot imagine what possessed Papa. I'm so angry I could spit.

Eden had met Liberty Bannister at a dance a few months before and had taken a shine to her. She and Caleb McHaney had sat across from the Bannisters when they'd gone in to eat. Since then, the Bannisters had been to the Chandlers' for dinner, and the Chandlers had been invited to dine at Rancho Bonito, the Bannisters' vineyard.

Eden, her chocolate-brown eyes still blazing, saddled up and climbed onto Spanner, wheeling him around. She headed toward the Bannisters' Rancho at a more circumspect pace than when she'd ridden to her hill, but only because she cared for her horse. The thought flitted across her mind that she should have told Gio where she was going, but in her state of agitation, she didn't care if she rode off the ends of the earth.

Eden rode down the long lane to Rancho Bonito, hoping Liberty was home.

Liberty and Matthew seem to be the happiest couple I have ever met—besides Mama and Papa, she amended. *Oh, how I miss Mama! I don't know if I can bear it.* Tears rolled down her cheeks, and she wiped them on her sleeve with impatience. She never cried, and now she couldn't seem to stop. *Wonder if I'll ever find someone who makes me sparkle the way Liberty does when her husband walks into the room. I've watched them together, and they seem to almost shine or something. It makes me want to be around them, whatever it is. Caleb is nice but more like a brother. Taylor, well, he's one of the best-looking men I have ever seen, but...*

The long drive was curved with grapevines stretching over the hills as far as she could see on both sides. She pulled up in front of the Rancho that looked more like a hacienda.

The roof was rounded red tile and the exterior a creamy stucco. Arches spaced themselves across its wide front and were painted a pale orange on their underside. A wide flagstone walk, or veranda, spread itself between the arches and the front wall of the house. Growing on either side of the entrance were neatly trimmed orange trees.

Eden slapped Spanner's reins on the railing and watched as they wrapped themselves around the hitching post, beginning to feel embarrassed she'd come.

She knew Bannister's vineyard was a growing concern and that Matthew had hired on more workers to care for the vines. Diego was foreman, but Matthew was owner and involved, working with his crew and overseeing every last detail. Liberty had told her that recently Matthew had hired on a man as bookkeeper to not only take care of the financial end of things, but also to oversee shipping. Rueben Stirling had come well recommended.

She saw Mr. Stirling, out of the corner of her eye, exit a small building newly erected next to the barn. She looked beyond him to the large office, containing a small apartment above it, where Reuben now resided. Eden knew Liberty had gone through Matthew's accounts and correspondence, neatly organizing everything, before they hired on Stirling. Her new friend liked things neat and tidy. Liberty told Eden that Matthew was a lot less frustrated knowing where he could find things.

Glancing back at Mr. Stirling, she saw him smile at her. They'd recently met at a dance, and she'd danced one time with him. He'd held her too close for comfort, and when she pulled back, he'd tightened his hold. She'd found a couple excuses not to dance with him when next he asked. Now here he was walking up to her.

"I was sorry to hear about your parents, Miss Eden. Please accept my deepest condolences. I feel badly for your loss. I can't say I know exactly what you're feeling, but I have also known the pain of losing a person I loved. It's devastating, and I am sorry."

Eden nodded, her eyes filling with tears. "Thank you, Mr. Stirling." She turned away, not wanting him to witness her loss of control. She took a deep breath as she walked up to the door.

There was a huge cowbell by the front door, and she rang it. It wasn't long before the door opened, and there stood Conchita, Liberty's cook and all-around help. Eden could hear the Bannisters' dog barking within the depths of the house.

"Why, hello, Mees Eden, please, you come een, and I weel get Mees Liberty. She lying down before lunch."

"Oh, is she sick? I don't want to bother her if she isn't well."

"No, she no seeck. I let her tell you why she lie down. Come een, Mees Eden. Mees Libbee, she weel be happy to see you." Eden followed Conchita into the large great room, and Conchita waved an expansive hand toward the area. "You seet there, an' I weel get Mees Liberty." She left hurriedly.

Eden didn't sit but prowled around the room. It was lovely, homey, and comfortable. The impression of natural woods and leather exuded a relaxed atmosphere full of contentment. Eden's anger dissipated. She took full measure of the room.

The floor was a smooth red-brown tile with a huge braided rug. One wall was all windows, two walls were of some kind of beautiful wood, and the fourth wall was painted a rusty red. There were end tables, a large square coffee table made of varying shades of wood, and deep leather chairs, sofa, and love seat. A narrow floor-to-ceiling bookshelf with staggered shelving held books, bibelots, and a few pictures. The rust-colored wall was short and acted as a divider to the front entry. Eden turned, hearing footsteps from the hall.

Conchita reappeared and said, "Mees Libby, she weel be here een a meenut. She say she want lunch. Haf you eaten? You like some too?"

"Yes, thank you. That sounds perfect. Do you know what time it is? I've been out riding and have lost track."

"Eet ees half past the noon hour. Funny time for a nap, huh? You excuse, please? I geet lunch ready." Conchita didn't wait for a reply but bustled off to the kitchen, from which wonderful smells were wafting into the great room.

Eden's stomach rumbled with hunger as she sat down in one of the deep leather chairs. She was not sleeping well and had skipped breakfast. This was the first time she'd felt hungry since her parents had been killed.

She no sooner sat than Liberty Bannister entered the great room from a long hall stretching to the back of the Rancho. She was a beautiful woman, and the sight of her never failed to take Eden's breath away. Winged eyebrows arched over moss-green eyes that seemed to hold an inner light. Coppery curls cascaded in a riot of beautiful color down her back. She wore a black split skirt, an exquisite white blouse trimmed with lace, and open-toed espadrilles. A large puppy galloped toward Eden and jumped up on her.

She has a figure women would kill for, but, Eden thought, *she is one of the sweetest women I know.*

"Down, Boston. Stay down!" Liberty ordered, and the puppy sat down with almost a thump, obeying with a tail that wouldn't stop wagging. Liberty smiled at Eden but spoke first to her dog.

"Good boy, Boston, good boy." She looked up with a smile on her lips. "Dog in training. Oh, Eden, I am so glad you came to see me!"

Eden knelt to pet the puppy. "I am sorry if I disturbed your nap."

"Not at all," Liberty replied. "I sometimes take a nap, but I call it a snap. It's only ten minutes, and then it's over. I don't, as a rule, take a nap, but I have lately."

Liberty walked over to Eden, who stood up.

She took both Eden's hands in her own. "I didn't get a chance to talk much with you at the funeral, but I am so deeply sorry about your parents. We only heard about it the day before the funeral. You must be devastated, Eden. I am terribly sorry. Has Sheriff Rawlins caught the person yet? Does he have any suspects at all?"

"No, I've had no word," Eden replied, tears trailing down her cheeks. "It's an unbelievable shock. My heart is broken, and now I have an added burden. Oh, Liberty, I didn't know to whom I could talk, and you were the first person to come to mind. I've always been able to talk to my mama. I could tell her almost anything."

"What is it, dear friend?" Liberty moved swiftly to take the younger woman into her arms. "What else have you to bear? How can I help you?"

Liberty held her as Eden sobbed in sorrow. "I already miss them so much, and I hate whoever did such a horrible thing. What a terrible way to die! I feel so alone." Eden pulled back and looked Liberty straight in the eyes. "Oh, Liberty," she gasped, "Papa's lawyer came this morning with a new will that Papa made out this past year. It leaves half the house, property…oh, half of all of Sunrise Ranch to a complete stranger!"

Liberty's green eyes widened. She spoke in a shocked voice. "To a complete stranger? Do you mean to tell me your father didn't know him?" She pulled a clean handkerchief out of her sleeve and handed it to Eden, who dabbed at her eyes.

"N-no, he knew him. I mean, I think he did. I don't know anything about it. He never told me a thing. Perhaps he thought he had plenty of time, or maybe he was going to have me meet the man. I have no idea what he was planning. I simply know that now for me to inherit my half of Sunrise, both the man and I have to reside *in* the house for the next five years and tend the business. After that amount of time, if one of us is able, we can buy the other out, but only if the other person is willing."

She ran her fingers through her hair, which had become loose again. "What in the world was Papa thinking? Why didn't he tell me about this? I've spent the entire morning trying to figure this out. I wonder if that man had some hold over my papa...perhaps he was blackmailing him. Maybe this was the only way Papa could get the man off his back! I am so angry at Papa for doing this to me and never saying a word about it. Then I feel guilty for feeling so angry! How can I be angry at my papa when he's dead?" Eden spoke almost hysterically.

CHAPTER II

As every man hath received the gift,
even so minister the same one to another,
as good stewards of the manifold grace of God.

I PETER 4:10

LIBERTY TRIED TO COMFORT EDEN and calm her down. "It sounds to me as if your father had a plan behind it all. Is this man married? Does he have a family? How old is he?"

"I have no idea. I know nothing about him. He's probably Papa's age, I'd imagine. I only know that my papa left half of everything to someone I don't even know. I have to deal with this, as if I haven't enough problems already. Can you imagine living in a house with a complete stranger?"

Liberty's expression seemed to become blank as she replied.

"In truth, I can imagine it. And as a matter of fact, I've done it. I'll tell you about that some other time." Liberty's eyes clouded with the memory of Armand, her first husband.

At her disclosure, Eden's eyes widened in surprise, but just then, Liberty's cook and also housekeeper came into the great room, and the conversation came to a halt. Conchita said, "Lunch, eet ees ready." She smiled and added, "You must come eat, Mees Libbee. Eet ees not good to go too long without eating."

13

Eden looked questioningly at Liberty. "Why is that?" she asked. "I'm expecting a baby. Oh, Eden, I am so happy! I'll tell you the whole story, but for now, let's go eat. Are you hungry?"

"Oh, how wonderful. A baby...congratulations. And yes, I am famished. It smells delicious!" They followed Conchita into the kitchen. "What is that smell?" Eden asked.

"Eet ees only the beef you smelling for the tacos. Eet mixed with the spices. They ees what makes eet smell so good. Come. Come. You eat now."

Boston followed Liberty at her heels, his nails clicking on the tiled floor and his tail wagging. He went over and lay down next to the open French doors leading to the courtyard. Putting his head between his paws, Eden could see that the dog had a clear view of outside as well as of his mistress.

Conchita showed Eden where she could wash up at the kitchen sink. Her hands still felt grimy from brushing Spanner down. She scrubbed with an olive-aloe-peppermint soap, which she suddenly realized came from her ranch. It was a Castile soap, and she smiled inwardly as she dried her hands. "You have very good taste in soap, Conchita," she said with a laugh.

Conchita laughed back.

"Eet ees good soap, an' I am buying eet from your business. Eet do good work cleaning, an' eet making my hands soft at the same time. I am liking eet *mucho*, Mees Eden." She smiled widely, her strong teeth white in her swarthy face.

Eden looked around the kitchen with pleasure.

It was not the first time she'd been in it, but it was beautiful, warm, and welcoming. Liberty told her when Matthew built his house, he had made it practical and utilized all of it. There was no formal parlor, no formal dining room, and everyone who visited the Bannisters' Rancho could be relaxed and entertained in a kitchen that was as beautiful as it was efficient, or in the cozy great room designed for comfort.

The kitchen was huge. Gleaming copper pots hung from a large rack over a wooden island serving as a counter and cutting board. Dominating one entire wall were windows, with a huge scrubbed oak table and chairs overlooking a courtyard. Another wall encompassed glassed French doors that opened to the courtyard. A roofed and tiled veranda, inhabited by several tables and chairs, extended past the end of the house. It was open, sunny, and cheerful.

"I remember the last time I was here with my parents. We enjoyed such a lovely afternoon and evening. You have quite a talent for entertaining. My mother said it was one of the most enjoyable evenings she could remember ever having."

"Thank you," Liberty said. She started to help set the food on the table, but Conchita waved her off and pointed to her chair, saying, "We do thees. You eet with your friend, Mees Libbee."

The two women sat down, and Liberty said, "I like to ask the Lord to bless our food."

"I know," replied Eden. "Go ahead. It's fine with me."

"Our gracious, loving heavenly Father. We thank You for this day. We are grateful for Your sovereignty and that Your ways are higher than our ways and Your thoughts than our thoughts. Please give Matthew a safe trip and enjoyable time with my brother. I also pray for You to comfort Eden's heart with the comfort that only You can bestow. May she find that You do care and You love her with an immense and measureless love. We ask Your blessing on this food and give You thanks for it. May You be honored. In Jesus' name we do pray. Amen."

"Thank you, Liberty," Eden said simply. "By the way, where is Matthew?"

"He rode to San Francisco this morning. He's spending a couple nights with my brother in the city and will return the day after tomorrow. I was supposed to go with him, but…I have morning sickness." Her eyes glowed as she spoke. "But I don't mind. I feel blessed to be expecting a baby."

"Congratulations! It's your first, isn't it?"

"Yes, it is. I thought for years I couldn't have children. You see, I was married to my first husband for thirteen years, and we were childless. I thought I was the reason we had no children. Armand died and I came west. Matthew and I have been married less than a year. At any rate, I seem to have had my share of morning sickness, and this morning I simply didn't feel like making the trip. I lost breakfast, and now I, too, am famished. I haven't been sick much this past month or so, but every once in a while, boom. One lady told me it was all in my head, and I just looked at her and said, 'No, you have it wrong, madam. It's all in my stomach!'" Eden chuckled and Liberty laughed. "Some people don't know how to give comfort and should refrain from trying, I think." Liberty laughed again.

"I'm sorry about your first husband," Eden said. "It must have been a terrible time in your life."

"The whole affair was tragic," Liberty said. "And sometime I'll tell you all about it, but not today."

Eden, not knowing if Liberty still mourned her first husband, changed the subject and asked, "When is your baby due?"

"October, I believe." Liberty grinned. "I am thrilled. I adore children, and to have one of my own...yes, I feel blessed."

"I can see how excited you are. Your face is aglow with happiness."

"I never knew I could be so happy."

"Your accent, it's Bostonian, isn't it?" Eden asked.

"Yes," Liberty answered in surprise. "Is it that pronounced?"

"Well, maybe not to some people, but I went to Wellesley."

"Did you? Why, we could have met a few years earlier, couldn't we?" Liberty grinned at her new friend. "I moved out here in December of eighty-two."

"I lived in Boston then," Eden replied, "and was going to school."

The afternoon slipped away, the two women becoming better acquainted.

Eden knew her foreman, Gio, would be worried about her, so with regret, she said good-bye.

Just as she was mounting Spanner, Reuben Stirling came out of his office, and Spanner danced sideways. She quickly threw her leg over the saddle, and with a wave of her hand toward Liberty, Spanner took off like a bullet leaving the barrel of a gun.

"What's got into you, boy?" Eden asked as she reined him in a bit. She slowed him to a walk because he kept prancing. "Was it Reuben Stirling? If it was, Spanner, I'll tell you something. You're not the only one. He gives me the shivers too."

She patted Spanner's neck, and he seemed to settle a bit. She headed for home at a good pace, but as she rode, she mused over her conversation with Liberty. *She's such an encouragement to me. Look at her, widowed and yet starting over with a new husband and now expecting a baby. I am glad I rode over there. I feel much better since talking with her.*

Giovanni Coletti came out of the dimness of the stable for the third time. He shaded his eyes from the glaring sun as he stared down the long empty drive. Removing his hat, he wiped his forehead on a kerchief he kept tucked in a back pocket. His stomach churned with nerves.

Now that Eldon is gone, it's going to be a tough job to keep Eden in line. She's headstrong in addition to the fact that she's now my boss. Anything I tell her won't be worth a tinker's dam unless she agrees with me. Eldon had a difficult enough time with her—she's so sure she's right about everything. I have no illusions as to how difficult it's going to be for me.

Giovanni had been with the Chandlers for years—even before Eden was born. Eldon had traveled to Italy when he was quite young. He'd just married Camilla, and the journey had been their honeymoon as well as a business trip. Eldon wanted to start an olive growing venture on the land he'd inherited from an uncle.

The two men had met when Eldon was touring Cavaletti Olives. Giovanni had been working the Cavaletti olive groves for several years. He'd grown up with olives and knew everything a body could know about them and then some. Giovanni had jumped at the chance to go to America when Eldon offered him a job. Eldon had hired him on the spot. Neither man had ever regretted their decision. Eldon had shortened Giovanni's name to Gio. It was a common nickname found in Italy, but an endearing one, as the two men became like brothers. Eldon would tell people that what Gio forgot about olives was more than most men ever knew about them. He was a walking encyclopedia on the subject.

This day he was dressed all in black, signifying his inner mourning. His heart ached, for he had loved Eldon deeply. He'd ridden into Napa several times in the past few days to talk to Sheriff Rawlins, but the sheriff was no closer to knowing who had murdered the Chandlers than when their bodies had been discovered.

He pulled his pocket watch out of his work trousers and wondered again where Eden had taken herself. He worried because she was still in shock about her parents. This morning's announcement by the lawyer, Stephen Hancock, who'd related the terms of the will, had been an additional blow.

I told Eldon not to do it, Gio thought. *When he insisted, I asked him to please tell Eden of his plans. He most likely thought he had plenty of time to tell her. Well, now the fat's in the fire, and I reckon we'll just have to see what happens. I can't see*

Eden kowtowing to anyone, let alone a man she'll consider her enemy. Giovanni squinted his eyes to see as far down the road as he could. There was still no Eden.

Wonder if I should go out looking for her? She wouldn't appreciate it unless she's been thrown or hurt out there somewhere. Reckon I'd better just hold tight awhile longer.

He went into the house and sat across from Dorothy, drinking a cold glass of iced tea Berry, the Chandlers' cook, had put in front of him.

"What do you think of all this, Dottie? Did Cammie tell you the plans for Sunrise Ranch? Did you know a stranger was to inherit half of it?"

"Frankly, I did. It's the reason I had Dolly get everyone else before she told Eden that the lawyer had arrived. I wanted Eden to have our support…little good that did."

"Eldon told me about it shortly after he got back from that trip last year. I begged him to tell Eden. I have no doubt he would have. He probably thought he had plenty of time."

"I've tried and tried to think who could have done this horrible thing." Dorothy started crying. "It's beyond my abilities, Gio." She pulled a handkerchief out of her sleeve and dabbed at her eyes. "I can't think of a single person who would do such a thing."

Dorothy's tears were more than Gio could bear. He felt stripped of self-control as his own eyes teared up.

"I know. I know. I can't think of anyone who would do such a *misero cosa*—such a miserable thing. I'm sure Sheriff Rawlins is sick of me riding in there to see if he's found anything. He adored Cammie, and I know this has taken him hard too."

"You're right about that. Cammie helped him through that bad patch with Jazzie. I think the man would have gone crazy if it hadn't been for her. And Eldon, my goodness, he was a rock, staying up all hours helping the sheriff get through the worst part.

"Trouble with Miss Eden is, she doesn't want our help. She's holding herself tightly together. I'm worried about her, that's certain."

"Me too, Dottie. Me too." His reply was soft spoken, and his heart was heavy.

In the late afternoon Gio led a mare out of the barn. He pulled all the nails out of one of her shoes. Working on one hoof from start to finish, he'd completed putting new shoes on all four hooves before Eden came home. He said nothing to her, but could see by her countenance she appeared a bit better than when she'd left. She was striking, dressed as she was, all in black, with her golden hair matching her horse's coat. She'd even gotten a new black Stetson. He straightened up and tipped his hat.

Eden nodded curtly at Gio but then took another look.

Seeing her own misery mirrored in his eyes, she felt a pang of remorse for not telling him where she was going. Her anger had lessened, but she felt bewildered. She'd made up her mind that the man who would share half of everything that was rightly hers was her enemy.

She slid off Spanner, and Gio reached to take the reins, but Eden said, "No, I'll take care of him. It's almost good medicine for me to brush him down. For some reason, it calms me."

He nodded. "I understand that."

"I should have told you where I was going, Gio. It was reckless of me not to."

Gio's eyebrows raised in disbelief at her comment, but he said nothing in reply. He simply nodded his head and listened closely to what she said.

"I ended up going over to the Bannisters'. I hadn't planned to when I left. I was so angry when that lawyer friend of Papa's stood there telling me about the terms of the will. Did Papa tell you he was going to leave half of Sunrise to a stranger? Did you already know it?"

Gio wanted to lie, but he didn't. "Yes," he said heavily, "yes, he did. I begged him to talk to you about it. I think he would have, *cara mio*, but..." His voice trailed off.

"It makes me so angry I could choke."

She walked Spanner into the dimness of the stable, glad the tears on her face would be hidden. She led her horse into his stall and undid the buckles of his saddle, heaving the heavy leather over the saddle stand. She removed the blanket and slid the reins over his head, removing the bit from his mouth. Spanner swished his tail, seeming to appreciate her ministrations. She scooped a big cup of oats into the manger as a treat and slipped her hands into a couple brushes.

Gio came in with the horse he'd just shod.

He said nothing but quietly began to brush the horse down, wondering if Eden had anything else to say, but the sound of brushing was all that met his ears.

CHAPTER III

He took away my birthright; and,
behold, now he hath taken away my blessing.

GENESIS 27:36b

ADAM HEARD THE CREAK of the stairs and knew someone was on the way up to the top floor of the hotel. He sat up, swinging his long legs over the side of the bed. A tap on his door brought him to his feet. He reached for his holster on the dresser and pulled out his revolver. A man couldn't be too careful. There'd been a rash of robberies in the area, and he was cautious.

"Yes, who is it?" he asked.

"You Adam Morgan Brown?"

"Who's asking?"

"US Postal at your service, sir."

Adam, bare chested, tucked his gun into his belt at the small of his back and pulled open the heavy door.

"I got a registered letter here for you if you can show me any proof you're really Mr. Brown." The gangly young man squinted at Adam, as if he needed glasses.

"Reckon it's been my handle for nigh unto twenty-three years," replied Adam. He grinned at the postal worker, who was younger than he was.

"Well, let me see your John Hancock on something, and you can have this here letter."

Adam reached for the beautifully tooled holster belt. The inside leather was burned with the name Adam Morgan Brown. He held it up for the postman to see.

"Yep. Must be you, all right. So just sign your John Hancock, or make your mark right there." He pointed to a line on his register. "An' I'll be on my way."

Adam signed on the specified line, his penmanship beautifully scripted. The postman handed him a thick envelope, and with a wave of his hand and a jovial farewell, he exited the room, closing the door gently behind him.

Adam stared a moment at the envelope. He wondered who in the world would send him such a fat missive. *Must be from Aunt Hattie,* he concluded. *But the handwriting's not hers.* The thought quickly crossed his mind that something could have happened to her.

He turned the packet over with more than a bit of curiosity. Above the waxed seal he saw the name of a law firm stamped on the back flap of the envelope: Stern, Hancock, Humphries and Edwards, San Rafael, California. He breathed a quick sigh of relief. It wasn't about his aunt Hattie. There was nothing else on the envelope, no return address. He'd been to San Rafael and figured a street address was, most likely, unnecessary. The town wasn't that big.

Sliding a finger under the waxed seal, it broke. He drew out a thick sheaf of folded-up papers and sat down on the side of the bed. Adam smoothed them out on his lap. They were dated June 7, 1885. He glanced down at the bottom of the first page. It was signed by a lawyer named Stephen Hancock, with the location of his law office in San Rafael, California, printed below his name.

What in the world, Adam wondered, *is this?*

He began to read the cover page. Running his fingers through his coal-black hair, he shook his head in stunned disbelief. *This must be some kind of jest!* He thought back to the day when he'd met Eldon and Camilla Chandler. It had been a little over a year before.

Adam had traveled back east to visit his aunt. He loved his aunt Hattie and tried, continually, to get her to move west. So far, she hadn't budged. He'd made the trip to Virginia, having been raised in Williamsburg, which was once the busy capital of that state. It had become a sleepy town after Richmond took over as the political center during the War Between the States.

Born during that time, he'd grown up in the quiet atmosphere where everyone knew the neighbors and most everyone was poor. His aunt Hattie still lived in Williamsburg, in the clapboard house where her parents had raised her. She told him if he ever found a place and settled down in San Francisco, she just might move west, but she didn't plan to live out the rest of her days in some hotel room in the big city.

Adam thought further back to the time when his father died. He'd barely turned eleven when his father had been killed in an accident. He'd worked on the railway, and a handbrake had disengaged on a railway car, which crushed him. Adam and his mother moved in with Hattie Hamilton, his mother's younger sister. Hattie was only fourteen years older than Adam, and he adored her. When he was fifteen, his mother had died jumping her horse. She'd ridden the same trail day after day, but Buster, her horse, had fumbled the jump. His mother had been thrown head over heels, never recovering. He'd continued to live with his maiden aunt, who lived comfortably but frugally. Attending a day school, he hadn't known she'd never touched a penny of the money realized from the sale of his parents' house. At sixteen he'd gone off to college and used much of that money for his education. He'd moved west and occasionally went back to visit. He'd made such a trip fourteen months ago—a relaxing two weeks visiting his aunt Hattie.

Upon his return to San Francisco, he'd struck up a friendship on the train with Mr. And Mrs. Chandler. They partook of their meals together and visited each other in their Pullman car compartments, passing the hours away in conversation. He remembered one time they'd touched on the subject of religion, and he shared his faith in Jesus Christ with them. They seemed quite interested but wanted to think it over before they made a decision.

When they arrived into Sacramento, they parted ways. He had told them, offhandedly, that his main address was the Bay Front Hotel in San Francisco. He remembered laughing and had amended his comment. "It's my permanent address because I travel around so much with my job. I plan to become more stationary in the near future and will most likely find a house and put down some roots."Now, here he was a year later, still living in the same hotel and reading the last Will and Testament of Mr. Eldon Chandler.

The Chandlers hadn't been all that old. I wonder what could have happened. He felt sorrow as he looked at the cover page again. He flipped through the remaining papers, scanning the documents quickly. Chandler had deeded half his estate to a virtual stranger.

Why would he do such a thing? I thought he had a daughter. Maybe she died too. Why in the world would he have included me in his will? He barely knew me.

He scanned the papers a little more thoroughly. *It's true—it's not a jest,* he thought. Reckon I'll just mosey on up there and see what's what. Got a few things I need to do first, but Friday I think I'll make a little stop on my way north and pay my respects to this lawyer, Stephen Hancock.

Adam Brown arrived at the law offices of Stern, Hancock, Humphries and Edwards just before lunchtime. The edifice looked more like a hacienda than a law office. The building stood alone. Huge recessed arches on either side of the front curved over broad flagstone walkways that led to an enclosed courtyard behind the building.

Adam tied his horse in front of an inn that served meals. He enjoyed a lunch of meatloaf and scalloped potatoes and wondered if he should pay for a room. He decided to wait and walked toward the law offices. He ambled leisurely down the wooden walk, his spurs jingling with each step. He passed one of the huge arches, glimpsing a large fountain behind the law office, and proceeded up the flagstone steps to a wide front porch.

When he entered, he saw several men seated behind a large mahogany reception counter. One stood as he approached, and Adam spoke to him as he removed his Stetson.

"Good afternoon. Is Mr. Hancock available?"

"Good afternoon," the young man replied as he came out a side door. "Do you have an appointment?" he queried, though he had to know full well Adam did not. Without waiting for an answer, he added, "Could you please state your business?" The clerk smiled, reached out, and shook Adam's hand. "My name is Karl," he said. "Karl Kepler."

Adam shook hands with the clerk and said, "My name is Adam Brown." He reached into his satchel as he continued to talk. "I live in San Francisco and received this letter from Mr. Stephen Hancock." He held the sizable envelope for the clerk to see. "I'd like some sort of explanation about it."

Karl, seeing the return address on the envelope, said, "Mr. Hancock left early this morning for a holiday and won't be back for about a month or more. Meanwhile, Mr. Elijah Humphries, one of our other lawyers, is taking care of Mr. Hancock's clients until he returns. Shall I see if he is available, or do you wish to wait and see Mr. Hancock when he returns in a month's time?"

"I'd gladly see Mr. Humphries if he's available. I don't care to wait a month to get some clarification on this." Adam waggled the envelope in his hand.

Karl turned and ran his forefinger down a ledger on the reception counter to see if Mr. Humphries had an appointment. "It doesn't look like he has anything on his schedule for another hour. Please wait one moment, and I'll check to see if he's back from lunch."

Adam watched as Karl strode down the long hall leading straight back to an exit at the far end of the building. The young man tapped on a door to his left, opened it, and spoke to someone. Returning to the waiting room, he said, "Mr. Humphries is able to see you. Please come this way."

He led Adam down to the end office and opened the door.

Adam entered and did a quick appraisal of Mr. Humphries as he was coming around his desk. He was unusually short for a man but looked quite fit. Except for around his ears, his gray hair was nonexistent. Adam saw sharp blue eyes looking at him, seeming to return the appraisal. He held out his hand to shake Mr. Humphries' and greeted him.

"Good afternoon, sir. My name is Adam Brown."

"Good afternoon. I'm Elijah Humphries, acting as a stand-in, so to speak, for my colleague Stephen Hancock.

"Please"—Elijah waved at a chair across from his desk—"be seated." He walked back to his desk chair and sat leaning forward, his hands clasped together on his desk. He smiled to himself, thinking, *He looks much like Matthew Bannister, with that gun slung low on his hip, and the leather vest.* "What can I do for you, young man? I understand you are Stephen Hancock's client—is that correct?"

"Well, yes and no," Adam replied. "You see, I've never met Mr. Hancock, but I received this notification from him and wanted some clarification on it." He handed Elijah the bulky envelope.

Before opening it, Elijah said, "Hopefully, I can help you. Do you not understand its contents?" He drew out the fat fold of papers from the envelope and looked at the letter Stephen had written to Adam. He flipped the page and perused the entire next three pages carefully. He looked up to see Adam staring at him.

"I don't see anything unusual about this. It's pretty straightforward, Mr. Brown. It was Mr. Chandler's desire that you inherit half his estate. The only thing I see that's a bit unusual is that you must first reside in the house for five years. At that time, you can decide to buy Miss Chandler out, or you can sell your half of the property to her. Do you understand this?" he asked kindly.

"Oh yes, I do understand what it says," Adam replied. "It's what brought me to this office. But you see, I met Mr. and Mrs. Chandler on a train coming back from Virginia last year. I only knew them for a little over five days. I am flabbergasted that he would leave half his estate to a virtual stranger when he has a daughter. What could he have been thinking?"

Elijah's clear blue eyes looked in shocked amazement at the young man sitting calmly across the desk from him. He had assumed this young man to be connected to Chandler in some way. He looked at the last Will and Testament of Eldon Chandler again, rereading the stipulation in the will, and was as amazed as Adam was.

"I don't know what to say, Mr. Brown, except you must have made a mighty good impression on Mr. Chandler. Sad about his death, isn't it? Mr. Hancock told me about it. He was shocked, and from my understanding, Sheriff Rawlins is still looking for the man or men who gunned them down."

Adam looked, to Elijah Humphries, mightily upset at his words, his eyes full of shock.

"I didn't know what happened to Mr. and Mrs. Chandler. I only received this"—he pointed to the document on Elijah's desk—"the day before yesterday, and it's all I know about the entire affair. I have not been in contact with the Chandlers since the train ride a year ago. What happened? Why were they gunned down?"

Elijah was a good judge of character and believed the young man. Adam's clear gray-green eyes reflected goodness within him, and Elijah perceived it. *This young man could be suspect when you read the will. Some men will do anything for a bit of money or property. I believe this man to be...ahh, now I do see! He's a believer...a child of God.* Elijah smiled inwardly at the realization and gave thanks to God for revealing it to him. He shook his head at the young Mr. Brown and said, "No one knows why they were gunned down. The Chandlers had been out to a friend's house, a fancy-dress dinner. The couple hosting were perhaps their closest friends. Because the Chandlers were dressed up, they rode in a carriage. They were found on the main road just outside the lane leading to their own house. Both were shot several times. One of the ranch hands found them early the next morning. Tragic affair, isn't it?"

"Yes, tragic and egregious," Adam replied softly. "I didn't know much about them. How could I in such a short time? I do know I liked them. What wretched sorrow for their daughter."

"Yes, yes it is. Before he left for his holiday, my colleague Mr. Hancock told me of his visit to the Chandlers' house. Mr. Chandler, you understand, was a personal friend of Mr. Hancock. When Stephen— excuse me, Mr. Hancock—revealed the contents of the will to the daughter, she was shocked and disbelieving. My understanding is her father never confided his intentions…never let her know he'd written another person into his will. Must have come as quite a surprise. Miss Chandler is an only child."

"What a shock that must have been for her, poor thing. How old is she anyway?"

"She just turned twenty, is well educated, and from what Mr. Hancock told me, adored her parents. I don't suppose you've been apprised of just what the Chandler place is worth?"

"N-no, I assumed it to be a house in Napa, but according to the paperwork, it's quite a large acreage."

"It's a lot more than a house. Have your heard of Chandler Olives?"

"Chandler Olives? Why yes, I have. No—you're not saying—no! Eldon wasn't that Chandler, was he?" Adam was stunned.

"Yes, yes he was. Over three hundred acres is in olives, I believe. Another sixty is in nuts. Mr. Chandler was a very wealthy man."

Adam could only stare. He was at a loss as to what to say.

Everyone in the area knew of Chandler Olives. They were a thriving business with exports to Europe and even South America, and widely spread across the United States.

Elijah waited for the shock to settle before he continued. "My colleague said Eden Chandler is quite headstrong and an independent thinker. She's a hard worker at Sunrise Ranch. In the will here at the end, and orally, Mr. Eldon Chandler told my colleague that if he needed to, he was to get on his knees and beg you to accept your placement in the will." He smiled and added, "He must have taken quite a shine to you, young man."

Adam was still in a state of shock, to Elijah's way of thinking.

"It's beyond my ken as to why he would do this," Adam stated emphatically. "He was a wonderfully knowledgeable man, but to leave me half of the Chandler Olives' estate is overwhelming. I simply don't understand it."

Elijah nodded his head in agreement but was beginning to understand Eldon Chandler's trust in this young man.

"Well, I need you to sign this deed of ownership, and then you should get yourself up to Sunrise Ranch and stake your claim. Please don't let any grass grow under your feet. Do you have a job?"

"Yes, I do, a good one. In truth, I'm an engineer and work mainly for the state of California. I have an office in San Francisco and design bridges. Sometimes I branch out and do tunnels or dams, and I also do some freelance work when I get the notion. I travel quite a bit but do much of the work in my office." His smile looked rueful as he continued. "I know nothing about olives except that they taste good and there are quite a variety of them."

CHAPTER IV

The righteous shall inherit the land,
and dwell therein for ever.

PSALM 37:29

ELIJAH LOOKED AT THE YOUNG MAN and suddenly realized he'd taken a real liking to him.

"It's getting a bit late to start out for Napa. Tell you what, how would you like to spend the night at my place, and tomorrow I'll ride up with you to Napa? My wife and I have someone who is as close to a daughter as we'll ever have, who lives in Napa. We could stop by there on our way up, and you could meet her and her husband. They would be a wonderful support and resource for you."

"Why, that would be fine with me," Adam replied. "I'd be happy and grateful for a place to lay my head tonight. I was thinking before I came in here that it was getting a bit late to ride north, and I should book a room at Three Hawks Inn. I appreciate your offer, and I'll take you up on it."

Elijah handed the young man a pen to sign his acceptance of the terms of the will. He looked on as Adam, his hand poised above the document, closed his eyes and seemed to breathe a prayer.

He looked up to see Elijah looking at him kindly, but he handed back the pen without signing. Elijah's surprise spread across his face as Adam explained his reasoning.

"I reckon I need to see exactly what I am committing to before I sign. I have been rather a free spirit, going wherever my job took me. I suppose what I am saying is that I don't wish to sign without first seeing."

Elijah felt an overwhelming impression that Adam would be a part of his life from this day forward. An inward warmth toward this young man for the decision he'd just made flooded through him. *He's not in this for what he can get out of it. If he were, he'd sign this immediately. He'd be half owner of all of the Chandlers' holdings...an extremely wealthy man. Instead, he is waiting on the Lord's direction.*

"Congratulations on that decision. I hope I would do the same." Elijah reached across his desk to shake Adams's hand, and with that handshake the two men forged a bond. "I have two more appointments, and then I'll be home. If you're comfortable enough, I can point you in the right direction. Ah...on second thought, my wife is not home yet. She's at the mission. I'll point you in the opposite direction. Are you on horseback?"

"Yes, my horse is tied up in front of Three Hawks Inn. I had a bite to eat there before I came here."

Elijah smiled at the younger man, still feeling a bond of warmth toward him.

"Good food, isn't it? That's in the right direction," he said. "You continue on down about three more blocks, and it's on the corner. You can stable your horse there or wait and stable him at our house. You'll be more than welcomed by my wife. Simply ask for Abigail. Bessie, our cook, is there too, which means you'll most likely get a piece of pie or something good to tide you over until dinner." He grinned at the younger man. "And if you think the food at Three Hawks is good, wait until you taste Bessie's cooking—there's nothing in the world like it."

Adam stood up. "Thanks for the invite. I always seem to be hungry, so I'll look forward to your Bessie's cooking. Thank you for clarifying all this for me, and I appreciate your help and for being so welcoming. Hope I haven't taken up too much of your time." He turned to head out the door, but Elijah followed him out and down the front steps. He clasped Adam on the shoulder and pointed him in the right direction. Adam thanked Elijah again, and donning his hat, headed toward his horse and the mission.

As he approached the mission, his eyes lit up at the architectural beauty of the building. He tied Locomotion to the railing and walked across the street, wanting to get a full view of the mission's exterior. He stood staring at the pulchritudinous structure, glad to see the integrity of the building had been kept when the exterior had been remodeled. Curved, pedimented gables spanned themselves across the front.

Whoever had taken on the project, he thought, *had been careful not to destroy the character and harmony of the building.* He strolled easily back across the street and let himself inside the heavy wrought iron gate. Tugging on the bellpull, he heard a deep sound echoing within the depths of the building.

"Hello. May I help you?" A pretty blonde opened the door of the mission, speaking up to him with a sweet smile on her lips.

Adam didn't know what he had been expecting, but it wasn't this. He'd been expecting someone more Mr. Humphries' age, and smiled inwardly at his mistake.

"Hello," Adam replied, surprise expressing itself in his eyes. He swiftly removed his hat. "My name's Adam Brown, and I've come to meet Mrs. Humphries. You're not Mrs. Humphries, are you?" he asked.

"No," the girl replied with a chuckle. "My name is Janne Greenway. I only work here. Please, come on inside. If you don't mind waiting here, I'll see if I can find Mrs. Humphries. Please do come in." She pointed him to an oaken pew flanked on one side by a huge plant and on the other by a large round end table with a vase of freshly cut flowers sitting beside a framed quote.

Adam stepped into a large open foyer and looked around in appreciation. He watched as the girl disappeared from a long hall. *Much thought has gone into the restoration of this building.*

Being an engineer, he was constantly aware of the character, tenor, and aura of his surroundings. Without conscious thought, he assessed the soundness of every structure he came across. The mission exuded charm and modern comfort blended with age and culture. It looked to him as if every effort had been made to preserve the history of the building and yet provide comfort within.

Adam picked up the framed quote from the end table and read it aloud. It was a quote from John Wesley written in a beautiful script. "Do all the good you can. By all the means you can. In all the ways you can.

In all the places you can. At all the times you can. To all the people you can. As long as ever you can." He smiled and set the frame back on the table. *I pray I can be that kind of person*, he thought.

Janne Greenway returned with a woman whose face caught one's attention. It was not a beautiful face but one that held a certain aliveness. A zest for living was somehow embodied in her features. Her bright-blue gaze looked in curiosity at the young man who stood up in respect for a female entering the room.

"Hello," she said. "I'm Abigail Humphries. May I help you?"

Adam grinned and said, "Yes, I think you can. My name is Adam Brown. I came to town to get an explanation of a legal letter I received from Mr. Hancock. He's out of town, so your husband gave me the explanation of the letter. Now, because of your husband's generosity, I reckon I'm your guest for the night. I met Elijah at the law office, and he said to come here and inform you of me." Adam smiled at his wording. "He invited me to dinner and said he had a place where I can lay my head tonight."

"Well, you're certainly welcome, Mr. Brown. Let me collect my things, and we'll walk to my house. My cook, Bessie, has already left to prepare dinner."

Abigail said she needed to get her satchel. She headed for the kitchen, and he heard her tell Janne she'd be leaving with Mr. Brown.

"I'm going home for the night, Janne. Thank you for all your help today. You go home soon. You've had a long enough day, and tomorrow will be busy with those new girls coming."

"I will, Abigail. I'll go just as soon as I finish this letter. Good night."

"Good night, dear girl."

Abigail returned to the front foyer, and Adam held open the door as he settled his hat back on his head. The two talked companionably as they headed toward the Humphries' house. Adam had taken the reins of his horse and led her down the road, and Abigail walked on the wooden sidewalk until it ended. They chatted amiably together.

"Have you always lived in the West, Mr. Brown?"

"No, I came out here just a few years ago. I hail from Williamsburg, Virginia. I hear by your accent that you're not from the West originally either, are you?"

"No," Abigail said with a laugh. "I'm from Boston, but oh, I do love it here! I've just taken up riding lessons." Abigail spoke with a wide smile and a twinkle in her blue eyes. "We moved west from Boston in the spring of eighty-three, and I learned how to shoot a gun last year. Now I'm learning how to ride. My husband doesn't like having to take the carriage all the time and says I need to learn. I'm finding it exhilarating. I never, in all my born days, thought to ride a horse and enjoy it."

"It makes sense to know how to ride and shoot in the West." Adam smiled, his gray-green eyes warm with laughter.

She glanced at him and grinned. "I told Elijah I could become another Annie Oakley." She laughed and Adam joined her. Looking for the first time at his horse, she exclaimed, "Why, is that a piebald?"

He looked surprised that she would know the breed, since she said she was just learning to ride.

"Why yes, it is. I reckon I'm a bit surprised you would know that."

"I confess. I know a young man who has a horse that looks quite similar. It's the only reason I would be able to guess what kind of horse that is. I believe Matthew's could be a twin to yours. He named her Piggypie. Funny name, isn't it?" She chuckled.

"Unusual to say the least," Adam returned. "I named my girl Locomotion. I smile when I say her name because it got shortened to Loco, but she's definitely not crazy. When she's full out, she seems to almost skim the earth, she's so fast."

"That's not much more dignified than Piggypie, is it?" Abigail asked. "Matthew said when his horse was a filly, she ate everything in sight. She was a regular pig! Since she was a piebald mare, he named her Piggypie. It also makes him smile every time he says it."

"I can see why. I would think you'd have to have a good sense of humor, and moreover, a good self-esteem to endure the ribbing that surely must come when he tells someone his horse's name."

Abigail stared at Adam, a bit of wonder in her eyes.

"I never thought of that, but it's true, isn't it? Matthew does have a good self-esteem, but I don't think he did when he named his horse."

"Why do you say that?"

"That part is not my story to tell, but I can say that since he's given his life over to Jesus to control, he's a man full of contentment and knows who he is in Christ."

Adam regarded her with surprise. He thought, *Most people don't speak so openly about the Lord.* He grinned at her, delighted she was a believer.

"So, you are my sister, Abigail Humphries," he said. "I'm glad, very glad, to get to know you."

They had arrived at the Humphries' house, located at the very edge of town.

She nodded her appreciation of his comment. With another wide smile, she said, "Well, Brother Adam, there it is!" Abby waved her hand at the house centered on the tee of the road, across the street.

Adam stopped walking as he looked at the Humphries' house. They stood across from it, and he regarded it with admiration.

"Beautiful house you have here. It's a wonderful example of an Adam-Federal house style."

Abigail nodded her head in agreement with the first part of his comment.

"I had no idea what kind of house it is. I simply fell in love with it when I first saw it. We've lived here for two years, and every time I enter this house, it seems to envelop me with a sense of belonging. It speaks to me. Please come on inside."

She led the way across the street and into a home that exuded not only comfort but peace, except for the barking.

"Oh, Polka, do hush!" Abigail admonished a beautiful dog with a mottled coat. Polka rushed up to Adam and sniffed his Levi's denims. "Mind your manners, Polka Dot. We have company."

Adam was thoroughly enjoying himself. He'd been so busy the past couple years that he'd made very few friends, and even those he didn't see often. He'd thrown himself into his work wholeheartedly. It was one of the reasons his aunt Hattie didn't wish to live with him. He was too busy to allow time for any other activities. He'd made up his mind a few weeks earlier it was time to ease up and enjoy life. He realized he needed to get out more to cement friendships. A real eye opener was when he realized he didn't have one person, here in the West, he felt was close enough to even care about him, or he them. With not one relationship to cement, he'd made the decision to settle down, do a bit more, and stop traveling so much. *Life is more than a job*, he thought.

The evening brought an even deeper realization for the need to develop relationships that were meaningful. Abigail and Elijah were charming. Abigail, witty and humorous, kept Adam on his toes. He couldn't remember the last time he'd laughed so much. He hadn't realized he was lonely, but he was. Because of his frequent traveling, he hadn't even gotten close to the people where he attended church.

Adam, always seeing the structure of a room, was pleasantly surprised by the parlor. It was understated elegance with a huge bay window, which made the room appear even bigger when he entered it. The far wall had a large fireplace with a beautifully carved oaken mantel above it. Two ornately carved wingback chairs, the upholstery a pale green, matched the pillows of the settee that separated the wingbacks facing the fireplace.

"Please make yourself at home," Abby said as she gestured to one of the ornate chairs. She and Elijah, who'd beat them home, sat together on the love seat.

With Adam's permission, Elijah filled Abby in on what had brought Adam to San Rafael. She too expressed shocked at the thought that a man could leave half of an estate, especially one as large as Chandler Olives, to an almost total stranger.

Abigail asked, "Do you have plans now you've inherited half the Chandler estate?"

"Frankly, I don't have any solid plans yet," Adam replied. "I thought, perhaps, to check things out, meet the Chandlers' daughter, and go from there. I packed a few clothes so I could spend a few days, but in truth, I haven't signed the necessary papers to inherit just yet."

Abigail looked at the young man in surprise. "You didn't sign the documents?" She looked at Elijah to see a smug expression on his face. "Elijah, doesn't he have to sign the documents to inherit?"

"Yes, he has to sign to inherit, but there's no rush. Do you know, Abby, my girl," he said, changing the subject abruptly, "this young man is a brother in Christ?"

"Yes, I do know that," she replied promptly, her blue eyes sparkling.

Adam turned to speak to Elijah. "Abby and I recognized we were brother and sister in Christ, but you, how did you know I am a Christian?"

Elijah cleared his throat before speaking. It was a habit he'd formed when nervous or, in this instance, preparing to relate something of import.

"I discerned it. It's one of my gifts from the Lord. He brought the thought to my mind when we were talking in my office. I was very proud of you when you didn't immediately sign the papers. You are allowing for

God's leading. So many people these days seem to go ahead with their own plans and later ask God to bless them. Many times the outcome is failure, and they blame God. They end up in trouble because they go ahead and make their own plan, assuming that because they want it, God does too. Instead, they should ask for guidance before they proceed. Again, I must say I'm proud of you, young man."

Adam didn't look embarrassed when he replied.

"Thank you. Do you also have the gift of edification? I feel quite encouraged by your words." He smiled at his host. *I feel a kinship with this man I've not experienced for a long time...not since I was eleven and my father still alive.* The thought startled him, and he took a long look at Elijah, who sat under his scrutiny with a twinkle in his eyes.

"Do I pass?" he asked.

"Sorry. I was staring, wasn't I?"

"It's all right, son. For some reason I feel it too." His eyes were warm on Adam's face.

Abigail regarded the two of them with a slight smile on her lips at the interchange. She listened and added a comment here and there but felt in her heart this young man would be like the son Elijah had never had. He had bonded with Liberty, and of course, Matthew, and also Liberty's twin, Alex. Liberty held a very special place in her husband's heart, and she felt Adam would do the same.

"I've been doing some thinking," Adam said, breaking her reverie. "If I decide to take Eldon Chandler's offer, I will beg my aunt Hattie to come out and live. It wouldn't be appropriate for me to stay in the house without a proper chaperone. What do you think?"

"And who is Aunt Hattie?" Abigail asked.

Adam proceeded to explain about the circumstances of his growing up and the special input his aunt had contributed to his upbringing. Abigail was entranced by the young man's conversation.

CHAPTER V

My son, if thine heart be wise, my heart shall rejoice, even mine.
Yea, my reins shall rejoice, when thy lips speak right things.
PROVERBS 23:15–16

"**WELL, SON, YOU NEED TA GET YOURSELF** over ta see that Chandler gal. I want you ta park yerself on the doorstep, so ta speak. That girl has a mind of 'er own, and I want her mind fixed on you! There's a lot of money that'll go with that girl. You listening ta me, boy?" Terrence spit a wad of chew out in a long stream.

"Yeah, Pa, I'm listening. She don't seem ta be that set on me. She goes out right regular with that Caleb McHaney. I reckon she might be sweet on him 'stead a me."

"Now you listen here, son. I'm not jestin' with you none. I want you ta make yourself indispensable ta that girl."

"Yeah, yeah, I plan ta go over there tamorrow. I'll be asking 'er if she'll go with me ta the barn dance next week."

"She ain't going ta be going ta no barn dance with you, Taylor! Don't you have a lick a sense between your ears? She's a mourning her pa and ma right now, an' I don't think she'll be a going anyplace real soon. So's you kin jest get yerself over there and give 'er what comfort yer able. She'll be right grateful fer your sympathy and be a leaning on you fer support, maybe even want some guidance on what she can do with all that wonderful money. An' afore you go over there, don't you go gettin' fortified at the saloon. She don't need no young man a calling on her with spirits on his breath. Are you listening ta me, boy?"

"Yeah, Pa, I hear you. I'll be a going over there tomorrow, like I said."

"Caleb, would you please go over to the Chandlers' tomorrow morning? I made a cake this afternoon, and you can take it over with our condolences." Mrs. McHaney wiped her hands on a towel and smiled over at her son as she spoke. "I know they have a very good cook, but I do think it's a good idea to let them know we care and we're thinking about them. It's a sad thing that's happened, and I want Eden to know she can count on us to lend some support and help in any way we can. Simply going to the funeral isn't enough. We need to let her know we care about her." Mrs. McHaney gave a lengthy explanation, knowing full well Caleb was not going to want to go visit Eden Chandler.

"I don't know if that's a good idea." Caleb's blue eyes looked serious. "Their cook is quite capable, and I know for a fact poor Eden is wild with sorrow. I don't know who would do such a vile thing. My heart aches for her. And, Mother, I'm telling you again, Eden and I are simply good friends. I am not romantically in love with her. I like her. I like her a lot, but I know I don't love her the way you loved Pop. It'll be a year next week, won't it? I miss him something awful."

"Don't change the subject, Caleb. We could use some of that Chandler money. I think Eden is a beautiful girl. She has quite a temper and knows her own mind, but I don't think that's a negative. It's a positive trait, not unlike myself." Mrs. McHaney pulled a lilac-colored handkerchief out of her sleeve and dabbed at her eyes. "You will go, won't you, Caleb? Please go, just to let them know we care."

"All right, I'll go tomorrow, but only because you want me to, Mother. I'll do it just for you."

Eden went up to her room to clean up before dinner. She removed her belt and holster before entering the bathing room. Pouring some water from a large ewer into a matching porcelain basin, she washed her hands thoroughly, dumping the water into the chamber pot. She poured some fresh water and splashed it onto her eyes and cheeks, which felt swollen and stiff from dried tears. She pulled a soft towel off the rack and patted her face dry, leaning closer to look at her reflection in the mirror. Dark smudges under her eyes revealed her lack of sleep. No sparkle in her eyes proclaimed her inner turmoil and sorrow. She looked closer, seeing a clear complexion looking pasty and washed out. Disgusted, she pinched her cheeks for some color.

She grabbed a silver-backed hairbrush off her chiffonier and brushed her hair out. Winding the honey-blonde mass back into a bun, she pushed some pins in and left her room. She had a sudden thought before she descended the stairs, and trudged the length of the hall to her parents' suite of rooms located at the far end.

Eden opened the door. The first thing that assailed her was the smell permeating the room. It smelled of her parents. Tears started in her eyes and trickled down her cheeks. Her mother used to make her own essence. It was a mixture of olive oil, orange, ginger, vanilla, and some other elusive scent Eden couldn't remember. She breathed it in, but the smell dissipated. She saw her mother's slippers by the bed, ready to slip on. Eden backed out of the room, shutting the door noiselessly behind her. She leaned back, her hands pressed against the door behind her. She closed her eyes, trying to swallow down her sorrow.

I'll deal with that later, she thought. *I don't have the fortitude I need to deal with it right now. There's plenty of time, years of time.* She wiped her tears on her sleeve and took a deep breath.

Gio happened by when Eden went to her parents' room. He was waiting for her at the bottom of the stairs. Offering her his arm, they went into the dining room but continued on to the kitchen, where Dorothy had Dolly setting the table.

Dorothy was waiting for them.

"Good evening, Miss Eden...Gio." She nodded her head as she spoke to Eden. "I had Berry fix one of your favorite dishes tonight." She smiled as she scrutinized the two of them. Both had deep sorrow etched in their eyes.

"Let me guess." Eden sniffed the air. "Umm, it's lasagna."

"No, no, it's not." Gio's nose almost twitched. "Dottie, you've had Berry make spaghetti, haven't you?"

"No, you're both wrong." Dottie laughed in delight. "It's ravioli, and it's delicious. I had to sample it, of course."

"Well, it doesn't matter what it is—it smells wonderful," Gio said.

Pulling out the heavy chairs, they sat with Dorothy as Dolly began to serve the meal.

Eden had been having trouble eating much the past few days.

It surprised her that she had eaten well at Liberty's and was hungry again. "This doesn't feel right, just the three of us and not having Mama and Papa here," Eden said. "It feels so empty, doesn't it?"

"Yes. I'm not sure it will ever feel right again," Gio replied. "Try as I might, I cannot understand anyone doing such a heinous crime without a motive. There has to be a reason behind it."

"Did you talk to Sheriff Rawlins again today?" Eden asked.

"No, not today. I had some work I needed to do, but I don't imagine he has any more news than he did yesterday. He told me he'd let me know soon as he found anything. He said whoever it was picked up their shell casings. It's going to be very difficult to find out who did this. They weren't robbed, so what was the motive? I simply don't understand."

"Maybe this man who was deeded half the property gunned them down." Eden's voice sounded bitter to her own ears as she continued to speak. "After all, he would stand to benefit the most from their deaths, wouldn't he? I already don't trust him. Wonder when he's going to show up and claim half of what should all be mine."

"I don't believe you should accuse a man you've never met." Gio's voice was soft, but the rebuke was clearly evident. "There had to be something about him your father appreciated, or he'd never have done what he did. I think we both should trust Eldon's judgement. Your papa wasn't someone to do something he didn't want to do."

"Maybe the man was blackmailing Papa. Maybe he had some sort of hold over him." Eden's voice rose. "I can't believe my business-minded father would ever give half of Sunrise Ranch and Chandler Olives to some man I don't even know, on a whim. It wasn't like him!"

"No, part of what you're saying is true." Eden saw the sympathy in Gio's eyes. "Eldon had to think over all the ramifications of deeding half the land to this man. As you said, he wouldn't do it on a whim. I told you this morning that your papa told me about it. I tried to talk him out of it, but he said to mind my own business on this one. He said he knew what he was about, and nothing I said was going to change his mind. When the man might show up, I don't rightly know. I do know Mr. Hancock said when he heard the news of your parents' death, he sent off a letter to apprise the man of the will's contents. According to Mr. Hancock, it will be as big a shock to the man as it was to you."

Eden stared at Gio, a frown wrinkling her brow.

"Well, I've already made up my mind. Whoever this man is, I consider him my enemy. Papa had no right to do this to me, not when I've worked my fingers to the bone on this property. I know everything about Sunrise Ranch from the ground up, and I don't intend for this man to ever buy me out. It's mine, and I don't intend to share it." Eden's mouth was set in a straight line, a sure indication of a deep determination burning within her.

Gio looked her full in the face and knew it was useless to talk to her. His heart was heavy for her losses. She'd find out soon enough that half of Sunrise was not hers—not anymore. He hoped whoever the man was, that he had a lot of patience. Eden, like her father, was not someone to be easily persuaded once she made up her mind about something. He took a deep sigh and began to eat.

Adam stretched, yawned, and stretched again. Lying flat on his back, he prayed, acknowledging God's glory and some of His attributes. He also had a few requests. The one foremost was a smooth meeting with Miss Chandler. He also prayed his aunt Hattie would come west to live at Sunrise Ranch should he accept the inheritance. He didn't feel inclined to accept. He couldn't imagine how disobliged Miss Chandler must feel, and he was quite keen on his job. He loved designing bridges and tunnels, so he prayed about the decision he must make…that the Almighty might make it clear. He didn't care to make a mistake. The decision would impact the rest of his life.

Adam sat up and swung his long legs over the side of the bed, looking around the room with pleasure stamped on his face. It was different from the usual colors of a room.

The wall containing the fireplace was painted a slate gray. A fantastic picture of the ocean crashing on giant boulders with rays of sunlight diffusing through the spray made him feel as if he were standing on a cliff overlooking the panorama. A lighthouse dominated the left portion of the oil painting and contained the colors in the room, which were gray and white with splashes of bright red in the pillows. A comfortable chair and accents throughout enhanced the beauty. The trims were done in stark white. *Abigail has good taste. This room is peaceful.*

He got up, stretching hugely, and entered a large, modern bathing room. He took care of his morning ablutions and dressed slowly, praying as he buttoned up his shirt. "Lord, please bless this day. Again, I pray the meeting with Miss Chandler goes well. If I were in her place, I doubt I'd feel very kindly to a usurper taking half my inheritance. I need direction from You, Father, whether to proceed or not. Give me guidance, I pray. And, Father, thank You for bringing about the meeting with Abigail and Elijah. I feel as if they are family. Lord, only You could bring this feeling of close connection so quickly. I know Elijah feels it too. Again, I thank You."

He threw his things into his satchel, pulled the sheets and pillowcases off the bed, and dropped them in a pile by the door, the way his aunt Hattie had taught him. She said it was only politeness to do that little bit of help when visiting someone. He folded the duvet and threw the pillows back on the bed. One more check to see if he had everything, and he made his way down the stairs, smelling wonderful aromas wafting from the kitchen.

He followed his nose and entered the large friendly room. The sight there made him stop and smile. Abigail sat at a huge oak table, glasses perched on the end of her nose as she read aloud from a large Bible. Elijah stood, hands clasped behind his back, looking out an open glassed door at a couple rabbits hopping across the grass as he listened to his wife reading scripture. Polka Dot was missing the action in the yard, as she was stretched out against the wall, sound asleep. Bessie, their cook, face flushed from the heat, was taking cinnamon rolls out of the oven. Adam walked over to the table, smiled, and nodded at Bessie as he slipped into a chair while Abigail continued to read.

"'He shall not fail nor be discouraged, till he have set judgment in the earth: and the isles shall wait for his law. Thus saith God the Lord, he that created the heavens, and stretched them out; he that spread forth the earth, and that which cometh out of it; he that giveth breath unto the people upon it, and spirit to them that walk therein: I the Lord have called thee in righteousness, and will hold thine hand, and will keep thee, and give thee for a covenant of the people, for a light of the Gentiles; To open the blind eyes, to bring out the prisoners from the prison, and them that sit in darkness out of the prison house. I am the Lord: that is my name: and my glory will I not give to another, neither my praise to graven images.'" Abigail looked across the table and said, "Good morning, Adam. I was just reading from Isaiah forty-two."

"Yes, I know. It happens to be one I've memorized. The next verse is, 'Behold, the former things are come to pass, and new things do I declare: before they spring forth I tell you of them.'"

Elijah turned and joined them at the table. "It's a good chapter, isn't it?"

"Yes, it is. I wonder if the 'new things' for me is a new life up in Napa. I've been praying for guidance." Adam smiled at his host and hostess. He felt a bond with this older man. He could feel Elijah's pleasure in him, and it warmed his heart. He listened closely when Elijah spoke.

"Perhaps you were meant to hear this particular scripture today." Elijah's blue eyes were warm on Adam as he counseled him.

"Yes," Adam replied. "Perhaps I was. I'd like to express my appreciation for last night. I enjoyed myself immensely. The food was spectacular." He smiled at Bessie and added, "You're a wonderful cook."

He turned to Elijah and Abigail. "I can't remember when I've had such a delightful evening of fellowship, and I slept soundly in a comfortable bed. Again, I thank you. If today goes half as smoothly, I'll be most grateful. I've been thinking how I'd feel if my father gave half my inheritance to a complete stranger. I don't think I'd be too happy to meet the person, that's for sure."

"It's interesting that you can put yourself in her position and see from her point of view. So many of us don't do that. We are blinded to any other way of thinking but our own. It gives us a lopsided view of the situation."

Bessie was spreading frosting over the cinnamon rolls. Thomas, Elijah's majordomo, came in to help serve breakfast. Elijah had mentioned Thomas was as close to family as Elijah would ever have.

Thomas poured out the coffee and began to serve bacon, omelets, and the cinnamon rolls. He poured small glasses of orange juice and asked, "Will that be all?"

"Just the peaches, and yes, that will be all. Thank you, Thomas." Abigail wiped her lips on a napkin and added, "Umm, Bessie, those rolls smell absolutely delicious."

"Well, son," Elijah asked, "would you care to ask the blessing?"

"My pleasure, sir." Adam bowed his head. "Dear Lord, how grateful we are for friendships and the unity we have in You. I pray Your blessings to rest on Elijah and Abigail and all they put their hand to. We pray Your continued peace to dwell in this house. Thank You for the warm hospitality shown me. Father, we thank You most of all for Your love. Thank You for this food and for Bessie who prepared it. We give You praise for this day. Amen."

Elijah said, "I think we should head up north as soon as we finish breakfast. I asked Pippie, my all around help, to have our horses saddled about eight thirty. Is that amenable to you? Do you have any other business to attend to here in San Rafael?"

"No, sir, I don't. I keep praying in my head about meeting the Chandler girl. I can only hope it will go smoothly. I can't help thinking it's a bitter pill for her to swallow. I thought during the night to refuse to sign and simply go on the way I have been, but then I thought of what you said to me yesterday, Elijah. The fact that Mr. Chandler told Mr. Hancock that if he must, to please beg me to accept. He saw more in me than I imagined if he foresaw that possibility. Most men would jump at this. I'm not so sure. I'll have to see how it goes today, I reckon."

CHAPTER VI

I, even I, am the LORD;
and beside me there is no Saviour.

ISAIAH 43:11

ELIJAH, ABIGAIL, AND ADAM ENJOYED a delicious breakfast, chatting as if they were indeed old friends.

Thomas entered the kitchen and said, "Mistah Bannistah ta see you, suh."

"Tell him to come in. He can have some breakfast." Elijah turned to Adam. "Perhaps I'll be able to tell you a great story of bringing a family together. Matthew Bannister has become like a son-in-law to me, his wife like a daughter."

Matthew came striding into the kitchen, wearing almost the identical clothes Adam had on. A checked shirt, black leather vest, denims, a kerchief around his neck, and a gun strapped to his hip completed his outfit. He held his hat in his hand, which he laid on a chair.

Elijah and Adam stood when he entered, and Elijah proceeded to introduce the two men, who were already taking each other's measure.

"Matthew, meet Adam Brown, an engineer who lives in San Francisco. Adam, meet Matthew Bannister, owner of Rancho Bonito in Napa, just north of here."

The two men shook hands.

Adam said, "Pleased to make your acquaintance, Mr. Bannister."

"And I can say the same. I'm pleased to meet you, Mr. Brown."

Abigail stood to give Matthew a big hug. "Where's Liberty?"

Matthew smiled a bit ruefully at Abby before he answered.

"Well, the two of us were supposed to visit Alex, Emily, and the children, but Libby woke up sick and opted to stay home. I told her I'd wait and see if she would feel better, but she shooed me out, so I went down to Frisco. We were supposed to stay a couple nights, but since it was only me, I stayed for one. I'm on my way home. I left Liberty House early so I could catch the first ferry. Breakfast sounds great." He turned to see Bessie dishing up a generous omelet, bacon, and a couple big fluffy cinnamon rolls. "I'll go wash up and be right back." He left the kitchen, whistling tunelessly as he went down the hall.

Abigail said to Adam. "Matthew's wife, Liberty, is expecting their first baby and is experiencing quite a bit of nausea. She's been like a daughter to us these past couple of years. It's a long story, and I'm sure Elijah will tell you all about it sometime."

Elijah said, "We'll wait for Matthew to eat, and then ride to Napa. I was going to have us stop there anyway on our way to Sunrise Ranch."

Matthew entered the kitchen and asked, "What's this about Sunrise? Wasn't that the saddest thing about the Chandlers? I've helped Sheriff Rawlins try to find who did it, but we found nothing. I can't think why anyone would do such an abominable thing." He sat down to a large plate of breakfast with steaming hot coffee and bowed his head to silently give thanks.

When he was finished, Elijah spoke.

"We're going to ride north with you, Matthew. Perhaps we can get a bit of lunch out of Conchita." Elijah made sure Bessie heard him. "Not that I'm hungry right now. Bessie, that was a most delicious breakfast. Thank you."

"You're welcome, Mr. Humphries," she replied.

He noticed she was cleaning up, getting ready to head down to the mission. He knew she loved to cook. Bessie had taught some of the girls at the mission, and he'd benefitted because she'd also learned new dishes from some of the Scandinavian and French girls.

"Need any help, my dear?" he asked Abigail as she gathered up a few things and her knitting. He knew she planned to walk to the mission with Bessie.

"No, I've got everything, I believe." She leaned over to give him a kiss, with no embarrassment that there were onlookers. "Perhaps I'll see you tomorrow. If you stay a couple days with Matthew, I won't worry. Have a safe trip, dear." She left the kitchen with a youthful stride.

Matthew cleaned his plate in short order and drank down the rest of his coffee.

He dumped his plate into some water sitting in a pan.

Thomas had Elijah's satchel packed, and the three men were ready to head out. They went out the door, and Pippie was waiting with Elijah's horse, Comet, and Adam's piebald mare, Locomotion.

Matthew pushed back his hat in near disbelief. At a glance, Adam's horse looked the twin of his Piggypie. He turned to Adam, a big grin on his face.

"Well, I'll say this for you, Mr. Brown. You have a sensational taste in horseflesh."

Adam looked Piggypie up and down and replied, "Thank you. Reckon I can say the same about you, only I'm not surprised by it. Abigail told me about your horse yesterday. She recognized the breed, and I was surprised she'd know it. By the way, you may call me Adam."

Matthew nodded. "And call me Matthew." He climbed onto his horse and watched as Adam stepped into his stirrup. "Are you looking to build something up in Napa, being an engineer and all, or is your business there private?"

Elijah wondered what Adam would reply as he swung up on Comet.

He grinned to himself as he looked at the other two men sitting their rides, and he thought, *They look so much alike it's amazing. The way they dress, their horses, and even their mannerisms. If Adam decides to take the Chandlers' inheritance, these two will be close neighbors.*

He imagined they'd become good friends. Kirk, Matthew's brother, didn't live close anymore. He was married and lived in Sonoma on a huge cattle ranch. Elijah smiled as he listened to Adam's reply.

"No, I'm not looking to build anything except some new relationships. I've gone far too long keeping my nose buried in my work. The Lord wants me to get outside myself and my work and get involved with people…build relationships that are meaningful." He looked at Elijah, who nodded at him encouragingly. Elijah thought in that moment that Adam would be signing his name on the inheritance papers.

"Are you bringing those papers with you?" Adam asked Elijah. "Reckon I've just made up my mind I'm going to sign them."

Matthew asked, "May I ask what papers? I won't be offended if you say it's none of my business." He smiled.

Adam nodded toward Elijah. "Go ahead. You're welcome to tell Matthew exactly what this is all about."

The three men headed out at a walk as Elijah began to explain.

"Last year Adam went back east to Virginia to visit his aunt. Coming back to San Francisco, he met the Chandlers on the train. For approximately five days, the three of them conversed and ate together. A few days ago, Adam received a letter from my colleague, Stephen Hancock, who is now on holiday. Adam showed up yesterday to ask about the letter he'd received. Since I'm overseeing Stephen's clients, I explained the letter to him. In short"—he paused to let the previous information sink in—"in short, Eldon Chandler left half his entire estate to Adam with the condition that he live in the house for the next five years. After that time, he can buy Miss Chandler out, or she can buy him out."

Matthew pushed his hat back off his brow and stared at Adam. His deep-set blue eyes looked at the other man in astonishment. "My wife and I knew Eldon and Camilla quite well. We've had them to dinner, and they've had us. That he left half of Chandler Olives to you must come as a real shock to Eden. As I live and breathe, that is really something! Whoever heard of such a thing!"

Elijah added, "Mr. Chandler also stipulated that should Adam decline, Mr. Hancock, his lawyer, was to get down on his knees and beg Adam to reconsider."

"You must know a tremendous amount about growing olives!" Matthew exclaimed.

"Not a thing. I know nothing about olives except that there are several different kinds. I know I like eating them."

"To answer your question, Adam," said Elijah, "yes, I do have the papers with me. I brought them home from the office. I had a feeling that you might come to a positive position. It's a good day for a ride, don't you think?" Elijah asked as he smiled at the other two men.

The day was pleasantly warm. No clouds marred the blueness of the heavens, and there was the slightest hint of a breeze.

"Uh-huh," Adam answered with a grin. "It's a beautiful day to be alive."

"Let's be on our way," Elijah said.

When they reached the edge of town, they kicked their rides into a steady lope.

It was nearly lunchtime, and Liberty, who was headed to the barn to talk to Diego, was surprised to see three men riding up the long lane. She shielded her eyes from the glare of the sun and saw that it was Matthew, Elijah, and someone else. *Is that Kirk? That's strange,* she thought, *I can't tell by looking which man is Matthew. Is he the man on the left or the right of Elijah? How peculiar. Whoever it is, he has a horse that looks just like Piggypie, and he sits his horse much like Matthew. Ah, Matthew's on the left. Well, goodness me. I am surprised he came back today. I thought he'd stay at least a couple days with Alex.*

Liberty was dressed in her normal attire of split skirt, long soft leather cowboy boots, and white blouse, which was gathered at the shoulders and wrists. The wide leather belt she usually wore was missing. She was showing her pregnancy but not all that much. She walked to the end of the flagstone path and stood by the hitching post to wait their arrival. Boston, her growing puppy, followed her closely. He was still in the process of learning good manners but was fast becoming an obedient dog. Reuben, their new office manager, came out of the office building and started toward her, but she turned away and looked only at the riders. He stopped, saw the riders coming, and went back into the office. Liberty breathed a sigh of relief. She didn't care much for Reuben. It wasn't that he was rude or disrespectful. It was because he was, as she called it, *oily, far too smooth. There's something about him that doesn't settle well with me. I don't like the smell of cigars either, and he reeks of them the way Armand did. I wonder if I should tell Matthew about my misgivings. I don't like to discredit someone without any real foundation. Just to go on feelings isn't right, and yet...*

As the riders pulled up, she smiled up at the stranger and Elijah, but her eyes caught and held Matthew's. *Will seeing him ever stop bringing my heart such joy? I hope not.* She added a quick prayer to her thought. *Lord, I do thank you for Matthew. I love him so much and give you praise for bringing us together.*

Boston wriggled and wagged, giving a couple yips in the excitement of Matthew's return and seeing strangers. He sniffed Elijah, whose scent was likely familiar, wagging all the while.

"I didn't expect you home today, Matthew. I thought you were going to stay at least two nights." She looked with curiosity at the man who still sat his horse, but Matthew blocked her view by taking her into his arms.

"One night away and it seems like forever," he said as his mouth came down on hers in a quick kiss. He hugged her to his side as he turned toward their guests.

Elijah was a bit slower getting off his horse, but he was smiling. Adam, clearly surprised at the public display of affection, had looked away but grinned as he stepped out of his stirrup and removed his hat.

Matthew made introductions. "Liberty, I'd like you to meet Adam Brown. Adam Brown, my wife, Liberty Bannister."

"I'm pleased—" Both grinned at each other as they had started to talk at the same time. "I'm pleased to meet you, Mr. Brown." Liberty's grin turned into a smile of welcome.

"And I you, Mrs. Bannister," Adam replied easily. "And please, just call me Adam."

"You may call me Liberty. We don't stand on formality around here," she said as she turned to Elijah. "Hello there, stranger! It's been a while. How are you?" She gave Elijah a huge hug and kissed him on the cheek. "I've missed seeing you. How are things going at the mission?"

"Fine, just fine. It's good to see you too, young lady," he said as he hugged her right back.

Liberty spoke to Adam. "I've never seen a horse look more like Piggypie." With a smile in her voice, she added, "I'll wager your horse doesn't have a name like Matthew's horse."

"No, but I can see why he named her Piggypie. It does make a body smile when you say it. My girl's name is Locomotion, but it got shortened to Loco. She can run like the wind, and I love her."

Liberty laughed. "Loco is a name to make one smile too." She liked the looks of this young man, feeling a connection and wondering why. "Where do you live, Adam? I suppose if I'm having you call me Liberty, I need to respond in kind. It's interesting when you grow up always being formal—it's a bit difficult to drop those habits."

Adam replied easily, "Right now I hail from Frisco, but I'm originally from Virginia. For some reason I feel as if we've known each other for some time, and yet I don't know you. Strange, isn't it?"

"It's because of our relationship in Jesus Christ," Elijah interjected. "We are all bonded in Christ…each of us brother and sister."

"Ah, so that's it," Liberty said as she took Matthew's arm. "You dress much like Matthew. It surprised me when you rode up on one side of Elijah. At first I thought you were Kirk, Matthew's brother. I honestly didn't know which one of you was my husband until you drew near. You sit your horse very much like Matthew. Well, come on inside. Conchita has lunch ready and is waiting."

The three walked up the flagstone path to the beautiful hacienda-looking house, where Conchita met them at the door. She wore a warm smile of welcome.

"You comed in an' you eat the deener now." She had a welcoming smile for Adam but spoke to Elijah. "Hello, Meester Humphries! You a welcome beeg surprise. How ees Mees Abigail? How does eet go at the meesion now? How many girls you haf now?" Conchita didn't wait for any answers. "We love to haf you come to veesit weeth us. You mens can wash up een the kitchen. Come, you follow me." She started to bustle hurriedly to the kitchen, but turned when the men didn't follow her.

Elijah said, "Wait, Conchita. First you must meet our guest. This is Adam Brown. He's a new friend of mine."

"You welcome to Rancho Bonito, Meester Brown. You hungry? You ready to eat?"

"It's nice to meet you, ma'am. And, yes, I'm quite hungry." He smiled.

Elijah asked, "I think we'd like to spend the night here, and tomorrow night too, if it's all right with you? I don't think we can get our business done in time to go back home tomorrow. Umm, it smells wonderful."

Liberty took Elijah's arm and led him to the kitchen.

"Certainly you are most welcome to spend both nights. I'll ride over after we eat and ask Papa and Granny to join us. It'll make the evening a party." Liberty smiled warmly but was curious to know what business Elijah was talking about. She didn't wish to be nosey, so she didn't ask.

Conchita pointed to a deep metal sink near the French doors of the kitchen, where several huge jugs of water sat waiting to be used.

"You welcome here, Meester Brown," she said. "You wash up an' you too, Meester Humphries."

Liberty and Matthew also washed up in the kitchen, which prevented Matthew from telling Liberty about Adam Brown.

Conchita said, "We having the *calabacitas con queso*—zucchini with cheese, but I add cheecken an' more cheese. Umm, ees so good."

They sat down to eat, and Boston padded over to the open French doors to lay with a clear view to the courtyard as well as the table and anything that might drop from it.

Matthew said, "Let's thank our Father for this wonderful meal."

They all bowed their heads, and he prayed, "Lord, how grateful we are for Your wondrous love. We thank You for friendships and how close we can feel to another who knows You as Savior. We pray that Adam's day tomorrow will go smoothly and all that transpires will be according to Your purpose. I pray Miss Chandler will be open and willing to abide by her father's wishes. Thank You for this food, for Conchita and Lupe and Luce who prepared it, and for the blessings of fellowship. May You be praised in all we do. We give You all the glory. Amen."

Liberty turned wide green eyes on Adam.

"You're not the man who's inheriting half of Sunrise Ranch, are you?" She asked, a bit incredulous.

"How'd you know about that, Liberty?" Elijah asked even as Matthew opened his mouth to form the question.

"Eden rode over here yesterday." She stared at Adam as she spoke. "She was quite angry and hurt that her father would do this without giving her any warning as to his wishes." Her eyes glanced at Elijah. "Evidently he told Giovanni but wouldn't or didn't enlighten Eden." Liberty's eyes fastened on to her husband's. "She's quite fragile right now. Her parents have been murdered, which in and of itself is an unbelievable shock, but then she loses half of Chandler Olives on top of it. I am moved with compassion for her."

She turned back to Elijah. "She's not a believer, you understand. She has no Savior to get her through this difficult time the way I did." Liberty turned to Adam and asked, "Are you by any chance related to a Simon Brown who was murdered in Boston about three years ago?"

"No, Brown is quite a common name. My only relative is a maiden aunt who lives in Williamsburg, Virginia. Other than that, I don't think I have any family."

"Did you know the Chandlers well?" Liberty asked. "How did you meet them? Have you known them for a long time? I'm sorry for all the questions."

CHAPTER VII

The Spirit itself beareth witness with our spirit,
that we are the children of God:

ROMANS 8:16

LIBERTY HAD MORE QUESTIONS, but only stated, "I'm simply flabbergasted that Eldon and Camilla would do such a thing."

Adam paused before replying, gathering his thoughts.

"You're not the only one!" Honest gray-green eyes met Liberty's. He nearly lost his breath seeing how beautiful Liberty Bannister was.

"I met them last year coming home on a train from Virginia. We struck up a conversation the first night in the dining car coming out of Williamsburg and ended up spending the entire trip eating meals together and simply talking on a wide variety of subjects. I found them a wonderfully fascinating couple. Eldon was an encyclopedia of information on a number of topics, but he never mentioned his owning a company such as Chandler Olives. We parted ways in Sacramento. I wrote them a letter, thanking them for making the trip so interesting. I received an invitation from them about four months ago—to a dinner—but I was down south at the time working on a project, and the date came and went before I returned to San Francisco. I wrote and told him how sorry I was to miss a dinner with them but never heard from them again. I am sorry to hear about their deaths."

His glance shifted to Matthew. "I'd like to help find the murderers if you wouldn't mind me tagging along with you. You're saying the Chandlers weren't robbed? I've never heard of anyone committing a crime of such magnitude without some sort of motive. There must be something behind it."

"I agree, but what?" Matthew asked. "You are welcome to come with me next time I talk to the sheriff, but so far nothing's come up at all. We did have several robberies a few months back, but there was motive. I was bashed over the head and robbed, but we caught all those involved. This business with the Chandlers is a conundrum for sure. I pray we can find who did this heinous crime."

"Well again, as I said, I'd like to help you in any way I can," Adam said.

"Of course, we'd like all the help we can get," Matthew replied.

"By the way, who is Giovanni?" Adam asked, turning toward Liberty for an answer.

"Giovanni Coletti is Sunrise Ranch's foreman. I don't know him very well, but he seems to be rock solid and a sweet man," Liberty replied.

Matthew laughed. "Don't ever tell him that. I don't reckon I know a man who yearns to be called sweet."

They all laughed and enjoyed good conversation as they ate the delicious meal.

Adam shared some of his immediate plans.

"I plan to meet Miss Chandler and then ride back the day after tomorrow to Frisco to pack up a few things. It'll probably take a couple days to get my affairs straightened out. This is an opportune time because I'm between jobs right now. I turned in the paperwork on the bridge down south the end of last week, and everything is finished. I received a letter two days ago asking me to take on another project. I'll send back the request form, turning down this next job, and see what it's like to grow olives."

Elijah turned toward Conchita and asked, "Are we having some of your famous sopapillas?"

"No, I no making sopapillas for lunch. I making the chocoflan. Your mouth weel tell you eet ees *delicioso*. Eet melt een your mouth."

Elijah had only stayed at the Rancho as a guest for a few days when he'd first come west, but it didn't take long to fall in love with Conchita's cooking. He was a great devotee of Conchita's sopapillas, which were filled with honey.

After the meal, Matthew asked Adam and Elijah if they'd like to ride over to Liberty's Land and meet Liberty's father and grandmother instead of Liberty riding over there and giving them an invitation to spend the evening.

Elijah replied first to the invitation. "Definitely. I'd enjoy seeing them again. Alexander is such a peace-filled man to be around. Are you sure we won't be interrupting anything?"

Liberty said, "They would love to see you, Elijah, and to meet you, Adam. They are glad to have visitors anytime, same as us."

"It's fine by me," Adam said. "I'd like to get to know people in the area."

Taylor Kerrigan dressed carefully, putting on his second-best shirt. It was a plaid cowboy shirt, but he was no cowboy. He buttoned it up slowly as he thought about Eden Chandler and how rich he'd be if she were to marry him. Walking over to the mirror above his dresser, he slicked back his hair, making sure his part was straight. *I would think any woman would want someone like me.* He grinned at his reflection, knowing he was a fine physical specimen but not realizing integrity and character were a lot more important than good looks. *She's a looker too, with her chocolate-brown eyes and that honey-blonde hair. Think I'll just mosey on over there and see what she's up to. She's been seeing too much of that Caleb McHaney, and I think he's a threat to our relationship. Wonder how I can get rid of the competition? Wonder if I...ah...I know what I can do.*

Sheriff Buckmaster Jacob Rawlins was a good lawman. He'd lived in the Napa Valley for nearly his entire life and knew most all the folks who lived there. When investigating, he was thorough and prided himself on his ability to solve cases. *Why*, he now asked himself, *why in the world would*

someone murder Eldon and Camilla for no apparent reason? What would a body gain by such a cowardly act? He was at a complete loss on the Chandler case.

Eldon and Camilla had been personal friends of his, and to be gunned down for no cause simply made no sense to him. His heart went out to their daughter, Eden. He knew she must be devastated. Being an only child, she'd been close to her parents.

When Buck's wife died, a little over six years before, Camilla Chandler had been there with food and a listening ear. Eldon had sat up with him many a night and tried to reduce the amount of alcohol he consumed to dull the pain of loss. Eldon had sat and listened to Buck talk and talk, rambling on half the night about Jazzy, short for Jasmine. She'd been a childhood sweetheart, and their love had only grown deeper as the years passed.

He'd just turned thirty-three when Jazzy had gone shopping in San Francisco with a friend. She was hit by an out-of-control carriage pulled by a spooked horse who'd jerked loose from the hitching post. The carriage had careened up onto the boarded walk. It was a freak accident and had left him feeling as if life had no more purpose, no meaning.

The Chandler murders had Buck at his wit's end trying to figure out a motive and the perpetrator. No robbery had taken place. No one stood to gain anything by it as far as he could see. *Why*, he asked himself for the hundredth time. *Why would anyone do such a beastly thing?*

Matthew, Adam, and Elijah went out to saddle up. Matthew nodded to his foreman and said, "Diego, I'd like you to meet Adam Brown. Adam, meet Diego Rodriguez, Conchita's husband. He's also the best foreman a man could have. He's my right-hand man, and like the Bible says, he's a friend that sticks closer than a brother."

The two men shook hands, eyeing each other. "I'm pleased to meet you, Mr. Rodriguez," Adam said.

"I am happy to meet you, Meester Brown. You have one fine horse. She look like Piggypie." He smiled widely, his strong teeth strikingly white in his darkly tanned face.

Matthew spoke to him. "We're riding over to Liberty's Landing and may not be back for supper. I forgot to tell Conchita."

"I weel tell her, Meester Bannister. I go eat now, an' I weel tell her."

"Thanks, Diego." Matthew smiled his appreciation.

Liberty came out to saddle up her horse, but Conchita had told Diego that Liberty would be soon be riding out, and Pookie was saddled and ready.

"Thank you, Diego. I appreciate it." Liberty climbed onto her horse and happened to glance at Adam, whose lips were twitching in humor.

"Is something funny?" she asked.

"No, sorry. I reckon I've never seen another woman beside my aunt ride astride. It just caught my funny bone. I have no doubt my aunt Hattie would take a real shine to you."

Liberty replied, "I rode side saddle while at boarding school and after I returned, but once I came west, I determined I would ride astride. I'm grateful Matthew agrees with me."

Elijah said, "Abigail is taking riding lessons, and she's riding astride too. She so admired Liberty's outfits that she's made some split skirts. I can see you women are going to refashion the West." He chuckled, and Liberty joined him.

Matthew looked around, "Everyone ready?" He wheeled Piggypie around and started out with Liberty riding beside him. Adam rode next to Elijah. Once they left the lane, Matthew kicked into a canter, and the rest followed suit. It would not take long to get to Liberty's Landing.

Taylor Kerrigan rode midafternoon to the Chandlers', knowing he'd be invited in for tea. As he rode up the long, winding drive at a leisurely pace, Gio saw him coming.

Giovanni Coletti did not like Taylor Kerrigan. He'd never said anything to his employer, but Gio knew a fortune hunter when he saw one. He knew Eldon hadn't liked Kerrigan either. Neither Cammie nor Eldon ever said anything to Eden, because she would take up Kerrigan as one of her causes. It had been a smart strategy.

Gio had wondered more than once where the Kerrigan money came from. There seemed to be no source of income. They lived in a decent house down the road a ways, but Terrence Kerrigan did not work and neither did his son. When Gio saw Taylor on the lane, he made himself scarce.

Taylor rode leisurely up to the house and tied his horse to the hitching post, whistling under his breath. He knocked on the door as he straightened his bolo tie, and Dorothy Jenkins, the Chandlers' housekeeper, opened the door.

"Why hello, Mr. Kerrigan," she said pleasantly. "What can I do for you?"

"Is Miss Eden home?" he asked. A frown marred his good looks. She didn't invite him in, and he noticed it. He was taken aback by the lack of hospitality.

"Yes, she is. I'm sorry, Mr. Kerrigan. She's in deep mourning and not accepting callers at this time. Perhaps in a couple months, but not now. So sorry." She started to close the door, but Taylor spoke up quickly.

"She'll see me if you'll just let her know I'm here. I'm a close friend, you understand."

"Evidently not that close, Mr. Kerrigan. She gave me the strictest orders not to allow anyone inside who is not on her list, and you, I am afraid, are not on her list. Sorry. Come back another time. Good day." Mrs. Jenkins gently closed the door in the young man's face.

Dumbfounded but extremely angry, Taylor stood facing the shut door. He felt like kicking it. He headed down the steps, his body stiff with rage. He thought he saw movement in the dimness of the stable but didn't wish to encounter the foreman. He didn't like the Chandlers' foreman and knew the feeling was mutual. He got on his horse and spurred it hard, heading down the long lane at a gallop and turning onto the main road to ride home.

Hattie Hamilton had packed up her house, deciding she'd had enough of not seeing her nephew, Adam, on a regular basis. For the past six months she'd felt the Lord tugging at her heart. It had taken her five months to finally respond.

Hattie spent a month getting ready to go west. She'd sold nearly all her furniture, keeping a few favorite pieces, which were held in storage as well as several trunks. For the entire month of May, she'd been a guest of her friends Emmaline and Josiah Danforth. Their house was listed on the historical register. Most of the acreage had been sold off, but the house retained huge grounds and some outbuildings. It was a stately edifice with tiered gardens leading down to the James River. The old colonial plantation had escaped the devastation caused by the War Between the States.

She sat in front of the window of her guest room, quill in hand, ticking off items on her list of things to do. Her hair, a deep-auburn color, gleamed from the sun streaming through the window. She stood and checked the tickets in her reticule, making sure she knew the time her train would leave in the morning. *Hope I'm not journey proud. I'd like to get a full night's sleep before heading west.*

She looked again through her satchel and felt she was prepared and ready. *I trust that man who owns the storage place remembers to get my things loaded tomorrow morning. I reckon all I need do is send off a telegram first thing tomorrow and pray Adam's not gallivanting off somewhere, and able to meet my train. I'm going to buy a house right there in San Francisco for us to live in. Oh, it will be good to see him again!*

Matthew pulled up Piggypie on the hill overlooking Liberty's Landing. His property abutted this land, which had belonged to Liberty. She'd deeded the land to her father, Alexander Liberty, when she married Matthew. A reverse dowry, she'd called it. *She is the best thing that ever happened to me*, he thought, resting his arm on the pommel of his saddle. *If it wasn't for her, I'd never have found Christ as my Savior or realized how good life can be. I carried such a grudge against God and life itself.*

"What a beautiful setting!" Adam exclaimed, drawing up next to him. "Wonder if the Garden of Eden looked like this!"

Liberty's heart warmed at his words. "Probably not, but my father has made this a veritable paradise with the way he put in the grapes and landscaped around the house. It is beautiful, isn't it?"

"It's a picture-book setting, Liberty," Elijah said. "I remember what it looked like before you started building. You picked a perfect spot. It reminds me of when Abby and I were in Italy."

"Thank you, Elijah. I think Papa missed Italy and fashioned the vines to look like Italy. Matthew staked out this property when he staked his," Liberty said to Adam. "I'm glad he didn't choose to stake out the property on the other side of his. I love this little valley."

Matthew smiled warmly at Liberty's comment and clucked to Piggypie to get going.

They started down the slope, and it wasn't long before they were pulling up in front of the stately house Liberty had designed.

Phoebe came out the front door, wiping her hands on an apron. "Welcome, welcome!" she said.

The riders tied up their horses, and Phoebe held out her arms to Liberty. They embraced, and Elijah stepped forward with a grin to say, "I'd like one of those too."

After they hugged, Matthew draped an arm over Phoebe's shoulders and said, "Phoebe Liberty, meet Adam Brown. Adam, meet Phoebe."

Phoebe proffered her hand, and Adam took it in a warm grasp and said, "Pleased to meet you, ma'am. Your granddaughter certainly looks like you."

"I'm pleased to meet you too, young man. You are welcome here at Liberty's Landing. And yes, even I can see the resemblance between Liberty and me."

"Is Papa in the vineyard?" Liberty asked. "We've come to spend the rest of the afternoon and evening. Adam is our guest for the night, and we wanted him to meet you, as he'll most likely be Napa's newest resident."

Phoebe replied, "No, your papa just came in a few minutes ago and is getting cleaned up. I'm sure he'll be down in a few minutes. We had planned to ride into Napa this afternoon, but it can certainly wait. We can do that any day, but it's not every day we have visitors." She looked at Adam, curiosity in her eyes. "So, you plan to reside in Napa? Come on inside and tell us all about it. Excuse me for a minute. I'll tell Cook to make a bit more for dinner."

"I can do that," Liberty said. "I'm going in to see her anyway." She headed off in the direction of the kitchen and came up behind Mrs. Jensen, whom she lovingly called Cook. Wrapping her arms around the substantial waist, she gave the woman a big squeeze.

"Ah, it's my Miss Liberty! Oh, I yam zo habby to see you! Velcome, velcome! How iz da little mama, huh?"

"I'm fine except for that dratted morning sickness. The rest of the day I seem to do all right. It's good to see you too. We'll be staying for dinner, and we brought Elijah with us as well as another man named Mr. Brown."

"Ya, I vill cook some good food for you, Miss Liberty." She patted Liberty's hand and swung around toward her stove. "I start right now!"

"All right. I hear Papa and want to say hello. I'll talk to you later." She went to the great room, which was styled after Matthew's but a bit more formal in appearance.

CHAPTER VIII

"**P**APA!" **LIBERTY STRODE TOWARD HER FATHER**, who met her halfway, and they hugged, her father lifting her off the floor and swinging her around a bit. Liberty loved her father deeply, although for twenty-nine years she hadn't known of his existence.

Introductions to Adam had already been made, and they all sat down to enjoy good conversation. Explanations were made about Adam and how he'd inherited half of the Chandlers' estate—although Elijah admonished them to not tell anyone just yet.

Cook came in with a tray of open-faced sandwiches and cookies she'd baked just that morning. Coffee and tea was served, and pleasant conversation ensued. They sat and talked for quite some time, and then, before going in to dinner, Alexander had taken everyone out to see his newest addition of a private screened bathing area of the hot spring that was on the property. He'd woven grape vines from the year before, and it resulted in a beautiful mesh fence, screening the area from any prying eyes. Although they hadn't grown much yet, he'd planted wisteria to grow up his grapevine fence.

"After the baby is born, you'll have to try it, Liberty. You'll love it!"

Liberty's moss-green eyes were full of laughter, thinking about a conversation, just a couple months previous, when her granny had said she wanted to bathe in the hot spring in the all-together. Liberty knew that meant no clothes. Her eyes, full of mirth, caught her granny's, and they both started laughing. The men, except Alexander, who grinned at them, had no idea what they were chuckling about, which just made them laugh harder.

The meal was wonderful, and the conversation stimulating. Adam sat back looking at everyone around the table, amazed how comfortable he felt. He'd never felt this way except with his aunt Hattie. He gave God the glory for his newly found friends.

Awaking very early the next morning, Adam lay thinking about the evening before. It had been quite late when they'd ridden back to the Rancho. Stars overhead had seemed so close he felt he could reach out and touch them. There'd been some shooting stars streaking across the heavens. He sat up, stretched, and looked at his pocket watch. He raised his eyebrows at the time and rolled over, falling quickly back to sleep.

Elijah was up early after the late night.

It didn't seem to matter when he went to bed—he was always up about the same time every morning. He had to be quite ill to sleep in. He divested himself of his nightshirt and dressed quickly. He was quiet in the bathing room, as it was shared by Adam in the next bedroom.

He walked down the long hall and let himself out the front door. He'd realized the night before that he'd left his Bible in his saddlebag instead of putting it in his satchel. In the morning, he normally read a chapter from a book of the Bible he was studying, and he always read a chapter in Proverbs that aligned with the date on the calendar before going to sleep at night. Last evening he'd skipped. Being extremely weary, he hadn't wanted to traipse over to the stable to get his Bible. He'd also not been able to keep his eyes open. On the front flagstone walk, he stretched and took a couple deep breaths. The view was fantastic, and although the air was quite cool, the sun was up before him, and it looked to be a beautiful day.

As he entered the stable, he saw one of the hired hands, a young man, already feeding the horses. Elijah didn't recognize him.

"Good morning," he said, "I'm Elijah Humphries."

"Good morning, sir, you're up early. Name's Donald Miller, but most folks around here just call me Donny."

Elijah stuck out his hand for a shake and met the hard, callused one of Donald Miller. He smiled into blue eyes that looked pure as a young child's, innocent of all guile.

"I'm pleased to meet you, Donny. You must be fairly new. I forgot to get my Bible. I left it in my saddlebag instead of my satchel."

Donny said, "I've been here about four months now. Got hired on because this place is growing and Diego needed help. He's the one who hired me." He watched as Elijah began to search his saddlebag. "The Good Book's the only one to live by, isn't it?"

"Yes, yes it is, Donny. Yes it is." He dug into his saddlebag, which sat on a stand, and pulled out his Bible. He left as Donny, whistling softly to himself, poured a few oats into a manger.

Elijah found a comfortable chair on the front veranda and sat to read and pray. He propped his legs up on the ottoman and let his body relax. He looked over the vineyard. Birds flitted by, and some were clinging to a suet ball hung on an orange tree. The sky was pure azure. It was a beautiful June morning, the air fresh and pure but still quite cool, and Elijah was glad for his frock coat. He sat where the sun could warm him, grateful to be alive and enjoying this moment. He pulled a checked blanket, on one of the chairs, over his legs.

He began to pray, always beginning his prayer time praising God and acknowledging His wonderful attributes. When he got around to his requests, his biggest supplication this day was about Adam and the situation he would face at Sunrise Canyon. He prayed for Eden Chandler and that God would help Buckmaster Rawlins find the person or people who'd left Eden an orphan.

When he finished, he sat and thought about the sheriff and what he knew of him. He'd met Sheriff Rawlins when Liberty had been kidnapped by her evil stepfather. Elijah knew the sheriff was a good man and would do his best to find who'd done this wicked thing.

It was less than an hour later that Matthew discovered Elijah on the veranda and invited him in to have breakfast. Elijah's stomach rumbled as the smells from the kitchen wafted his way.

Breakfast was bacon, eggs, onions, and green peppers wrapped up in a tortilla served with salsa, sour cream, and guacamole.

Adam and Elijah spoke about their plans for riding over to Sunrise Ranch, meeting with Eden Chandler and coming back to Rancho Bonito for dinner.

"I'd like to ride over with the two of you—that is, if you don't mind me tagging along," Matthew said to the two men.

"Make that a party! I'm coming too. Just let me get my hat and gun," Liberty said.

Adam's eyebrows rose at her comment, but Matthew grinned and said, "I reckon whether the two of you like it or not, the Bannisters are coming too…all three of us."

"Three of you?" Adam asked a bit bewilderedly.

"Liberty's expecting our first baby," Matthew said proudly. "We're due in four more months."

"That's right, Abigail mentioned that to me. Should she be riding a horse? I know she did yesterday, but what I mean is, is that healthy?"

Liberty came back from her room, her hat already in place; she was fastening her gun belt. "I've been riding a horse since I was three, so yes, I can ride a horse."

Adam laughed but sobered when he saw her strapping on a gun, "I didn't mean that. I meant since you're expecting a baby, is it all right for you to ride?"

"Frankly, Dr. John disapproves, but it doesn't seem to hurt anything. I love to ride, and as long as I seem to be all right doing it, I will continue. When Matthew has to boot me up, I'll quit," Liberty replied with a smile. "Let's get going."

Their horses were saddled and ready. Liberty stepped into the stirrup on Pookie and was up with no help.

Liberty saw Adam's look of surprise. She knew she looked feminine, but here she was wearing a gun and riding astride. "It must come as a shock to you," she said.

Elijah grinned when he saw Adam's expression.

"You should have seen her back east in her mansion and formal attire. You'd never believe it was the same woman." He looked at Liberty with eyes full of love, thankful he'd been a part of freeing her from a life of misery.

"I had no idea life could be so good or that I could be so happy," Liberty said. "God has been gracious to me."

They headed out with a wave to Diego and Donny. The ride was short, and it didn't take long for them to arrive at their destination. It was midmorning when the four started up the long lane to the Chandlers' house.

Gio, who had come out of the stable, spotted them as he climbed the steps to the house. He had planned to talk to Dottie but decided to wait and see who was coming. Gio always called Mrs. Jenkins Dottie, short for her real name of Dorothy. He wanted to know what she'd said to the Kerrigan boy the day before. Instead, he shaded his eyes to better see who might be coming up the lane and stood waiting patiently until they arrived.

Matthew smiled at Giovanni, slid off Piggypie, and tied her to the railing.

"Hello, Giovanni." Matthew strode up the walk. "Good to see you. You've been through a difficult time, and I'm sorry for all that has happened. I've been praying for you, sir." He shook the older man's hand with his right and clapped him on the back with his left.

The older man teared up and said, "I cannot begin to tell you the sorrow of my heart." As he spoke, the rest of the group came up the walk.

Liberty took his face in both of her hands, kissing one cheek and then the other, European style. "Oh, Giovanni, I am so sorry for your loss. My heart mourns for you. As Matthew said, we are praying for the good Lord to comfort your sorrowing heart." She stood back, her hands resting on the shoulders of the older man. Her green eyes gazed into his brown ones, hers filled with compassion and tears. "May God comfort your heart, Gio," she said quietly.

"Thank you, madam. Thank you." He looked curiously at Elijah and Adam, and Matthew made the introductions.

"Giovanni Coletti, this is Elijah Humphries, a lawyer from San Rafael and a great friend of ours, and this is Adam Brown, an engineer for the state of California. He lives in San Francisco when he's not out on a job."

Gio wondered why they had come.

The men shook hands as Gio looked each man in the eyes. He liked what he saw.

Adam glanced at Matthew and cleared his throat as he spoke to the older man.

"Mr. Coletti—"

"Giovanni, just call me Giovanni," the older man said, his posture dignified and proud.

"Giovanni." Adam spoke with hesitance. "I reckon I don't understand all that has transpired. I am sorry for your loss. I met Eldon and Camilla last year on the train—"

"So, you are the man!" Gio's eyes showed their surprise, yet understanding filled them also. "I didn't realize you'd be so young."

"Yes, I am the man. It's come as a shock to me. I have no idea why Eldon would do this. I only knew them for a little over five days. They were a wonderful couple."

Gio looked the young man up and down and stared into gray-green eyes that were honest and clear. He knew exactly why Eldon had done such a thing. He'd explained to Gio that as soon as either Eden or Adam married, Eldon would change his will back to solely Eden. In the meantime, in case of an unforeseen accident, Eldon Chandler had picked Adam for a son-in-law. He had planned for the young man to come for a visit and meet Eden. He was sure the rest would fall into place quite naturally. The will would be in effect even if Camilla were still alive. Gio hoped Eldon's faith in this young man was not misplaced.

"He must have had his reasons," Gio said succinctly, "but it doesn't come as a shock to me. Eldon apprised me of his plans when he returned last year from his trip east. I will tell you straight up you're going to need the patience of Job." He gave a small, tight smile as he thought of Eden and her headstrong ways. "Come, I'll introduce you to Eden and let you do the rest. I'd have thought that lawyer, Stephen Hancock, would have come with you."

"Stephen is on holiday, sir. He is my colleague," Elijah said. "It's fortunate that I know the Bannisters, as it makes things a bit smoother, don't you think?"

"You will need all the help you can get, Mr. Humphries," Gio responded sagely. With a nod of his head, he said, "Come." He opened the front door just as Mrs. Jenkins was entering the large front foyer from a door further back in the hall.

A beautiful parlor opened on the right of the hall. It had no wall facing the foyer or hall, only a massive column midway down that delineated the hall from the parlor. A grand piano stood in an enormous bay window on the right. The room had an air of distinction and was far more formal than the room on the left. The wide door to that room was open and revealed a comfortable open-concept great room with a huge kitchen at the far end of it. It was here that Gio led his guests.

"Good afternoon, Mrs. Jenkins," Liberty said. "I hope it's all right that we come at this time—"

"Oh yes, it is perfectly fine, Mrs. Bannister. Eden filled out a list of those she would like to see, and you are on it…both of you, right at the top." She smiled warmly at Liberty. "I understand she rode over and spoke with you yesterday. Thank you for being such a comfort to her. I'd also like to say"—Mrs. Jenkins blushed as she continued —"congratulations as well, Mrs. Bannister. How excited you must be to have a baby." She glanced over at Elijah and Adam, clearly embarrassed speaking of such a delicate matter in front of strangers.

"Thank you, Mrs. Jenkins. Yes, I am excited. I have three and a half more months to wait. Meanwhile, I'm furiously knitting, crocheting, and tatting."

Liberty looked over at Matthew to perform the introductions.

Matthew stepped up and took Mrs. Jenkins' hand. "I'd like to introduce you to a couple of friends of mine. Mrs. Jenkins, please meet Elijah Humphries from San Rafael and Adam Brown of San Francisco. Elijah, Adam, meet Mrs. Jenkins, who keeps the house running like clockwork."

The two men shook the hand she proffered. Dorothy, though obviously not used to being introduced to guests, graciously said, "It's a pleasure to meet you. Please, do make yourself at home, and I'll get Berry to rustle up some tea, unless someone prefers coffee?"

"Tea will be fine, Dottie." Gio spoke for the group. "But we need Eden to come down to meet our guests."

Mrs. Jenkins took a second glance at Elijah and Adam. Gio figured his tone alerted her to the fact that this was not a sympathy visit for Eden.

"I'll have Dolly get her," she said with another glance at the two men.

"*Grazie*, Dottie," Gio said softly. She inclined her head and left the room.

Gio said, "Please, be seated." He indicated a couple deep chintz-covered chairs and a love seat. He seated himself in a wingback. Looking straight at Adam, he said, "So, you are an engineer for the state. I don't suppose you know anything about olives, do you? Eldon was a bit sketchy about you but said you would fit the bill just fine."

Adam looked at Gio in amazement. "Fit the bill? I know nothing about olives. In truth, the subject never came up. I enjoyed my conversations with both Eldon and Camilla, but neither one spoke about olives. I had no idea they were the owners of Chandler Olives. We spoke on a variety of topics, and I found them to be one of the most delightful couples I'd ever met. But fit the bill? Me? No, I don't believe I do."

CHAPTER IX

Let no man seek his own,
but every man another's wealth.

1 CORINTHIANS 10:24

HATTIE HAMILTON MET A SWEET OLDER LADY on the train. The second time she had gone to the dining car there had been another lady sitting across the aisle from where she'd been seated. They struck up a conversation, and Hattie invited the other woman to come back to her compartment. The two passed the time talking about their respective lives and found comfort in going to the dining car together instead of alone. Now, the two ladies sat across the table from each another, conversing comfortably. Although Hattie had been in the dining car several times, it never ceased to amaze her how pristine the tablecloths were and how spacious the car seemed.

She was a bit anxious about arriving in San Francisco without having heard back from Adam. She told Bertha she felt a bit of a dunce that she hadn't wired him earlier on, when she had time to receive an answer. Her new friend, Mrs. Bertha Morrow, told her not to fret. If Adam didn't appear, she was more than welcome to stay with her until Adam could be notified.

"I live north of San Francisco. You are entirely welcome to stay with me. I'm a bit lonely without my husband. He went home to be with the Lord two years ago. We never did have children. Now I ramble around in my house and keep busy with sewing bees, church, and various other activities."

"It sounds as if you must be quite busy. What other activities?"

"Well, let me see. I belong to a sketching club, which I find quite enjoyable. I've always loved to draw, and although they are expensive, I very much enjoy using those wonderful colored pencils. I also belong to a women's suffrage group and play whist with several other ladies once a week. I also belong to a knitting group that gets together once a week."

"My, you must be one busy lady. Where do you live?"

"Oh, for nigh unto twenty-two years I've lived in up in Napa, California, just on the outskirts of town. It's just short of forty miles north of San Francisco, but it don't seem far to me."

"Well, I appreciate the invitation, Mrs. Morrow, and I will be delighted to stay with you if Adam doesn't meet our train. Now that I'm on my way to California, I feel silly I didn't notify Adam earlier. It took me long enough to finally make the decision to pack up and go west. I simply had a difficult time selling the house my parents lived in. I reckon that didn't sound the way I meant it. It sold right away, mind you. It was difficult for me emotionally. I was raised there and have lived in it all my life. I reckon the good Lord has other plans for me, as He's been tugging at my heart for nigh unto six months now, wanting me to join Adam. It's just that Adam's never home, and when he is, he lives in a hotel. I finally came to the place where I realized I could buy a house and keep a nice place for him whenever he's in town, and when he's not…well, I'll just have to get involved in activities such as you do yourself, Mrs. Morrow."

"Please, just call me Bertha. I have been with you every day for the past three, and I don't wish to stand on formality."

"Well, then, thank you, Bertha, and please, you may call me Hattie."

With the offer of a place to stay, Hattie Hamilton felt relieved and thankful to the Almighty for providing this woman for her.

Dolly climbed the stairs to the second floor. With dragging footsteps, she walked down the hall to Miss Eden's suite of rooms and tapped lightly on the door. She knew her mistress had cried a lot over the last few days, and she didn't wish to intrude, but a command from Mrs. Jenkins was not to be taken lightly. There was no answer, so she knocked louder. It wasn't all that often visitors came to actually visit the inhabitants of the big house. Most visitors were shown the office and olive production, people who wanted a tour of the grounds.

"Come in," Eden said softly as Dolly opened the door. "What is it?"

"Guests come ta visit, miss."

"Who?"

"Mr. and Mrs. Matthew Bannister, and they brought two other men with 'em, miss."

"Liberty's here? Goodness, help me with the back of my dress, Dolly. I was just about to put on my denims and go riding. Never mind. That blouse will do. Button it up please."

Buttons ran down the back from the neck to below a fitted waist. It was new and entirely black. Eden hurriedly slipped her arms into the puffed sleeves, and Dolly buttoned the square jet-black buttons. As Eden pulled on the black denim split skirt, Dolly grabbed her espadrilles. Her hair was brushed out, and she twisted it around into a fat bun while her feet moved to slip on the shoes. Dolly stuck a couple curved combs into either side of the bun to hold it in place. With a glance in the mirror, Eden pinched her cheeks for color and bit her lips, hoping to not look so pale.

"Thanks, Dolly girl. Reckon I'll do." She exited with quick strides toward the stairs, wondering who the two men were who'd come with the Bannisters. It didn't really matter. Liberty was here, and Liberty cheered her up. She ran lightly down the steps. Gaining the bottom, she straightened her blouse, lifted her chin, and walked into the parlor to find her guests were not there. She heard voices and walked on to the great room.

"Liberty! What a wonderful surprise!" She held out both hands to grasp Liberty's, and pulling her friend toward her, she gave Liberty a hug. Turning graciously toward Matthew, she said, "I thought you weren't coming back from San Francisco until tomorrow. Good morning, Matthew Bannister, it's good to see you again." Her smile was welcoming, although she knew dark shadows circled her eyes.

"Miss Eden, it's good to see you. I didn't get much of a chance to speak to you at the funeral, but again, I offer you my sincerest condolences. I'd like you to meet a couple friends of mine. This is Elijah Humphries, owner of the mission for women in San Rafael."

Eden proffered her hand, which Elijah took tenderly. "I am pleased to meet you, Miss Chandler, and I am deeply sorry for your loss."

"It's nice to meet a friend of the Bannisters," she replied.

"And this is Adam Brown, a state engineer from San Francisco."

Eden again proffered her hand. "Welcome, Mr. Brown. Any friend of the Bannisters is welcome here." Eden was not short, but Adam was at least five inches taller, and she looked up into beautiful gray-green eyes. She retrieved her hand hastily, wondering at the effect the man had on her.

"I too am sorry for your loss, Miss Chandler, but I'm pleased to finally get to meet you. I feel as if I know you. I've met your parents, and they were wonderful people."

"You knew my parents?" Her brown eyes widened in surprise.

"Yes. Last year I was coming home from visiting my aunt in Williamsburg, Virginia, and your parents and I shared every waking moment on the train together. They told me a lot of stories about you. Again, I am so sorry for what has happened. What a horrible tragedy. They were wonderful folk, and I'm sure you must be devastated." He looked into her cocoa-colored eyes, and she wondered if he saw the pain etched there as well as dark smudges underneath. She wasn't sleeping well.

"I feel as if I'm in a nightmare and I'll wake up to find it all untrue. It doesn't seem possible." She looked at her guests. Why was Gio there? "Please, be seated. I'll see if Berry can rustle us up something worth eating." She left with a smooth stride and no self-consciousness as she walked to the other end of the gigantic room where Berry and Mrs. Jenkins were both busy making tea and coffee to go with the cherry pies that had just come out of the oven. Cherries were just beginning to ripen in the lower valley, and Berry had made a couple delicious-looking pies.

Gio turned to Elijah, saying in a low voice, "I think it best if you or one of the Bannisters would relate the truth about this young man *after* we've had something to eat. Otherwise, we may not get to eat it, and I can assure you, Berry can concoct wonderfully tasty desserts."

Elijah glanced over at Matthew and Liberty, a question in his eyes. "I'll tell her after we've had tea," Liberty said in a low voice. "This is not going to be easy for her, so please say a prayer in the next few minutes. She's been devastated by all the events of the past week. I feel sorry for her."

Eden returned to the group. "Mrs. Jenkins has it all under control. Berry was making a couple cherry pies, so you're in for a treat. Please"— she gestured to the settee and chairs—"sit down."

The men had all stood when she came back to join them. She glanced at Adam Brown and then at Matthew. "You two look a lot alike, the way you dress." She smiled at her guests and then spoke rapidly in Italian to Gio. *"Che succede, Gio, perché non sei fuori per lavoro?"* (What's going on, Gio? Why are you not out working?)

Gio replied, *"Voglio un po 'di torta di ciliegie."* (I want some cherry pie.) He smiled winningly, and she had to smile back. She turned to her guests, and Adam replied to her comment.

"I guess we do dress a bit alike, but you should see our horses."

"Why is that?"

"Have you ever seen Matthew's horse?"

"Yes, of course I have," she replied.

"Well, I have Piggypie's twin."

Eden looked startled. She went to the front door, opened it, and saw the horses tied to the hitching post. As she did so, another rider came into view down the long lane. She took a quick glance at the two piebald mares tied to the rail and was surprised to find she didn't know which one was Matthew's. She looked up again to see that the rider was Caleb McHaney. She closed the door quickly and went to get Mrs. Jenkins, who was still in the kitchen helping Berry.

"Caleb McHaney is riding up. I think we have enough company, and I don't care to see him right now, so could you please take care of it?"

"Certainly, Miss Eden." She wiped her hands on a towel, and as Eden headed back across the expanse to the great room, Dorothy Jenkins went to the front door.

Suddenly Eden changed her mind. Caleb was her good friend, and Eden decided she wanted him to meet her other guests. When Mrs. Jenkins opened the door, Eden was standing behind her to welcome Caleb into the house. Mrs. Jenkins glanced at her in surprise, smiled at

Caleb, and took the cake he offered. With a thank-you, she headed back to the kitchen.

"Caleb! How nice to see you," Eden said. "Come on inside and meet some people."

"Are you sure you don't mind, Eden? I know you must be suffering mightily, and I don't want to butt in where I'm not wanted. I came by to bring the cake my mother made, not to bother you."

"Thank you for your consideration, but as I already have guests, one more won't matter. Besides, you're practically family. Come on with me, and I'll introduce you to a couple of them." She pulled at his arm, and he came in halfheartedly, looking as if he didn't want to be there.

"Matthew, Liberty, you both remember Caleb McHaney, don't you?"

"Good to see you, Caleb. How's that beautiful paint coming along that you were trying to break?" Matthew grinned at the younger man.

"You can see for yourself. She's hitched to the railing outside. Good strong mare she is too, even if I do say so myself!" Caleb replied. The two men shook hands, and Liberty stepped forward, her hand outstretched in a warm greeting.

"How nice to see you, Caleb. We'll have to arrange for you and your mother to come to dinner sometime."

Caleb shook her hand and said, "We'd both be honored, Miss Liberty."

Eden took Caleb's arm in hers and turned him to face Elijah and Adam.

"I'd like you to meet our other guests. This is Elijah Humphries from the women's mission in San Rafael, and this is Adam Brown, a state engineer from San Francisco. Mr. Humphries, Mr. Brown, Caleb McHaney from just down the road."

Elijah looked keenly into the young man's eyes and smiled pleasantly as he held out his hand to shake.

"Pleased to meet you, Mr. McHaney."

"Likewise," Adam said, a smile on his face as he also shook Caleb's hand.

"The honor is mine," Caleb replied.

"Please, be seated. It looks like cherry pie and, umm, is that an upside down pineapple cake? Yum, it's one of my favorites. Be sure to thank your mother," Eden said.

"I will, Eden, but I have some chores to do. I only wanted you to know my mama and I give you our deepest condolences," Caleb said.

"I'll just mosey on home and tell mama you're doing the best you can under the circumstances. Thanks for the invite though." He turned to the others. "It was nice to make your acquaintance."

Matthew said, "We really would like you to stay, Caleb. Chores will always be there."

Caleb looked pleased that Matthew wanted him to stay. He glanced at Eden and said, "Thank you. Reckon you're right. Chores *will* always be there. Besides, I love Berry's cooking." He sat down in an empty chair, and everyone else did likewise.

Mrs. Jenkins, along with Berry, served the coffee and tea. There were open-faced sandwiches and cherry pie as well as the pineapple upside down cake Caleb had brought.

"Thank you, Berry, Mrs. Jenkins. This looks delicious," Eden said, and the rest agreed. The conversation turned to the new president, who'd only been in office for three months.

Elijah said, "I've met the previous president, Chester Arthur, but I've never met Grover Cleveland. He won by popular vote, and I like it that he's conservative about spending money. I read last week in the *San Francisco Chronicle* that he's vetoed unnecessary spending bills eight times in his first two months of presidency."

"What do you think about the new vice president, sir?" Caleb asked. "It's been quite a while since we've had one."

"Well, son, I know he ran with Samuel Tilden for vice president back in seventy-six and lost, and I also know he's not a very healthy man. He's a National Democrat, and I think we'll just have to see."

Conversation continued until they were finished eating. Liberty glanced over at Elijah, who gave a slight nod of his head.

"Eden," Liberty said, "the reason we all came to visit you, besides offering our condolences, was to introduce you to Adam—"

"For goodness' sakes, Liberty, whatever for?" She nodded toward Adam as her face colored slightly. "Are you familiar with olive groves?"

Liberty didn't let Adam reply but spoke soothingly. "Eden, please let me finish. Adam Brown, as he said, met your parents on the train last year coming back from Virginia. For some reason your father was very taken with him. Adam is the man to whom your father deeded half of Sunrise Ranch."

"What?" Eden's eyes widened in stunned disbelief. "You're saying this man's it?"

"I am, Miss Chandler." Adam stood and took a step toward her. "I am as surprised as you, and quite frankly, I can't believe Eldon did this," he said humbly.

Eden's eyes hardened as she stared at him. "Why did you come here? You have no business being here! My father had to have been coerced! What were you doing? Blackmailing him?" Her voice rose to a fevered pitch. She picked up her plate and hurled it at the wall, where it smashed into bits. She ran out of the room and up the stairs. Her heavy door slammed with a huge bang.

There was a stunned silence which Caleb broke.

"Whew!" said Caleb. "I hate to tell you this, but once Eden forms an opinion about something, it's like yanking teeth to change it." He picked up his hat and turned to ask Adam, "What man is it that you're supposed to be, anyway?"

Adam, obviously upset, replied, "Eldon left half of Sunrise Ranch to me with stipulations for both Miss Eden and me."

Caleb's eyes widened, and his hands involuntarily crushed his hat. "No wonder she's upset! I would be too. Oh my, what a shock that must have been for Eden." His eyes misted over, and he noticeably swallowed. "Reckon I need to be going home now." He went over to the kitchen, where Berry was cleaning up. "Thanks for the pie, Berry. It's surely the best I've ever had."

Returning to the great room, he said with a nod at Giovanni, "I enjoyed the conversation. It was nice to meet you all...good-bye." Caleb started for the door in near embarrassment for Eden's behavior and the stunned silence that pervaded the room.

Matthew joined him at the front door, and Caleb turned to him, a question in his eyes.

"I've been sticking around to see if I can be of some help to Eden, but it looks like she has help from several different directions," Caleb said. "I was wondering, Matthew. Do you think Kirk could use me on his ranch? I've always had a hankering to do real ranching, and I'm looking to hire on if he could use me."

Matthew, clearly surprised by Caleb's question, replied, "Kirk could always use more help. I know when I worked there, they would hire men who simply showed up with a desire for a job. If they proved to be a good worker, they were kept on. Kirk knows you which is a bonus. You just need to ride over to Sonoma and see. You're a hard worker, Caleb, and I'm sure my brother would be happy to have you work for him."

CHAPTER X

*Cast thy burden upon the LORD, and he shall sustain thee:
he shall never suffer the righteous to be moved.*

PSALM 55:22

GIO HURRIED TO THE DOOR, followed by Dorthy Jenkins, who handed Caleb the cleaned cake plate, which had a couple pieces of cherry pie on it. "Thank your mother for us, won't you, dear? I know Miss Eden enjoyed it. And you're more than welcome to drop by anytime. We love having you."

Gio shook his head in regret and said, "I'll see you out, Caleb." He opened the door and ushered the younger man out, with Matthew at his heels. "Tell your mother we appreciated the cake. What a beautiful horse!" Gio appreciated good horseflesh. "I see what you mean, Matthew. That's one splendid-looking horse you have there, Caleb."

Caleb lifted his hat and said, "Thanks. I think so too. Mother will be glad you liked the cake...I'll be seeing you both later. Bye." He set his foot into the stirrup and turned his pretty black-and-white mare to head down the road. Gio went back into the house to join the rest of the guests in the great room. It was still silent, and no one seemed to know exactly what to do.

Liberty stepped close to Gio, took his hand, and said, "I'm sorry we upset Eden. She has had enough to bear. Would you mind if I go up and talk to her?"

"No, not at all. Please do, although I don't believe it'll do any good. It'll take more than you talking to her to make her see there's nothing to be gained by acting the way she did. She has to work it out for herself. She told me yesterday whoever the man was, he was her enemy." He glanced at Adam, wondering what kind of man he was. His eyes looked clear and honest. "Sorry, Mr. Brown but—"

"Adam," he interrupted, "please, just call me Adam."

"Adam—I'm sorry for the outburst. She's always been headstrong and a very independent thinker."

"Excuse me," Liberty said. "Which room is it?"

"Make a left turn at the top of the stairs. It's the third door on the right," Gio replied.

Gio nodded at Liberty, glad she saw the need to talk to the poor girl.

Liberty left, her lips moving, as if in prayer. She climbed the stairs, her focus on how to bring comfort to the hurting girl.

Adam turned to Gio, but before he could say anything, Elijah spoke up. "Mr. Coletti—"

"Giovanni," the older man said.

"Giovanni," Elijah said with a smile, "I would like to vouchsafe a little information about the conditions of the will."

"Before you do, could you please tell me where the outhouse is?" Adam interrupted.

Gio answered, "Just go down that hall there, second door on the right. There's one of those newfangled flush toilets begging to be used." He smiled and pointed Adam in the right direction.

"Thanks," Adam said.

When he left, Elijah continued to speak. "I not only help run the mission, I am Stephen Hancock's colleague. I'd like you to know that Adam has not signed the will. He wanted to think about it first. Yesterday, the realization hit him that he needs to make friends and not bury his head in his work all the time. Although he hasn't signed the papers yet, I believe he will now his mind is made up. Giovanni, you will not find a nicer young man to help out around here. You will need to teach him, of course, but I'm wagering he'll be an asset once he learns the ropes."

Gio nodded his head. "I have looked into his eyes, sir. I can see he's a good man. It's not fair for Eden to blame him for something her father did. She needs to accept the circumstances and go on. There's nothing to be gained by acting so childish."

"That is something you and I can agree on, but she's young and seems impetuous. Couple that with the shocks she's had lately, and I think we can easily excuse her behavior. Liberty will talk to her, and I'm sure she'll come around."

"You don't know Eden Chandler," Gio said.

"You don't know Liberty Bannister," Elijah replied with a smile.

Liberty took a left at the top of the oak staircase and walked at a slow pace down the hall, praying as she went. The hall had skylights to light her way. Her unconscious mind took in family pictures and decor, but her thoughts were wholly centered on the Lord and what He would have her say. She took a deep breath and tapped lightly on the door. There was no answer, so she turned the knob softly and opened Eden's door.

Eden lay curled into a ball of misery in the middle of a huge canopy bed. Liberty's mind flashed back to the night she arrived at Matthew's Rancho. She'd been newly widowed with no grief for it, only a deep relief from years of torment from an evil husband. She'd cried in anguish, pouring out thirteen long years of suffering and misery. She had felt let out of a cocoon of evil that had bound her. Conchita had ministered to her and created a bond between them that even death would not sever. She blinked away the memory and prayed she could be of comfort to Eden.

Walking swiftly into the adjoining dressing room, which contained a dresser with an ewer and pitcher of water, she poured some into the basin, knowing Eden was unaware of her presence. Libby's heart wrenched with compassion at the heartrending sobs. She wrung out a cloth of cold water, and going back to the bed, placed it on the nightstand and sat down on the bed. She pulled Eden into her arms and rocked her as if she were a baby. Tears formed in her own eyes at the grief Eden bore. Mixed with Eden's grief was anger, and Liberty understood it. She sat there rocking the younger girl, not saying anything until the sobs died down. Eden pulled back and lay against her pillows.

"Oh, Eden, I'm so deeply sorry. What a sorrow and a burden you bear," she said, as she took the cool cloth and wiped Eden's face of tears. Lovingly Liberty took her Eden's hands and washed them as if she were a baby.

Eden sat up away from her pillows and looked at Liberty, speaking bluntly. "When I came to see you the day before yesterday, I had no idea you already knew the man who was to inherit half my estate. I can't believe you let me rant on like that—you never said one word about him. I'm angry, Liberty. Angry at Papa for doing such a deed and never preparing me and angry at you for what I consider a slap in the face!"

"Eden—"

"I thought you were my friend," Eden spoke harshly. "It's why I rode to your Rancho!" Tears still streamed down her cheeks. She looked bereft and beaten, as if she hadn't a friend in the world.

Liberty didn't answer the girl immediately, seeing how distraught she was. In all probability, Eden wouldn't hear what she had to say until she settled down a bit. Liberty simply sat still and waited, praying that she would have the right words.

When Eden saw she was getting no response, she leaned back again, looking dejected, but the tears had stopped. She closed her eyes in exhaustion and took a shuddering breath.

Liberty started to wipe her face again, but Eden's eyes flew open, and she grasped Liberty's wrist in a tight grip.

"Don't," she said. "I don't need *your* help." She flung Liberty's hand away from her.

"Eden, I met Adam for the first time just yesterday, when Matthew and Elijah Humphries came home with him. I've never met the man before in my life, and I certainly didn't know him when you talked to me the other day."

Liberty let the import of her words sink into Eden's mind. She took another big shuddering breath but didn't reply. Finally she said, "I ask your pardon, Liberty. I reckon I can't see straight with all I've been through lately. I thought you knew him, and I felt angry and hurt—betrayed that you hadn't said anything to me when I rambled about the will and all."

"No, I don't know him, and yet because he's a believer in Christ as I am, I feel a definite affinity with him. I can't explain it, but there's a peacefulness about him that touches me. Did you notice the way he is dressed? When Matthew, Elijah, and Adam came riding up yesterday, I didn't know until they got close who was Matthew and who was Adam. You saw their horses. It's a bit uncanny how much alike they are."

Eden evidently wasn't paying attention to Liberty's words. She said scornfully, "*Your* God allowed my parents to be murdered! I thought after meeting you that I too would like to become a Christian. My mother and father asked Jesus into their hearts not more than a couple months ago. Look at the protection God gave them. If that's the kind of God you have, I don't want any part of Him. I've seen some horrible things happen in this life, and I can't believe in a loving God who allows it!"

Liberty, shocked by Eden's statement, breathed a prayer for help in speaking to her.

"God didn't make us puppets, Eden. He gave us the freedom to choose. He doesn't always step in and stop things from happening that are bad. Sometimes He does, but all the evil you see, all the wretchedness here on this earth, is not from the hand of God. There's a scripture in First Peter five about the devil going about like a roaring lion seeking whom he can devour. Satan loves evil. He wants us to live in misery. Man himself is born to do evil. Yes, it is true that God could stop all the bad things from happening, but then it would be Him controlling our lives, breaking from the fact of freedom of choice. I realized just recently that had I not had a miserable first marriage, I'd never have known the fullness of joy in my second. If everything in life was always good, we wouldn't recognize how good it is." She wiped a tear from Eden's face and continued to talk.

"In truth, there's only one answer as to how God does things, and it's that He doesn't do things our way. He does not have limited thinking the way we do, and He never violates the personalities He's made. He doesn't push His way in, make our decisions for us, nor make us do anything. He gives us the freedom to choose. The sad thing is, most people don't want to be under His authority or don't recognize the love He has for them. So they go their own way, messing up their lives and everyone around them. God created us because He wanted relationship. He wants us to love and enjoy Him forever. He loves you, Eden, far more than you can even imagine, but He loves Adam too."

"I already determined that whoever Papa deeded half of Sunrise to was going to be my enemy," Eden said, her eyes hardening. "How did your Adam inveigle his way into my papa's heart? Did he have some kind of hold over him?"

"Eden, listen to me. He's not *my* Adam. He's a young man who is as bewildered as you. He hasn't even signed the papers yet, as most men would have done, but I think he will sign them. I should tell you that Elijah is not only the owner of the women's mission in San Rafael, he is also one of Stephen Hancock's business partners. Elijah is a lawyer, and back in Boston he helped me when I was in dire need. I love Elijah as if he were my own papa. He told me that your papa stated in his will that if Adam decided not to sign the papers, Stephen Hancock was to get down on his knees and beg him to reconsider."

"Why?" Eden whispered brokenly. "Why would he do such a thing? It makes me so angry I can scarcely contain it. It's burning in my gut."

"You'd better let it go, Eden. It'll only make you ill. As to why he did it, I don't know, but what's done is done. I think you should make an effort to abide by your papa's wishes. Your mother must have known about it. I know Gio said he did."

"Is Adam that knowledgeable about growing olives or nuts? Does he know anything at all about ranch life?"

"Perhaps you should ask him."

"I suppose if he's going to be residing here, I will have to talk to him, but just because you trust him doesn't mean I do." Eden looked away, her fingers plucking at the front of her blouse in nervousness. "I can be decent, but to have a stranger live in the house without my parents being here doesn't even seem circumspect."

"Well, I'm certain things will iron themselves out. You need to give it time to do so. I'm grateful you're no longer angry at me, Eden. I need a friend like you. Would you mind if I prayed with you for this entire situation?"

"Do you really think it'll do any good?"

"Oh, Eden, if you only knew the solace I have received from the Almighty throughout my life, you'd be amazed. Only God knows how much I've been held in His tender care since I was fifteen and found His saving grace. Someday, we'll make a time when I will share with you about my late husband and stepfather. All I'll say for now is—I never knew people could be so evil."

Eden's eyebrows rose at her statement.

"Whoever killed your parents," Liberty continued, "is in the same category as them. Let me pray for you." The two women bowed their heads. Liberty took Eden's hand and gave it a gentle squeeze as she closed her eyes.

"Almighty Father, how grateful I am for Your wondrous love. I pray Eden will come to know You the way I do. We pray together for her to find peace throughout this horrible time in her life. Only You can know how hurt and distraught she is. I pray You will help Sheriff Rawlins find who did this heinous crime. May some evidence or happenstance occur to bring the evil person or persons to justice. Thank You in advance for what You plan to do. We pray Your will be done. In the precious name of Jesus, amen."

Liberty released Eden's hand, and they hugged as Liberty said, "I'm going to love you, Eden, like the younger sister I never had. If there is anything I can do to help ease your burden, please, please let me know."

While Liberty and Eden were upstairs, the four men were still in the great room conversing quietly, formulating a plan of action for Adam.

Elijah said, "When we get back to Matthew's Rancho, I want you to sign the papers, Adam, unless you'd like to do it right now."

"No, I'll wait. I think it might upset Miss Chandler to sign them here in front of her. I will sign them though. Now I've made up my mind, I won't let any grass grow under my feet."

"You don't have to be worrying about signing them in front of Eden," Gio said. "She won't be coming back down to see you off."

Matthew stood silently watching the other three men talk. He usually waited to form an opinion about someone, but he was quite taken with Adam.

"I'll be right pleased to have you as a neighbor," he said. "If there's anything you need, I'd be glad to be of help."

"Thanks, Matthew. That's kind of you and a comfort to know."

"When do you think you'll be back here?" Gio asked.

Adam turned to Gio and replied, "I'll need to spend at least a couple days getting my affairs in order, but I'll be back as soon as I'm able. Do you have a book or anything I could read for the next couple nights, on growing olives?"

"No, we have no books to learn how to grow olives. All we do is from head knowledge, things we've learned from trial and error. However, I can give you the recording of things we have done in the past to give you a better idea of the process. We record what steps we've taken each year, always looking to better our crop. Besides myself, Eden is the most knowledgeable."

CHAPTER XI

A faithful man shall abound with blessings:
but he that maketh haste to be rich shall not be innocent.

PROVERBS 28:20

JUST THEN THE TWO WOMEN ENTERED the room, and Eden asked, "Most knowledgeable about what?"

Gio's face showed surprise at her return to the great room, but his voice was full of compassion as he spoke.

"I was saying that besides myself, there is no one here at Sunrise Ranch more knowledgeable about growing olives than you." He turned back to Adam to say, "Of course, we have many workers, and some are very well schooled in what they do. Most know their own particular job well but do not know how the entire process works."

Eden said, "I would like to apologize for my earlier behavior. I have no excuse other than I have quite a temper, and I am angry that my father would leave half of this"—she waved her hand to encompass the house and grounds—"to an unknown man. He should have left half to Gio, who has been his faithful friend all these many years, not you," she said bluntly to Adam.

Giovanni's eyebrows climbed up his forehead in astonishment. Eden knew it was because she had apologized to someone she vowed would be her enemy.

"I agree with you, miss," Adam said promptly. "Wholeheartedly. But Eldon didn't leave it to Gio, and I plan to do the best I can to learn and be an asset rather than a hindrance. I know it will take time to train me, but I plan to do my best to help."

"We will see," Eden replied. Her eyes were full of distrust, thinking that somehow he must have swindled her papa or had some hold over him. "Do you know anything about growing olives or nuts?"

"No, in truth, I don't," Adam replied ruefully.

Eden stared at the young man in disbelief. "You're saying my papa deeded half his holdings to a man who knows nothing about olives?" She continued, her words clipped, "When do you plan to move in?"

"As soon as I settle my affairs in San Francisco," Adam replied easily. "I reckon I'll be spending tonight with the Bannisters again and wrap things up in Frisco in the next couple days. I haven't signed the papers yet, but Elijah has them."

Eden turned to Elijah. "Liberty told me you're a lawyer and that you also own the mission is San Rafael."

"I do, along with my wife, of course. I am Stephen Hancock's colleague. At present, I am taking his clients while he is on holiday." Elijah reached into his satchel and handed the papers to Adam but spoke to Eden. "This states quite clearly your father's wishes concerning the estate."

Eden reached for the sheaf of papers, and Adam handed them over to her. "It is beyond my ken why Papa would do what he has done," she whispered, her voice choked with emotion. She flipped through the paperwork and saw the instruction toward the end where Stephen Hancock was to get down on his knees and beg Adam, should he refuse to sign. Tears started in her eyes, and she angrily blinked them away. "I was so furious when Mr. Hancock came to tell me the contents of the will I didn't even take the time to look at these. I will reiterate that I don't understand why Papa would do this and not tell me. What would have happened if Mother had not been killed? Would all this"—she waved the papers in her hand again expansively—"have gone to her or only half? What in the world was Papa thinking?"

Gio said, "Eldon told me that if your mother should survive him, half would still go to Adam. Your mother, for some reason, was quite agreeable to this. The three of us talked about it. Your papa was insistent that you not be apprised of the terms of the will."

Eden allowed the distrust to show on her face as she looked at Adam. He clearly saw it, but unflinching, he stared steadily back at her. He met her chocolate-brown eyes with his clear honest gray-green gaze.

Eden held his eyes with hers for a full minute, but she looked away first.

Hattie Hamilton and Bertha Morrow arrived into San Francisco late midmorning.

Wonder why it's taken me so long to pack up and move? I should have done this a couple years ago. It's silly to live so far from your loved ones just because you're comfortable. What's more important than family? Oh, how I do look forward to seeing that young man. It's been a whole year. Won't he be surprised!

The two women were ready to alight when the train came to a full stop. They headed for the back of the train where men were already offloading the trunks, furniture, and other paraphernalia that people had brought west.

Disappointment flooded through Hattie's being when she didn't see Adam waiting for her. She swallowed it down, reminding herself that at least she had a place to stay and wouldn't be out on her own, not that she couldn't do quite well by herself, but she was grateful for the offer Bertha had made.

Hattie stood waiting as the men put things into piles. She wondered where Adam might be. Having never married nor having any other relations, Adam was the mainstay of her life. *Probably out gallivanting around the state, drawing up a new bridge or tunnel*, she thought. *How I do love that boy.*

After collecting their luggage, Hattie asked, "Bertha, do you mind waiting for me while I write out a message to my nephew, Adam? Most likely he's out on a job somewhere and hasn't gotten my telegram. I have no idea how to get in contact with him other than to send a note to his hotel address. I'll let him contact me whenever he gets back."

"I don't mind at all. Go right ahead and write your message. Frankly, my friend," she said with a smile, "I hope he doesn't find out about you right away. I'm looking forward to your staying with me in Napa. Tell you what I'll do. I'll go collect my carriage, which is just down the street, while you write out your note to your nephew. I have a place where they stable my horse and store my buggy whenever I get a hankering to travel. If you don't mind keeping a lookout for our things, I'll go get the buggy."

"No, I don't mind at all. It'll give me time to write this out." She sat down on a bench near the door of the station.

Bertha, who was quite tall, strode off with purposeful steps. She spoke aloud to herself, "I do hope Taffy will be fit to take us up to Napa. That old nag is getting up there." Taffy was fifteen but still performed well for all that was needed. Because of lower back pain, Bertha had stopped riding her horse, but Taffy seemed just as content pulling a carriage. Bertha found her horse and paid off the stable owner, grateful to have a clean stall and an honest man care for her horse when she took trips. He hooked up the traces, and she made her way back to the station in short order.

Meanwhile, Hattie had dug into her satchel for some money to have the stationmaster store the majority of her luggage, which he said he could do for up to two weeks. She separated out a large grip packed with immediate necessities, along with the two satchels she'd carried on the train. She wrote her note, included Bertha's name and address, and found a messenger boy to take it to the Bay Front Hotel near the Embarcadero, where Adam resided.

Bertha returned, secretly glad to see the huge pile of trunks and paraphernalia were gone.

"I was wondering how we were going to get all your luggage and that furniture into this buggy," she said with a laugh.

"Oh, I suppose I should have said something," Hattie replied. "I see no reason to drag all my things north when I'll most likely be settling here in San Francisco with my nephew. I just hope he returns before the two weeks are up. If he doesn't, I don't know what I'm going to do with all the things I brought west."

"We can come down with a wagon and collect it, if need be," Bertha replied. "Don't fash yourself, Hattie. Everything will work out just fine."

Hattie loaded the remaining luggage onto the back of the buggy, and they were off, heading for the Sausalito ferry, which ran five times a day regular as clockwork.

Caleb, on his way home from Sunrise Ranch, planned to stop at the mercantile store to buy a few items his mother said they needed. He tied up in front of the post office to see if there was any mail. His mother said she was expecting a letter. It had arrived, and he picked it up. He stood outside the post office on the boarded walk as he perused it to see whom it was from. It was addressed to his mother and looked like it was from Montana, where his aunt Naomi lived. He looked up to see Taylor Kerrigan heading down the boarded walk toward him.

Taylor looked Caleb up and down and said, "I heard tell you've been trying, awful hard, ta cozy up ta my girl, an' I don't appreciate it, not one bit, Caleb McHaney!"

Caleb looked at Taylor more in surprise for what he said than his tone of voice, which was quite disparaging. His tone, usually amicable when others were around, was never agreeable when it was just the two of them.

"Really, Taylor, you need to stop jumping to conclusions. My mother and you seem to think alike. You both have me nearly wed to Miss Eden, and both of you are as far from the frying pan as you can be. I'm—"

"I don't have you wed to 'er, McHaney!" Taylor interrupted. "As I said, she's *my* girl! I just don't like the way you've been flirting with her every chance you get!"

"I'm only friends with her, Taylor. We are not, as you put it, cozying up to one another. I enjoy her company, and she enjoys mine. Eden is like a sister to me and a really good friend wrapped up into one. Furthermore, she is not, as you put it, *your* girl! Believe me that I happen to know. I've just now been out at Sunrise Ranch visiting her, and I'm—"

"That housekeeper let you into the house?" Taylor interrupted again. Clearly livid, his neck turned red, and his cheeks seemed puffed up, with color climbing up into his face. He looked a far cry from his usual handsome self.

"Why yes, she did," Caleb replied. "I had a nice chat with Eden as well as her new friends." He decided not to say anything to Taylor about the will nor that Adam Brown would soon be a resident of the Chandlers' house. He thought, *I'd better leave well enough alone. Eden may not like the terms of the will bandied about, and I am quite sure Taylor Kerrigan doesn't know how to keep his big mouth shut.* Caleb was thankful he hadn't spoken out of turn and remembered a proverb he'd memorized when he was young. *The one who guards his mouth preserves his life; The one who opens wide his lips comes to ruin. It's true*, he thought.

Caleb was ready to move on, but Taylor stopped him with a question.

"What new friends?" Taylor asked, his voice sharpened.

"Well, of course you know she is a friend of the Bannisters?" Caleb was trying not to be too sarcastic, but Taylor grated on his nerves.

"No, I don't know that. You mean the Bannisters of Rancho Bonito?"

"I thought you said Eden was your girl? Surely you'd know who her friends are if that is the case. And, yes, Matthew Bannister and his wife are good friends of Eden's. They were good friends of Camilla and Eldon, too. Are you saying that Mrs. Jenkins wouldn't let you into the house? Surely if you are Eden's beau, she'd let you in."

"That ain't none of your business neither. What's she doing seeing people when she just lost her parents? It's not right."

"I don't think that's for you to say. Frankly, you're correct for a change. It isn't any of your business, nor my business, what she does."

"It *is* my business, I'm telling you. She's *my* girl. We have an understanding of sorts. She's quite sweet on me, I'm telling you."

"I don't think you're telling the truth, Taylor. If it was true, Eden would have said something to me about it."

"That's because it's none of your business, like you said." Taylor sneered.

Caleb lifted his hat and said, "Be seeing you around, Kerrigan." He left abruptly before Taylor could say anything more.

Whew, Eden better be careful seeing that man. He's unstable, Caleb thought. *I'd better warn her next time I see her. Before you know it, Kerrigan will be saying they're engaged.* Caleb strode down the sidewalk toward the mercantile store.

Liberty was pleased when Eden invited the Bannisters, Adam, and Elijah to stay for dinner. Before eating, Liberty peeked into several rooms, interested in the decor and the layout of the house. Eden told her to go right ahead. Liberty was enchanted with Camilla's beautiful sitting room. The walls were done in a pale apricot. Thick crown molding, stained a dark mahogany, covered the breach between the wall and the ten-foot-high ceiling. All the trim board and casing around the windows and door matched the deep stain of mahogany, as well as the mantel over the small fireplace. A huge picture of apricot-colored poppies, blowing in a breeze, graced the wall over the mantel. Two long, narrow pictures on either side of it was of a single poppy, its delicate pale green stem bowed to hold the bloom. Long drapes in chartreuse flanked the huge window looking out to the fields behind the stable. The rest of the room was done in apricot, pale chartreuse green, and cream. It was inviting as well as charming.

Liberty exclaimed to Eden, "This is so unusual and lovely. I can imagine your mother sewing and reading in here, enjoying the view."

"Ye-es...I haven't been able to come in here and use the room yet. It was such a part of her. She decorated it herself, you know." Tears stood out in her chocolate eyes, and Liberty hugged her closely as if she could take some of her sorrow to bear.

"Oh, Eden, I can't imagine your sorrow. I lost my mother when I was seventeen. I'd been married to Armand for a year, but I knew she was dying. To have the sort of shock you've had...I can only say, I am so sorry, and any time you need or want to talk, please come on over or send for me, and I'll come."

The tears that had threatened, spilled over, and Eden tried to blink them away. She wiped her eyes, and Liberty waited before they headed back to the great room.

It was time for dinner, and Eden and Liberty headed to the huge great room and to the table where the men were standing around waiting for them. They sat, along with Gio, around the homey table. The talk was desultory, jumping from one subject to the next until Adam spoke directly to Eden.

He cleared his throat and said, "I clearly understand your being upset about the terms of the will. I would be too—very much so, if our places were reversed. I was wondering, if I may be so bold, I know you have a housekeeper here, and that me being here would be circumspect with Mrs. Jenkins present..." Adam looked around the table and saw a couple nods of assent but continued. "I wonder, if my aunt Hattie is willing, would you mind her coming to stay also? I know she—"

"It's half your house, Mr. Adam Brown," Eden replied flatly. "As soon as you sign those papers, half of Sunrise Ranch is yours. You don't have to ask me permission for anything you do." Her words, although softly spoken, were clipped. Her eyes, looking bruised, were fastened on his. "You want a whole party of people staying here, it's your right. I don't believe my opinion has much bearing on what you do."

Elijah cleared his throat, knowing that Eden was vulnerable but also volatile. "Miss Chandler, I understand your position, but I beg you to try to understand Adam's." He cleared his throat again, which he was wont to do when nervous, and said softly, "He didn't plan to sign those papers. He thought he'd walk away, but the words your father used in the will gave him pause. Most men would jump at the chance of being half owner to such an estate—not so, Adam. He sought the Lord's will first. I don't know what your beliefs are, and I know you don't know me, but please believe me when I say that once Adam knows his way around, he will be an asset, not a drain, for your business."

"Well, I reckon you're telling me the truth, but I don't care for a stranger barging in and taking half of what rightly belongs to me. I feel betrayed by my parents, and I have no recourse for my father signing away what should be all mine." She nodded at her foreman. "Gio deserved to inherit more than a stranger. I suppose I have to accept it, but I don't have to like it. Let's change the subject so we can enjoy this meal Berry has fixed for us, shall we?"

Berry had prepared a delicious dinner. Roast pork with saffron flavored rice tasted delicious. Asparagus dripping with cheddar cheese and pickled beets made a splash of color on the plates as well as a pleasing impact on the palate. Applesauce with a touch of cinnamon was an appetizing side to the pork. Everyone enjoyed the meal, and even Eden did more than toy with her food.

CHAPTER XII

In the multitude of words there wanteth not sin:
but he that refraineth his lips is wise.

PROVERBS 10:19

AFTER ELIJAH, ADAM, AND THE BANNISTERS left Sunrise Ranch, Eden, whose back had been ramrod straight during their visit, slumped in her chair. "I just don't understand it, Gio. When you discussed this with Papa, did he ever explain why he was giving half the estate to Mr. Brown? Did he give any explanation at all?"

"No, Eden…uh, not anything he'd like me to share with you. No, he did not. I asked him, more than once, to tell you about it and to give you a reason for it, but he would just smile and said the way he was handling it was best."

Eden picked up her fork and stirred the cake crumbs on her dessert plate. "Mr. Brown seems like a nice man, but for Papa to give him half of Sunrise after only knowing him for five or six days…oh, Gio, I don't know what to think!" Tears made their way down her cheeks, and she wiped them away angrily with the back of her hand. She'd done a lot of crying in the past week but never in front of anyone, until today. It embarrassed her, but she couldn't seem to stop as the tears slid silently down her face.

"Oh, how I wish he were here! I could find out what he was thinking. Adam doesn't know the first thing about olives. Wonder if he even knows there's more than one kind? I am so angry at Papa, and then I feel so guilty for my anger."

"Why don't we just make the best of a situation neither of us understand?" Gio said quietly. "We can see if he'll work out. Did you get a look at his hands? There's not a callus on them—he's not used to a lot of physical labor. He's an architect, and perhaps he'll get tired or not like the work that's required here. He's used to a drawing table, not manual labor. If he leaves before the five years are up, the terms of the will are that you will get it all. And there is the fact that if you wait out the five years, you can buy him out. I know it's not your strong suit, Eden, but this time you're going to have to be patient."

Eden stared at Gio, knowing he was absolutely right.

More upset than he'd let on to Caleb McHaney, Taylor Kerrigan felt in need of a stiff drink. He entered the saloon in Napa, pushing past the swinging doors that led into the darkened interior. He ordered a shot of whiskey, and while he waited for his drink, he thought about what Caleb had said.

If Miss Eden put that Caleb on her list of people allowed ta visit her and not me, it sure don't bode well for a future relationship. My parents expect me ta marry 'er. Now that her parents are dead, she's got money and position in Napa. It's exactly what I want...money and position. I'll show my pa I'm not just another mouth ta feed. Sides that, she's not hard ta look at. He stared at himself in the huge mirror, which covered the back wall of the bar, and slicked the side of his hair back. *Reckon I'm not hard ta look at neither.* He smiled at his reflection, but as he looked away, a scowl replaced the pleasant look he'd given himself.

The bartender took a look at the scowl on Taylor's forehead and said nothing as he placed the shot glass on the long, stained counter. Taylor took the glass and downed it in one swig, setting it down with a plop. He wiped his mouth with the back of his hand and dropped fifty cents onto the counter. Turning, he glanced around at some men sitting at a table,playing cards, as he strode out the swinging doors. Not paying attention, he ran straight into Sheriff Rawlins. "Whoa there, Kerrigan. What are you up to today?" the sheriff asked as Taylor bumped into him.

"I'm on m'way home and thought I'd have an appetizer afore I get there."

"Whew, pretty strong appetizer," Buck Rawlins said as he smelled Taylor's breath. "Hope you're keeping yourself out of trouble, young man. You need to find yourself a job and take on some responsibility. I don't believe in young men gallivanting around the countryside with nothing better to do but start drinking in the middle of the day." He stared at the younger man, his steady blue gaze willing the younger man to look him in the eyes.

Taylor glanced up at Buck but quickly looked down. He felt the sheriff must know every thought he had in his head with that brilliant, clear blue gaze that seemed to pierce him.

"Well, I'm expecting ta be coming inta some money afore too long. You don't need ta be worrying 'bout me, nor preaching ta me either, that's for sure."

"How are you coming into money?"

With no thought at all for the truth, Taylor replied, "Reckon I'll be marrying Miss Eden, that's what."

"You asked her yet?"

"Nah, but I will, soon's her mourning is over. She needs a man like me ta take care of 'er. I got patience. I'll be awaiting fer a year when she's done being sad fer her parents."

"Now you listen to me, Taylor Kerrigan. Don't you go bandying about that you're marrying Miss Chandler until you have a tight little ring on her finger and she's said yes to you. Do you understand me?"

Before he could answer, Buck Rawlins saw Bertha Morrow's buggy wheeling down Main Street. He lifted his hat, and Bertha pulled up in front of him.

"Good afternoon, Sheriff Rawlins, Taylor," Bertha said pleasantly.

"Welcome home, Mrs. Morrow. We've missed you," Buck said cordially as he settled his hat back onto his head.

"Thank you, Sheriff. I'd like you to meet my friend Miss Hattie Hamilton from Williamsburg, Virginia. She will be staying with me for a few days." Bertha turned to Hattie and said, "This young man is Taylor Kerrigan, and Sheriff Rawlins is a close friend of mine."

"I am pleased to make your acquaintance," Hattie said with a glance at the younger man, but her deep-blue eyes caught and held Buck's. Something almost startled her. Her eyes widened in some unfathomable knowledge that stirred within the depths of her being.

"Welcome to Napa, California, Miss Hamilton," Buck replied as he lifted his hat again and surreptitiously bumped Taylor on the arm.

Taylor lifted his hat and said, "Pleased ta meet you, ma'am, I'm sure."

Bertha said, "Nice seeing you, Sheriff. I'd stay and chat awhile, but I'm eager to get home. I enjoy my rambles and traveling immensely, but it's always good to get back home. Good day, gentlemen." She expertly flicked her riding crop with a little snap, not even touching Taffy's backside, but the horse, conditioned to hear the little pop of the whip, began to pull the buggy forward.

Hattie nodded her head and quickly averted her eyes as Buck slowly touched the brim of his hat respectfully.

His eyes rested on Hattie's face as the blood crept up and into her cheeks.

Caleb McHaney led the horse, Dalmatian, into the barn, setting the cake plate on the sawhorse. He opened her stall door, and she pranced in. He hung the bridle up on a post and threw the saddle over one of the saddle stands. He dropped a generous helping of oats into the manger as a treat. Dalmatian swished her tail in clear appreciation. Caleb grabbed a couple brushes, slipped his hands under the straps, and began to brush her down. He looked up, surprised to see his mother coming into the barn. She had a slim cigar in her hand. He didn't like the fact that his mother smoked them. He noticed the cigar was lit, and it angered him that she would flagrantly disobey a cardinal rule his father had set down years ago—nothing lit in the barn except a lantern when necessary.

She entered the dimly lit barn, which was unusual for her. Usually she waited for him to make an appearance inside the house. "Hello, Mother," he said with a tight smile, but his gut started to churn a bit at the look on her face. The two of them had been at loggerheads for the past year over Eden Chandler. She kept pushing him to have more than a casual friendship with the girl, but he just didn't like Eden that way. He couldn't say exactly why. He liked her. He liked her a lot, but he wasn't in love with her. He didn't think he ever would be.

"Hello...I didn't happen to see the cake anywhere. Did you take it over to the Chandlers'?"

"Yes, I did. I don't think she would have seen me, but she already had company." For some reason that he couldn't fathom, he didn't care to elaborate about the contents of the will nor the stipulation in it. "The Bannisters have become quite good friends, and they were visiting her along with a couple friends of theirs. Trying to cheer her up, I imagine. I got invited to tea and had a good visit. Berry had made cherry pies, and Mrs. Jenkins gave you this." He took the plate and handed it to her.

"That was right thoughtful of her. You know how I love cherry pie."

Caleb nodded and said, "I saw Taylor Kerrigan in town, and he said Eden was his girl. Sure surprised me. You could have knocked me over with a feather. Eden is not his girl, and I told him so."

"How do you know? She was out with him last week, the night before her parents were killed. Maybe she is his girl."

"How do you know that, Mother?"

"Know what?"

"That she was out with him last week."

"Oh, I keep up on what's happening in Napa," she replied airily.

"Well, I don't believe she's his girl. She's got more sense than that. And mother, remember what Papa said about smoking in the barn? An ash could drop and smolder in the hay, and you wouldn't know until it's too late."

"Yes, I'll take it out in a minute, but as far as Miss Chandler having sense, maybe she has, maybe she hasn't. Taylor Kerrigan is a nice-looking young man. I happen to know that she still sees him on occasion." She turned to go back to the house and added, "Supper's nearly ready. I fixed roast beef since it's your favorite." Caleb stared after her, wondering just what she was up to now.

Matthew, Liberty, Elijah, and Adam rode up the long lane to the Bannisters' Rancho. It was dusk, and the Rancho was lit up. Liberty had a quick flashback to when she first arrived at Matthew Bannister's

Rancho Bonito. It looked much the same. The drive swept around in the front. She smiled to herself as she remembered she'd thought it must look like a hacienda. *It doesn't only look like one, it is a hacienda.*

The entire place blazed with lights, as if a party were taking place. Liberty breathed a prayer. *I thank You, Father, for the changes You've wrought in my life these past two years. I thank You that this is home and a place full of love and laughter. I pray we can encourage Adam. He will need much support and prayer to put up overlong with Eden's biting comments. I pray she finds You as Savior. Thank You, Father.*

Diego came out of the Rancho and said, "I weel groom the horses."

"Not Piggypie," Matthew said. "I can groom her. You've had a long day, Mr. Rodriguez." He smiled. Throwing Pookie's reins to Diego, he added, "You can groom Liberty's horse or have Donny do it, and thanks." He turned to Liberty, who dismounted. "You, little girl, go get yourself a cup of tea or a glass of wine or something. You must be exhausted, having no nap today."

Liberty's eyes misted up at his thoughtfulness. "Thanks, Matthew."

"You're welcome, sweetheart. Now go." He squeezed her shoulder and turned to Adam. "Come on. Your Loco must be ready for dinner." He led the way into the stable.

Liberty smiled at Diego. "Thank you, Diego, for grooming Pookie. I *am* very tired. I feel like a flower looks when it hasn't been watered. I'm drooping." She headed up the walk and went straight to the bedroom and washed up before greeting Conchita. She splashed water on her face and thought she'd like nothing better than to crawl into bed right now.

She headed for the kitchen to find a cup of tea brewing and coconut bars on the table. Hugging Conchita, she said, "Thank you, dear friend. You are so thoughtful."

"You seet, Mees Libbee. Not here—you go inna great room. I breeng your cookies and tea. You need to relax before you go to the bed."

"I can take my tea, but you're right. I am exhausted," she said as she headed for the great room and settled herself into one of the deep leather chairs, her legs curled up beneath her. "It's been a long day. We didn't plan to stay for dinner, but Eden invited us."

Conchita nodded her head and asked, "How she doing weeth Meester Adam?"

"I don't think she'll be easy to live with, at least for a while, but she knows she has no choice but to accept Adam and make the best of the situation. She's an intelligent girl. She should figure it out."

"*Sí*, she a smart girl. *Mi corazón* aches for her. She haf too much to bear."

"Yes, and I know how you feel. My heart aches for her too." The two women talked until the men came in from the stable.

Adam spent another enjoyable evening with Matthew, Liberty, and Elijah. They played whist, drawing straws for their partners. Liberty and Elijah had fun soundly beating Matthew and Adam.

Just as they were finishing up, Conchita came into the great room with plates of warm sopapillas. Elijah smacked his lips in appreciation.

"You sure know the way to a man's heart, Conchita, my girl. I've had sopapillas made by other people, but for some reason yours are by far the best."

"Oh, Meester Humphries, you ees always saying that! Thank you. I am liking the sopapillas too. Eets my favorite dessert. Maybe eets because I am liking the honey so much."

"She goes through quarts of it." Matthew laughed. "I never mind getting more honey for her because it means sopapillas for us, and they are so delicious."

Adam sank his teeth into his first sopapilla and could well understand the conversation. The deep-fried pastry was filled with honey, and he chewed in appreciation.

"Delicious," he said.

They all needed to wash their hand after the sticky dessert.

When they had settled back in the great room, they talked on a variety of subjects, but the conversation drifted back to Sunrise Ranch and Adam's plans.

"Adam, I think it's time," Elijah said meaningfully as he drew papers out of his satchel. He looked at them and said, "You sign here and here." He pointed to the first and last sheets of the paper.

"Here's a metal pen," Liberty said as she handed it to Adam.

Adam bowed his head and said a quick prayer before signing *Adam Morgan Brown* on the sheet of vellum. He signed again and breathed a huge sigh. "Well, I am now committed," he said. "Think I'll send a telegram to my aunt Hattie tomorrow rather than wait on the trains to take the mail back and forth. It'll take some time for her to pack up and sell her house, if she's willing to come, that is."

"It must be quite exciting for you to change everything you've known and been comfortable with to begin a new adventure. I did that very thing just about two and a half years ago," Liberty said. "I'd never have done it if it hadn't been for Elijah. He arranged the entire trip west. He told me back in Boston I'd find a freedom I'd never known before, and he was absolutely right."

Liberty slipped her arm through Elijah's and gave him a pat on the shoulder. "My entire life is different, and I am grateful and thankful for it! It's actually quite a long story, but sometime I'll tell you all about it. What I can say is, that if this move and change is right for you, Adam, grab it with both hands."

CHAPTER XIII

Iron sharpeneth iron; so a man sharpeneth
the countenance of his friend.

PROVERBS 27:17

BERTHA AND HATTIE, EVEN WITH their stop to talk to the sheriff, had made good time. They turned off Main Street onto North Hampton Road. As they turned into the lane to the house, Hattie drew in a big breath of surprise. Bertha Morrow was quite wealthy. Hattie looked around with interest as they entered the wide gates of the lane up to the house.

Hattie's indrawn breath caused Bertha to smile inwardly. She never talked about money, but was grateful to a husband who had left her well off.

Hattie's eyes darted from one thing to another.

"My, but this is beautiful." A succession of flowering plum trees lined the long drive. A huge two-storied house came into view, fronted by a wide circular driveway that sported a rounded green lawn within the circle. Flowers lined a walk to the steps of the front door, and hydrangeas, smoke plants, azalea bushes, and clematis decked the walls under the stately windows, but Bertha drove alongside the house to the back where a large cobblestone courtyard connected the house with the stable and barn.

"Welcome home, Mrs. Morrow," Chester said, as he took the reins from her. "Glad you're back safe and sound." Chester was an all-around help, living in a small house situated by the front gates. The exterior of the gatekeeper's house matched the grand mansion. The gates were kept wide open most of the time.

"Thank you, Chester. It's good to be home, although it was a wonderful trip. I'd like you to meet Miss Hattie Hamilton from Virginia, who will be staying with us for a while. Hattie, meet Chester Wilson, head stableman and definitely irreplaceable, besides being a very nice man. He has a good listening ear when I need it." She smiled down at him with affection from her high perch.

Chester raised his Stetson and looked into a pair of the bluest eyes he'd ever seen. Hattie could not be considered beautiful, but she had an arresting face, full of life yet full of peace. She must have been in her late thirties. Still slender, it made Chester wonder what the men of Virginia were thinking. She smiled at Chester, and it lit up her face. There was a small quirky dimple at the top of her cheek that caught his attention.

"How do you do, Mr. Wilson?" she asked in a low voice.

"I do quite well, ma'am. Welcome to Morrow House. There's not a person in all of Napa that'll make you feel more at home than Mrs. Morrow. I hope you have a long and pleasant stay."

"Why, thank you for that warm greeting," she replied with a wide smile.

"You are quite welcome, ma'am," Chester said as he stood holding Taffy's head while the two women descended the carriage.

Bertha led Hattie up the back stairs, leaving the carriage for Chester to unload. Before he did, he stopped at the pump and filled two jugs of fresh water to take up the stairs, one for Bertha's room and one for Hattie's.

The two women entered a large entry room, which seemed more like an enclosed back porch, it was so spacious. It had a clean, scrubbed look to it and contained a wash washtub, wringer mangle for squeezing water from wet clothing, and a large drying rack as well as a clothesline, which was strung across the high ceiling. The room was full of light. Wainscot from the floor up to about two and a half feet was topped by windows on three sides. Double doors led to a large, airy kitchen.

"Hello, hello, Mrs. Morrow! Welcome home!" A large woman with gray hair scraped back into a tight bun turned at the sound of their entry. She had big dimples in her cheeks, and everything about her seemed larger than life. In spite of that, she moved swiftly to take the satchels weighing down Bertha's arms.

"Thank you, Fern. Oh, it's good to be home! I feel as if I've been gone for a year instead of merely a few weeks." With her hands now free, she took Hattie's satchels and placed them on a chair as she spoke. "I'd like you to meet my new friend, Hattie Hamilton. Hattie, this is Fern, my chief cook and as indispensable as Chester."

Hattie smiled and stuck out her hand to grasp the cook's. "It's nice to meet you, Fern. I look forward to knowing you better."

Fern, surprised at the gracious words and the handshake, smiled hugely and squeezed Hattie's hand. "It's nice to meet you too, Mrs. Hamilton."

"No, not Mrs. Hamilton, Fern. Miss Hamilton. I'm an old maid," Hattie said with a sweet laugh.

Bertha chuckled and asked Fern, "Can we have a cup of tea? I'll show Hattie around while you get it ready. We'll have it in the parlor, thanks. Where's Faye?"

"I gave her the day off, Mrs. Morrow. I wasn't sure if you'd be back today or tomorrow."

"Oh, well then, we'll have that tea in here at the table. That way we can chat with you too." Bertha began picking up her satchels, as did Hattie, and they exited out of the kitchen into a wide hall.

"Let's take our things upstairs, and I'll show you to your room. We can both freshen up a bit before we have our tea."

Hattie looked around with interest. The wide hall looked even wider with an open staircase doubling its width. The staircase had a bookshelf that stretched itself the entire outside length of the stairs. Its top was stepped to match the staircase. Books, pictures, a couple plants, and bibelots filled the shelves in a pleasing array of color and interest. The opposite wall had several large paintings of landscapes and a beautiful painting of a horse in a field of grass, daisies, and forget-me-nots. The colors were bright and made Hattie feel as if she were standing at the fence of the pasture, looking in.

As they climbed the stairs, large pictures of family climbed the wall along with them. At the top of the steps, facing the wide staircase over a marble-topped credenza, was an imposing picture of a man.

"That's my Edwin," Bertha said proudly. "He was the love of my life, and I miss him so. He worked hard all his life and left me well off, but I'd give it all up in a flash to have him back again. We had such good times together. Ah, well, he's in a much better place, I reckon."

At the top of the stairs, the stair railing curved to the left, spanning the width of the foyer below, so Hattie could see down to the front door and part of the front entry. A great crystal chandelier hung from the second-story ceiling, its top below them once they crested the stairs. Light from a fan-shaped window reflected off the crystals, creating a peaceful glow.

"What a beautiful chandelier," Hattie said. "Look at the prisms of light dancing on the wall."

"That chandelier was a gift from Edwin on the occasion of my fortieth birthday. He had it shipped from France especially for me. He was so thoughtful. How I do miss him."

Bertha led Hattie down the hall and into a beautiful room. Palest of lavender walls rose to the thick cornice stained a dark-chocolate walnut. The trim and door were stained dark walnut, and the light-colored rich lavender gave the room an elegant yet peaceful air. A pair of plush purple chairs flanked the fireplace, and a bit of green mixed with purple and cream in the duvet, pillows, and Turkish carpet created a look of tasteful charm.

"What a lovely room," Hattie said, looking around appreciatively. Over the large bed hung three long, narrow paintings of Tuscany. Purple hills in the distance, with a touch of vineyards in one, ripe grapes with thick green leaves in the second, and a Tuscan villa in the third, created a look of charm mixed with refinement. "This room is simply gracious yet peaceful."

"Thank you, and just look at the view, my dear. You are going to love the view," Bertha said as she pulled back the heavy purple drapes. A door led onto a balcony and overlooked the Napa River. She opened the walnut door, and they walked onto a large balcony replete with wicker chairs and a glassed-top table between them.

"My, this is simply lovely. Thank you for sharing your home with me. I cannot tell you how much it means to me not to have to struggle on my own in an unknown city such as San Francisco, waiting for my nephew to show up. I pray I won't become a nuisance to you."

"Nonsense! Besides being happy you're here, I'm grateful for your company. We'll have a good time, Hattie Hamilton, and no mistake!" Bertha smiled happily at her sweet guest.

Taylor Kerrigan arrived home tired and irritable from his encounter with Caleb McHaney. He climbed off his horse and led her into the dimness of the stable, where he found his pa cleaning out the hooves of his beautiful black-and-white horse, a paint. It looked to Taylor much like the one he'd seen Caleb McHaney riding earlier in the day.

"What'd she say, son?"

"What?"

"I asked you, what'd Miss Eden Chandler have ta say to you?"

"I didn't get to see her, Pa."

"Wa'al, whyever not?"

"That housekeeper of hers wouldn't let me in the house ta see 'er," he answered in a disgusted tone. "She's a bossy one, and that's no jest. Why, she shut th' door right in my face." He could see his pa was not happy with him. "It's cause she said Miss Eden had a list o' visitors she'd allow an' I wasn't on that list. Turned me away right at the door, she did. Closed it on my face, as a matter of fact. Sure made me mad. Then, I come to find out that Mrs. Jenkins let that Caleb McHaney in without a bye your leave, an' Miss Eden, she already had company there ta boot. I can't see why one more body would make any difference."

"Now you listen here, young man. We're a needin' that girl in our family, an' I don't give a hoot as ta how you go about it, but ya'll need ta git it done, ya hear me, boy? I'm glad her parents are daid. Never did like 'em anyways. Hoity toity, they was, lookin' down their noses at us folk. Well, now they don't be a standin' in the way of you a courtin' 'er. I expect you ta get 'er done. The money from yer granpappy is near gone." Terrence Kerrigan glared at his son. "You git that horse brushed down. I knowed you didn't do nuthin' last night. Didn't even feed yer horse. You keep it up, an' me an' your ma'll be kickin' ya out on yer back side, ya hear?"

After a delicious breakfast of diced potatoes, eggs, bacon, onion, cheese, and green peppers wrapped in a tortilla and topped with salsa, sour cream, and guacamole prepared by Conchita, Adam pushed back from the table with a groan.

"That was delicious, Conchita. I don't know if I can move, I'm so full."

Elijah grinned at him but spoke to Conchita. "I agree. That was *el perfecto*. Is that the right term? I'm trying to learn a bit of Spanish, but I'm hopeless when it comes to a foreign language."

Liberty grinned. "As a lawyer, I'm sure you know plenty of Latin. That should be helpful in learning Spanish."

Matthew said, "I've been able to pick up some Spanish because of Diego, but mine's pretty weak when it comes to communicating." He looked over at Adam and added, "Maybe you need to learn Italian. I seem to have heard a bit of that yesterday."

"I think the first order of business isn't learning a language, unless the language is immersing myself in olive talk. I reckon I'm going to eat, sleep, and live olives for quite some time," he said with a rueful laugh. "And now, I suppose we need to be on our way." He stood up and thanked Conchita again, heading toward the door to go out and saddle up the horses. He found Locomotion ready and waiting beside Elijah's Comet.

"Thank you for saddling us up, Diego. Elijah will be here in a minute. I reckon I'll be seeing you around since I plan to be your newest neighbor."

Diego looked over at him in surprise. "You are welcome, Meester Brown. And, *sí*, eet ees a good thing you do. Conchita, she tell me all about eet. Mees Eden, she need a steady man besides Giovanni. She look at Gio as foreman who take orders, not someone who know what he do."

Adam nodded in agreement, "I think so too, but I understand Gio is a walking encyclopedia when it comes to growing olives and nuts. I want him to take me under his wing, so to speak, and help me learn the business. I doubt I'll ever know half what he does, but I plan to try my best. I know nothing of growing olives. I understand, from Matthew, that you are a man of prayer, and I'm asking you to pray for me, please."

"I weel do eet. I weel do eet faithfully," Diego responded solemnly with a slight nod of his head. "You ees wise not to go in as eef you know everything. Gio, he a good man, an' he weel teach you all you need to know."

"I appreciate that advice, and thank you," Adam said. He unwrapped the reins from the hitching post and stood talking to Diego until Elijah joined him, followed by Liberty and Matthew.

Adam reached out to shake Matthew's hand. "I want to thank you both," he said with a smile and a nod in Liberty's direction, "for the enjoyable time I've had with you, good fellowship, a comfortable bed, and delicious food. What more could a man ask for? I'll be looking forward to getting to know you both better in the near future. I'm glad we'll be neighbors."

"Well," said Matthew, "you're welcome here anytime. I want you to know that we will be praying for you and the situation at Sunrise Ranch."

"Yes," added Liberty, "we certainly will."

"Thank you. I certainly need it, and so does Miss Eden. I reckon I'll be dropping by here in a couple days or so on my way back to Sunrise Ranch, if it's all right with you."

"As I said," Matthew replied, "you're welcome here anytime, whether we know you're coming or not."

Elijah said his good-byes in the Rancho but gave Liberty another hug. "You rest up, young lady. You need to be resting more with that little one on the way. We'll be seeing you soon. Abigail has been busy at the mission, or she would have come with us. She keeps saying she plans to take a few days off and come visit you."

"I wish she would. We'd love to have both of you come stay."

Elijah said, "I'm fortunate I could come for a couple days. Standing in for Stephen Hancock has kept me at my desk for some long hours." He turned to Adam. "Are you ready?"

"Ready as I'll ever be." He stepped into the stirrup and swung his long leg over the saddle. "I've had such a good time here that I hate to leave. Reckon I've been missing out on socializing. It feels good, and if Miss Eden is up to it, we'll have you both over real soon. And by the way, Matthew and I will make a comeback playing whist. I'm not used to losing and need a makeup game," he said with a grin. "Thanks again to both of you." He tipped his hat and with a look at Elijah, who'd settled himself comfortably on Comet, turned his mare toward the long drive through the vineyard to the main road.

"Be seeing you soon," he said, and the two men set off.

They rode steadily for a while and then pulled up to a walk as they talked about the recent happenings. Soon the conversation turned to faith and their spiritual walk.

"Yesterday, I was thinking about how powerful our words are. We can either tear down with our words or build up with our words," Elijah said. "I read from Proverbs every day the chapter that corresponds with the day of the month. If it's a thirty-day month, I read two chapters on the last day of the month. That book has words to live by."

"Interesting," replied Adam, "you saying that, about building up or tearing down with our words. Just last week I was thinking about a man who lied to me. A person who tells a lie is, in truth, most hurt by it."

"How so?"

"Well, we become what we say. The man who lied to me becomes a lie. In other words, he has to live with himself...someone he cannot trust. The opposite is true when we speak positive, loving things. Jesus said, 'For by your words you will be justified, and by your words you shall be condemned.'" Adam nodded his head sagely at Elijah. "You saying we either tear down or build up by our words is so true. I always say, 'A clear expression deepens impression.' When I talk over some idea that is difficult to understand with another person or go over something several times myself, it makes more sense than it did the first time. It's the same with our words. When we say something, we need to be careful and ensure that it is guarded by truth, integrity, and kindness."

"Good thoughts," Elijah responded. "It's also important *how* we say our words, isn't it?"

"Yes. I am convinced that most of the time it's not necessarily what we say so much as how we say it."

"Exactly."

Adam and Elijah rode comfortably as they enjoyed sharing their thoughts with each other. The time slipped away, and it seemed like no time at all when they were pulling up in front of the mission.

CHAPTER XIV

For without cause have they hid for me their net in a pit,
which without cause they have digged for my soul.

PSALM 35:7

ABIGAIL MADE THEM WELCOME, giving Elijah a big hug and kiss as if Adam weren't standing there looking on. The women at the mission were just about to sit down to luncheon prepared by Bessie, and the two men joined them. Bessie fussed over them as if they were children.

"I didn't think I wanted to eat again today after that breakfast of Conchita's. Here I am ready to eat again. Hot roast beef sandwiches with gravy…umm, you know the way to a man's heart, Miss Bessie!" It'd been a while since Adam had enjoyed such good food. He knew he was in for good meals when he moved into the Chandlers' house. Berry was a good cook too.

When they finished their repast, Adam pushed back from the table with a big sigh.

"That was delicious, Bessie. I could get used to your cooking, but I mustn't. Boarding room food simply doesn't have the flavor yours does. Ah, well…reckon I'd better get going. I've been enjoying myself immensely and now must get back to reality. Thank you, Elijah Humphries, for all your help, and you too, Miss Abigail. You've made me feel so welcome."

They rose from the table, and Elijah stuck out his hand, but Adam pulled the older man into his arms for a good hug.

"You are most welcome," Abigail said. "Stop by on your way north. Perhaps we can scare up a meal for you," she added with a smile.

Elijah said, "You are welcome here anytime. We love having company, and you seem more like family than company. So, please do come again."

"I'll do that, and thanks."

The couple followed Adam out the front door and down the walk to the iron gates of the mission. He stepped into the stirrup and with a wave of his hand was on his way.

Adam rode south with much on his mind. He thought about what needed to be accomplished in the next couple days and began to line them up in proper order in his mind. When he arrived at the Sausalito ferry, he had to wait for half an hour, so he got his satchel off the horn of his saddle and sat down to write a list of things he must do before heading back to Sunrise Ranch.

When the ferry docked, he was ready and enjoyed the freshening breeze that blew across the strait. Whitecaps splashed against the sides of the ferry, and looking up, he saw white fluffy clouds scudding hurriedly across a sky so blue it nearly took his breath away with its beauty. On his left was the island of Alcatraz rising above the bay with its stark prison spreading across its width. Seagulls swooped down hoping for a bit of fish or bread, and they screamed in the breeze that blew coolly on his face.

He arrived at his hotel by midafternoon, stopping by the front desk to pick up his room key and mail. The concierge handed him a sealed note and two telegrams. Climbing the stairs, he reached his room at the top of the second flight and unlocked the door, throwing his mail and satchels on the bed. He went down the hall to use the restroom and wash up. As he returned to his room, he wondered about the telegrams. *Another job? Well, it'll be the first one I turn down.* He locked his door, picked up his mail, and sat down on the bed. He tore open the oldest telegram carefully and read it with some astonishment.

ARRIVING SAN FRANCISCO JUNE 11 STOP MEET TRAIN FROM CHICAGO STOP I LOOK FORWARD TO SEEING YOU STOP AUNT HATTIE STOP

He ran a hand through his hair and thought, *She arrived yesterday! She's already here! Wonder, is she staying in this hotel?* Quickly, he picked up the other telegram but tossed it down, knowing it was from the state of California. A sealed note was in his aunt's hand. He opened it too quickly, tearing the missive a bit in his haste. It was dated the day before.

> *Dear Adam,*
>
> *Sorry to have missed you. I reckon you're out on a job. I've been invited to stay in Napa, California, which I understand is just north of here. Bertha Morrow's house is located at 912 North Hampton Road. Whenever you get back, I'll be happy for you to come get me. Or, send word and I'll come to San Francisco.*
>
> *With love and looking forward to seeing you,*
>
> *Aunt Hattie*

Adam laughed and said aloud, "Lord, You sure do have a sense of humor. Thanks for smoothing the way. Don't know if she's coming to stay or visit, but I know Your hand is in this, and again, I thank You. This will make things a bit easier." He ran his hand through his hair and thought, *I've accumulated a few things, but packing up should be easy. Reckon I'd better go downstairs and let them know I'm leaving.* He pulled a watch out of his vest and checked the time. *It's almost time to eat,* he thought. *Think I'll pack up my clothes and then go down. I should be able to head back up north by midday tomorrow.* He chuckled again. *What are the chances of Aunt Hattie staying in Napa?*

Eden went out to saddle up Spanner. She needed to get away and think. She tried to clear her mind of thought and concentrate on her horse. He whickered softly as she opened the stable door, and she had a carrot ready to give to him. He took the treat delicately with his lips. Rubbing his cheek as he crunched the carrot, she crooned love words to him before picking up his saddle blanket. As she threw it onto his back, she heard the door at the back of the stable open and close.

It was the door to Gio's living quarters. She didn't want to talk right now; she simply needed to get away, to think about what Liberty had said to her and to think about what she should do. After meeting Adam, she didn't believe he had anything to do with coercing her father into giving him half of Sunrise. No man could have made her father do something like that unless her father wanted to do it. *No, it must be as Gio said*, she thought. *It was all some scheme of Papa's for some reason unknown to me.*

Gio asked, "Where are you going, Eden?"

"For a ride," she replied curtly. "I need to think, and I'm tired of people right now."

"I understand, but be careful. We still don't know who—"

"I know. I know!" she interrupted. "But what would anyone gain by killing me? For that matter, the only person to gain by my parents' death is Adam Brown. I never thought of it before, but if something did happen to me, Adam Brown stands to inherit everything, doesn't he? Doesn't that give you pause at all, Gio?"

"It did occur to me before I met him," he replied, "but I don't believe he had any inkling of Eldon writing him into his will. You need to watch your words and think this through before you go accusing someone of murder."

"I'm not accusing him of anything, yet. I simply wonder about it. A body can wonder without making an accusation. I don't understand any of it, but I'm quite certain whoever did kill my parents isn't walking around with a placard saying 'I'm a murderer' or that they're acting any different from anyone else. Perhaps it was a random act of violence, but to me, until we find out who did it, the person who stands to benefit is suspect."

"I see your point, *bambino*."

Eden's eyes filled with tears, and she whispered, "You haven't called me that for years."

"I love you, Eden, as if you were my own daughter. Please don't forget that. You are my family, I have no other. And, you're not alone in your questions nor in your sorrow. I'll ride into town again tomorrow and see if Sheriff Rawlins has found out anything. I don't see how he can have found anything with all the shell casings picked up and horses' hooves brushed out. Whoever did this heinous thing planned it out well. No, I don't believe it was a random act of violence, nor was it a robbery.

Nothing was taken. Whoever did this evil planned it out right down to the last detail. I believe it's someone we know, right here in Napa. No, if it had been Adam Brown, he'd have signed those papers when he first had the chance in San Rafael. Instead, he came up to check everything out first. He believes your father wanted it this way." Giovanni squeezed her shoulder with a sympathetic hand and walked toward the house. She stared after him, realizing for the first time that his grief must cut as deeply as her own. His normally ramrod-straight shoulders were bowed, and for the first time in her life she thought he looked old. She knew of the love that had existed between her father and Gio. Tears slid silently down her cheeks.

She yanked the girth tighter and wiped away her tears with an impatient hand. Leaning her head against the stallion, she whispered, "I wish this was a nightmare and I could wake up and all would be well. Oh, how I do wish it!"

She stepped onto the slat of the stall and threw her leg over the saddle. Leaning forward, she hugged her horse's neck before backing Spanner out of the stall. Instead of jumping over the corral fences, she walked him sedately down the lane until she was out of sight of the house. Kicking him into a gallop, she felt the wind on her face and wished she could ride off the face of the earth rather than deal with the pain that pierced her heart and the questions that would not allow her to rest.

It was very early morning, and a lone rider entered into a back trail leading up the steep path to the bluff above. The opening to the trail was obscured by heavy brush and scrub oak. Unless a body knew where it began, the trail was difficult to find. Once atop the bluff overlooking the valley, the rider sat quietly astride a beautiful black-and-white paint. The horse and rider were so still that if one could see them they'd look like a painting. Huge boulders topped the bluff, and it was easy to sit within their cover without being seen from below. With eyes trained on the main road, a single rider came into view. He never noticed the still figure watching him as he loped along.

Fingering the trigger of the rifle held loosely in hands that were quite capable, the lone rider sitting atop the bluff knew patience and timing were a strong asset. The lone rider took aim and fired the rifle.

It was still dark when Buckmaster Rawlins rode out of Napa. He'd decided to get an early start and look a bit further out from the area where the Chandlers were murdered. Perhaps there was a hideout or someplace where a stranger could stay without being noticed in town. His gut told him the murderer was a person known in Napa, not a stranger. It was someone who had to have known about the Hardings' party that night. As difficult as it was to believe, most anyone was suspect.

Streaks of light made their way over the hills, and the sky was lit by a beautiful dawn. Buck looked at the horizon as the Almighty's paintbrush seemed to paint a swath of red stretching out across the heavens. All of the sudden, the sun peeked its bright orb over the bluffs lining the road. He saw a flash of light and instantly turned to see what it was. Pain ripped through his chest. *I've been shot!* he thought in astonishment as he heard the report of the rifle. He tumbled from his horse and lay there. He needed to staunch the flow of blood. He tried to undo his neckerchief with fingers that fumbled and grew weak and clumsy as he lost consciousness…

Buck opened his eyes to see Dr. John Meeks bending over him. He felt the pain in his chest, and although he was foggy about the events, he remembered he'd been shot.

"How bad is it, Doc?" he asked.

"You're lucky, Buck. The bullet went clean through. Do you have any idea who might have done this?"

"Most likely someone who doesn't want me snooping around. Truth to tell, I have no idea who, but I did catch a glimpse of reflected light on a bluff overlooking the main road just afore I was shot. I turned to look and heard the shot, but I don't remember much else. How did I get here?"

"Well, if you hadn't turned in your saddle at that exact moment, I'm sure it would have been worse," Dr. John said grimly. "We've got us a murderer out there on the loose and have no clue as to who they are. I reckon one good thing is that Theo Harding was riding down the road right after you were shot, and picked you up. He said not a minute behind him was Matthew's new bookkeeper, who helped him bring you into my office. You could have lain there and bled to death, or the culprit could have come to finish the job. Yes, it was quite fortuitous that Harding and Stirling rode up when they did. I helped them get you into the office. Did you know both those men ride a black-and-white paint? Looked strange having the two of them tied up side by side."

Buck grinned slightly, uncomfortable on Dr. John's medical exam table. "I thought I'd ride over toward the Hardings' and carefully search out the place where Eldon and Cammie were shot. I know I've done that a half dozen times, but I keep feeling I've overlooked something, some clue as to whomever did it."

"What I don't understand is why someone killed the Chandlers in the first place and why they would go after you. That it's the same person goes without saying."

"Maybe I was getting too close for comfort. Maybe whoever did it is afraid I'll find something." Buck winced as he tried to sit up, but Dr. John forestalled him, pushing him back down. "Whoa there! You're not getting up just yet, sir. You lost a bucket of blood, and you need some rest before you go gallivanting around the country trying to find your attacker. Problem is, you're not going to find out who did this unless you catch them in the act, so to speak."

Buck grimaced with the pain of movement. "I reckon you're right, but I sure as the dickens don't have to like it. Do you think you could get Bannister in here so's I can talk to him?"

"I'll do that. I'm also going to get Bertha to come over and cluck over you like a mother hen. I heard she's back."

A slow grin spread out over Buck's face, and he said, "I'd like that... I'd like that just fine, and yes, I saw her riding into town yesterday."

"You surprise me, Sheriff. I thought you'd start kicking and screaming at the thought of someone hovering over you."

"Nope, not at all, not this time," Buckmaster Rawlins said with a grin.

Well, you'll be comfortable in your own bed. We'll try to get you there with little fuss. Sorry this happened. I sure hope you will be able to find out who's gone crazy."

"Crazy?"

"Yes, anyone who murders or shoots someone for no good reason is wicked and has to be insane," the doctor replied grimly as he stood up, finished with his ministrations.

Buck had no comment to add to that statement but asked, "When do you think you'll ask Bertha to come over?"

Dr. John looked at Buck, surprise written all over his face. "She's a bit old for you, don't you think?"

Buckmaster started to laugh, but gasped and grimaced with pain instead as he rasped out, "You do know how to jest, Doc. I'll be fine, really. I don't need anyone."

"Yes, you do. As a matter of fact, think what I'll do is have you moved over to Bertha's. That way she can enjoy her own bed, and you'll have a cook and people to wait on you. I still don't understand why you let everyone go after Jazzie died. You still needed a cook and housekeeper."

"Too many memories, Doc. Too many memories. It's why I moved into another house too. I couldn't take comfort in the memories—I only found pain. I was so angry at God for the longest time, until I finally came to realize His ways are best even when we don't understand them. I do wonder, though, was it her day to die? If she hadn't gone to Frisco that day, would she have lived longer, or was that, no matter what, the last day of her life?"

"Hmm, I've never thought of that before. I'll have to think about that for a while before I give you my thoughts on it. Off the top of my head I'd say only God knows the answer. Meanwhile, I'll find a stretcher and a couple men who can haul you to Morrow's house."

For some reason, unknown to the doctor, Buck could not stop grinning.

CHAPTER XV

Though I walk in the midst of trouble, thou wilt revive me:
thou shalt stretch forth thine hand against the wrath of mine enemies,
and thy right hand shall save me.

PSALM 138:7

HATTIE OPENED HER EYES and stretched. Sitting up, she plumped a couple pillows behind herself and leaned back. Glancing toward the window, she could see it was still quite early. She'd opened the curtains and cracked the window before she blew out the lamp the night before. She hated sleeping in a room with all the windows closed. She didn't believe she was claustrophobic. She simply enjoyed fresh air.

Leaning back, she closed her eyes, but all she could see was a pair of cool blue ones staring at her in a bemused fashion. Even now, the blood climbed into her cheeks.

"Lord," she whispered, "what in the world is the matter with me? I've never reacted like that to a man's perusal in my entire life. I can't seem to think about anything except that man standing there on that walk, lifting his hat and staring right back at me. Well, help me to concentrate on You right now. I do need to pray and thank You, Father, for this new day. I thank You for providing me a place to stay until Adam contacts me. I suppose I could have stayed at his hotel, but this is so beautiful, and I've found a new friend. Lord, I ask You to bless Bertha for opening her home to me. What a delightful woman she is, and I thank You for the friendship that has sprung up between us. I thought it'd be a long time before I could call a new acquaintance a friend, but you provided for me before I even asked. Thank You, and may I be a blessing to others this day. In the precious name that is above all names, amen."

She slipped out of the bed and pulled on her robe, hoping it wasn't inappropriate to not dress before breakfast. She went downstairs in search of a cup of coffee. She didn't expect anyone to be up yet, but she was mistaken. Hearing noises coming from the kitchen, she entered and saw that Fern had already made coffee and was making breakfast.

"Good morning, Fern. Umm, it smells wonderful in here. There's nothing like the smell of frying bacon to whet one's appetite, is there?"

"No, miss, bacon always makes my mouth water." She smiled. "Good morning to you. Did you sleep all right?"

"Yes, I slept wonderfully, thank you. Is there anything I can do to help?"

Fern took a good look at this woman who seemed so youthful, surprised she'd offer to help. "No, I believe I have it all under control. Mrs. Morrow is usually an early riser, but like you, she dresses later. I suppose you could take her cup of coffee upstairs for me, if you don't mind."

"I'd be happy to do that. She showed me her room last evening. It's beautiful. I love the view from her balcony," Hattie said as she took two cups from Fern.

"Yes, it is beautiful. Although we live here on the edge of town, when you look out the back, it feels as if we're in the country."

"It does give that impression." Hattie smiled in agreement. She headed up the stairs and wondered how she was going to knock on the door. She tried knocking with her foot, and Bertha opened the door.

"Good morning, Hattie. Thank you, dear, and come on in," she invited as she took her cup from Hattie's hand. "Let's go sit and enjoy our coffee on the balcony. It's looking to be a glorious day. Come on in, my new friend," Bertha said with a warm smile as she led the way through the already opened door to the balcony.

"Good morning, Bertha. I slept well last night, quite different from being on that train. I didn't miss the click of train wheels on tracks one bit! Again, I want to thank you for opening your home to me."

"Well, this house is too big for just me anymore. I've thought about taking in boarders, but I don't care for the hassle, nor do I wish to hire on more help, which I'd need to do if I opened a boardinghouse." She waved to a cozy-looking wicker chair with faded floral print cushions. "Sit down and make yourself comfortable. Most mornings, at least until the rainy season, I have my coffee right here and have a nice chat with the Lord."

The two women sat, the chairs at a slight angle toward each other but facing more toward the view of the backyard and grounds. There was a low glass-topped wicker table between them.

"My, this is lovely, isn't it?" Hattie enjoyed the feeling of contentment as she sat comfortably looking at the gardens below that ended in a thick line of trees and shrubs. Birds flitted by, and a family of quail strutted across the grass. In the lead was a beautiful male, his plume bobbing importantly.

"Yes, it's a wonderful place for uninterrupted quiet time," Bertha said.

"I know what you mean. I simply don't understand how a body can get through the day without some quiet time and direction from the Lord."

"Oh," said Bertha, "I don't know how some people get through life when they haven't got the sense that God gave geese."

Hattie laughed and Bertha joined in.

The two women chatted happily, sipping their coffee and enjoying relaxing conversation until Bertha made a comment.

"I think you really caught Buck's eye yesterday."

"B-Buck?" Hattie asked faintly, knowing what was coming.

"The sheriff you met yesterday, Buckmaster Rawlins. I do believe he took quite a fancy to you. I've never seen him ever look at another woman since his dear wife, Jazzie, died. Jazzie, short for Jasmine, was killed in a freakish accident in San Francisco about, hmm, let me see, it's been nigh unto six years ago now. My, how the time does fly. Poor man, he was devastated. They'd never had any children, and the two of them were the best of friends since childhood. A real tragedy it was...such a shock. You told me you were thirty-seven, didn't you? He's just turned thirty-nine. We had a birthday party for him just afore I left to go back east.

"Yes, my dear friend Camilla Chandler had the celebration at her house. Lovely place...Chandler Olives, you know. Buck was that surprised, he was. Didn't know it was a party for him. Eldon and Camilla Chandler helped him through the bad time of losing his wife. Well, as I said, I've never seen the man take a second look the way he did yesterday."

Hattie blushed to the roots of her deep-auburn hair. Her thoughts scattered, and she couldn't think of a single thing to say in reply, so she said nothing.

Bertha, noticing the blush, smiled inwardly and continued to talk. "Yes, poor Buckmaster. Jasmine and he grew up together…childhood sweethearts, they were. Never could see one without the other. Now, he's all alone, poor man."

Hattie, the blush receding, stared unseeingly out at the beautiful view. Still not saying anything, Bertha's last comment went round and round in her head. *Now, he's all alone, poor man.*

"Let's go down and have breakfast," Bertha said. "I'm sure it's ready." The two women went to the dining room, where the table was set for two. Still in their robes, they sat down to the delicious breakfast Hattie had seen Fern preparing.

Bertha said, "Let's pray. Lord, how blest we are. We thank Thee for this food and for good fellowship. May our conversation be pleasing to Thee, and may our thoughts and attitudes also please Thee. We thank Thee for providing more than we could ask or think. We bless Thy name this day. Amen."

Faye heard a knock and went to the front door, wondering who would come calling at such an early hour. She opened the door to find Dr. John standing there and two men behind him with a stretcher. She looked in amazement into the doctor's face.

"Good morning, Faye. Is Bertha in? I need some help. Sheriff here has been shot, and I need her to tend to him."

Faye stood staring as if rooted to the floor, and the doctor said a little impatiently, "Faye! Go get Bertha, now!"

Startled, she turned and ran to the dining room, where Bertha and her guest were having breakfast, without asking the men on the steps to come in.

"Oh, ma'am, Doc's at the door! The sheriff's been shot and needs nursing. Come quick!"

Bertha stood abruptly and headed to the door, Hattie right behind her. "What happened, Dr. John? Come in. Come right in. Take him up the stairs, second door on the left. Hattie, get Fern to heat some water."

Hattie walked swiftly to the kitchen. "Fern, the sheriff's been shot, and the doctor is taking him upstairs. I took a good look, and it appears to me the doctor has already attended to his wound, but just to be sure, could you please heat some water?" Hattie spoke calmly, but her heart beat a fast tattoo against her ribcage. "Oh, Lord," she whispered, "please, please let him be all right," she said as she quickly ascended the stairs.

She stood back out of the doorway, as the men had already shifted the sheriff to the bed and were coming out. Hattie entered quietly and stood out of Buck's sight, listening to what the doctor was saying to Bertha.

"Buck was traveling out to the place where the Chandlers were murdered to check—"

"Murdered! The Chandlers murdered? Oh my!" Bertha's face paled as she put her hand over her heart. She sat down with a plop on the plush armchair.

"I'm sorry. I thought you knew," Dr. John said apologetically. "News like that travels fast, and I supposed Fern would have told you about it. Again, I do apologize. What a shock for you. I know you and Cammie were the best of friends. I am so sorry for telling you like this."

"When did it happen? All of them? Oh my goodness, what a tragedy!" Tears formed in her eyes, making runnels down her cheeks.

Buck spoke up from the bed. "It's worse than a tragedy. There's at least one lunatic, and maybe more, going around shooting and murdering people, and I can see no reason for it, so far. Maybe I was getting too close to a hideout or something. I feel frustrated that I haven't been able to find one single thing related to Eldon and Cammie's deaths. And no, Eden wasn't with them. The Hardings had a dinner party. It was late evening, and Eldon and Cammie had left and were returning home. They were attacked and killed on the main road."

Buck turned his head, seeing movement by the doorway, and felt a sense of contentment warm his insides. *Ah, there she is*, he thought.

Dawn came swiftly, the red streaks turning quickly into a pure cobalt with not a cloud marring the horizon. Matthew was up early. It was the day after Adam had gone back to San Francisco. He had several things he wanted to get done before he headed into town.

He stood outside the barn, giving Diego some instructions, when he saw his beautiful wife come across the stable yard, heading straight for him.

"Good morning, Diego. Gorgeous day, isn't it?" She turned to Matthew. "Breakfast is ready, Mr. Bannister," she said with a wide smile, her full lips curved up into a gamin grin.

He put an arm around her and pulled her to his side, giving her a tight squeeze. "Be right with you, sweetheart," he said as he released her.

"All right. Just want you to know we're eating in the courtyard," she said as she headed back toward the house. He finished talking to Diego and went inside the Rancho to wash up. He was hungry.

Sitting across from Liberty, he began eating a breakfast of omelets, toast, and coffee. Liberty kicked off her espadrilles, and her bare feet rested between Matthew's crossed ankles under the table. The two were so in love; it was evident for all to see. They each made the other a priority, and keeping Jesus the center of all they did caused their love to be sweet and deep. There was a contentment, knowing each put the other's welfare first.

"I love you, Liberty Alexandra Corlay Bouvier Bannister!"

"Goodness, that's a mouthful, isn't it? I love you back, Matthew Aaron Bannister. I love you with all my heart and will never stop being grateful for the plan God had for me to come out west and meet you. If I had never experienced unhappiness, I wouldn't know what real joy is, would I? It's a wonderful thing to know that God gave you to me." She smiled at her husband and thanked God in her heart for His goodness.

"I reckon I don't know the answer to that. Seems like everyone has to go through hard times. It's part of living, I suppose. What's important for us to remember is that God is with us through those hard times. He will never leave us nor forsake us," Matthew quoted softly.

Liberty, finished with her breakfast, got up and went around the table. She put her arms around Matthew's neck and sat down on his lap.

"Whoa, Libby," he teased, "you're getting heavy!"

Liberty, her green eyes laughing into his blue ones, said, "Not as heavy as I'm going to get. I'm so excited to have this baby, so thankful I am *able* to have a baby, and grateful that you will be the daddy. I've watched you with Sally Ann's little Hannah. You will be a good father, Matthew. Our child will have lots of good memories of growing up. My mother tried to make up for the lack of love from my stepfather, but a body can really never take the place of another, can they? Children were meant to have both a mother and a father. If you weren't around, I'd find a man that would be willing to spend time with my children to give them the image of a good father. I'm so grateful for my father, even if we didn't know about each other until I was nearly thirty. He's a good man, and children need a good man in their lives."

Matthew's eyes sparkled at Liberty's speech. "I plan to be a good papa, but you're right, Mrs. Bannister. And now on to my plan for today. I've got a bit of work to do around here, and then I plan on riding into Napa and seeing if the sheriff has found out anything more. I decided last night to start praying we find the person or people who killed the Chandlers. I believe we're going to need the help of the Almighty on this. I've been thinking, too, that we need to pray first. So many times we seem to pray as a last resort rather than pray first."

Liberty nodded her head in agreement. "You're right about that. As far as my plans for this day, I'm going over to Granny and Papa's. Granny and I are making a tablecloth together. I showed her how to tat, and it's been fun working on such a huge project with her. We haven't decided who will end up with the tablecloth when we're finished, but it sure is a lot of work." She kissed Matthew's cheek and then slipped off his lap, picking up their dirty plates to take into the kitchen.

Matthew got up slowly, thinking about Eden and Adam and how they were going to get along. He shook his head, glad he wouldn't have to put up with Eden's sarcastic comments. He headed out to the barn.

Adam had a restless night's sleep. Waking up often, he'd pray and hope he was doing the right thing. *I'm journey proud*, he thought. *Wonder if I should send a letter of resignation and make a clean break of it or take a leave of absence from my job and see how things go at Sunrise Ranch?* Because he didn't know exactly what to do, he wondered if he truly believed that Sunrise Ranch was the right choice. Was God leading him there? *Am I showing a lack of faith to not end the state job?*

He got up early and decided to play it safe and take the leave of absence. Perhaps it was a lack of faith. On the other hand, perhaps it was being wise. He'd already written a reply to the state building commission's telegram and packed his few belongings into a large valise. He went down to eat a hearty breakfast and felt fortunate to be packed and ready to go so early.

He paid up his bill, turned in his room key, and loaded up Loco's saddlebags. The manager came out onto the boarded walk with him.

"I'm sorry to see you leave, young man, You've been a good and faithful resident these past two years. We'll miss you, that's for sure. Please keep us in mind if you ever come back to San Francisco to live."

"I'll do that, sir. I've enjoyed my stay, but I reckon it's time for me to move on." Adam shifted two satchels to his left arm to take hold of the manager's hand. "Thank you for always being so helpful," he said.

He looped the heavy satchels over the saddle horn, and with his valise strapped behind his saddle, he was ready. With a nod of his head toward the manager, he stepped into the stirrup and clicked his tongue to Loco, who set out at a sedate walk. She was heavily loaded, so he didn't plan to travel fast.

It took over twenty-five minutes for him to get to the ferry landing, but his luck held, as the ferry had just come in. He boarded with a sigh of relief that he didn't have to wait. He dismounted and led Locomotion onto the packet with ease.

CHAPTER XVI

Thou art all fair, my love;
there is no spot in thee.

SONGS OF SONGS 4:7

FOR THE FIRST TIME HE NOTICED the brilliance of the day.
San Francisco was often socked in with fog, but not this morning. It was
the beginning of a glorious day. The sky was pure azure. Looking up, he
saw not one blemish on the horizon. A breeze blew in across the strait.
The wind, a bit cool, seemed to caress his face, and he stood with long
legs spread to keep his balance on the wave-tossed ferry. Alcatraz stood in
the distance, a prison that, he knew, had housed Civil War prisoners as
early as 1861. More than that, he didn't know. He turned to look at the
Golden Gate, so named by John C. Fremont, who wrote in his memoirs
about it. The wind whipped up whitecaps, and the ferry plowed through,
finally arriving on the Marin side of the bay.

Climbing back on Locomotion once he'd led her off the ferry, Adam
headed toward the Humphries' house.

"Thank you, Father," he said aloud. "What a spectacular day to
begin a new page in the story of my life. How I do love you, Lord! May I
be pleasing to you this beautiful day, which you have created. I pray you
will help the sheriff find who killed Eldon and Camilla Chandler. Father,
help me to be long on patience with Eden Chandler. I know I wouldn't

like it if I were in her shoes. I pray You flow through me so that I can be Your ambassador to all who come in contact with me. May I be of use to You today."

Abigail was late leaving the house to walk the few blocks to the mission. Over her arm she carried a basket full of sweet rolls Bessie had made for the girls. As she opened the door, she was surprised to see Adam Brown poised to knock.

"Oh, Adam, you startled me!" she said. "Do come in. We didn't expect you until later tomorrow."

Adam pulled off his hat. "Yes, ma'am. I didn't plan to be here until tomorrow either, but I didn't have as much to do as I thought."

"Well, let's not stand here in the doorway. Come on in. We're late getting around today. I was just heading for the mission."

Elijah smiled broadly, standing up from the kitchen table as the two entered. He'd been reading a bit more in his Bible. He came across the kitchen, meeting Adam halfway, his hand outstretched, and with a clap on the shoulder, he propelled Adam toward a chair.

"Have a cup of coffee with me." He turned to look at Bessie, who'd just removed her apron, planning to go with Abigail to the mission. "Can we have a couple more of those cinnamon rolls before you go?"

"Of course." Bessie plopped a couple cinnamon rolls onto a plate and set them on the table. She poured a cup of coffee, still hot from the big woodstove. "Enjoy, Mr. Brown. I'm going down to the mission with Mrs. Humphries. Is there anything else either of you want before I go?"

"No, thank you. This is fine," Elijah responded. "We certainly couldn't do without you, Bessie."

"Pshaw, Mr. Humphries. You'd just find someone else to cook for you."

"But no one like you, Bessie. There's no one like you."

Bessie's face was glowing from the praise when the two women left, each with a basket over her arm.

"Well, young man." Elijah turned to take a good look at Adam. "That was fast work. We didn't think you'd be back until tomorrow at the earliest."

"I didn't think I'd be here this early either," Adam said with a grin. "You'll never guess what I found when I got back to my hotel, so I'll just tell you. I had received two telegrams and a sealed note. One of the telegrams was from my aunt and the other from the state. The note was also from my aunt, who is already here in California, staying with a woman named Bertha Morrow of Napa, California. Doesn't God have a wonderful sense of humor? She is staying right in the town of Napa. All I need do is pick her up and take her to Sunrise Ranch—that is, if she's willing. It's amazing when God is orchestrating events how everything seems to fall into place. I don't know if she's just here for a visit or moving out here, but either way, it's nothing short of a miracle that she's here."

"I do understand what you're saying. This house just happened to be on the market when we were looking for one. It was exactly what we wanted, and the location perfect. We moved here from Boston because we felt God's leading and followed it. The events leading up to our packing up are tied up in Liberty Bannister's history too. I feel grateful for God's mighty provision in our lives when we trust it all to Him."

"I agree. I just keep praying that I am following His lead. The circumstances surrounding this change in my life are horrible. Someone had to plan the whole thing out. I don't believe the Chandlers' deaths were achieved by a stranger. It had to be someone who knew them, but to what end?"

Elijah responded, "I know what you're saying. I have prayed much and thought much about this whole affair. I believe you are right in your assessment, but I also believe the crime is not yet finished. I—"

"What are you saying, Elijah! Do you think the person will strike again?"

"Yes, I most definitely do. They can't have finished their plan by simply doing away with the Chandlers. Either they must do away with Eden or...well, I haven't worked that all out yet, but Eden is the key to all of it."

Adam chewed on his cinnamon roll, thinking while Elijah spoke. What Elijah was saying was true. "This is going to be more difficult than I thought," he said. "She certainly won't appreciate me sticking close to her nor admonishing her to be careful."

"No, no, I agree with you, but you *can* tell your aunt and Gio and the housekeeper, Mrs. Jenkins, and whomever that Eden needs to be guarded, and most carefully."

"Yes, I can do that, but you and I both know she's not a person who will submit willingly to someone hovering over her. I peg her as being quite an independent young woman."

"Yes, I concur," Elijah responded. "What she needs is the sweet touch of the Master's hand in her life to give her some direction and support, poor girl."

Adam stood up, and taking his plate, dumped it into a pan of water sitting in the sink.

"Well, I'd love to stay and talk a spell, but I need to get a move on if I'm to get to Matthew's and then into Napa to pick up my aunt. I'm excited to see her. She's only fourteen years older than me and quite an individual. I hope she'll approve of our new living circumstances." He shook Elijah's hand, but it turned into a bear hug. They headed out the front door.

"I didn't realize your aunt was so young. For some reason I thought her to be more my age."

"Yes, Aunt Hattie was my mother's only sister, but she was quite a few years younger than my mother. They were still close. I understand that there were a couple more siblings in between them who didn't make it to adulthood. I lived with Aunt Hattie from the time I was eleven until I went off to college. We've always been close and more like friends. She's a real character and yet a very godly woman. You'll love her."

"Well, I'll come up and visit you real soon to see how things are going for you. This won't be an easy venture, but I have no doubt the good Lord's hand is in it," Elijah said seriously. He looked at Locomotion. "Your horse looks loaded down."

"Yes, it's quite a load, but we're taking it easy," he replied as he set his boot into the stirrup. "See you real soon, Elijah, and thank Bessie again for the second breakfast." He tipped his hat and turned Loco's face toward the way out of town.

The lone rider sat on the beautiful horse and wondered if it'd been too hasty a reaction, gunning down the sheriff. It had been a quick impulse, nothing more. The sheriff was getting too close to the bluff, and the rider didn't want the area searched. *That sheriff is poking his nose in it…wonder if I should have finished him off. Now I'll have to find another place to watch the road, and none's as good as this bluff. Perhaps I'd best not even scout around for a while…let things rest a bit. I reckon I'm in no hurry.*

Adam rode Locomotion down the wide road to the Bannisters' house. He passed row upon row of grapevines extending out as far as the eye could see. Coming to a stop at the long hitching post, he didn't see anyone around and sat on his horse, thinking how beautiful the facade of the Rancho was. On either side of the entrance, orange trees grew with fruit in every stage of ripeness, hanging on branches that were neatly trimmed. Matthew had told him how the Valencia orange was ready to be harvested between February and October. The fruit could ripen and hold on a tree for more than six months, and the longer it held, the sweeter it got. Adam thought it strange that the rind regreened, and it was hard to differentiate between fruit just turning orange and ripe fruit regreening.

Dismounting, he slapped the reins around the railing and unhooked the heavy satchels from the saddle horn, placing them carefully on the grassy area under the rail to give Loco a little relief from the weight. He started up the wide flagstone walk but heard his name called. Turning, he saw Matthew leading Piggypie out of the barn, and switching direction, Adam headed toward his new friend.

"You certainly have taken me by surprise," Matthew said with a smile lighting his deep-set blue eyes as he stuck out his hand to shake Adam's. "I didn't think you'd be here until tomorrow at the earliest."

"I know. Elijah said the same thing earlier this morning. Reckon I didn't have as much time-consuming business to attend to as I had supposed. It didn't take me any time at all to pack. There's all my worldly goods right there." He gestured to his horse and the satchels under the hitching post. "I've been so busy working I haven't had time to collect many things." Adam suddenly realized Piggypie was saddled and ready to ride. "Are you heading out somewhere?"

"Yes, I've decided to go into Napa. I want to talk to the sheriff and see if he's found anything. I also thought I'd take another good look at the area around where the Chandlers were attacked."

"Well," said Adam, "matter of fact, I'm heading that way. Mind if I tag along?"

"You're going to Napa? I thought you'd be going only as far as Sunrise Ranch, but of course, you're welcome to ride along with me."

"No, not Sunrise Ranch yet. I'm heading to Napa first. I believe God is orchestrating these events. His timing sure is a lot better than mine," he replied with a grin. "When I got back to my hotel room, there was a telegram from my aunt who lives in Williamsburg. My aunt Hattie is in Napa, staying with some woman named Bertha Morrow."

"Bertha? Ah yes, she went back east. I saw her at the sheriff's birthday party just before she went on her trip to Virginia. Sheriff Rawlins and Bertha Morrow are great friends. What a coincidence, your aunt staying with her." Matthew smiled. "Well, let's be on our way. I can introduce you to Bertha. She's a wonderful woman. Lost her husband a few years back. She's involved in many activities in Napa and is the only woman on the city council. Liberty adores her." He settled himself on Piggypie, and Adam, after hooking his satchels back over the horn of his saddle, got on Loco. Because of Loco's heavy load, the two men set off for Napa at a comfortably slow pace. They stopped at Sunrise Ranch and dropped off the things Adam did not need right away, handing them over to Gio, before they traveled on to Napa.

"Well, Bertha, I think you're stuck with me for a bit," Buck said. "Dr. John thinks this is where I need to recuperate."

"Stuck with you is right," Bertha teased. She turned to Dr. John. "How bad is he, anyway?"

"Any lower and he wouldn't be with us. He happened to turn in his saddle, and it saved him. He's lost quite a bit of blood and needs nourishing soup and plenty of liquids, and I might add, plenty of rest."

"I'll have Fern make her chicken soup. It's delicious as well as strengthening with all those vegetables in it." She turned and held out her hand to Hattie. "This is my guest, Hattie Hamilton from

Williamsburg, Virginia. She will be staying with me until her nephew comes for her. We don't exactly know how long that will be. Hattie, meet Dr. John Meeks. He tends to all of us around these parts, and when he's not available, we ride to Sonoma and get Doc Addison. John, be pleased to meet Hattie Hamilton."

The two eyed each other. Hattie felt color rising up her neck and into her face, knowing Buckmaster Rawlins was watching her every move.

"I'm pleased to meet you, Dr. Meeks," she said primly.

"I'm happy to meet you too, Mrs. Hamilton."

"Miss, that's Miss Hamilton," she corrected him, her cheeks now in full bloom.

"Sorry, my mistake, Miss Hamilton. You may call me Dr. John like everyone else in these parts." He wondered at her reddened cheeks, until she turned to greet the sheriff.

"It's good to see you again, Sheriff Rawlins, even under such wretched circumstances," she said. "I'm so sorry this has happened to you."

The sheriff gazed at Hattie and spoke slowly. "It's nice to see you again too, *Miss* Hamilton." He held out his hand for her to shake, and as he took her hand in his, he felt a sense of satisfaction, as if her hand belonged in his. He smiled lazily, not letting go of her hand, as was proper.

Finally, Hattie recovered her hand, but not before she was completely discombobulated. Her cheeks were a rosy red, but she looked steadily into the clear, light-blue eyes of Buckmaster Rawlins as if mesmerized. The spell was broken by a tap on the opened doorjamb. It was Fern who spoke to Bertha.

"You have company in the parlor, Mrs. Morrow."

"Company! Why, who is it?"

"It's Mr. Bannister and another young man come to call."

"Well, send them up, dearie. I'm sure Matthew will want to be talking to Buck here."

Fern left, descending the stairs quickly. "Please," she said to the two men, "Mrs. Morrow wants you to come upstairs. Follow me."

Matthew looked at her in surprise, wondering why Bertha would want them to come up the stairs. He glanced at Adam and nodded his head for him to follow as he started after Fern. Going up the steps, Matthew heard voices and wondered who else was visiting. He hadn't noticed any horses tied up out front.

Fern stood aside and gestured for him to go in. Matthew entered the large bedroom that seemingly grew smaller by the minute. He assessed its occupants but couldn't see who was in the bed. Surprise etched itself on his face as he saw Dr. John Meeks. Before he could say anything, a woman rushed past him with a cry, and turning, he saw Adam pick her up and swing her into his arms, making a complete circle, her skirts flying outward.

As Buck watched, his face was stoic, but his heart felt tight. He didn't realize he was holding his breath until he heard the young man's speech. His air came out in a slight whoosh of relief, but pain seared through his chest from his wound.

CHAPTER XVII

Though I walk in the midst of trouble, thou wilt revive me:
thou shalt stretch forth thine hand against the wrath of mine enemies,
and thy right hand shall save me.

PSALM 138:7

"**A**UNT HATTIE!" ADAM CRIED. "What the blazes are you doing here?
I thought you said you'd never come out west!"

"Land o' Goshen, Adam, put me down!" she said, giggling. "Right
this instant!" she commanded as a wide smile spread across her face, and
the small quirky dimple at the top of her cheek appeared.
Embarrassment flooded through her, as her silky auburn hair had lost its
pins and cascaded down her back.

Adam, his eyes twinkling, set her down, but not before her slim
ankles and calves had been exposed to the occupants of the room.
She straightened her skirts, her cheeks scarlet, and scrambled to
gather up the pins off the floor, sticking them between her lips as she
twisted the long hair back into the semblance of a bun. She thrust the
pins in while Adam introduced her to Matthew, who clearly wanted to
laugh but contained himself.

"Aunt Hattie Hamilton, I'd like you to meet Matthew Bannister of
Bannister Vineyards. Matthew, my aunt, Miss Hattie Hamilton, recently
of Williamsburg, Virginia."

Matthew switched his hat to his left hand and stuck out his right as she proffered her hand to him. "Pleased to meet you, ma'am. Adam has spoken most highly of you, and you are a godsend to us all, being the answer to our prayers, Miss Hamilton."

"It's nice to meet you too, Mr. Bannister, but I don't quite follow what you mean," she replied in a puzzled tone.

"I'll tell you all about it, Aunt Hattie, but first introduce me to your hostess," Adam said, replying for Matthew.

Matthew turned back to the main part of the room and for the first time saw Buckmaster Rawlins in the bed.

"What's going on here?" he asked in amazement.

Dr. John replied, "Buck's been shot—"

"Shot! You've been shot?" Matthew bit out the words.

The jovial atmosphere of the room immediately cooled.

"Yes, I think by the same person who killed the Chandlers. I was out snooping around early this morning and was out by Eagles Bluff. Think I was getting too close for comfort, and someone shot me."

"If Buck hadn't seen the reflected light off the rifle and turned when he did, I don't believe he'd be with us," the doctor interjected. "Whoever the shooter is, they're quite accurate with both a handgun and a rifle."

Matthew turned to Adam. "Mind if I tell them what's going on here?"

"No, go right ahead. I'm just thankful that Aunt Hattie's here. It makes things a bit more proper. I don't want any rumors to get started that might cast any aspersions upon Miss Eden." All eyes became trained on Adam, who waved a hand toward Matthew to explain what he meant by his statement. "You tell them," he said.

Matthew nodded. "Eldon Chandler met Adam Brown on the train coming back from Virginia a year ago. Both Eldon and Camilla Chandler enjoyed his company for about six days. When Eldon was killed, his lawyer, Stephen Hancock, came up from San Rafael to let Eden, Gio, and the rest of the household know about the terms of the will. It seems Eldon took such a shine to Adam and that he left half his estate to him, with conditions. Both he and Eden must live in the house for five years, at which time one of them may buy the other out."

Hattie gasped. "You're not going to take him up on it, are you, Adam? Why, it's not yours!"

"You're right. It's not mine, and I wasn't going to sign the paperwork, but the will stated that if I decided not to, Stephen Hancock was to get down on his knees and beg me to accept. I prayed and feel I've made the right decision. I have accepted the terms of the will. Miss Eden, of course, is beside herself with grief and also anger. I can't say I blame her. I wouldn't like it if my father had done such a thing and never told me. Evidently he told Giovanni but never his daughter.

"I took a leave of absence from my job and intend to see how this works out. I'd like to see whoever killed the Chandlers caught. Perhaps, in some way, I can protect Miss Eden. I don't understand Eldon doing this, nor do I understand why anyone would want him dead, but I intend to see this thing out now I've made my decision."

Buck looked carefully at Adam while he spoke. He stared into Adam's eyes, looking for deception or something furtive, but his gut told him the young man was telling the truth.

"You're saying half of Sunrise Ranch is now yours?" Dr. John asked in astonishment.

"Yes, it is. I plan to learn the business from the ground up. I also had planned to write Aunt Hattie and see if she'd be willing to come out and be a live-in chaperone just to stop any possible gossip...make my being there a bit more proper."

"Well, that's news to me," she said. "You don't know, do you, that I am not here for just a visit. I packed everything up, sold the house, and took a train out here. It's how I met Bertha. She was sweet and hospitable and offered me a place to stay until you showed up."

Adam was stunned. "You have moved out here? Why, that's perfect," he said.

"I have belongings still at the station in San Francisco."

"We can get those for you," Adam said quickly.

Matthew turned to Buck. "So what's next, Sheriff?"

Buck took his time, deliberating Matthew's question. "Well, I don't rightly know. I sure don't want you getting shot, but I'm sure someone is using Eagles Bluff to keep eyes on the road and what's happening around here. I think I got to looking too close for someone's comfort."

Adam walked closer to the bed and looked Buck straight in the eyes. "I am pleased to meet you, sir. Matthew speaks quite highly of your abilities. I'd like to find out who shot you, but more, who killed the

Chandlers. Matthew and I are committed to finding out. I believe you're going to be out of commission for a while, and Matthew and I will do whatever you think necessary to find the cowards who did this despicable thing. You just say the word, and we'll do it."

Bertha, with a tiny wink at Buck, turned toward Adam and asked innocently, "Do you have to take Hattie away right now, Mr. Brown, or can she stay here and help me nurse Buck back to health?"

"Please, just call me Adam. Of course you can borrow her for a few days. I need to settle some things first." He glanced at his aunt, who was blushing to the roots of her hair. All the sudden he sensed something he couldn't quite put his finger on, and he looked at her quizzically. "Is it all right for you to stay here for a few days, Aunt Hattie?"

"Yes, I can stay here and help out," she answered. She glanced over at Buck and saw him close his eyes, as if he was very tired. "Saying that, I think it's time for us to clear out of here and let Sheriff Rawlins rest."

Dr. John, with another good look at the patient, nodded his head in agreement. "I concur," he said. "Everyone out. Buck needs to rest. He's lost a lot of blood and needs to rest."

"Just one more word of advice before you leave," Buck said, opening his eyes. "Please, Matthew, Adam, please be very careful. The shooter has a deadly aim."

"So do I, Rawlins. So do I," Matthew said grimly.

The group filed silently out of the overcrowded bedroom. Hattie walked over to the bed and stood looking down at the sheriff, her deep-blue eyes caught by his frosty cool ones.

"I don't know exactly what is going on here, Buck. I may call you Buck, mayn't I?"

"Of course, and may I call you Hattie?"

"Yes, certainly." She turned and dragged a comfortable armchair close to the bed. "I'm not going to sit just yet. I need to talk to my nephew before he leaves, but this conversation isn't over, is it?"

Buck closed his eyes and said, "No, sweetheart, it's not." Hattie blushed again. Her heart was singing as she hurried down the stairs. Adam and Matthew were heading out the front door.

"Wait a minute, Adam!" She hurried to the foyer. "You weren't going to leave without talking to me, were you?"

"No, of course not. How long are you planning to stay here?"

"I'm staying right here until the sheriff is able to be up and about," she replied unabashedly.

He stared at her, wondering what it was about her that seemed so different, but he couldn't seem to put his finger on it. "All right. I'll make sure of arrangements at Sunrise Ranch and see that you have a room to stay in. It seems like a big house, so there should be no problem."

"It's a huge house, and there's plenty of room for you," Matthew interjected. "My wife and I have had a tour of the downstairs but were told there are eight suites upstairs, two for the family and six for guests. I don't reckon you'll be using more than two for the pair of you."

"N-no," Hattie replied. "I wouldn't suppose so." She looked at Matthew and asked, "Is Miss Chandler a Christian?"

"My understanding is that she is not. It's a pity she doesn't have that resource to draw upon. She has no idea of the comfort God could bring to her heart," Matthew replied.

"Sad, isn't it?" Hattie murmured.

"I'm going to go water Loco while the two of you talk," Adam said. He went out the door, closing it quietly behind him.

Bertha and Dr. John came into the foyer from the kitchen. Bertha had been giving directions to Fern about the prescribed meals for Buck.

"I'd better be going," Dr. John said. "I have a baby to deliver sometime this afternoon or evening, and my Sally will be wanting to give me a late lunch." He turned to Bertha. "Don't allow Buck up for anything other than the chamber pot. I can see him wanting to go out and find the man who did this to him, but he's to be in bed at least two full days, and then he can be up in a chair for a total of a week. You'll most likely have to hog-tie him."

"Actually, I don't think so," Bertha replied airily with a quick glance at Hattie. "I know he enjoys my company, and he'll most likely enjoy getting to know Hattie. Thanks for bringing him here, Dr. John. We'll be sure to take good care of him." She looked meaningfully at Hattie, who didn't bat an eyelash.

"Yes," Hattie said graciously to the doctor, "we'll be sure to take good care of him. Will you be back to change the dressings, or should we do that?"

Bertha looked abashed. "I didn't even think to ask."

"I'll be over tomorrow to take a look at him. Mostly, I want him to rest and drink plenty of liquids. I tried to get him to take some laudanum for the pain, but he said if it got to hurting too bad, he was going to raid your liquor cabinet."

"But I don't have one!" Bertha said in astonishment.

"He knows that," the doctor said with a laugh. "Don't worry. He's tough. Good day, ladies. I'll be seeing you tomorrow." He picked up his hat from the coat tree and opened the front door. He left, tipping his hat to the two women as Adam came indoors with a couple satchels.

"Would you and Matthew care to have a late lunch with us?" Bertha asked him. "There's plenty, and I'd love to have you stay."

Matthew replied for the two of them. "Yes, we'd like that very much, thank you."

Adam asked, "Where's your room, Aunt Hattie? I've got a couple things I'd like to stow there until we move to Sunrise Ranch. I left the heavier things there with Gio, who is foreman of the ranch, so Loco wouldn't have to carry such a heavy load."

"Follow me," she replied and led him up to her room. Once there, Adam laid the satchels in the clothespress and then plopped down on one of the plush chairs.

"Aunt Hattie, I'm thankful you're here. What made you leave Williamsburg? Did you sell your house or rent it out?"

"I simply got tired of not seeing you, Adam. You know how I love you, and I missed you more and more as the days went by. I realized that time was a wasting, and without you, well…I just want to be closer, that's all. I thought you'd still be working your state job and be gone a lot. I knew I could make a home for you when you weren't traveling. So I sold up the old house. It sure seemed forlorn after I packed up the things I wanted to keep and sold the rest. I stayed for a nearly a month with the Danforths while I emptied the house and put it up for sale. It sold quickly. Probably sold it too cheap, but I wanted everything done before I moved out here. I'm glad you're happy to see me." She gave Adam a hug. "Now, we'd better join the others for lunch, but I want to hear all about this business with the Chandlers. What a horrible thing to happen to Bertha's friends."

As they started down the hall, Hattie said, "Just a moment, Adam. I need to tell Buck he'll get some soup after we've had lunch." She peeked in on the sheriff to give him that information, and with rosy cheeks she went sedately down the stairs with her nephew.

Eden picked at her lunch. She was beginning to lose weight, and already having a willowy figure, she couldn't afford to, but she didn't feel hungry. Food seem to almost choke her. Her throat constricted as she spoke.

"So, we have one more day before the usurper comes."

Gio ignored her comment and dug into the casserole as if there were no tomorrow. "This is delicious, Berry," he said. "You've outdone yourself. I believe this is the best lasagna you've ever made."

"Same recipe, Gio. Made the same as it ever was. I do believe you say that every time you eat it." The cook laughed at him.

"Well, this time it really is the best," Gio assured her. "You need to eat, Eden. You'll end up ill if you keep playing with your food like that and not eating anything."

Eden made a face at her foreman, stood up abruptly, and threw down her napkin. "I'm going for a ride," she said and left the dining room, heading for the stables.

Eden saddled up Spanner and led him outside. He was obviously eager for a ride and stamped his feet and swished his tail in anticipation.

"I know, big boy. I know. You want to be racing across the canyon as bad as me." She stepped into the stirrup and turned him. They went into an immediate canter and cleared the corral fence next to the barn and then the second one on the further side. She kicked him into a gallop, and they were off and away.

Gio's face was downcast after she left. "What am I to do with her?" he questioned Dorothy Jenkins. "She's so angry and hurt, and I have no idea how to help her."

"I know. I know. It's simply going to take time," Mrs. Jenkins replied. "Frankly, I think it's a good thing that young man, Adam Brown, will come here to live. He will most likely make her so angry that she'll get back to normal faster than if she simply sits around by herself, angry and mourning. I have a feeling he's going to upset her applecart."

Gio, with speculation in his eyes, said, "Perhaps that *would* be the best thing for her. I've never seen her so despondent. I doubt if she'll ever get over losing her parents the way she did. It's a tragedy. One thing about the death of a loved one, is that time lessens the pain but never the loss. I sure hope the sheriff finds out who did it and that they hang for it. It's an evil act that will never be made right. Eldon was like a brother to me, and Cammie, well, the good Lord broke the mold when He made Cammie. She was one of a kind."

"That's true. I've never known a nicer woman." Tears stood out in Dorothy Jenkins' eyes, and she took the corner of her frilled apron to wipe them. Gio got up and took her into his arms as she cried and cried.

CHAPTER XVIII

Two are better than one;
because they have a good reward for their labour.
A threefold cord is not quickly broken.

ECCLESIASTES 4:9 and 4:12b

HESTER McHANEY RODE INTO TOWN with her son, Caleb. They had taken the flatbed wagon to get foodstuff and grain for the chickens.

"Mother, I know we never talk about it, but how is Pop's money holding out? I know the chickens bring in some, but I have no idea at all about our finances."

"Well, son, it's one reason I keep after you to see that Chandler girl. We have steadily depleted your Pa's money. If we watch it, we'll be all right, but I don't like being so tightfisted. I wish you'd just marry that girl. Then we'd never have to worry about money again."

Caleb's lips thinned. "If wishes were horses, we'd all ride." He glanced at his mother's set face. "I'm not interested in her that way. She's a good friend but nothing more. I'm tired of the constant harangue over the same subject. You need to stop pushing for something that's not going to happen. She's got enough on her mind right now, anyway."

"What do you mean by that?"

"I wasn't going to say anything, but Sunrise Ranch and Chandler Olives no longer belongs to just Eden."

Hester looked at her son in shock. "Did Eldon leave part of it to that I-talian foreman of his?" Her face paled, and she put her hand onto her heart, feeling it pound more than what was good for her. She glanced down at her fingernails, which had a blueish tinge to them, and knew, too, her lips were blue from lack of air. Dr. John had told her several months ago that her ticker wasn't doing well. She'd said nothing to Caleb, not wanting to worry him, but she did wish to see him married and settled before her heart gave out. Dr. John had told her it could be soon, or she might last a long time. One just never knew with a heart condition. She wanted desperately for Caleb to marry the Chandler girl.

"No, no, he didn't leave it to Mr. Coletti," Caleb replied. "He left half of all of it to a complete stranger. His name is Adam Brown, and he's coming the end of the week to live at Sunrise Ranch. Eden is beside herself with anger. Her father never told her a thing about his plans, and she, of course, resents it. I feel sorry for her. She's mourning her parents but also is very angry with them for never telling her of their plans, poor girl."

"How do you know all this?"

"I was there when the Bannisters brought Mr. Brown over and introduced him to Eden."

"The Bannisters! Do they know this Adam Brown?"

"Yes, and he's seems to be a nice, even-tempered man. I like him. He's young, about my age, I'd say."

"That young? My...wonder what in the world Eldon was thinking. Well, you just be sure to keep your oar in. You never know when you might change your mind and fall in love with the girl. She's quite attractive, and although headstrong, she's nice enough."

Caleb, his face stony, stared at his mother for a moment, wondering why she couldn't or wouldn't understand, but he said nothing more.

Matthew and Adam rode down the main road toward Eagles Bluff.

"This isn't where the Chandlers were killed," Matthew said. "That happened closer to Sunrise Ranch. The Hardings live about three miles further in this direction." He nodded toward a huge bluff in the distance. "That's the bluff the sheriff was talking about. See the huge boulders on the top? Good place for a body to hide and spy on the comings and goings on this road. Whoever's been up there won't be happy the sheriff now knows about it. Most likely they won't be lurking up there anymore." He nodded again toward the bluff. "Let's ride around it and see if we can find a path up that isn't from the main road on this side."

The two men rode around the bluff, and Matthew, who was an excellent tracker, found the hoofprints of a horse even though the area was mainly pebbly from several screes that stretched themselves down the bluff. Most of the area was covered by bushes and scrub oak. He pointed silently toward a visible print, and then he saw a slight breaking of bush ends and rode toward it, spotting a narrow trail leading upward. He gestured for Adam to follow him.

"Come on," he said. "I think I've found it."

Adam followed Matthew's Piggypie up the narrow trail, which was rough and steep. Matthew pointed to obvious broken foliage along the rugged track. The trail suddenly widened, grew more level, and the rocks turned into a sandy soil as they reached the top. The two men drew abreast and traversed the top of the bluff; the view of the road and surrounding area was spectacular. They sat and gazed in silence at the beauty surrounding them. Not a cloud marred the blue expanse, and a slight breeze helped to alleviate the heat radiating off the rocks.

Adam slid off his horse, and as he did so, he noticed cigar butts on the ground.

"Look at this, Matthew! Know anyone around here who smokes cigars?"

Matthew got down and knelt on one knee, picking up a couple of the butts. "Actually there are quite a few men who smoke them. I can tick a half dozen right off the top of my head, but it's something we should look into. We could take these into town and see who buys this brand. This was careless of someone, but carelessness is usually why a body is caught. We've had no clues at all until this." He stood and pulled a piece of newsprint from his saddlebag. "I'd tucked this in here from a couple tamales Conchita made me a few days ago." He carefully wrapped the slim cigar butts in the paper and put them into his saddlebag. "That should keep them safe. I wonder if the person who smoked these will remember they left the butts here and come back to pick them up." He looked around at the ground, which was what Adam was also doing.

"All I can see is hoofprints, but there's no brand on them. I reckon I'd better be heading for Sunrise Ranch before it gets too dark. Thanks, Matthew, for riding with me to the Morrow house. She seems like a nice lady. My aunt was acting strange, but I couldn't quite figure out what was going on. She seemed on edge or excited or something."

"I think I can tell you what was going on." Matthew's eyes glinted with humor as Adam looked at him, totally bewildered.

"What? You noticed something too?"

"Yes, I did. Sheriff Buck Rawlins and your aunt are attracted to each other. You should have seen Buck's eyes when your aunt went running into your arms. He was figuring you two were a couple, until you started talking. I wanted to laugh but didn't dare," Matthew added.

"I don't remember my aunt ever looking twice at a man. She's been quite popular at soirees and dinner parties. Seems it's easier to find a single man than a single woman for different functions. I do know she's been courted by several men, but nothing ever came of it." He looked in amazement at Matthew. "You sure it wasn't just the sheriff attracted to her?"

"You said yourself she was acting strange." He laughed, his face split with a huge grin. "No, it was definitely a two-way attraction—I can guarantee you that." Matthew sobered and went on to relate to Adam about Buck's late wife and the tragedy that had occurred several years ago. "I've never seen him look twice at another woman until your aunt. And believe me, there have been numerous females who have thrown themselves at him. He's a good man and a great catch for some woman."

Eden rode up to her favorite place to think. It always seemed to calm her to ride like the wind and then go sit quietly under the spreading red leaf maple tree at the very top of the hill, where the view overlooking Sunrise Canyon was magnificent. She gained the hill, which had a fairly flat top and was grassy. There were a few low-lying boulders, and wildflowers of all colors and sorts dotted the hilltop. She dismounted and undid Spanner's saddle, laying it and the blanket under the tree. She sat down to have a clear view of everything in all four directions, if she wanted. A slight breeze kissed her cheeks, and the sky overhead was seamless, not a cloud marring its deep-blue expanse. She couldn't see the main road from where she sat—all civilization seemed held at a distance. *It feels as if I'm the only person alive on the earth when I'm up here*, she thought. *Maybe it's one of the reasons I like it so well.*

She pulled at a clover stem in full bloom, and breaking it off, she pulled the little purple flowers out, sucking the sugar out of the ends. As she sat there, she thought about where events were taking her. Her heart ached for her parents, but the tight knot of anger seemed to be dissipating. In its place was growing a firm resolve to find out who had done this to her. *Papa had to have some reason for leaving Sunrise Ranch to a complete stranger. I don't understand why anyone would murder him or why he'd leave the property to someone else. Adam Brown, it seems to me, is the only one to profit from these events. I'm not sure he had anything to do with all this, but he's certainly going to benefit from my parents' death. That in itself makes me angry. He stands to gain a fortune, and it rightly belongs to me. I reckon if he owns half of it and anything happens to me, he'll own all of it. I'll be on my guard around him.*

With this decision made, she leaned back against the saddle. She knew her gut churned a lot and wondered if Liberty ever felt that way. *Liberty seems so stable; she's such a lady. I probably gave her a real shock the way I acted that day.* Her thoughts swung to another friend, Caleb. He was a rock in her life. She enjoyed his friendship as much as anyone she knew. He was like a brother and had a level head. He was interesting and fun to be around, but she didn't care much for his mother. She seemed overbearing. Then there was Taylor Kerrigan. She realized she'd seen too much of him lately, which might give him the impression she was sweet on him. Nothing could be further from the truth. He'd been someone she went out with simply to annoy her father. *He is terribly good looking*, she thought. *His speech doesn't bother me either. I don't even mind how he says things, but I do mind that he never seems to have an original thought in his head. Face it, Eden. He's an arrant boor.*

She closed her eyes and took a deep breath, thinking about her new circumstances. Because she was incredibly spent, both emotionally and physically, she fell soundly asleep. When she opened her eyes, Spanner was standing over her, lipping her cheek. She reached up and rubbed his face with both hands.

"I love you, Spanner. Reckon you think it's time I got up, don't you? I can't believe I fell asleep." She felt disoriented. The sun had traveled across the heavens while she slept.

Eden stood up and reached into her pocket for her watch. It had been a gift from her parents on her last birthday. It was square shaped and had a cover that was set around the edge with tiny topaz stones and diamonds. She pushed a little button, and the lid flew open. *My goodness! I can't believe I slept that long...over two hours! Gio will have a conniption fit. I need to get home.* She closed the lid with a tiny snap and stood up abruptly, shoving the watch back into her pocket. Her hair had come down and straggled around her face. She quickly took out the pins and wrapped her long, honey-colored hair expertly into a bun, thrusting the pins into it as fast as she could. She grabbed her Stetson and jammed it on her head, tightening the strap under her chin. Quickly saddling Spanner, she yanked hard on his girth, but even in her haste, her fingers were sure and steady with the buckles.

Eden rode down to the main road, surprised to see Matthew Bannister and Adam Brown heading her direction. She pulled up and waited as the two men drew near, smiling a little to herself because she could see exactly what Liberty had meant the other day when she said she had trouble distinguishing who was Matthew and who was Adam.

The two men approached, and Eden said, "Well, looks like you're here already, *Mr.* Brown. Didn't let any grass grow under your feet, did you?"

"I reckon I didn't, did I?" He smiled obligingly back at her, even though her tone had been discourteous.

His reply surprised her. She had expected, with her comment, for him to be on the defensive, but good humor lurked in his eyes, which because of her tone toward him, shamed her. She held his eyes, trying not to flinch at his clear, transparent gaze. She swallowed and looked away, but her blood boiled.

"That's not all," Matthew said with a laugh. "Remember he asked if his aunt who lives in Virginia could come to stay?" He chuckled. "She's already here. She met Bertha on the train and ended up in Napa because she couldn't find Adam. She figured he was out on a state job, and because she didn't know when he'd be back, she took Bertha up on an invitation to visit until Adam showed up."

"Your aunt is at Bertha Morrow's? That sure is convenient, isn't it?" She sneered. "Everything right in place, ready for you to take over," Eden said sarcastically. *It's just too pat*, she thought. *As if he knew he'd be moving in.*

Adam didn't reply to her comment but said, "No, it's not everything." He leaned forward, his arm on the pommel, as he replied, enunciating clearly so she would hear what he said. "While I was in San Francisco getting ready to ride up here, Sheriff Rawlins was up and about early this morning. He was riding out by Eagles Bluff and got shot—"

"Shot!" Eden exclaimed. "Is he all right? He's not dead, is he? This is insane! Buck...shot? Everything seems so out of control!"

Adam, seeing her agitation, tried to soothe her. "The sheriff will be all right, barring infection. He's also a guest at Bertha's, to recover. My aunt is going to stay and help Bertha nurse him."

"He was shot in the chest," Matthew added grimly. "Adam and I scouted around Eagles Bluff but found nothing but a few cigar butts. The shooter is bold as brass and has no scruples, as you well know. It has to be someone who knows the area and knows the people. What's worse is I'm sure we most likely know the shooter. We're most likely friends with him, or them. It's disheartening to think someone we rub shoulders with is a murderer. Most anyone could be suspect. There has to be some plan behind it, some motive, but we haven't worked that out yet." He paused to let that sink in, then continued. "You need to be very careful, Miss Eden Chandler. Whoever gunned down the sheriff has some sort of plan in mind, and you must be an important part of it."

Eden stared at him in surprise. She leaned forward, now resting her own arm on the pommel of her saddle as she said thoughtfully, "Gio said the same thing to me. Do you really think so?"

Adam answered, "Yes, and Mr. Humphries thinks so too. He's the one who said you shouldn't be left alone. Someone may be gunning for you, ma'am, and until we find out who, you need to be very careful."

Eden stared at him as her blood boiled up again. "Don't you dare tell me what to do, Mr. Brown. You may now own half of Chandler's, but you don't own me!"

Matthew, surprised at her outburst, looked in the direction of the sun and said, "I'd better be heading home. Reckon it's about time for supper, and Liberty will be waiting." He tipped his hat toward Eden and reiterated, "Be safe, Miss Eden. Be safe. I'd also caution you to be sensible and not end up sorry for being otherwise." He looked at her meaningfully and added, "I'll be dropping by tomorrow to check on the sheriff and see how things are going. Be seeing you soon. Adam, thanks for riding out here with me.

I will appreciate having you as a close neighbor." He tipped his hat respectfully and kicked Piggypie into a canter.

"Well, *Mr.* Brown—"

"Adam, just call me Adam, please. If we're going to be living in the same house, we may as well be friends, don't you think?"

"No, in truth, I don't think so," her voice clipped out. "I'll tell you straight up—I resent you, *Mr.* Brown. I keep wondering if you had some kind of hold over my father that he'd give you half of Sunrise. Nothing else makes any sense, and my father was a very level-headed, sensible man." Her voice rose, anger and frustration filling her soul. "I'll tolerate you because I have no choice. To accept you as friend? No, not anytime soon!"

She raised her arm to bring her quirt down on Loco's rump, but Adam grabbed her arm, his grip like steel.

"Not my horse." His voice was low...calm but commanding. His eyes bored into hers as he removed his grasp.

With a quick thrust of her hand, Eden threw the quirt away in disgust. She kicked Spanner, who took off like a newly branded cow out of the chute, toward Sunrise Ranch.

Adam rode Loco at a much more sedate pace. He did not plan to compete with Eden. He didn't care to give her additional reason to resent him, but he prayed as he loped along, asking for protection, guidance, and most of all for patience.

CHAPTER XIX

Blessed are the undefiled in the way,
who walk in the law of the LORD.

PSALM 119:1

AFTER **A DELICIOUS LUNCH AND SEEING** the two men off, Bertha and Hattie went back to the kitchen to get some soup for the patient.

"It's not quite ready, Mrs. Morrow," Fern said. "I'll have Faye take it up when I'm finished."

Bertha peeked into the pot. "It smells delicious, and I'm not even hungry. You are such a good cook, Fern. I've missed your wonderful meals. It's good to be home. I'll check on Buck and make sure he wants to eat before we take it up."

Once upstairs, Bertha saw Faye was busy unpacking her luggage, smoothing out her clothes and sorting what needed cleaning. She spoke quietly to her maid. "Soup's not quite ready for Buck. Fern will let you know when to bring some up."

She walked on down the hall and motioned Hattie to follow her. The two women entered the sheriff's room. He was sound asleep. Bertha, who had some catching up to do after being on vacation, put a finger to her lips to be quiet and gestured for Hattie to sit in the chair close to the bed.

Hattie obediently sat down, and Bertha left the room, eager to attend to her stack of mail.

Hattie sat back comfortably in the plush chair and studied Buck's face, memorizing every detail. His hair, cut shorter than was the custom, was thick and sandy colored. His eyebrows, smooth and well defined, were a bit darker than his hair. He had a small scar over the left brow. She knew the deeply lined indentation in his right cheek turned into an elongated crease when he smiled. His lashes were dark but short and spiky. He was clean shaven, his sideburns a little shorter than fashionable. After perusing him for a while, she leaned back against the chair and closed her eyes. Feeling drowsy but full of contentment, she fell asleep.

Sometime later, Buck awoke to a constant throbbing in his chest. He was glad it was on his left side, knowing the healing would be slower if it was on his right, which he'd use a lot more. He lay there, eyes closed, and prayed for God to bring speedy healing to him and an extra measure of patience. He felt so frustrated not having any clues to point him in the direction of the Chandlers' murder.

All the sudden, he smelled a faint orange-lemon, citrusy-ginger smell. He opened his eyes and turned his head on the pillow. There sat Hattie Hamilton, and she was sound asleep. He swallowed as he stared at her, wondering if he had the right to look while she slept.

He could see a slight indentation at the top of her cheek, which he knew turned into a quirky dimple. Her wide lips were well formed, the lower a bit fuller than the top. She had a pert upturned nose and thick, dark lashes that curled up, blonde at the tips. Her deep-auburn hair was pulled straight back into a bun, but tendrils escaped and curled around a minxish face. *Lots of personality there*, he thought. *However has she escaped marriage? However did she creep into my heart so quickly? One look and I was a goner for sure.*

The door stood open, and Bertha stepped into the room, but Buck held his forefinger up to his lips as he smiled at his hostess. She stopped abruptly and grinned back at him.

"I'll get some soup," she said in a soft whisper, backing out the door.

Buck nodded.

Hattie awoke slowly and blinked her eyes open. Buck stared at her boldly. The blood began to climb up and into her cheeks, but she couldn't seem to look away.

He decided to face this head on. "How has this happened?"

She didn't play coy, as if she didn't understand what he was saying, nor did she look away or act embarrassed. "I don't know. It's insane. I've never, not in my entire life, been so bowled over by a man."

He wasn't surprised at her straightforward answer. He, for some reason, felt as if he knew all about her, and yet there was a lifetime left to explore and find out if what he thought was true.

"I never thought to fall in love again. This has taken me as much by surprise as you. I knew yesterday, when I met you. I love you, Hattie Hamilton," he said simply. "It's not just a childish infatuation or a figment of my imaginings. I don't reckon I know how this has come to be, but I know it for the truth."

"I know it too, but I've never been in love before. I can't seem to think straight for thinking about you. I know nothing about you. Are you a Christian, Buck Rawlins? I ask because this is over, right now, if you're not."

"I accepted Christ as my Savior when I was eight years old. He's been my source of strength since I was about sixteen. I live by His Word," he replied simply. "I went through a real bad patch in my faith when Jazzie died, but I came through it with a stronger faith and knowledge that God's ways are definitely not our ways."

Hattie beamed at him and said, "All right then, I accept."

"Accept what?" he asked teasingly. "I haven't asked you anything yet."

"No, but you will, and I'm simply saying, yes. I believe I love you back, Buck Rawlins. I never thought I'd fall in love. I always thought it was folderol and nonsense. It's taken me less than twenty-four hours to know differently. This is the real thing, and I don't plan to let it slip through my fingers. I cannot believe this incredible feeling of lightness and rightness. I feel all shimmery and shiny inside."

He lay staring at her, enjoying her forthright speech. Most women he knew would never reveal their heart this way. She was an all-or-nothing kind of woman. He'd take the all, knowing if he didn't grab this with everything he had, he'd never know contentment in this world again.

"I plan to court you, Miss Hattie Hamilton. I'm going to do it up right, and I *will* ask you to marry me, but not today, not when I'm in this condition." His light-blue gaze stared into her deep-blue one, and both looked at the other in complete satisfaction. There was a feeling of blessing in this thing that had happened to them…blessing and rightness and God's loving hand. They were in complete harmony.

Adam rode slowly up to the Sunrise Ranch stables, thinking of how he was going to need a patience he knew within himself he did not possess. *I reckon I'm going to need the patience of Job. Miss Eden Chandler has made me the enemy, and I'm going to have to accept that as a fact.*

Even the information that he hadn't been around when the sheriff was shot didn't seem to change her opinion any. He determined he would not be drawn in by her baiting him. He'd just have to remember she was hurting and lashing out because he was the recipient of Eldon's decisions that left her with half of Sunrise belonging to a stranger.

His thoughts then switched to Matthew's observation of the sheriff and his aunt. That really caught him by surprise. He grinned to himself. "Reckon it doesn't matter how I feel about it," he said aloud. "My aunt Hattie has definitely always been a woman who knows her own mind. I pray, Lord, that Your hand will guide her and my aunt isn't hurt in any way."

As he dismounted, Gio came out to meet him.

"Eden told me you were on your way. Come on into the stable, and I'll show you around. Dinner is always at six, so we have a bit of time." He was dressed all in black, as was fitting for mourning, but he looked quite distinguished. Although he was only in his midforties, his hair was prematurely white and gave him an air of distinction and sophistication. Gio exuded an aura of integrity mixed with refinement, and Adam looked at him respectfully.

"I'd be happy to look around, Gio, but poor Locomotion is plumb tuckered out. She's had a long, hard day. As you know, I dropped off the heaviest of my load, but I lightened it for Loco even more in town with my aunt."

"Your aunt is already here?"

"Yes." Adam laughed. "She's staying with Bertha Morrow. I'll tell you about it later, but I really want to get Loco comfortable. She needs a good brushing and an extra bit of oats for her hard work today. Truth to tell, I wouldn't mind the same treatment," he said with a smile.

"Come," Gio said. "Pepe can help you with the horse part." He smiled as he led Adam into the stable, where a boy of about twelve was brushing down Spanner. "Pepe, come meet your new boss, Mr. Adam. He is now part owner of Chandler Olives and Sunrise Ranch, along with Miss Eden."

Pepe's eyes widened as he absorbed Gio's words.

"His horse needs some special attention. Mr. Adam, meet Pepe, the best horse handler this side of the Mississippi." Gio ruffled the boy's hair and gestured for him to shake Adam's hand.

"I'm happy to meet you, Pepe. It's good to know that someone who understands horses will be caring for my Locomotion. She's a good horse, and I call her Loco for short."

Pepe grinned as he shook Adam's hand. "I'm pleased to meet you, Mr. Adam. Loco, she one fine-looking piebald mare," he said, his eyes full of laughter. "You know loco means crazy, yes?"

"I do, but she's not *loco en la cabeza*, or crazy in the head. It's just that she can run like crazy. It's why I called her Locomotion—her speed and endurance are remarkable. Thank you for caring for her. She'll appreciate a good rubdown and extra oats."

"Come," said Gio. "I'll show you where I work and live, then you can go in and rest a bit before dinner. There's plenty of time for you to see everything else. You notice we have many outbuildings. We not only can the olives, but we make the olive oil, fragrance soaps, shampoo, and cream to soften the skin. Because it's close to dinnertime," he said, "I just show you the stable office and where I lay my body down at night."

Adam nodded. He would be spending a lot of time with this man, and whatever he wanted to share, Adam was willing to learn.

After Gio had shown him his own quarters, he led him to the house. Dorothy Jenkins opened the door for them.

"Hello, Gio," Dorothy said as she put her hand on Adam's shoulder, giving it a slight squeeze. "You, Adam Brown, are very welcome by the staff of Chandler House and, I would imagine, all who work at Chandler Olives as well. We are in need of a steady hand here at Sunrise Ranch." She leaned closer and lowered her voice to nearly a whisper and added, "Miss Eden will come around to a more agreeable disposition. You just need to give her time. I'm sorry for her behavior, but please look at her side of this. She's been very hurt. I know you're a good man, Mr. Brown.

Please be assured of your welcome by us, regardless of Miss Eden's feelings." She straightened and said in a normal tone, "Let me show you to your room. I understand you aunt plans to move in too. Is that correct?"

Eden, descending the stairs, answered before Adam could. "Yes, she does, and she's already in Napa. Now isn't that just convenient?"

Adam looked her straight in the eyes and said, "It's very convenient. I am thankful I don't have to send telegrams back and forth and wait for her to sell her house and travel out here." He turned toward Dorothy. "Thank you, Mrs. Jenkins," he said a bit pointedly, "for your hospitable welcome. It is much appreciated." He didn't look back at Eden to see if she got his not so subtle message.

"You are welcome, Mr. Brown. You say your aunt is planning to move in, so where is she?" Dorothy asked.

"She's in Napa, staying with Bertha Morrow. She will join me here once Sheriff Rawlins heals up enough to get around by himself," Adam replied.

"What's wrong with the sheriff?" Gio asked, his words clipped.

"I forgot to tell you." Eden glanced at Adam, but she went ahead and answered. "Sheriff Rawlins was shot early this morning. He thinks it's the same person who killed my parents and that the person may be after me too."

The silence in the foyer was complete.

"Where did this happen?" Gio asked Adam.

"The shooter was on Eagles Bluff," Adam replied. "Buck said if he hadn't suddenly turned when he saw the glint of sun on the rifle, he'd be dead. Mr. Harding and Matthew's new hire, Mr. Stirling, helped get him into town to Dr. John's office. After dressing his wound, Dr. John had him moved to Mrs. Morrow's house. So now, my aunt Hattie wants to stay at Mrs. Morrow's and help nurse him.

"Aunt Hattie sent me a telegram notifying me of her arrival, but I never got it until yesterday. She luckily had met Mrs. Morrow on the train coming west, who invited my aunt Hattie to stay at her place until I got her messages and could let her know I was back. She thought I was out on a job somewhere."

Berry entered the front foyer and said, "Dinner is ready, and I'd not like to keep it warm overlong. It's fish."

Dorothy said, "Thank you, Berry." She turned to Adam. "Mr. Brown, please follow me so you can wash up. You can get settled in after

162

dinner." She led the way down the hall, obviously not realizing he'd used the room before.

The days sped by, and for the first time in memory, Buck Rawlins was content to stay the invalid, enjoying the tender ministrations of Bertha, Faye, and Fern, but of course most of all, Hattie. He'd spent two days in bed, as Dr. John had ordered, and the rest of the week he was up sitting around. His chest, after the first couple days, didn't really bother him so much unless he forgot and made quick movement or if he coughed or sneezed. He had done a lot of thinking, jotting down ideas about who the shooter could be, but he still had nothing of any import. He felt frustrated and wondered who could be the next victim.

He was amazed by his feelings for Hattie. He kept thanking God for sending this woman his way. She was a feisty female and yet full of peace. He felt contentment in her presence but more alive than he'd felt for years. It was a conundrum, but a welcome one.

Dr. John checked on him almost daily, and since today made a full week, Buck was ready to get back to the business of finding his shooter and the murderer of the Chandlers. That they were one and the same, he had no doubt. The night before, he'd sent a message to Matthew to please meet him at the sheriff's office and to bring Adam with him.

It was early morning, and Buck, fully dressed, descended the stairs, heading for the kitchen and hoping for a good cup of coffee. His nose told him breakfast was ready, and he was glad to get started on his day. He also hoped for a glimpse of Hattie before he left. It was the first day he'd gotten out of bed before eight thirty.

He entered the big roomy kitchen, admiring the sunny warmth it exuded. He was surprised to see Hattie and Bertha already having breakfast.

"Good morning!" He smiled and caught Hattie's gaze.

"Good morning to you. You're up early," she replied, an answering smile spreading over her face.

He stared at her, noticing the blush climbing up into her cheeks. His eyes were warm and knowing on her face. Both women still wore robes, and Buck's eyes warmed even more, seeing how feminine his Hattie looked.

Bertha echoed, "Yes, you are up early. You're not thinking of going back to work yet, are you?"

"Yep, sure am. I heard Dr. John and followed his advice right down to the last nubbin and quite patiently, I might add. Now it's time to get back into the saddle, so to speak. I'll take it easy and probably take a break after lunch and rest. Would you two mind if I came here to eat and rest? I could go home, but this way someone else cooks my meal and makes my bed." He grinned winningly, knowing neither woman would say no.

"Of course—you're welcome anytime," Bertha said, "but please, whatever you do, don't overdo it. We don't need a relapse. I think you should continue to stay here until you are completely healed up."

"Thank you. I'd welcome that, and no, I won't overdo it. As a matter of fact, I'm going to get someone to ride my horse first thing, or she'll be too frisky for me to handle. She'll be needing some exercise after a week in the stall."

"Oh my goodness!" Bertha's hand flew to her mouth. "I forgot to tell you that Dr. John arranged for your horse to be ridden every day. He told me to tell you, and it completely slipped my mind. At least that's one less thing you'll have to do."

"I appreciate that. Dr. John never used to think much about anything but medicine before he married Sally Ann. She seems to have caused him to be a bit more aware of life in a different way, hasn't she?"

"Yes, I believe that's true. He seems a much nicer person and a bit more humble. Being married should rub the rough edges of selfishness off a body, don't you think? You can't have everything the way you want it. You have to consider someone else's feelings, and I think Dr. John is finding that out," Bertha said. "Do sit down, Buck, and have breakfast with us."

CHAPTER XX

A merry heart doeth good like a medicine:
but a broken spirit drieth the bones.

PROVERBS 17:22

BUCK LOOKED OVER AT HATTIE, and his eyes lit with pleasure. "Thank you. Reckon I'll do just that," he said as he pulled out a chair.

The two of them explained to Hattie about Sally Ann's first husband having been murdered in Boston a couple days after Liberty Bannister's first husband.

"Oh my, what a tragedy for those two women," Hattie said in response to their story.

"Well, from what I've gleaned from the story, yes, it was a tragedy for Sally Ann, but for Liberty Bannister it was an introduction into freedom. She was married to an evil man and suffered mightily for years. She's never talked about it to me, but Matthew told me a few things," Bertha said.

Fern handed Buck a cup of coffee, the steam curling out of its rim. He took it with a thankful nod. "Thanks, Fern. You're a wonderful cook. So wonderful I don't want to give you up. I'm not sure when I'll be back for lunch. Is it all right for Matthew and Adam to come for lunch too?"

"Of course," Bertha said. "I'm sure Hattie would like some time with Adam. She'll be moving to Sunrise Ranch soon, since you're so much better."

Buck's eyes rested on Hattie's face. "Reckon I'll be a regular visitor to Sunrise Ranch," he said with a smile.

Conversation flowed easily between the three, with Fern adding comments and little tidbits of news. When they finished eating, Buck said he needed to be on his way. His chest felt tight, the skin pulling where it had healed. He ignored it and headed out for the sheriff's office.

Buck's message had Matthew and Adam and Gio in the sheriff's office at eight in the morning. The four men discussed their dilemma.

"First off, I'd like you boys to show me exactly where you found the entrance to the trail leading up to the bluff where I saw that flash of light before I was shot off my horse," Buck said. "I could've died out there had Harding and Stirling not come along when they did. Harding's wanting to find whoever did this heinous crime. You do realize anyone could be suspect. It could be Harding himself…he so far seems to be a common thread. He smokes cigars too." Buck ran his hand through his thick, sandy-colored hair. "I'm sorry, but don't you smoke cigars, Gio?"

Gio, looking startled, replied, "Yes, I do. A couple a day, as a matter of fact. You think I did it?" Gio stared at the sheriff, disbelief stamped on his face.

"No," Buck replied, "no, I certainly don't. I'm simply saying anyone could have done it who knew about the Hardings' party and smokes cigars. I've lain in bed and sat around for a week pondering this thing, and I'm no closer to knowing who did it than when it happened." Buck clenched his jaw in anger and frustration. "I don't even know why I called you to meet me today. I just have a feeling we're missing something —some important clue that would point us in the right direction."

"Well," Matthew said, "I say we go ahead and ride out to the bluff and over to Sunrise and start from there. You can tell us exactly where the Chandlers were attacked. We'll spread out and see if there's anything we missed."

Adam spoke up for the first time, having stood back and carefully assessed Buck.

Buck had felt his perusal.

"I don't know when it will happen," Adam said. "The Good Book says, be sure your sin will find you out. I believe whoever did this will be found out. I say let's have a word of prayer before we set out, and we'll let the Lord have His timing on this. It's frustrating, to be sure, and I'm glad I don't smoke cigars." He clapped Gio on the shoulder and grinned at the older man, who smiled back and nodded.

Buck said, "I'll pray. Let's bow our heads." Each man had already removed his hat as he entered the sheriff's office. They stood with bowed heads as Buck prayed.

"Dear Father…how grateful we are for Thy wondrous love. It's a love so high, so deep, and so wide we can't fathom it. Your Word says if we were to count the number of precious thoughts You have of us, they would outnumber the grains of sand. It is beyond our comprehension, oh Lord, why You love us so much and sent Your only son to die for our sins. We give pause this morning, Father, to give you thanks and praise for Who You are. And now, Lord, we ask Your guidance. We ask for You to help us find out whoever did this heinous crime and bring them to justice. We thank You in advance for Your leading and for what You will do. We also ask for protection for anyone who travels the main road. We do pray and ask these things humbly, in Thy name. Amen."

"Amen," the other men responded.

Adam's heart sang knowing his aunt Hattie had chosen a man with a close relationship to Jesus. He caught Buck's eyes on him as he lifted his head, and he looked, with glowing eyes, back at this man who'd fallen in love with his aunt. The two men forged a bond right there that even eternity wouldn't erase.

Buck picked up his gun belt and buckled it. He felt pain in his chest as he bent forward to tie the leather thongs but said nothing about it. "Let's be on our way, men," he said.

They silently filed out and climbed onto their rides.

Eden awoke and stretched. She pillowed her hands behind her head and stared at the ceiling. Speaking out loud to no one, she voiced her innermost thoughts. "Mr. Adam Brown is terribly good looking, intelligent, and speaks with a pleasant voice. He's also a usurper. I feel so torn, not knowing what to think. I hate myself for being so angry with Papa...he's dead! How can I be angry at my own father when he's dead? It's a deep anger in me that he'd give half of my inheritance away. I know I need to be nicer to Mr. Adam Brown, but when I'm around him, I feel irritated beyond measure. All right, if truth be told, what would I do if someone handed me half of a very wealthy estate? I reckon I'd take it no matter who was opposed to it. In my heart of hearts, I don't think that's what he did. I think he weighed what Papa said about begging him to sign the will. I feel so confused. Why am I kicking at someone who for all appearances just happened to have a windfall from my father, when I should be helping him look for the murderers of my parents?" She sighed, and tears started in her eyes when she thought about never seeing her mama or papa again. She wiped them away with the back of her hand and took a deep, shuddering breath. "I need to stop this. I reckon the best way is to immerse myself in work."

As she lay there, she thought of all that needed to be done. *I'm thankful Papa has such a well-organized crew. Everyone knows their jobs, and every supervisor knows his section and the work there like the back of his hand. Still, it's not good to go too long without checking on each crew.* She decided it was time she got back to work and stopped moping. Swinging her long legs over the edge of the bed, she stripped off her gown and performed her morning ablutions. As she patted her face dry, she spoke to her reflection in the mirror. "I feel guilty for being angry at my papa, but I can't seem to let it go. He could have at least let me know he changed his will. I don't understand why he did it or what he was thinking."

Braiding her honey-blonde hair with nimble fingers into a single long braid, she wrapped it around her head in a crown and shoved long pins into it. She pinched her cheeks for color because she looked so wan and knew Gio would say something. She reached for a clean black split skirt and a black blouse with black lace ruffles down its front. She fastened the tiny, square jet buttons, but suddenly realized she was looking forward to an encounter with her new guest. "Reckon he's not a guest. He's half owner, and I'd better get used to it." She descended the stairs still mumbling to herself.

Eden entered the kitchen, fully expecting Gio and Adam to be there. "Where's Giovanni and Mr. Brown?"

"They rode into town. Sheriff Rawlins sent a message asking them to join him in trying to find some clues as to who killed your parents and who probably shot him," replied Mrs. Jenkins. "They left about an hour ago."

"I would have liked to have joined them," Eden said. "I was planning on going out to oversee workers today and catch up on some things that need doing. Instead, I think I'll ride over to the Bannisters'."

"My understanding is that Matthew Bannister was also asked to meet with the sheriff."

"Well, Liberty will still be home. It's her I want to talk to, not Matthew," Eden said shortly. "I'm sorry, Dorothy. I apologize for my tone," she said wearily. She was tired of life and wondered if she'd ever be really happy again.

She stood by the huge kitchen table. "Where does happiness come from?" she asked abruptly.

Dorothy Jenkins turned to look at Eden with startled eyes. "Happiness is a byproduct," Dorothy replied succinctly. "You can't say, 'I'm going to be happy,' and then be happy. No, happiness comes as a byproduct of doing something. It can come from some work or activity or simply enjoying nature or being with other people. I reckon my greatest happiness comes from doing things for other people." She nodded her head toward Eden. "Usually the greatest happiness, to my way of thinking, is in relationships...being or doing for other people. Whatever you do, don't confuse joy with happiness. Real joy, I believe, comes from a personal relationship with Jesus Christ. I don't share with you much about that because you've told me enough times that you're not interested, but it's true. We were created to have a relationship with Jesus, not substitute any other thing for that. Nothing else in all of life is lasting or permanent except that one thing...a relationship with Jesus Christ. I thank the good Lord your parents came to realize that and made the commitment to live for Jesus. They talked about it a lot with me before making the decision. Evidently Adam spoke to them about it on the train ride they shared."

Eden didn't reply but simply stared at her housekeeper, who always seemed unruffled by the unexpected, as if she had some internal regulator that kept her on an even keel. Eden sat down at the table, and Berry had a cup of coffee in front of her before she could ask.

"I made a quiche for you, Miss Eden." Berry knew full well Eden hadn't been eating breakfast for the past couple weeks, but Eden's stomach rumbled this morning.

Eden glanced at Berry and said, "That's thoughtful of you. Berry. You know that's one of my favorites, don't you? I'd like to have a small piece." She smiled at her and was startled at the tears forming in her cook's eyes. *I reckon I've taken the love of my servants for granted, never thinking how they must mourn my parents too. It's a humbling thought to realize I am now responsible for all the hired help. I don't think I can do this alone. On second thought, I reckon I don't have to do this alone. I have Mr. Adam Brown, who is also responsible, don't I?*

Matthew led the way around the bluff that Sheriff Rawlins wanted to see. He started up the incline with the other three men following him. The going got really steep, with underbrush nearly obscuring the trail up. When they got to the top, they dismounted, and each man was captivated by the view.

"Pretty awesome view, isn't it?" Adam stood spellbound by the beauty of the morning.

"A body can have a pretty clear sighting of anyone on the road for as far as the eye can see," Matthew replied. "And yes, it's a glorious day. Bet it's going to get hot. There's not a cloud to be seen."

"I was right there"—Buck pointed down to the road—"when I saw the flash up here. The sun was coming up, and I think the barrel of rifle caught the sun's rays."

The view from the bluff was unbelievably beautiful. The sky was so blue it made Adam catch his breath with the deepness of color. The sun was beginning to warm up, and it felt good on his back.

"Well, let's look around and see if there's anything we can find," Buck said. "If I hadn't been shot, I would have tended to believe the Chandlers' deaths were a random act. Now I believe there is some plan behind this. Someone wants something, and I'm thinking Miss Eden is a key player, so to speak. I've gone over and over this in my mind, and it's all I could come up with." He nodded at Adam. "You stand to gain the most, but you weren't around when I was shot, and I don't think you had previous knowledge of the will's contents."

"I didn't know of the Chandlers' deaths until I received the legal papers by US post. It was registered mail, if you care to check on where I was. You do realize whoever began this most likely didn't know that I was to inherit along with Miss Eden. Are there any fortune hunters out there that could have done this? I met Caleb McHaney, and he seems a good man. Is there anyone else who would be looking to marry Miss Eden?"

The silence after his question was deafening. Light dawned in Buck's eyes, and Gio whistled softly between his teeth. Matthew looked at Adam with respect clearly stamped in his eyes.

"Now that you've stated it, it seems obvious, doesn't it." It was a statement, not a question, Matthew vouchsafed.

"I also think you hit the nail on the head, Adam. It has to be someone who wants a cut of the Chandlers' estate," Buck said quietly. "We'll head on over to where Eldon and Camilla were shot and scout the area one more time. Then I'd think it'd be in our best interests to sit down and figure out who could be behind all of this. We'll make a list of eligible bachelors in the area and go from there."

Taylor Kerrigan was in the middle of saddling up his horse when his father entered the stable.

"Where're ya going, son?" He stood with his thumbs hooked in the front of his suspenders. Terrence Kerrigan was not a happy man. He likely figured Taylor was going into town to drink. It was becoming a daily ritual.

"I'm going into town, Pa."

"What for?"

"I'm bored. I need something ta do, and I thought I'd ride inta town and play some cards or have a jaw with some of my friends."

"You'd do better ta be a visiting that Miss Chandler. She must be feeling pretty low, and you'd do well ta comfort 'er."

"I told you afore, Pa—her housekeeper won't let me inta the house."

"Yore jest gonna haf ta wait for her ta come out, then. Just you park yerself down the road and wait for her ta appear. Getting that Chandler money is worth putting yourself out a bit, son. Sometimes we have ta work ta get what we want. Shore too bad 'bout her ma an' pa, but maybe it'll be a good thing fer us."

Taylor's eyes widened at his father's words. It made him wonder just who shot Miss Eden's parents. He'd never thought about there being a motive, but now he did.

"Wonder who killed 'em? I wouldn't think they'd be able to sleep at night for the evil they done."

His father didn't bat an eye. He only nodded his head.

"I sure am going to miss you, my dear girl," Bertha said as she helped Hattie pack up her things.

"I'm going to miss you too," Hattie replied. "I'm not excited about moving to the Chandlers'. I haven't even met the girl, Eden, but I feel like I will definitely be intruding. I suppose the conversations I've listened to haven't endeared her to me, although I'm very sorry for her loss. It's difficult, isn't it, when a body hears something negative about someone, it stays in the mind and niggles there. I believe a negative comment about anyone, even if untrue, colors our perception of that person. I don't like to hear the negative." She folded a lovely silk blouse the color of her eyes, placing it carefully into a large satchel. "I must say, Bertha, I don't care to leave, because I've felt so at home here and welcomed. Thank you for being so hospitable. I have no doubt it's one of your gifts. You've been kind and have provided an unexpected balm to my heart. It wasn't easy for me to pack up and leave everyone near and dear back in Williamsburg, but you've given me friendship, and it's touched me. Again, I'm thankful."

"Oh, my dear girl, you are entirely welcome. I am glad to call you friend, Hattie Hamilton, and no mistake!"

The women continued to chat as Bertha helped Hattie.

"Meeting you on the train was no coincidence, Hattie. The good Lord knew both of us were in need of friendship. Sure, I've lots of acquaintances here in Napa, but I have lost my best friend, Camilla, and it's hit me hard. I too am grateful for the Lord bringing us together. Speaking frankly, I think you'll be living in town before too very long, if I'm any judge of relationships. That Buck will not let any grass grow under his feet, I can tell you for sure." She laughed as she saw the blood climb into Hattie's cheeks.

Hattie laughed with her and said, "I don't know about that, but we already have an understanding of sorts, and I can tell you whenever he asks me, I'll say yes!"

Bertha had a smugly satisfied look on her face. "I'll enjoy having you as a neighbor, and I predict it will happen within the year."

Hattie merely smiled. "Well, I think that about does it," she said as she closed her satchel. "I'm ready whenever Adam comes to collect me."

"Most likely they'll be back from their ride afore too very long. Let's go down and have a nice cup of tea. Perhaps it'll cheer me up." Bertha hugged Hattie. "Oh, girl, I will miss you!" Arm and arm they went down the stairs.

CHAPTER XXI

He that walketh uprightly walketh surely:
but he that perverteth his ways shall be known.

PROVERBS 10:9

LIBERTY BANNISTER WAS HOME when Eden arrived at the Rancho. Spanner was lathered up because Eden had ridden him hard all the way. She was grateful Diego was there and would take care of him. Spanner was a friendly horse most of the time, but every once in a while, he'd take a dislike to someone; then that person couldn't get close to him. Eden knew he liked Diego and that a treat was in store for him. Her horse started to followed the foreman into the stable but balked when Reuben Stirling came out of the office building. Spanner became stiff legged, and his head came up as he stared at Reuben, who was oblivious to the disturbance he caused. It surprised Eden, who stood watching Diego trying to get Spanner to move. Her eyes glanced over to see Reuben heading her way. She didn't care for Liberty's new accountant, or whatever he was. His manner was almost too deferential. Seeing him advance, she turned quickly and went into the front door without knocking. Closing it gently, she turned, peeking out the front window, and gaped in astonishment. Spanner reared his front legs in a dangerous arc, flailing the air. Diego let the stallion have a long length of rein, and as Spanner came down, Diego quickly shortened the length, his head turned toward Rueben. Eden could see Diego saying something. Reuben flipped his cigar, ground it with his heel, and turning, went back into the office. Diego stroked the quivering horse's neck, and with a swish of his tail, Spanner docilely followed the foreman into the stable.

Eden gave a great sigh but knew there was something about Reuben that her stallion didn't trust, and she felt the same way. She heard footsteps and turned in embarrassment as Liberty entered the great room, clearly startled that Eden stood by the front door and had let herself in.

Color flooded into her cheeks as she blurted out without thought for her words, "I...I'm sorry I startled you. I let myself in without knocking. It's just that Mr. Stirling was headed my way, and...and I...I didn't wish to talk to him. I don't like him, Liberty. I don't like him at all!" Eden spoke in a rush, her words tumbling over each other.

Liberty replied, "I don't either. I haven't said anything to Matthew yet, but for some reason, I don't trust him."

"Must be that woman's intuition thing, for I don't trust him either," Eden said. "My horse doesn't like him at all. I just witnessed him stand on his hind legs and flail his front hooves at Diego because Stirling had come out of his office. Spanner loves Diego...there's never been a problem with him before. How long has Mr. Stirling been working for you?"

"Only about three weeks. Matthew was looking for someone to take care of shipping and work the bookkeeping end of things, as we are beginning to get a lot of orders. Word of mouth seems to be the best advertisement for our wine. Mr. Harding met Reuben and recommended him to us."

"The Hardings were great friends of my parents. They were devastated when they got word of what happened. They had just left the Hardings' dinner party."

"Come, let's sit awhile and talk." She indicated a chair to Eden. "I'm glad you came over. I was thinking of riding your way this afternoon. Excuse me just one moment while I tell Conchita you're here. Would you like tea, coffee, or some lemonade?"

"A glass of lemonade would be wonderful. I got really hot riding over here. It's unseasonably warm, isn't it?" Eden responded as she sat down with a huge sigh of contentment, making herself comfortable in a deep leather chair.

Liberty headed for the kitchen, answering over her shoulder. "It *is* really warm. Since I've only been here one other summer, I wondered if this was normal, but Matthew said it's not.

"Eden Chandler is here," Liberty said to Conchita. "I don't know if she plans to stay for lunch or not. Can we both have a glass of lemonade, please?"

"*Si*, I weel get you the lemonade. You go veesit your friend." Conchita was making sopapilla*s* for dessert. "Meester Bannister, he no come home for lunch. He halp Meester Brown move to Mees Eden's house. I theenk that Reuben, he ride to town for some supplies for the office and to geet the mail."

"I know. He told me the same thing, but I thought just maybe Matthew might end up coming back earlier if Buck wasn't up to riding yet. He must be feeling much better. And by the way, Reuben is already back." She returned to the great room.

"Would you care to stay for lunch?" she asked Eden. "I'm not sure what we're having, but I do know we're having sopapilla*s* for dessert." Liberty smiled. "They are delicious."

"Thank you. I'd like that." She took her handkerchief and wiped her forehead. "Whew, I'm still warm from my ride over here."

"I'll be right back," Liberty said as she went back to the kitchen.

"I've invited Eden to stay for lunch," Liberty said as she took the two cold glasses of lemonade from Conchita.

"Eet be ready soon," Conchita replied.

Taking the glass from Liberty, Eden said, "Um, that looks delicious." She took several swallows. "It tastes as good as it looks." She smiled over at Liberty.

"How are you doing, Eden?" Liberty asked, deep concern in her voice.

"Frankly...I'm not doing well. I can't abide the fact that a perfect stranger has invaded my home. And using the word *perfect* describes him. He's just a bit *too* nice. He's got to be covering something up. I don't think for a second my father would give half our entire estate to a man he knew for a few days on a train. It is totally out of character. No, there's something behind all this, and I'm going to find out what it is! One good thing is that I haven't seen much of him except at dinner. Today he's to bring his aunt Hattie out to live at Sunrise. Have you met her?"

"No, but according to Matthew, Buck and Hattie Hamilton are in love."

"In love! She's only been here since—"

"Love doesn't always take a slow path," Liberty interrupted with a smile. "My friend Maggie's husband was a goner the first time he laid eyes on Maggie. I think that's what happened with both Miss Hamilton and Buck Rawlins. I'm happy for him. I don't think he ever thought to fall in love after Jasmine. I can't wait to see them together."

"Well, that is fast work. Wonder what that means for having a chaperone. Maybe Buck would be willing to live at our place too. He'd keep things on an even keel," Eden said. "I hope Adam's aunt is amenable. It'd be horrible to have someone living in the same house that you don't get along with."

"So you're saying you're getting along all right with Adam living in the house?"

"N-no, not really. As I said, I haven't seen much of him since he moved in. How old is his aunt, anyway?"

"I don't know. I haven't met her yet either, but she sounds like someone I'd like to know. Matthew said she sold up her house in Virginia and moved out here without Adam having a clue. Even when he saw her, he still didn't know she'd sold her house. He thought she'd just come out for a visit. She had some of her things in San Francisco that needed to be hauled up here, and Adam went down the other day and collected them. We have them stored in the barn."

The two women had much to talk about. They had lunch together and never ran out of things to discuss. It was with real regret in her voice that Eden said she must be going.

Conchita went out to tell Diego to saddle Eden's horse while the two women said good-bye. Liberty walked out to the hitching post with Eden, where Spanner was saddled and ready to go.

When Eden stepped into the stirrup, Reuben came out of the office, and Spanner quivered all over but stood and let Eden mount him. Reuben didn't walk closer when he saw Spanner. After Eden was ready to ride, Spanner pranced and swung his head up and down.

With a final wave of her hand, Eden set off at a more sedate pace than when she arrived.

Liberty nodded and smiled at Reuben, but she headed up the walk to the front door with a quick step. Struggling with the idea that Reuben reminded her of Armand, she chided herself. *I need to get a grip on my emotions. For some reason I simply can't abide that man. He's too ingratiating, and Armand was always that way when he wanted something from someone. I need to sit down and have a good talk with Matthew. I can't continue to skulk around in my own house, hiding from that man.*

She went to the kitchen and poured herself another glass of lemonade. She sat down at the huge round oak table. Putting her chin in her hands and resting her elbows on the table's smooth top, she asked, "Conchita, what do you think about Mr. Reuben?"

Conchita turned quickly and looked Liberty straight in the eyes. "I doan know yet how I feel about heem. He seem nice, but I am seeing a very unhappy man under all his smiles and bravados. I doan know heem enough to say how I feel, except I am sorry for heem."

Liberty looked at Conchita in surprise, feeling a little chagrined. "Perhaps I've been too quick to judge him. He doesn't look like Armand, but he smells and acts a bit like Armand, and I have been avoiding him because of it. I know better than to judge a person, especially when I don't really know them, but I find it difficult for some reason to like that man."

"*Sí*, it is very hard sometimes to separate our past hurts from our feelings about someone who seem to be the same type of person as the one who hurt us. Many times we judge weethout knowing. I have learned we are not to judge but to love. We must leave the judging to Dios."

Liberty nodded her head in agreement. "That's true, Conchita. Thank you for reminding me of it."

Taylor Kerrigan had ridden into Napa. He pushed through the swinging doors of the saloon. Several of his card-playing buddies were there. He drank a couple whiskeys, played poker for about an hour, and decided he'd better head for home. His father was showing signs of kicking him out. He didn't like to think he'd have to get a job to support himself.

Taylor wasn't a deep thinker, but he thought about what his pa had said to him and how he needed to see Eden. He began to think about what his pa said about the Chandlers. He thought aloud as he slowly rode along.

"Pa wouldn't murder th' Chandlers on the hope that I'd marry Miss Eden, would he? I heard th' sheriff was shot last week too. I'm wonderin' jest who did it? It's gotta be someone around here." With that thought, he kicked his horse just as he heard the report of a rifle. He spurred his horse into a swift gallop and rode as fast as he could.

"Someone just tried to shoot me," he said in astonishment.

The men standing on top of the bluff heard the boom of the rifle and, looking down, saw Taylor Kerrigan crouched low over his horse, riding at a blistering speed down the road.

"Come on!" Buck said. "Someone just shot at Kerrigan. Let's see if we can find 'em."

Because of the steep terrain, they couldn't descend as fast as they'd have liked, but the thought crossed Buck's mind that whoever shot at Kerrigan must be having the same problem getting down another bluff. Buck could feel the strain on his chest, and sweat broke out on his brow from the pain.

When they reached the bottom, they split. Gio and Adam rode south, and Matthew and Buck rode north. Each group traveled about a mile in the opposite direction, but they saw nothing. Turning back, they met just about where the trail came down from the bluff.

"These hills, as you know, are riddled with caves. It'd be impossible to find someone if they're not wanting to be found," Matthew said. He turned toward Adam. "The Napa Valley has many undiscovered caves. Some are natural and others have been dug out specially for aging wine. Some of the caves are quite deep, and if a body knows where they are, they could easily hide a horse inside as well as themselves."

Buck nodded. "You're right, Matthew. You should know. Do you age your wine in a cave on your property?"

"No, I don't. There are caves in the area around my property but none right on my land. This past year is the first time I've stored wine. I had a huge cellar dug out behind the barn, where I'm storing it.

Bannister Vineyards is becoming known by word of mouth, but I really haven't tried to market it yet."

"I can help you with that," Gio said. "I have several places that have inquired if we produce wine along with our other products. I've kept records of letters sent us that I can lend you for contacts. When you do start selling seriously, I can help you with marketing if you're interested. Adam will be able to help you too. He'll be learning all about Chandlers and Sunrise Ranch from the ground up, soon as we can find out what's going on around here." He nodded to Buck. "Do you plan to ride on out to Kerrigan's place?"

Buck shook his head. His pressed his hand to his chest, where the bandage peeked out of the vee in his shirt below his neckerchief. "No, I doubt Taylor knows any more than we do about it. Truth to tell, I think I need to get back to Bertha's and lie down."

Adam said, "I'll ride with you. Today is the big day. Aunt Hattie is moving into Chandler House. I'll probably need a wagon to move her belongings from Bertha's to Sunrise. Tomorrow I'll get her trunks and things that are stored at Matthew's. I went down to San Francisco the other day and collected the rest of her belongings. She has a few pieces of furniture she brought too."

Buck said, "You're welcome to come with me." He tipped his hat to Gio and Matthew. "Reckon we'll be going."

"Mind if I tag along?" Matthew asked. "I can help you, Adam."

The four men rode together until they were abreast of Sunrise Ranch, where Gio said his good-byes. They pulled up their horses at the start of the long lane to the house.

Gio spoke to the other three men. "I don't think I probably know anything more than you about who is a bachelor and stands to gain by marrying Miss Eden. Frankly, if Taylor Kerrigan smoked cigars, I'd say it was most likely him, but he doesn't smoke at all. You all know it's not going to be easy tracking down who the shooter is. I feel I have too many things to attend to and not enough time."

He turned to Adam. "I'll be watching for you and your aunt to arrive. Don't expect a warm welcome from Miss Eden, but Dottie will make her welcome. She's looking forward to meeting her. Will you be here in time for supper? I can let Berry know to expect your aunt to be dining with us if you plan to be here by then."

"Yes, I'm hoping we'll be here by late afternoon. It depends on whether Aunt Hattie is ready or not. Knowing her, she'll be ready. And, Gio, I let Berry know about Aunt Hattie this morning." He smiled at the foreman, but his eyes met Buck's cool blue ones, where humor lurked in their depths.

Buck said, "She'll be ready—you can count on it."

Adam tipped his hat respectfully. "Reckon I'll see you later, Giovanni."

Hester McHaney rode into the stable yard and dismounted, leading her horse into the stable where Caleb was mucking out stalls. Her breath came out in short gasps of air, and her lips were blue.

"Where have you been, Mother?" Caleb tried to steel his face against the shock of seeing his mother looking so ill.

"I rode over to the Hardings. Theodore was coming back from town when I got there, and Francis had invited me to tea. Why do you ask?"

"The sheriff came by with Matthew Bannister, Giovanni, and the new man, Adam Brown, who's part owner of Sunrise Ranch," Caleb replied. "I wanted you to meet our newest neighbor. He said his aunt is moving into the Chandlers' house today. She came west to be with Adam. Eden, of course, is dead set against it, but this is what her father evidently wanted."

"Sorry I missed them, son." Hester handed the reins of her horse to Caleb. "I reckon it'd be a hard thing to have a stranger inherit half your property. I can't imagine it. Thanks for taking care of my horse, Caleb. You did a good job breaking her in. She's a good ride and very obedient. Reckon I'll go in and lie down a spell. I feel right tuckered out." She moved slowly toward the house.

Taylor Kerrigan almost skidded to a stop. His father was in the barn, unsaddling his horse.

"Where've you been, Pa?" Before he could answer, Taylor exclaimed, "I just got shot at on the road a few miles back. I'd just kicked into a canter. If I hadn't, I wouldn't be here to tell the story."

Terrence looked at his son and snorted disbelievingly. "Well, did you go after 'em?"

"No, I have no idea where the shot came from, but I heard it whiz past me. It would'a got me if I hadn't just started to ride hard for home." He took out his handkerchief and wiped his brow and upper lip, his hand still shaking from fear.

"You shore hit's what happened, boy? Mayhap you've bin drinking too much and just imagine ya'll were shot at."

"I don't understand! Why can't you ever believe me, Pa? Why do you always question m——"

"Because you've lied to me, son. You've lied when the truth would'a fit better. I don't trust your words. How can I trust what you say when you're a liar?"

Taylor turned his back on his pa and began brushing his horse down with hard, angry strokes. "I reckon what your saying's true, but I ain't lied fer a long time."

"Well, it don't seem so long ago ta me, son." He spit out the end of his cigar that he'd chewed off and stalked off toward the back door.

Taylor stared at his back, wondering if his father had taken a potshot at him to scare him. If he had, he'd accomplished his purpose.

CHAPTER XXII

If a wise man contendeth with a foolish man,
whether he rage or laugh, there is no rest.

PROVERBS 29:9

BUCK, ADAM, AND MATTHEW RODE up to Bertha's mansion. Adam watched as Buck pressed a hand to his chest. Even though Buck didn't grimace, Adam knew the older man was in pain.

"Let me take your horse, sir," he said, but Chester came out of the stable and took the reins from Buck.

"That's my job, young man. I'll take all three of your horses if you like."

"No need," Buck replied. "These two will be riding out again after lunch. If you just stable them out of the sun and give them a bit of water, they'll be happy. Mine needs a good brushing down." He turned and began to make his way slowly up the stone steps of the back of the house.

Matthew took Loco's reins from Adam and led their horses into the stable. Adam strode quickly across the cobbles, moving behind Buck just in case he had any difficulty as they entered the huge utility room. Adam walked ahead of Buck and pushed open one of the double doors to the kitchen.

"Why, hello there," Bertha said, turning to greet the men. She had just tasted the dressing Fern had made for the salad, and nodded her head at Fern. "It's perfect," she said. She wiped her hands on her apron and taking a good look at Buck said, "Lunch isn't for another half hour. You go have a toes-up for a bit, and I'll let you know when it's time to eat."

Buck held himself very still. He was to the point where movement was almost making him nauseous. "See you later," he said to Adam. "I'm going to take Bertha's advice." He headed slowly out of the kitchen and up the stairs.

Hattie stepped out of her room just as Buck reached the top. Taking one look at Buck, she smiled and quickly went to his good side and slipped herself under his arm. She walked him to his room.

"Reckon I don't need to tell you that you've overdone it, do I?" She smiled, her deep-blue eyes warm on his face.

He turned her toward him and said, "Nope, no need, no need at all." Pulling her into his arms, his mouth came down gently on hers. Hattie's arms crept around his back, and she molded herself against him, feeling protected and very alive.

His kiss deepened into passion as he poured his love for her into it; Hattie's response surprised him. Her kiss caused a fire to lick through his veins. He held her away and said simply, "Hattie, will you marry me? Sooner would be better than later."

"Yes, you know I'd marry you at the drop of a hat, but I need to also see this thing through for Adam. I can't go back on my word to act as a sort of chaperone for him. Wonder if we married, could we both live out at Sunrise for the time being?"

"I don't know what Miss Eden would think about that."

"Well, she mayn't like it, but then, so far, it seems to me she doesn't much care for anything. Can't say I blame her, losing both of her parents like that and half her property."

Buck sat down on the side of the bed and said, "I want to marry you regardless of where we live. As far as Miss Eden is concerned, I reckon Adam has a say now as to whether I can live there or not as much as Miss Eden does."

Hattie walked over to the bed and knelt to untie Buck's boots. She pulled them off and said, "Buck, would you please pray for me? I want to have a loving attitude toward Miss Chandler, and I'm afraid that some of the comments I've listened to haven't endeared her to me. I usually try not to listen to negative comments about a person because of that very reason. It changes the way one thinks, and it's hard to undo preconceived notions."

"I've never thought about that before, but you're right. It's true. Yes, I'll certainly pray for you. I've known Eden all of her life, and she's really a wonderful girl. She's always been a bit headstrong, but being an only child, I think Eldon and Cammie were happy to let her do whatever made her happy. She's been through a terrible time, and I do hope you will care for her. She needs a woman she can look up to."

"Thank you, Buck. I know it's been hard for her, but I also know I'm very protective when it comes to my nephew. Enough said now, sir," Hattie said as she stood back up. "It's time for you to rest. You can have lunch later." He obediently laid his head on his pillow, his eyes warm on her face.

"I love you, dear girl," he said as he closed his eyes, glad to be prone and without gravity pulling at his wound.

"I love you back," Hattie said with a smile. She leaned over and kissed his closed eyelids and then his mouth. "I'll talk to you later." She covered him with a lightweight blanket and left the bedroom, closing the door gently behind her.

Buck took a deep breath and fell asleep before a thought could intrude.

Once Hattie closed the door on Buck, she hurried down the stairs to see if Adam still planned to take her to Sunrise Ranch today. She found him talking to Bertha and Matthew in the parlor.

"Ah, there you are, my dear," Bertha said. "Let's go in for lunch, shall we? I'll give lunch to Buck when he gets up."

They made their way to the generous-sized dining room and sat down to eat.

"Matthew, will you please ask the blessing?" Bertha asked.

"Sure, can do," he replied. They bowed their heads, and when he finished, Fern came in with a casserole. A bed of rice was covered by chicken and broccoli and a thick layer of creamy chicken-and-cheese sauce with a slight hint of curry. Croutons covered the top, making it a delectable meal.

"Umm, what is this?" Matthew asked.

"I call it Chicken Scrumptious. Good, isn't it?"

"It's delicious!" Adam said.

"Well, I haven't heard anything out of you men. Did you find anything of any import on your ride to Eagles Bluff?" Hattie asked.

Matthew's eyes flickered to Adam, who gave a slight nod.

"Yes, Taylor Kerrigan was on his way home when we were on the top of Eagles Bluff. We heard the report as someone fired on him. They missed, but I wonder if that was intentional," Matthew said.

"Why intentionally miss?"

"Not quite sure. I haven't figured that out yet, but Adam did come up with the most plausible theory as to the Chandlers' deaths."

"What's your theory, young man?" Bertha wondered.

"It only makes sense that whoever did this horrible deed is after Sunrise Ranch and Chandler Olives. I think we need to sit down and figure out all the eligible bachelors in the area who'd marry Eden to get their hands on the estate."

Bertha's eyes widened at the sensible explanation. She nodded her head in agreement and said, "That certainly makes sense to me."

Hattie turned to Matthew. "Perhaps that Kerrigan boy's father shot at his own son to take suspicion off him."

Adam nodded his head in agreement. "That's a good point. Wonder if that's what happened? Up till now, the shooter has had quite a deadly aim. We'll stick around and have a talk with Buck and see what he thinks when he wakes up. I sure hope he didn't overdo it. It was a pretty strenuous ride down that bluff and then trying to see if we could find the shooter. I'm tired," he said with a smile, "and I don't have a hole through my chest."

Matthew said, "Meanwhile, we'll finish this delicious chicken concoction and we'll make a list. Reckon, Adam, your name will go at the top." He chuckled at the startled look on his new friend's face.

Dr. John rode down the long lane to the McHaneys' to check on Hester. He'd been called farther out that morning to set a broken leg on a ten-year-old boy. Since he was close, he thought he'd see how she was faring. She hadn't looked too good the last time he'd seen her.

Riding up to the wide hitching post, he looked around at the neatness of everything. It surprised him every time he visited, for some reason, how the little picket fence always looked as if it'd just been whitewashed. The barn looked freshly painted, a deep red with the trim white, and clean looking. There were never any farm tools left lying haphazardly around nor anything that ever looked out of place. It was refreshing to him.

He wrapped his reins around the post and walked up the steps, knocking on the doorjamb since the door stood open, probably to allow for a cross breeze through the house. Hester came to the door and smiled widely at him. "Welcome, Dr. John, welcome. Come right on in."

John Meeks had to school his face not to show the shock he felt when he saw her. She looked gaunt, and her lips very blue. Her hair had grayed in the short time since last he saw her. It was scraped back into a generous bun, and her large, beautiful hazel eyes looked at him curiously.

"Hello, Hester. Thought I'd drop in for a glass of water since I was going right by. Had to go out and set the leg on one of those Johnson boys. Seems like I am forever going out there to set something or stitch one of those young 'uns up. Those kids are into everything—jumping out of the haymow into a wagon, climbing trees, playing stretch with knives, jumping out of trees—but they're hard little workers too."

Hester asked him to come in, and he entered with alacrity. The front door opened to a large, comfortable living room. Floral chintz pillows decked the settee, and she gestured for him to have a seat.

"I'll go get that water. Sure you wouldn't like a cup of tea or coffee?" she asked.

"No, a glass of water would hit the spot. It's unusually hot, isn't it?"

"Yes, we don't normally get so hot. I told Caleb he needed to order another block of ice for the icehouse. Caleb dug a deep hole a couple years back and put in an icehouse. It's been right nice to have a block of ice in there to cool things down a bit. You just sit, and I'll get that glass of water for you."

She left the living room, and Dr. John looked around appreciatively. The room wasn't overly large, but it was tastefully done. He knew money must be an issue now that Phillip McHaney had passed on. The man had been a carpenter, had grown chickens, and sold eggs in Napa as well as raised a couple steers for meat. He'd been a hard worker.

The fireplace was cleaned out and looked as if it hadn't been used in a while. Over the birch mantel hung a painting of a wheat farm. A darkened sky with darker clouds contrasted with the golden wheat. An old farmhouse with a barn and silo to one side, and a lane continued past the house and into the distance. It was a peaceful scene, and Dr. John never tired of looking at it.

The settee was the same shade of wheat, and the floral pillows picked up colors in the painting. Two other wingback chairs in gray, matching the clouds, flanked the fireplace. Books and bibelots sat on a single bookshelf painted the darker gray color.

Hester came back with a cold glass of water, the glass sweating from the cool water inside. She placed it on a coaster next to him and had another glass for herself. Sitting comfortably in one of the wingbacks, she looked over at him expectantly.

"Well, Dr. Meeks, I'm not doing so well, am I?" She sat there, a woman not forty years old, and he felt sorrow for her.

"No, Hester, you're not. Have you told Caleb?"

"No, I—" She closed her lips on what she'd been about to say.

"Whyever not, woman? Don't you think he has a right to know?" Dr. John looked horrified. "Would you like me to tell him?"

"Tell me what?" Caleb had come out of the barn and was standing in the open doorway.

Hester looked upset and then simply shrugged her shoulders at the doctor's questioning look.

"I think you need to get yourself a glass of water and join us, Caleb," Dr. John said.

Caleb nodded to the doctor and headed for the kitchen. He knew what the doctor was going to tell him, and his heart felt guilty. Perhaps he should ask Eden to marry him and ease his mother's mind. He knew the two of them would get on well together. He'd been in such discord with his mother over the past year, and he didn't want to be. Up until his mother had decided he should marry Eden, they'd had, for the most part, gotten along quite well, but they'd never had a close relationship for as long as he could remember. Every once in a while she would go into one of her raging tempers, and then there was no peace. He swallowed hard a couple times and wiped his tears with the back of his hand. Pouring himself a tall glass of water, he took a deep breath and went back into the living room. He sat down in the wingback opposite his mother and let the doctor struggle to tell him his mother was dying.

Theo Harding met Reuben Stirling on Eagles Bluff. The two men looked at each other, distrust clearly stamped on both faces.

"Why did you want to see me?" Reuben asked. He sat his horse easily but spoke with almost a sneer in his voice.

"I want you to leave. I want you to clear out," Theo said, not mincing his words.

"Now, after all I've done, gotten myself a job and all, why would I do that?" Reuben asked in almost a wheedling tone.

"I got you the job, you little pipsqueak! I've got some money tucked away I can give you. It's time for you to move on. We have nothing further to talk about."

Reuben sat his horse and laughed shortly at Theo and then stared bitterly at him. "I'll think about it," he said in a rancorous tone, his eyes dark and hard on the older man. Without another word or a bye-your-leave, he turned his beautiful paint horse and began the steep descent.

Theo Harding sat staring at the gorgeous view laid out before him without seeing any of it. He cut the end of a cigar and lit it. While he smoked the cigar, he rubbed his aching forehead and wondered what in the world he was going to do.

After the doctor left, Hester turned to Caleb. "Sorry you had to be told this way, son. I didn't want to say anything and have you feel sorry for me or change your thoughts about marrying Miss Chandler. Now you can see why I wanted you to court her. I'm not going to be around much longer, and I had it in my mind to see you settled afore I go. Reckon that isn't going to happen, is it?" She looked at him hopefully.

"Would you have me marry someone just for their money, mother? I can always find a job. I know you wanted me here on the farm, but I think I'd probably hire on with Kirk Bannister over at McCaully's and do a bit of ranching. It's something I've always been interested in. I like Eden, as I've told you before, but I don't like her in the way you'd like me to." He got up and went over to squeeze her shoulder. She was angry, and he could tell it. It made his gut churn.

"Yes, I would have you marry her just for her money. The two of you get on together right well. You're a hard worker and would be an asset to Chandler Olives and Sunrise Ranch. I don't want you scrabbling around for every dime the way I've had to for years. You father tried to make a decent living, but besides selling chickens and eggs, I had to take in laundry just to make ends meet. I don't want that for you, son."

"Don't you think it's rather selfish to foist on me your wishes and ignore what I'd like to do with my life?"

"Pshaw, son. You've got no clue what you'd like to do with your life. I can't see why you can't abide by a dying mother's wishes." She pressed her lips together in a thin line and pressed a hand to her heart as if it hurt.

He looked at her sorrowfully. "All right, Mother. I'll ask her to marry me." He walked out the front door and went to saddle up his horse.

CHAPTER XXIII

*In the multitude of my thoughts within me
thy comforts delight my soul.*

PSALM 94:19

BUCK AWAKENED SLOWLY AND FELT much better for the rest. His chest felt stiff, but the feeling of deep-seated pain was gone. He lay there for a few minutes to get his brain functioning properly. He'd never been one to take naps during the day. It only made him feel discombobulated and headachy rather than rested.

Since being shot, naps have been a good thing, he thought. Reckon a body needs rest to heal. His thoughts turned into a prayer. Lord, I am so thankful for Hattie coming into my life. What a feisty little bundle of joy she is. I'd thought to grow old alone and wasn't looking for someone to take away the ache of losing Jazzie. I pray I'll be good for Hattie—give her the joy and laughter that can come if we do it right. Lord, I also pray she'll not be biased against Eden from the things she's heard. You can make her see Eden with eyes that are clear and a heart that's willing to help. Thank You, Lord, especially for this second chance at happiness.

He sat up carefully and stood, making his way to the bathing room. Bertha had recently converted the original dressing room, connected to the large bedroom, into a bathing room. There was a tub and a new flush toilet that Buck delighted in using. "No more chamber pots," he thought aloud. "Why didn't someone think of this a long time ago?" He dumped some water into a large basin and washed his face and hands, feeling a bit better for having done so.

He made his way downstairs and was surprised to see Adam and Matthew hadn't yet left. He nodded at the two men and Bertha, still seated at the dining table, but his eyes caught and held Hattie's until her cheeks became warm and rosy under his perusal.

She didn't look away, and Matthew, Adam, and Bertha all felt they should be somewhere else and yet were held captive by the magnetic attraction emanating between these two people who were surprised by love. Time seemed suspended.

Adam, now fully aware that his aunt was in love for the first time in her life, could only hope he fell in love with someone as deeply as his aunt Hattie seemed to be. Her face was radiant with it. She looked shining, and his heart warmed that she had finally found someone to love. He had no doubt Buck would cherish his aunt Hattie until the day he died.

Fern entered the dining room with a fresh pot of coffee, and the spell was broken, but peace and contentment seemed to fill the room.

Buck sat down at a place already set for him next to Hattie, and Bertha asked Fern to fetch his lunch. He bowed his head and gave thanks for his meal in silence.

"I see you are working on a list of names. Who do you have so far?"

Matthew replied because he knew every man on the list. "First we have Adam, then Caleb, who doesn't smoke cigars. There's Gio, Taylor Kerrigan, the oldest Johnson boy—I've forgotten his name."

"Johnny," Buck supplied. "John Johnson is what he likes to be called since he's all grown up. Do you have the Bliesner twins written down?"

"No, forgot about them."

"Well, I do know Miss Eden danced with both of them the night afore her parents were killed. Neither one smokes, but they both chew."

Adam busily wrote down the suspects' names while Matthew continued to read off the names to Buck.

"Let's see. Then there's Kenneth Grub. He doesn't smoke either, and he's always got his nose to the grindstone, working himself to death."

"He's not in any need of money either. I wouldn't even put his name down," Buck added.

"There's Chester."

Bertha looked aghast. "Chester! Why, he won't even kill a spider!"

Matthew laughed. "I don't really think most of the men on this list are involved, Bertha. There's always the possibility that we could be barking up the wrong tree. Perhaps we should add all cigar smokers that we know."

"Ah, Matthew, we forgot your new hire, Reuben Stirling. He's young, single, and smokes cigars," Buck said.

Matthew's eyes widened at the import of Buck's words. Matthew had hired Reuben on because of Theo Harding, but the man rubbed him the wrong way, and Matthew didn't think Reuben would last long.

They added a few more names, when there was a knock on the door. Faye, who'd been helping Fern with the dishes, hurried to the front door.

"Why, Dr. John, how nice to see you. Come right on in. You're just in time for a bit of dessert."

The doctor greeted her cordially, following her into the dining room. After Faye left the room, he spoke.

"Glad to see all of you here together," he said. "I was just now riding back from the McHaneys'. I was approaching Eagles Bluff, and who do you think I saw come riding around and onto the road in front of me but your new hire, Matthew." He wiped his sweaty brow with a large white handkerchief and continued. "I rode my horse into the undergrowth right next to the side of the bluff until he was out of sight. I was just about to come out, when lo and behold, here comes Theo Harding riding out and onto the road after him. Now what do you think about that?"

Stunned silence pervaded the dining room. Everyone could hear the rattle of dishes and silverware, previously unnoticed, emanating from the kitchen. Bertha cleared her throat to say something, but closed her lips, for once at a loss for words.

Buck's normally relaxed demeanor visibly changed without him moving a muscle. The lazy look sharpened into steel.

Matthew said quietly into the stillness, "Theo recommended Stirling to me. Said he was an excellent bookkeeper, and although he writes legibly, I haven't seen any great ideas or new way of doing the books out of him. I've had to show him in minute detail what to do. Frankly, I don't think he's ever kept books."

Adam tapped his teeth with the pencil. He looked at the list again, laid the pencil down, and folded his hands. "It looks pretty cut and dried, but there could be another explanation. We will need to tread softly here, lest we jump the gun and end up with the wrong person or persons."

Buck nodded. "I concur wholeheartedly. It does look mighty suspicious, but what would Harding's motive be? He does seem to be a common denominator, doesn't he?"

"I don't know. I just don't want us to act too hastily and perhaps miss the real culprit," Adam said.

Buck, with conviction behind his words, said, "I'm thinking a good thing to do would be to beat them at their own game. What other bluff gives protection from being seen from the road, but a clear view?"

"There are several—none as good as Eagles Bluff, but what about Sandpiper Ridge?" Matthew asked. "It has a clear view of the main road and has a few boulders on top where you could stay out of sight, if need be."

Buck's eyes lit up. "That would be perfect," he said. "If you boys don't mind, we could take turns doing a surveillance of the road and surrounding area. We could see if the two men meet again or if anyone else uses the bluffs around there to watch the road. We wouldn't have to do it every day, I don't suppose, but—"

"I think we do," Matthew interjected. "We don't want to see those scoundrels get away with what they've done."

"All right, we'll post guards. Problem is, I don't know whom to trust," Buck said.

Hattie said, "I could help. It might be better to post two people just in case you need one to go for help. Also, there must be a lot of law-abiding citizens who don't smoke cigars, who would be willing to help."

"Not just another pretty face, are you?" Buck said with a smile.

"Now that's one adjective I would never claim to have." Hattie laughed.

"Personality and character are a lot more important than a pretty face," Adam said, "and frankly, I think you have both those plus a pretty face."

Bertha said, "I can help too, as well as Chester. Then, too, there's Gio and others you can certainly trust. But mark my words—this needs to be kept under wraps. If anyone thinks the road will be watched and they're involved in this, well, they won't be showing their face, if you get my meaning."

The men looked at her respectfully.

Dr. John said, "I need to be going, but I thought what I saw should be reported to you right away, Buck. I sure hope you catch them."

"Thanks, Dr. John," Buck said. "This is the first break we've had, and even if it doesn't pan out to be Stirling and Harding, at least we've got a plan of action. I do believe we're going to get 'em."

Matthew, after helping load up the wagon with Hattie's things, rode home wondering if he should tell Liberty what he knew. He didn't wish to alarm her unduly. On the other hand, she should be aware about Reuben Stirling, should he end up being the killer. He knew he certainly couldn't fire the man, or he might leave without them knowing if he'd done the heinous deed. He prayed God would give him an answer.

Diego was waiting in the stable yard as he rode up. How I do appreciate this man, Matthew thought. Diego took Piggypie's reins and said, "Welcome home, Meester Bannister. I weel brush your Piggypie down. Eet ees very hot, si?"

"Yes, it is that." He looked carefully at his foreman. "Something bothering you, Diego?"

"How comes you always seems to know eef something bothering me?"

"Well, we've been together a good many years, and you're my friend. Now tell me, what is it?"

"Mees Eden, she comed today and she geeve me her horse, Spanner. That horse no like Reuben. He ees pawing the air and muy loco when Reuben comed out of the office. That man know nothing. He just keep walking toward Mees Eden, and she hurry an' go inside. I yell at Reuben to make heemself scarce, but he ees taking hees time about eet. I no happy with heem, Meester Bannister."

"Yes, I'm not happy with him either. I hired him because he came highly recommended by Theo Harding, but I can't let him go just yet." He dropped his voice and told Diego about the afternoon's events and how it was important to keep Reuben on until they had proof he was involved with the Chandlers' deaths.

Diego nodded his head sagely. "I unnerstand, Meester Bannister. Believe me, I unnerstand.

After Matthew left Bertha's house, the talk went back to discussing Sunrise Ranch.

"When are they expecting you to arrive?" Bertha asked Adam.

"Sometime before dinner. I don't want to be too late, as I want Aunt Hattie to get settled in before dinner and not feel rushed."

"I never thought to ask," Bertha said to Hattie, "but do you ride?"

Adam didn't even let his aunt reply. "Does she ride? You should see her on a horse. She never was married, you know, and there were no restrictions on her behavior. She was the gossip of Williamsburg when she refused to ride sidesaddle. She even had ladies from a women's club come visit her and tell her it wasn't proper for her to ride astride like a man, that her dresses were not meant to be split over a saddle. But Aunt Hattie is not easily intimidated when she's made up her mind about something. She told those ladies that she knew their intentions were good, and she would think about their admonition. My mother rode sidesaddle and was thrown jumping a fence. It ended up killing her. Aunt Hattie is my mother's sister, and I wouldn't have her riding sidesaddle either."

Hattie's cheeks burned under Adam's rendition.

"So what did you end up deciding?" Bertha was intrigued.

Adam again answered for his aunt. "She went to the tailor and had special split skirts made and continued to ride astride." He laughed, and the others joined him. He added, "Aunt Hattie, you're going to love Liberty Bannister. She has split skirts, wears a holster and gun, and rides like the wind."

Hattie replied, "Sounds like my kind of girl."

"Well, sir"—Adam turned to Buck—"we need to be on our way." He turned to his aunt and said, "I'll go collect your things while you say your good-byes."

He left the dining room, and Bertha mumbled something about having to talk to Fern. She headed for the kitchen.

Buck said, "I love you, Hattie Hamilton. I'll be out to check on you regularly and make plans for a wedding." He smiled and swept her into his arms. He kissed her long and hard and set her away from him so he could look into her blue eyes.

Before he could say anything more, she put her hand to his cheek and caressed the crease in it. "I love you, Buckmaster Rawlins, the forever and ever kind. Don't worry about wedding plans just yet. You need to get a murder solved and not have your attention divided."

He laughed, catching her hand in his and squeezing it gently. "Too late, my dear. My attention is already divided."

Hattie laughed and stood on tiptoe to kiss Buck again.

She went upstairs for one last perusal of her room. She opened the armoire and checked under the bed, but all was cleaned out save her one satchel on the bed. She took a deep breath, straightened her skirts, and breathed a prayer. "Lord help me show the love of Jesus and not spit fire at that young woman if she's nasty to my Adam." She smiled a little at her prayer, reached for her satchel, and left the room with her head held high.

Buck was waiting for her at the foot of the steps, and Bertha came out of her bedroom, descending the stairs with a big package in her arms.

"This is for you, Hattie. I loved having you stay here. If you don't feel welcome at Sunrise Ranch, you come right back and take up residence here. I'd love it and would pray to that end, but that wouldn't be nice." She smiled and wrapped her arms around Hattie, giving her a big hug and a kiss on both cheeks. "You take care now."

"Thank you, Bertha. I'm grateful we both found satisfaction in me being here. You are a gracious hostess, and I'll miss those early morning coffee chats on your balcony."

Adam took the big gift and stowed it in the wagon and stood patiently while his aunt said her good-byes. Buck took Hattie's arm and led her down the walk to the wagon.

"I'd normally swing you up, girl, but I'll have to forego that for another time." He grinned at her.

"Yes, I reckon you will."

He handed her up into the wagon. "I'll be out there in a day or so and will stop in to see you, my girl." His eyes were warm and lazy on her face, which grew rosy under his gaze.

"If you don't, I'll be riding into town to see you!" She laughed, and he joined her.

Adam climbed into the driver seat and took the reins. "Reckon I'll be seeing you tomorrow as we finalize plans for watching the road," he said.

Buck nodded at him. "For sure we need to keep an eye on Stirling and Harding. Be seeing you."

Adam clucked to the horses and slapped the reins slightly, and they started to move.

Hattie didn't say anything more, but her blue eyes spoke volumes to Buck, who loved her back with his.

Adam and Hattie headed down the wide driveway and out onto North Hampton Road, then turned onto the main street of Napa and headed out of town.

"Aunt Hattie, I want you to know that Miss Eden Chandler is—"

"Difficult. That's already been made quite clear," Hattie interrupted. "I promise to be on my best behavior, Adam." She patted his arm reassuringly. "Honestly, you don't have to worry about me spouting off. On the other hand, gross rudeness will not be tolerated." Her lips were set, and Adam knew that was that. He did breathe a sigh of relief because he didn't think Eden would be rude to him in front of his aunt— at least he hoped she wouldn't.

The two of them talked and caught up on past events. Hattie told Adam all about how the Lord had been tugging at her heart for months to move west. Adam explained about the will and how he'd met the Chandlers on the train coming home the year before. He told her about receiving the legal papers and riding up to San Rafael. He gave her a clear picture of Abigail and Elijah Humphries, making her want to meet them. He also told her about Matthew's wife, Liberty, and meeting her father and grandmother. Because of Adam's rendition of all that had transpired in the past few weeks, it seemed like no time at all to make the journey to Sunrise Canyon and the ranch named after it.

"Why is this called Sunrise Ranch?" Hattie asked as they drove under a huge wooden sign that stretched across the road and was held up by huge posts.

"Beautiful sign, isn't it? This entire area right here is a wide canyon called Sunrise Canyon. Giovanni, the foreman of Sunrise Ranch, told me that the sun rises during the summer months right at the canyon's mouth on the east end, and that's how it got its name."

"Yes, it is lovely here. After living in Williamsburg, this seems quite remote to me. There's no neighbors close, are there?"

"No, the closest neighbors are about a half hour down the road. Matthew and Liberty Bannister."

Hattie changed the subject to that which was foremost on her mind. "Adam, do you think Miss Chandler would allow Buck to live at the ranch too? I want to be the chaperone you hoped I'd be, but I also want to get married." She spoke plainly.

Adam laughed. "You never were one to mince words or sidle up to a subject. Frankly, I don't see why she'd mind, but you certainly can have your wedding and live in my half of the house."

"Have the two of you split up the house, then?" Hattie was aghast at the thought.

"No, not the house, but we did split up the upstairs. Eden didn't want me down where she sleeps nor where her parents slept. I don't blame her. Actually, it makes it a bit simpler, as I know which rooms I can use for my guests or you, for that matter." He looked down at his aunt Hattie with a twinkle in his eyes. "Don't worry, Aunt Hattie. I think you will enjoy yourself. You're going to love Dorothy Jenkins. She's the housekeeper and a believer, and Bernice Anderson, whom everyone calls Berry, is the cook. Well, here we are."

CHAPTER XXIV

Bear ye one another's burdens,
and so fulfil the law of Christ.

GALATIANS 6:2

COMING TO THE END OF THE LONG DRIVE, the house stood proudly, an imposing edifice surrounded by trees and shrubs. Hattie liked the look of the house. It was huge, two storied, and solid. It seemed to hold an air of stately elegance.

Adam jumped off and went around to help his aunt down. She stood up in the wagon to better take in her surroundings. There were many outbuildings and sheds, but everything looked orderly and homey. She held out her hand to her nephew, and he helped her descend.

The front door stood open, and Dorothy Jenkins was there to welcome Hattie.

Gio came out of the stable. He'd been watching for them. Knowing Eden was not there to greet Adam's aunt, he felt relief rather than consternation. Her arrival would be peaceful without Eden there. He was tired of the tension and Eden's rude curtness.

"Oh, you must be this young man's aunt Hattie," Dorothy said. "Welcome, welcome to Sunrise Ranch. We've been looking forward to your arrival," she said as she walked down the front steps and held both hands out to the newcomer. Dorothy was a bit surprised Hattie was so young. They were most likely close in age.

Hattie looked Dorothy in the eyes and immediately realized she would have more than Bertha for a friend. Dorothy's eyes were warm and welcoming, with no reservations.

Hattie took both her hands and said, "Thank you for the warm welcome, Mrs. Jenkins. I look forward to getting to know you better."

She turned and said, "You must be Giovanni. Adam has great regard for you."

Gio took off his hat and made a sweeping bow. "Giovanni Coletti, madam. Nice to make your acquaintance."

Hattie took one of his hands, which charmed him, and said, "And I am Hattie Hamilton and very pleased to meet you, sir."

"Let's get your things inside, Aunt Hattie."

"I'll help you with that," Gio offered.

Mrs. Jenkins and Hattie reached into the wagon and grabbed a few of the lighter satchels, and Hattie followed the housekeeper into the spacious front foyer.

She looked around appreciatively. A beautiful parlor, open to the foyer and the hall, no wall along the foyer side. Halfway down the hall was a huge column. There was a large bay window with a grand piano sitting in it. Hattie was delighted; she played quite well, but had not shipped her piano. On the left of the foyer was a set of glassed French doors that opened into a comfortable great room. She peeked into the room and saw that it was open to the kitchen, which lay behind it.

"This is beautiful," she exclaimed, "yet very inviting and homey too."

Dorothy nodded her head in agreement. "Mrs. Chandler had good taste and always kept this house on an even keel. We miss her greatly." Tears filled her eyes, and she bit her lip in consternation.

"I am sorry for your loss, Mrs. Jenkins. It cannot be easy for you, losing someone you cared so deeply about." Hattie squeezed Dorothy's shoulder with compassion.

"Dorothy, just call me Dorothy, or Dottie, as Gio does. We're not so formal here on the ranch." She smiled and blinked away her tears. "Thank you for your kind words. Now, please follow me, and I'll take you up to your suite."

Hattie followed Dorothy up the oak staircase, and they turned right at the top. Dorothy pointed left and said, "Those are Miss Eden's rooms, and her parents were at the end of the hall. She and Adam split the rooms down the middle, her taking the left of the stairs and him taking the right of the stairs. He took the bedroom at the far end, which is identical to Eden's parents'."

"I have never seen a hallway with skylights. It surely brightens this hall, doesn't it?"

"It is different," said Dorothy, "but it was something Camilla wanted when they built the house. She said dark halls were morbid and boring.

"Adam wanted you to have this suite of rooms," Dorothy said, and she opened the door to a lovely sitting room with doors opening to a modern bathroom, a huge bedroom, and a large dressing room.

"Oh my, this is huge, and it's lovely!" Hattie exclaimed. Before she could say more, Adam, along with Gio, came trooping in with her first trunk. He walked straight into the huge dressing room and set it on the floor.

"We'll be back!" he said with a grin.

The room was painted a pale salmon color. Two plush chairs flanked the fireplace, done in a dark-apricot color, with pillows done in salmon, fresh green, and white. The mantel and trim were stark white and looked fresh and clean with the salmon as their backdrop. A vase was filled with snapdragons, daisies, carnations, and roses.

"Thank you for the flowers," Hattie said. "They always make a body feel welcome, don't they?"

"Yes, they do, but I didn't pick them. Eden did. She said it was something her mother always did for guests and she wanted to carry on the tradition. I thought she'd be back by now. She went over to visit Liberty Bannister."

"Oh, that must be Matthew's wife. He's such a nice man. Adam was telling me about his wife. Well, I'll be sure to thank Eden for the flowers. Oh, there's a balcony!" French doors led to a wide balcony with white wrought iron fencing. Two chairs sat side by side with a table between, reminding Hattie of Bertha's house. She stepped out onto the balcony.

"What a gorgeous view! Look at the hills there in the distance. Oh my! A body could sit here and never get tired of the scenery." She reentered the sitting room and said, "It is beautiful, and I thank you again for your warm welcome."

Dorothy looked Hattie in the eyes and said, "Miss Hamilton—"

"Hattie."

"Hattie, I hesitate to say this, and I'm not sure your nephew has enlightened you, but Eldon Chandler giving half of Sunrise Ranch to a total stranger has put his daughter in an untenable situation. She is angry with her father and yet feels guilty she is, because he's dead. There is no recourse for her."

"I do understand. I was surprised Adam took the half offered him. I'm not sure it was wise to do so, but I support him in whatever he does as long as it's not contrary to the good Lord's Word, of course."

Dorothy murmured, "Of course. Eden is very fragile right now, but along with that, she is quite headstrong. We are grateful for Adam's calming presence and feel after things settle down a bit, Miss Eden will come to realize it's for the best. She looks at us as merely hired help, not capable of helping her make decisions. Having you here along with your nephew is, in truth, most welcome by the staff of Sunrise Ranch."

Hattie looked at Dorothy with surprise in her eyes. "I thank you for that, Dorothy. I have been praying for the situation here, even though I don't know all the details."

Dorothy linked her arm through Hattie's and said, "I am delighted to know you are my sister in Christ, Hattie. It simplifies many things. Let's go downstairs. Dolly can help you unpack while we get acquainted."

The two women walked side by side down the wide stairs, chattering as if they were old friends.

Gio, helping Adam carry a large trunk into the front doorway, looked up as they were coming down, and it warmed his heart that Dottie had taken a shine to Adam's aunt. He knew her heart was aching over Camilla.

The two women went to the kitchen, where Dorothy introduced Hattie to Berry.

"Hattie, I'd like you to meet one of the best cooks this side of the Mississippi. Bernice Anderson, meet Miss Hattie Hamilton. Lately of Williamsburg, Virginia. Miss Hamilton, Bernice gets shortened to Berry around here, and it fits because she makes the most delicious berry pies in the whole world."

Berry inclined her head as her deep-set eyes took in the newcomer.

Hattie stuck out both hands and grasped Berry's in hers, saying, "I'm delighted to meet you, Berry."

Berry, surprised by her friendliness, warmed up to her right away.

Dorothy looked on in satisfaction, knowing Berry could be difficult if she took a dislike to someone.

Eden arrived, having just returned from Liberty's house, fully prepared to resent Adam's aunt as much as she resented him. She stalked into the big kitchen.

Hattie turned to see her bearing down on the group of three.

Oh my, Hattie thought. *Oh my goodness. Why, she looks like a wounded deer just waiting for the hunter to finish her off. Oh, Lord, help me to help her find her way. Is that why You brought me here?*

Every preconceived notion Hattie had about the mistress of Sunrise Ranch fled out the window with one look at her. All Hattie's motherly instincts rose to the fore, and when Eden drew near, she said, "I'm Hattie, and you must be Eden."

Tears stood out in Hattie's eyes, and Eden, looking into them, saw such love and compassion, she was undone. She reached out to take Hattie's hand, but Hattie pulled the younger woman into her arms and held her tightly. "Oh, you poor child. What you've had to endure—I don't know how you've done it. Oh, dear girl, you must be very strong."

Hattie held Eden, stroking her hair, and Eden began to cry at her words, her entire frame shaking with sobs and sorrow. Hattie, for the first time in her life, took the burden of sorrow as her own and sobbed right along with Eden.

Dorothy and Berry looked on at first in consternation and then with glad hearts, knowing Hattie Hamilton was going to be exactly what Sunrise Ranch needed. More than that, she was what Eden needed.

Hattie and Eden pulled back from each other, but a friendship had been established between the two women. Eden gave Hattie's arms a squeeze and spoke softly. "I was prepared to hate you. I'm sorry. Instead, I wish to be your friend."

"We will be just that, Eden Chandler. We shall be friends." Both women took handkerchiefs out of their sleeves and wiped their eyes and blew their noses.

Dorothy said briskly, "Now that we've all been introduced, would you two like a cup of tea before dinner?"

"That would be lovely," Hattie said.

"I'd enjoy that too, Dorothy," Eden said, "and it'd be nice if you'd join us."

"We'll sit right here and talk while Berry finishes up dinner."

Gio and Adam finished hauling the trunks up the stairs. Adam would get Hattie's few pieces of furniture and a couple more trunks from Matthew's Rancho on the morrow. She was glad her new suite of rooms would easily accommodate the few pieces she'd brought. She would have hated to part with them. Her parents had been frugal, but when they did buy anything, it had been of exceptional quality.

Eden was startled when Berry rang a huge bell on the porch, signaling it was time for dinner. It hadn't been rung since the deaths of Camilla and Eldon. Besides signaling dinnertime, Eden felt it also signaled a big change in her life.

Dorothy, Gio, Eden, Hattie, and Adam gathered at the huge table. It was round and could accommodate fourteen without the huge leaf that could be put into the middle of it.

It's time for me to stop making everyone around me miserable because I'm miserable, Eden thought. *Hattie thinks I'm strong, but I know I'm not. I feel like my insides have shattered into little bits and the pieces will never come back together again.* She sighed, glancing at the table. *One good thing about a huge round table is that there is no head nor foot of the table and my parents sat down wherever they felt like. I won't have to deal with the idea someone is usurping their place.*

With new eyes, she peeked over at Adam. Hattie had told her while they were drinking tea that his father had died when he was eleven and since then, she'd helped raise him. Then his mother, Hattie's sister, died from a horse-jumping accident when Adam was fifteen. *Reckon every one of us has a story to tell of sadness or tragedy. I never thought about it much before, but sadness is part of happiness…without one, you can't have the other.*

Eden started to sit, signaling the others to take their places. No one spoke for several seconds.

Adam said, "I know my Aunt Hattie and I are the interlopers here, but we—"

"No, not interlopers. You are half owner of Sunrise, Adam. I know I don't pray before eating, but my parents did for a little over a month before they died, and I'm quite sure you do, as well as Hattie and Dorothy. So, Adam, will you please ask the blessing?"

Adam looked stunned. He swallowed, his Adam's apple going up and down. "Certainly, with pleasure, ma'am," he replied, his eyes serious; he bowed his head. "Let's pray. Lord, how grateful we are that You love us with an everlasting love. We praise You for being trustworthy and good. We pray You help us find the wicked person or people who took Eldon and Camilla's lives before their time. Father, may good prevail and not evilness, that Your glory may shine and be honored. We also ask that You bring comfort to Miss Eden's heart. Lord, may she feel Your compassion and loving-kindness. Thank You for this food. Thank You for Aunt Hattie's safe travels and that we are together again. May we ever be mindful of Your provision for us. We thank You. Amen."

Adam looked over at Eden, who was flanked by Gio and Dorothy. "You said your parents began asking a blessing for the food?"

"Yes, I did, Adam. My parents asked Jesus into their hearts a little over a month before they died. They told me they'd met a man on the train last year who told them about having a personal relationship with Jesus. They started reading the Bible, as neither one of them had a clue about anything. Neither of them was raised in a God-fearing household. I reckon you were the man they met, aren't you?"

Adam said, "I am the man." His heart sang with joy over the news.

Berry, along with Dolly, began to dish out a clear mushroom soup served with tiny yeast rolls stuffed with a mushroom and rice concoction.

"Umm, this is delicious!" Hattie said. "These rolls melt in your mouth. I'd have more and just make this my meal. Berry, this is absolute perfection!"

Berry beamed but admonished, "You don't want to be eating too much, Miss Hattie. We're having chicken fricassee, and its flavor is so delicious that you won't want to stop eating, and then there's dessert."

"I certainly see I'm going to have to be watching my waistline, eating Berry's cooking. This is simply scrumptious."

Dorothy breathed a sigh of relief, watching Eden eat. She didn't pick at her food, and although she didn't eat her normal portion, she ate more than she had since her parents died. She'd never seen Eden take to someone the way she had with Hattie, and it warmed Dorothy's heart that Hattie would be a good influence on Eden. She wondered about Hattie leaving once she was married. Dorothy had gleaned from Gio that Buckmaster Rawlins had fallen head over heels for this woman, and Dorothy could see why.

Hattie brought life and laughter to the table, and by the time dinner was over, everyone adored her.

Adam, since staying at Sunrise Ranch, hadn't eaten with anyone except Gio, and once with Gio and Eden. He watched his aunt charm the inhabitants of Chandler House and was thankful for her bubbly personality and loving ways. He glanced over at Eden, surprised to see her eyes on his face. He gave her a long look, which she returned in full measure, but he could see the animosity was gone. He surreptitiously drew a big sigh of relief. He hated living with tension.

Caleb McHaney tossed and turned, not able to sleep. An engagement was serious business. He'd told his mother that he'd have to wait a year for Eden's mourning to be up before he could ask her to marry him. She started yelling at him, her lips becoming bluer, until he thought she'd die right in front of him. She yelled and fumed, ranting on and on, saying she wanted him settled before she died. He had slammed out of the house and saddled up the paint he'd broken for her. He'd ridden like the wind on a horse that seemingly had wings for feet. When he felt the heat of anger and frustration had subsided, he'd gone back home only to find the door locked on him. It wasn't the first time in his life she'd voiced her displeasure in that way. He was now trying to sleep in the hayloft, a heavy saddle blanket to protect him from the pokes of straw. The loft had been a refuge he'd had since he was young, when things in the house were a stomach-churning caldron. Sometimes his father had slept with him when things became unbearable in the house. His father told him that most of the time his mother was pretty easy to live with, but once her temper flared, it was almost as if she was deranged and didn't know what she was doing. It was just better to stay out of her way until she cooled off. Sometimes it took more than one night for her to unlock the door.

He remembered a verse his father taught him. His father was forever quoting Proverbs from the Bible, and Caleb had begun memorizing them at a young age. He quoted softly to himself, "'The rod and reproof give wisdom, But a child who gets his own way brings shame to his mother.'" He lay thinking about it. *I'm not a child anymore, and I certainly don't bring my mother shame by not marrying Eden. I'd bring more shame by marrying someone I don't love.*

Caleb made up his mind to talk to Eden about the whole affair. She was his best friend, and he was not going to ask her to marry him just to suit his mother. His mother was going to die, and he'd be stuck in a loveless marriage. He turned on his bed of hay again and wondered how he was going to go about it. He thought maybe he should pack up and ride to the McCaullys' and get himself hired on there. He always had liked Kirk Bannister. One thing certain—he wasn't in love with Eden Chandler, and although he'd told his mother he'd marry her, he didn't plan to. *I can just make sure things around here are caught up so it won't be any extra burden on her. If the door is still locked tomorrow, I'm going through the window to get my things. I'm done with living this kind of life.*

CHAPTER XXV

A fool uttereth all his mind:
but a wise man keepeth it in till afterwards.

PROVERBS 29:11

THEO HARDING TOSSED AND TURNED and finally got up, not wanting to wake Francis. He went to a cabinet in the great room and took out a bottle of whiskey. He looked at the amount in the bottle in shock and put the bottle back into the cupboard.

I can't believe I've drunk that much. It's certainly not going to help with finding a solution, and most likely will only add to my problems. What in the world am I going to do? Reuben Stirling is a thorn in my side. I should never have recommended him to Matthew. Matthew is sharp and is going to know Reuben has never been a bookkeeper in his life.

He grabbed a blanket off the settee and sat down in a big leather easy chair. He drew the ottoman closer and eased both legs onto it, throwing the blanket over him and pulling it up under his chin. He leaned back and closed his eyes. *What will Francis do when she finds out? The way Reuben talked, I'm sure she's bound to find out.*

Theo sat pondering what he should do, as he had every single night for the past three weeks.

It was very early morning, and Buck rode out of town, heading for Sunrise Canyon. He'd written a note and left it on the table for Fern to find. He figured he'd get breakfast at Chandlers'.

The sun was just coming up over the horizon as he made his way into the canyon, and the beauty of it nearly took his breath away. Streaks of light fanned out from its source, which was just starting to rise over the other end of the canyon's entrance in the far distance. He'd heard about this phenomenon but had never witnessed it. He stopped his mare and just sat, his arm resting on the pommel, taking in the most gorgeous sunrise he'd ever seen. Red, gold, orange, and yellow streaked the skies like a fan. He sat mesmerized by the sight as the fingers of light began to reflect their glow on the rocks and bluffs inside the canyon, turning them from deep purple to gold. The light seemed to invade his soul with gladness that he had seen such sight, and he felt as if he were the only person alive to witness such an awesome display.

He spoke aloud as he kicked his mare into a lope. "Thank You, Lord, for that beautiful spectacle. You're still creating—don't reckon I ever thought of that before, but You never stopped creating, did You." It was not a question but a statement.

He kicked his mare into an easy canter and headed for Sunrise Ranch. He turned into the long lane and rode up to the wide hitching post. Hearing a noise, he turned to see Gio coming out of the stable.

"Good morning, Giovanni," he said. "Reckon I'm early, but I thought we'd get busy on a schedule for watching the main road. Plus, I have another reason for riding out here. I'll probably be a regular visitor for the time being." He smiled, the crease deepening in his cheek.

Gio grinned back at him. "Yes, your princess charmed us all last night at dinner. She is quite the lady."

Buck lowered his voice. "Did Eden seem to take to her at all? Hattie was quite worried that the two of them might not get along."

"No worries there, sir. Eden and your Miss Hattie will be the best of friends, I'm sure. Somehow having that woman here has already changed the atmosphere that has hung heavy on Sunrise for the past three weeks. Come on in and have some breakfast." He led the way up the steps, and Buck followed him. "If you plan to stay for a bit, I'll have Pepe take care of your horse."

"I reckon that would be nice. I don't know how long this will take, but we do need a concrete plan and list of men to watch the main road."

"Go on in, and I'll be right back," Gio said. He went back down the steps and took Buck's horse, leading him into the stable.

Buck, who'd been a guest at the Chandlers' many times, let himself in the front door and headed for the kitchen. The smell of frying bacon put a smile on his face.

Hattie was sitting at the table, chatting with Berry, a mug of coffee sitting in front of her.

Buck leaned against the doorjamb of the great room and watched, unnoticed by the two women.

Hattie, dressed in a mint-green silk robe, looked utterly feminine. Her hair was formed into a loose knot on the top of her head, and a few strands of curls had escaped notice and framed her minxish face. Buck took a deep breath and let it out slowly. It still amazed him that he'd fallen for this woman. He'd taken a glance that turned into a gaze that would last the rest of his life

Hattie was answering Berry's question. "Why, I slept like a baby last night. Maybe I shouldn't say that. Babies don't always sleep through the night, do they? I slept like a contented baby," Hattie amended with a laugh, and Berry laughed with her.

"I'm glad you slept well, dearie. How do you like your eggs?"

"I like mine over medium," Buck replied from the great room, making his way to Hattie like a bee to honey.

"Buck! I didn't expect you out here this soon!"

Hattie stood up, and with no thought for Berry, Buck swept her into his arms, and his mouth came down hungrily on hers. He murmured into her ear, "I can't stay away from you, me darlin'."

Hattie's cheeks were aflame, and Berry was grinning widely as she expertly flipped a pancake, a stack of them staying warm on the back of the woodstove. Plates also warmed on the back corner, and the smell of frying bacon and maple syrup heating up made Buck's mouth water.

"Welcome, Sheriff Rawlins. I haven't seen your face around these parts in a while. How are you feeling? Reckon you're feeling much better these days, aren't you?"

"I'm healing up nicely, if that's what you're referring to," he replied.

"Well, sit yourself down and have some breakfast with Hattie," Berry said as she sat a steaming mug of coffee in front of him. "I don't imagine it'll be long before the others are up. Adam has usually made an appearance by now, and Gio is always here by this time. Don't know what's holding him up this morning."

"He's taking care of my horse. I plan to stay a bit this morning and get a schedule written down of trustworthy people we can get to watch the main road."

The sun stretched out fingers of light that curled themselves over the horizon. The Bannisters were not up yet. Matthew and Liberty had lain long into the night, talking. The conversation had begun at dinnertime.

"Matthew, I know you've been so busy with Rancho Bonito and all that comes with a growing concern, as well as you're taking time to help out the sheriff. I hate to bother you with things that most likely aren't important, but ah…" Her voice trailed off, and Matthew knew whatever Liberty had on her mind was important to her. She now had his full attention.

Liberty glanced over at Conchita, who seemed not to be listening, but Liberty knew she was.

"Well, I'll just lay it on the table. Conchita feels that Reuben is a very unhappy person and is sorrowing in his heart. She feels very sorry for him. Frankly, I can't abide the man. He almost makes my skin crawl, and I know it's because I'm projecting my past feelings about Armand onto Reuben. I don't mean to do it, but the man puts me so much in mind of my former husband that I can't seem to shake this feeling of complete distaste for him. I'm even beginning to hide in the house if I know he's around. I know I shouldn't judge the man on my feelings for Armand, but I can't seem to help it. My mind says it's wrong, but my heart doesn't trust him at all. There! Now that I've finally told you, I feel much better."

Matthew looked back at Liberty, his deep-set blue eyes serious in his tanned face. "Well, my dear, I didn't know whether to worry you about what I found out yesterday or not," he said. "In light of what you've just said, both you and Conchita should know that Reuben Stirling could be connected with the Chandlers' deaths. We don't know for sure yet, but because of what Dr. John saw yesterday, guilt seems to be riding in that direction." He told the two women all that had transpired the day before.

"I know you can't go gunning for someone on Dr. John's observations, but can't Sheriff Rawlins arrest him?" Liberty asked.

"No, he can't. What would be the charge? Talking to Theo Harding is hardly proof of anything. It just looks suspicious. On top of that, you know Theo recommended Reuben to me, and the man knows next to nothing about bookkeeping. I can't figure out what's going on, but I also can't fire Reuben and have him ride off somewhere, when he could very well be our shooter."

Conchita said, "Maybe dere be another reason Meester Stirling, he meet with Meester Harding. Maybe eet have nothing to do weeth the Chandlers."

"Yes, maybe you're right, Conchita, but what if you're wrong?" Matthew drummed his fingers on the table, trying to figure out just what his plan of action should be.

The door was still locked when Caleb tried the knob the next morning. He'd slept poorly but still woke up early. He removed his spurs from his boots and went around to the back of the house, where he knew his window was open. He silently climbed over the sill, and grabbing a couple satchels out of the bottom of his clothespress, he stuffed his clothes, a couple knives, leather gloves, and a few other nonessential items into both bags. He was very quiet, having lots of practice growing up. He'd been caught sneaking out once and got the tanning of his life.

Throwing his leg back over the sill, he made his way stealthily to the barn, where he put his spurs back on, saddled his horse, and quietly led her out of the barn. He walked quite a way down the road before he climbed on and headed for Sonoma and McCaully Ranch. He hadn't even left a note for his mother. *She'll figure it out*, he thought.

It was quite a long ride, but before midday, he pulled up in front of the McCaully-Bannister Ranch. He'd seen the sign coming onto the property and grinned at the name change. Caleb didn't know Caitlin, Kirk's wife. Until about a month before, he hadn't even known they were married.

He wrapped the reins around the hitching post and made his way over to the barn first, thinking someone would be able to point him in the right direction. He looked around with interest. There was a barn, stable, and several other buildings he figured were bunkhouses and a chow hall.

He found a man shoeing a horse, and Caleb stuck out his hand. "Howdy, name's Caleb McHaney, and I'm looking for Kirk Bannister."

The other man dropped the hoof, wiped his hand on his chaps, and took Caleb's hand in a callused palm. "Name's Sneedy," he said. "You've comed ta th' right place. Kirk's over in th' corral, but y'all don't want ta be gettin' too close. There's a stallion in there thet ain't too friendly ta strangers." He grinned and jerked his head in the direction of the corral.

"Thanks," Caleb said. He strode over to the corral, and climbing up on the bottom slats, resting his arms on the top, he watched Kirk put a beautiful horse through his paces.

Kirk glanced over at Caleb and took a second look. "Caleb! Good to see you!" Kirk slid off the stallion, who wasn't saddled. He slipped the reins over the horse's head, removed the bit, and looped the reins over his arm. He strode over to his visitor.

Caleb's face split into a wide grin. "I'm always amazed when I see how much you look like your brother!"

"How is the ole man anyway?" Kirk asked with a twinkle in his deep-set blue eyes.

"Well, right now, everyone's frustrated around Napa. I reckon you heard about the Chandlers, right?"

"Who hasn't? It was a terrible thing." He stuck out his hand for Caleb to shake and asked, "Have you had lunch? Come on in and meet my wife. She'll be coming in anytime now. She's been working fence."

"Your wife repairs barbed wire?"

"Yep, she loves the out of doors. What brings you to these parts anyway?"

"I've always had a hankering to ranch. I can rope almost anything, and I...well, truth to tell, I've left home, and I'm in need of a job."

"Lit out, huh? Well, I can ease your mind. You're hired, Caleb. I know you to be a hard worker, and I can use that around here. We have some cowboys who come and go, and then we have the ones who stay and become part of McCaully-Bannister. So, let's go in and have lunch and talk terms. I'll get you set up in the bunkhouse after we eat. Now, tell me about that brother of mine, and how's Liberty doing? This is her first baby, you know."

The two men walked toward the huge ranch house, and Caleb felt better than he had in a long time.

After a delicious breakfast of bacon, pancakes, and eggs, Hattie went up to get dressed. Adam, Gio, and Buck sat around the table to write out a list of possible people they could ask to help with keeping an eye on the main road.

Eden came down, still in her robe, to have a bite to eat. She was surprised to see Buck there, but glad too.

"Adam told us last night at dinner about what you found out yesterday from Dr. John. Pretty incriminating, isn't it?" she asked Buck.

"Yes, but it's certainly not proof of anything. We thought we'd station some people on bluffs above the main road and see if the two meet anymore, or if we can find who's up there taking potshots at people. Did anyone tell you someone shot at Kerrigan?"

"Taylor or Terrence?"

"Taylor," Buck replied.

"Someone shot Taylor?" Eden was aghast. "I can't believe this. We have a madman on the loose. Someone has gone completely crazy, but to shoot Taylor...why?"

"No, they didn't get him, but someone either tried to shoot him or tried to scare him, or as some of us think, maybe tried to cast the blame on someone other than the Kerrigans for this mess," Buck said. "It could have been Terrence. He smokes cigars. Maybe he's hoping you'll marry Taylor and they will have a chunk of Sunrise."

"Tell me what happened!" Eden's nerves were stretched tight and wearing thin. She sat down with a plop.

Adam got up to get a cup of coffee for her. He set it down in front of her, and she looked up with surprised appreciation in her eyes. She picked up the cup, and it rattled a bit on the saucer.

Buck didn't notice.

But Adam did.

"Eden," he said, "take a deep breath. We talk about all these things that have happened without thought for how you must be feeling. Is Kerrigan a beau, that you should worry about him, or just a friend?" Adam was curious, but he also wanted to get her mind off people riding around shooting other people.

"He's, ahh, he's...well, I've danced with him a few times, and I know him. Frankly, if the truth were known, I don't care for him much at all, but I went dancing with him to irritate my father, who could barely stand having him around. My papa had little patience for people with no original thought in their head, and that typifies Taylor and his pa in every respect."

"Wonder," Buck said meditatively, "wonder if Kerrigan took a potshot at his son to make us think they have nothing to do with all this, or to scare Kerrigan from going into town. He's been a regular lately at the saloon. I don't approve drinking like he is during the day, when he should be working like a man. Wonder where all their money comes from?"

"Maybe there was an inheritance. Maybe they robbed someone, or maybe they robbed a train before they moved to the Napa Valley." Eden laughed shortly. "Who knows why anyone does what they do— case in point, my papa. No one knows why he did what he did. But back to the matter at hand. Do you still think it's only one person doing this, Sheriff?"

"Your guess is as good as mine," he replied.

Eden started to get up, but Adam's comment stopped her.

"You haven't eaten. Here." And he set a plate with one egg, two strips of bacon, and one pancake in front of her.

She looked up at him, incredulous, and started to say something, but just then Hattie walked into the dining area, dressed in a split skirt and fitted white blouse with tiny lacy flowers on it.

Eden closed her mouth, wanting to see Buck's reaction, and was not disappointed. Buck swooped Hattie into his arms, and turning her so the two of them faced away from the occupants at the table, he bent her back and kissed her.

"It feels like forever since I've done that," he said.

Hattie, blushing to the roots of her hair, grinned at him and said, "I believe it's been all of a half an hour, sir."

Eden, not even thinking of what she was doing, began to eat as she watched the pair. She glanced over at Adam to see a look of satisfaction on his face, and suddenly realized he was caring for her needs before she asked. She blushed, but once she'd started eating, she found she was hungry, and breakfast had always been her favorite meal. She continued to watch Buck and Hattie, but her mind stayed on the man across the table from her.

CHAPTER XXVI

The Spirit itself beareth witness with our spirit,
that we are the children of God: And if children, then heirs;
heirs of God, and joint-heirs with Christ.

ROMANS 8:16–17a

EDEN SAT CONTEMPLATING ADAM and tried to see him without the constant bias she had against him. *He's even tempered, even when I've been harping at him. Wonder why he's so different? I'll bet it's because of what Liberty said. He's a Christian like she is, like Buck and Hattie and Dorothy and Matthew. He's tremendously attractive, to my way of thinking.* She looked around the table and realized these were people she admired. They were honest, hardworking, and true to their beliefs. *I want that kind of peace...*

"I want that kind of peace." Eden hadn't realized she'd spoken out loud.

All movement stopped, and suddenly she recognized what she'd done. She looked almost defiantly at the occupants in the room and repeated her statement.

"I want the kind of peace you all seem to have. I want to be a Christ follower the way my parents were their last month of life. I saw such a contentedness in them. It doesn't mean I'm not still unhappy with the choices my father made, but..."

Adam, instantly by her side, said, "We all would be delighted to help you with that. Could you pray, or would you like me to pray and you repeat after me?"

"I'll repeat whatever you say," she replied.

"Let's pray then." Everyone bowed their heads, and Adam began a short prayer. "Lord, I recognize I'm a sinner. I repent of everything I've ever done that is contrary to Your ways. Please come into my heart and help me to love You and follow You all the days of my life. Amen."

Eden had repeated after him, and she looked up in surprise. "That's it? That's all I have to do? What if God doesn't think I'm worthy of being His follower?"

"None of us are worthy," Hattie said. "Not one of us *was* worthy, but the blood of Jesus makes us worthy. You are now like a princess. Romans eight tells us that as believers, we are joint heirs with Christ. It's kind of like Adam here. He doesn't deserve half of the Chandlers' estate. He did nothing to earn that right, and yet it was freely given to him by your father. Now he's a joint heir with you, although you were born to it. That's what the blood of Jesus does. It makes us joint heirs of the kingdom of God though we've done nothing ourselves to earn it. Jesus is prince, and you are a princess because of your inheritance in the kingdom. You don't have to feel any different. You just need to trust that what God promised has now been done in your heart. It also doesn't mean you won't make mistakes. You simply ask for forgiveness, turn away from doing it again, and go on."

"A princess, huh? Thank you for the explanation. It helps. Frankly, I realized the other day that Sunrise is too big for me to handle all alone anyway. So, I'll be glad for Adam's help."

Everyone in the room looked at her in surprise, especially Gio.

He felt he was capable of running the Chandler Olives part of the ranch, but he'd never get the opportunity. He'd help Adam all he could and be satisfied with that.

Adam spoke up. "I think I told you I know nothing about growing or the process of producing Chandler Olives. Gio will be making the decisions along with you, Eden, not me. I'm going to be learning for a long, long time before I'm able to make important decisions about this business."

Gio's eyes glowed with the knowledge of Adam's deferential attitude. Adam would treat him with respect, and that was all Gio needed. He would be loyal to Adam until the day he died.

Eden blushed at Adam's statement. "Sorry, Gio, you do know more than I ever will about growing olives."

Gio simply inclined his head in acknowledgment of her comment.

Eden continued to talk. "Also, I talked to Liberty, and she thought I should ask you, Buck, about living here. I know you two are already planning to marry. You, sir, are welcome to stay here, if it doesn't bother you to be so far from town."

Buck, grinning from ear to ear, said, "I'll be happy to take up residence here for the time being. We need to set a date for a wedding. How about tomorrow?"

Everyone laughed. Hattie replied, "Maybe not tomorrow, but next week?"

Buck said, "You're all witnesses. We're getting married next week!"

Hester awoke slowly. She lay very still, feeling an intense, painful squeeze in her chest. It crawled up her neck, and her jaw felt numb, like it was caught in a vise. She didn't move, wondering if this was it. *I reckon I'm not ready to die yet. Got a few things I need to do first. I should have known better than to put it off.* Although she was not a believer, she said, "OOOOhhhhh, God, help me! I can't take the pain!"

She lay in an agony of suffering with hardly any other thought than she'd locked Caleb out, and he'd never know she lay here dying. "OOOhhh, the pain," she panted as she lost consciousness.

Once the list was made up and analyzed thoroughly, Buck took his leave from Sunrise Ranch. He had a long day ahead of him. He needed to notify everyone on the list about the plans. He prayed no name written down on it was involved. Until he had proof, he just couldn't be sure that Harding and Stirling were the culprits. It made a tiring day for him, riding to each person and taking the time to fully explain exactly what the plan was and what part the individuals would play in it. His last stop was the Bannisters'. He was hoping for dinner, as he'd forgone lunch. He'd drunk several glasses of water and cold tea offered him at different stops, but now he was hungry. His stomach growled at its mistreatment. *I'm getting used to my creature comforts, staying at Bertha's.*

He rode up the long, winding lane, admiring the neatness and beauty of Rancho Bonito. Grapevines spread out on either side of him and up the hills that surrounded Matthew's land. The house was gorgeous and always seemed to have a welcoming air about it. As he rode up to the hitching post, his mind swung to Hattie and what kind of home they'd have together. He wasn't interested in growing grapes, but the layout of the house was something he wouldn't mind copying. He decided he'd bring Hattie out and see if she liked the layout and design of the house. For all he knew, she might like a big old clapboard. He hoped not.

He and Jazzie had picked out a piece of property years ago that he'd consistently made payment on. He'd paid it off several years back and still had ideas to build there even though Jazzie was gone. It lay not far from town and yet felt as if it was in the country. In truth, it was just down the road from Bertha's place. *Hattie might like that. It's going to be an adventure finding out what Hattie likes.* He smiled.

Dismounting, he slapped his reins around the hitching bar. Out of the corner of his eye, he saw someone come out of the new building next to the barn, and he thought it might be Reuben Stirling. He'd never met the man before.

"Hello," he said cordially.

"Good afternoon," Reuben said.

Suddenly Reuben's eyes lit up, seeing the badge pinned to Buck's vest. "My name's Reuben Stirling," he said as he approached Buck. He continued, "How are you feeling? I thought you were a goner for sure when Theo and I stopped to help you. You were unconscious and bleeding like a stuck pig. Looked as though you'd tried to get your neckerchief off but didn't make it afore you passed out."

"Well, for sure I want to thank you. I have no doubt the two of you saved my life." He looked closely at Reuben's eyes and added, "I think had you not come along, whoever shot me would have come to finish off the job."

Reuben reached out to shake the sheriff's hand. His eyes looked back at Buck, dark and inscrutable, but his voice was pleasant enough.

"Well, I'm certainly glad we were there and could help. I heard tell from Matthew that you haven't caught the person yet. Got any clues as to who it might be?"

"Well, I'm working on a couple, but I've got no real proof yet. Wouldn't like to accuse anyone until I'm sure about it." He saw movement and raised his eyes to look over Stirling's shoulder, his face splitting into a wide grin

"That makes sense to me," Reuben said. "I hope you catch them." He turned as he heard footsteps behind him. It was Diego coming to welcome the sheriff.

"Good to see you, Sheriff Rawleens! You come to veesit just een time. Conchita, she fixing the *chimichangas* tonight. You stay and eet some, ees very good." He slapped Buck on the back with his left hand and reached to shake Buck's hand with this right.

"Long time, no see, Diego! And thank you. I'll take you up on that. Came over to have a chat with Matthew." He walked toward the front door and glanced back to see an inimical look on Reuben Stirling's face as he stared at Diego. Diego was staring back at Reuben. The bookkeeper turned abruptly and headed back to his office. Buck's glance took in the fact that Diego Rodriguez did not like Reuben Stirling, not at all.

Buck was about to ring the big cowbell beside the door, but the door opened just as his fingers grabbed at the thin rope. It startled him, and he grinned widely in response to Conchita's smile.

"Welcome, Meester Sheriff Rawleens. You welcome to Rancho Bonito!"

"Thank you, Conchita. It's a pleasure to come here. Everyone is always so friendly and welcoming that it's like being with family." He heard a dog barking within the depths of the house and looked questioningly at Conchita.

"Eet's nice you say that. We welcome you like family. Come. Come in. Eet much cooler een here weeth the door closed. Come. I tell Mees Libbee you here, but I am sure she already know we haf company. We haf a dog now from Mees Libbee's nephew, Xander. *Sí*, Meester Humphries, Mees Libbee's papa, Meester Bannister's brother, *sí*, they all have the puppies from Xander." She smiled warmly, her teeth strong and white.

She continued to talk. "Matthew, he out in the veenyard, but I am sure Diego, he weel tell heem you are here."

She walked down the long hall to let Liberty know Buck was visiting, but Liberty was already straightening her hair from the warning she'd had from Boston.

"Thank you, Conchita. I'll go talk to him. Would you mind getting some lemonade, please? I'm sure he's fairly parched being out in that hot sun." She followed Conchita down the hall, but Boston was in the lead.

He gamboled over to Buck and began sniffing and smelling, wagging all the while.

"Beautiful dog, Liberty," he said as he stroked Boston's head. "Conchita told me it's a gift from your nephew."

"Yes," she said, smiling, "a most welcome gift, but Xander had to part with all of Daffy's puppies, which was a wrench on his little heart, I'm sure." She gestured to a chair. "Please sit down and rest a bit. How's your wound healing up?"

"Oh, I'm feeling fair ta middling. I find I wear out by afternoon, which I've never done since I can remember. The pain is more a pinch now than a real pain." He smiled at her, his eyes twinkling.

Liberty wanted to ask about Adam's aunt but didn't, although she was very curious.

"You have a lot on your mind right now, I understand." She smiled her gamin grin at him. Her ploy worked.

"Yes indeed, I do have a lot on my mind. Have you met Adam's aunt Hattie Hamilton yet?"

"No. I've heard from Adam that she's moved out west. Is that correct?"

"Yes, and this coming week she'll be Mrs. Buck Rawlins. I've asked her to marry me, and she has accepted."

"Congratulations, Buck! My goodness, that's pretty fast work, isn't it?" She couldn't for the life of her stop grinning.

"One look and I was a goner. I never saw it coming. I am completely bowled over by her, and what is so special is she feels the same way. She's never been married, you understand. We both feel the Lord's hand in this miracle that has happened, and it's perfect for both of us!" Buck had no problem sharing his heart with Liberty. She and Matthew were very close friends.

"What's perfect?" Matthew walked in just as Conchita entered with lemonade. "I'll have some of that too, please," he said to Conchita. His eyes caught and held Liberty's. *Love you.* His lips formed the words silently; aloud he said, "I'll just be a minute. I need to go wash up." He whistled going down the hall as he went back to the bedroom.

Buck smiled and said, "Whistling like that is the sign of a happy man."

"Yes, I think he is a happy man," Liberty replied. "Have you been out to Sunrise lately? Do you know what's going on there?"

"Yes, first thing this morning. In fact, I had breakfast there. I also proposed there in front of witnesses this morning. Another great bit of news is that Eden Chandler accepted Christ as her Savior this morning!" He beamed at Liberty's gasp of surprise.

"That really is awesome news. You have all kinds of good things to tell me." Liberty's mind was thanking God for Eden's commitment to Him. *Thank you for answering my request, Lord,* she said silently. Aloud she said, "I'll ride over there and talk with her tomorrow."

"Ride where?" Matthew came into the great room, and Conchita arrived with another glass of lemonade. "Deener ees nearly ready," she said. "Maybe ten more meenuts." She handed the glass to Matthew and bustled back to the kitchen.

"To answer your question, I'm going over to visit Eden tomorrow. Oh, Matthew, listen to what Buck has to say. It's all good news." Liberty patted the seat on the sofa next to her, and Matthew sat down close to her.

Buck related all that he'd told Liberty, and Matthew exclaimed over each revelation.

"You're a fast worker, Buckmaster Rawlins." Matthew grinned.

"As I told Liberty, one look and I was a goner for sure."

"Time for you to come eat," Conchita called from the kitchen doorway. "Eet all ready for you. I making the chimichangas tonight," she said. "You wash up here, Meester Sheriff Rawleens." She pointed to a deep metal sink in the kitchen with a large jug of water next to it.

Buck washed up, and after praying, the three talked about the events of the day, Buck making sure Matthew was up to snuff on all that had transpired. Buck showed them the list he had made that morning with Gio's and Adam's help.

"What are your thoughts about Harding and Stirling?" Matthew asked.

"Well, it's like Adam said yesterday. We have no proof of anything. I reckon if I were a betting man, I'd say most likely those two were up to something, but whether it's the Chandlers' murders and shooting me, I reckon I just don't know. Harding stands to gain nothing as far as I can see. Stirling, sure, he'd have motive. Sunrise Ranch is worth a pretty penny. He could woo Miss Eden and try for her hand in marriage, but I don't see him getting anywhere. She doesn't care for him at all. Then there's Taylor Kerrigan. He told me outright a couple weeks back that he planned to marry Miss Eden, but he hadn't even asked her yet. She'd be a fool to be misled by his good looks, and she's no fool. She told me flat out this very morning that she danced with him and saw him mainly to irritate her father. Taylor is fast becoming a drunk, to my way of reckoning."

"He's drinking?" Matthew asked.

"Yes. He comes into town almost every afternoon and drinks the hard stuff. I've thought about it and wonder if it isn't Terrence Kerrigan wanting a cut of Sunrise for his son. He'd benefit, for sure."

"He smokes cigars too," Matthew added. "Wonder…I reckon it's beyond my ken that anyone would murder the Chandlers. They were such good people."

"I know. I know. They were the best kind of people. I can't think it was Harding or Stirling. After all, it was Harding and Stirling who took me into town. If they shot me, wouldn't they have just let me lie there and bleed to death? Unless one of them shot me, and the other one didn't know it." Buck sighed heavily. "I just don't have a real clue yet as to our murderer."

CHAPTER XXVII

See now that I, even I, am he, and there is no god with me:
I kill, and I make alive; I wound, and I heal:
neither is there any that can deliver out of my hand.

DEUTERONOMY 32:39

IT WAS LATE AFTERNOON WHEN HESTER McHaney regained consciousness. She lay quietly assessing her heart and physical condition. *Reckon I'm not dead yet, but I don't think I have much time.* She sat up slowly, knowing she'd had a real episode with her heart. Wearily she drug herself out of bed. The first thing she did was unlock the door. She opened it to a hot sun, but there was no water in the bucket by the door. *Caleb must be paying me back*, she thought. *It's unlike him though. He never does that.*

She picked up the pail, which felt heavy even though it was empty. Walking very slowly, she got to the pump and pumped the handle, grateful it wasn't stiff. Water gushed, and she caught some of it in the pail and turned back to the house. She felt that fleeting bit of work had sapped what little strength she had left. Hester plodded back to the house, putting one foot in front of the other methodically. The sun beat down on her head, and she felt lightheaded from the heat and the exertion.

She poured some of the water in a basin, splashed some on her face, and washed her hands. *I'll dump that out later.* Every little task seemed a herculean effort.

She opened the cooler and took out a couple eggs but put them back, as she thought she'd have to make a fire in the stove to cook them. It was too hot, and she knew it would be too much for her. She took out a piece of cooked ham, cutting a thin piece off the bone. She sliced some bread and poured herself a glass of water. Her feet shuffling as she walked across the floor, she sat down to eat, although she didn't feel hungry at all. After a couple bites, she pushed the food back and sat thinking for a while. Everything seemed such an effort. She wondered where Caleb was and if he had come around to her way of thinking.

She rose slowly and took a piece of vellum from her desk. She could feel the pain in her chest again, but it was bearable. Hester sat down to write a missive to Caleb. She wrote slowly, but her words didn't look like her normal writing. It was quavery, and it made her angry. *Looks like an old woman's handwriting.*

It took her a while to finish it up, although she didn't write all that much. She picked up an envelope, and folding the letter with shaking fingers, she slid it in. She took a taper and lit it, melting a bit of wax to seal the flap. Her hand shook, and the pain in her chest nearly took her breath away.

She went to set it on the dresser in Caleb's room. She placed it carefully and all the sudden realized his room was empty. None of his clothes hung in the clothespress; the door had been left hanging open. She slowly looked around the room as it dawned on her that he was gone. He'd really left this time, as he'd threatened to do so many times before.

She felt a huge vise clamping her heart closed and clutched at her chest as the pain dropped her to her knees. Without a sound, she went down to the floor, still holding her chest, and then was still.

Buck's trusted people began their vigilant watch over the main road. Several days passed, and still nothing out of the ordinary occurred. Because it was so hot, each pair watched for only a couple hours a day. With the amount of manpower Buck had garnered, it was working out well, but Sheriff Buckmaster Rawlins was frustrated. He'd hoped to have seen some action early on. He wondered if it could be Terrence Kerrigan who was the shooter. He fit the bill as far as Buck could see. Also, there was the fact that Taylor had bragged to him about marrying Eden. Never, in all Buck's years as sheriff, had it taken him so long to solve a case. He took a deep breath to ease his irritation.

He turned into the lane of Sunrise Ranch, surprised to see Matthew's and Liberty's horses already tied up at the rail. It was still early.

They were all sitting in the great room. Hattie got up as soon as she saw him, and grabbing his arm, led him to the parlor.

"I need a kiss," she said, "and I want it private this time." She laughed up into his face.

"You're a real piece of baggage," he teased, "but I'll be glad to oblige." He swept her into his arms and kissed his fiancée most thoroughly. She returned his ardor in full measure.

"Five more days," he said. "Five more days and you'll be Mrs. Rawlins for all time."

"I can hardly wait. Eden and I have been busily sewing from morning till night, and now Liberty has offered to help and offered her grandmother's help as well. My dress is coming along quite nicely. Bertha helped me with invitations, and we've decided to have the wedding at her place. It's perfect for a wedding, don't you think?"

"Anywhere would be perfect. I love you, Hattie Hamilton. I love you so much!" He kissed her again.

"I love you back, Sheriff Rawlins. What a miracle this is, and I am so grateful for it. I suppose you know I am really an independent woman of independent means, and it most likely won't be easy for us to get along sometimes. I'll try my best, and I'm sure you will too."

"As long as we keep the Lord in the center of what we do, we shouldn't have too difficult of a time. I was thinking I'd like to take you out to see a piece of property that Jazzie and I picked out years ago. It's down the road from Bertha, and if it's amenable to you, I thought we could start building a house on it."

"Oh my, that sounds exciting. So much is happening so quickly. I've been praying you find the Chandlers' murderer so you can get on with your regular work."

"Thank you. I've been praying that way too. I also thought I'd like to take you over to the Bannisters' Rancho and see how you like their house. If you do, I'd like to pattern our house off their design. It's somehow elegant yet homey. It's hard to explain, but I think you'll see what I mean when you see it."

They kissed one more time before returning to the great room.

With a feeling of contentment, Liberty looked at Buck and Hattie as they entered the room. Hattie's face was rosy with happiness, and Buck seemed to glow with love. Ever since Liberty had met the sheriff, she'd felt sorry for him losing his wife the way he had. She'd taken a real shine to Hattie, who was little more than six years older than she was. She knew she'd have another friend who, at least for the time being, would live close.

The room was full of talk about the wedding, and there was much laughter and high spirits. Soon the subject changed to the business at hand. Buck began to relate his frustrations.

"I don't believe we're going to find out anything this way," he said. He took a sip of the elderberry juice Mrs. Jenkins handed him. "This hits the spot. Thank you."

"The problem is, I can't think of any other way to do this," Adam said. "We have no leads except the fact that there are cigar butts, but I've been thinking about that. Dr. John said he saw Harding and Stirling coming down from Eagles Bluff, where we found the butts. Both of them smoke cigars, so the butts may have no connection with the murderer unless they themselves are the culprits."

Buck looked at Adam, a light dawning in his eyes. "I never thought about that. So picking men to help us who don't smoke cigars may have been a wasted effort. We could have the murderer watching the road for us." He gave a bark of laughter that was self-deprecating.

Eden looked at Adam, knowing he could be right. *I'm actually beginning to really appreciate this man*, she thought. *He thinks things through and doesn't shoot off his mouth about things unless he knows about them.*

A loud knock sounded on the door, but the visitor didn't wait for Dorothy to answer it. The person let himself in. It was Dr. John, and he was sweating profusely. He grabbed at his hip pocket and wiped his forehead with his handkerchief.

"Just came from the McHaney's," he panted. "Hester's dead."

Eden gasped. "Oh no! Poor Caleb! Oh, this is horrible! Why would the murderer go after her?"

"No, no, I'm sorry, Eden. Didn't mean to upset you. Where *is* Caleb, anyway? Do you know? Hester had a heart condition, and I'm sure she died of a heart attack, but it had to have happened at least three days ago." He wiped his head again, and Dorothy handed him a glass of cold elderberry juice.

Matthew spoke up. "He said something to me about hiring on with my brother over in Sonoma. Maybe that's what he ended up doing."

"But he knew his mother was dying. I just told him the other day. Why would he light out like that when he knew she was so ill?"

Matthew stared at Dr. John but didn't say anything. He pressed his lips together.

Liberty knew that was a sure sign Matthew knew something about it, but it was negative information, and he wasn't about to share it.

Buck said easily into the silence, "You know when a man gets a hankering to make a change, it's a pretty powerful pull, no matter what your circumstances."

Eden said, "Caleb and his mother weren't getting along so well lately. He wouldn't tell me the reason. He just said living at home was becoming unbearable. Frankly, I've never cared for his mother that much. She was almost intimidating, but I am sorry she passed away. Caleb's going to feel guilty for not being there for her."

"Most likely he will," Dr. John said. "I knew her ticker was giving out. Rode out there last week and told Caleb right in front of her. She knew it, of course, but I had no idea she was this close." He shook his head ruefully. "I sure wish we knew more of how to help people. Medicine can only do so much, and there are so many things we don't know about the human body." He smacked his fist into his palm. "I always feel so inept when I can't help someone. I liked Hester. She was a strong-willed woman, but I liked her. She wasn't yet forty, you understand."

"I'm sorry, John," Liberty said with sympathy in her voice. "We all know you do the best you know how. Look how you helped Cabot, and if you hadn't tended Buck, he would have died. We couldn't do without you and your expertise. We know you keep up to date on the latest *New England Journal of Medicine* and the newest method of doing things. You couldn't do more than you do, and we're grateful for what you do."

It was silent for a moment. Dr. John, feeling humbled, bowed his head under the accolade.

"Thank you, Liberty. I needed that. Most of the time I just go from one thing to the next without time to think. This has hit me pretty hard. Hester had a rough life, and yet, so do a lot of other people. What causes a body to have heart problems? Perhaps one day we'll know." He wiped his forehead again with his handkerchief. "Why are you all gathered here anyway? Still looking for the shooter? Do you have any leads yet? Is it Stirling and Harding?"

"We don't know who it is, but your reporting of them has, hopefully, put us on the right track," Buck replied.

Before anyone could ask him questions, there was a strong knock on the door.

"I'll get it," Dorothy said, walking swiftly to the front foyer. She came back in a hurry with Joseph Woitt, the owner of Napa Mercantile. He was wringing his hat between his hands. Buck stood up in amazement. Joe was supposed to be on guard right now.

"You need to come quick, Sheriff! Stirling is atop Eagles Bluff, and Harding is coming down the road heading in that direction. I left John Johnson watching and came as quick as I could to tell you."

"Thanks, Woitt! Come on, boys," he said to the room at large. "We're going to Eagles Bluff."

"I'll pass," said Dr. John. "I think I've had enough excitement for one day, and I need to get someone to haul Hester's body into town. I'll get someone to ride over to Sonoma and notify Caleb. It's still early. Maybe I should do that myself."

Matthew, Adam, and Buck went to get their horses.

Gio saw Adam leading Locomotion out of her stall.

"Where are you going?" Gio asked.

"Harding and Stirling are meeting again on Eagles Bluff. We're going to go see just exactly what is going on," Adam replied. "Want to come?"

"I believe you have enough men. I don't think I'm needed, and there is much to be done around here. I've let things slide since Eldon's death. I do hope you find who murdered my best friend."

Adam nodded his head. "I hope we do too. Eden will have no peace of mind until we do." He finished saddling up and climbed on Locomotion. Joseph Woitt, Buck, and Matthew were already down the lane a ways, and Adam kicked Loco into a gallop, catching up in no time. As he approached, everyone kicked into a gallop and despite the heat rode at a hard pace, arriving at Eagles Bluff in short order.

Buck gestured for Matthew and Adam to circle the bluff and go up the steep track. He and Joe would ascend up the normal trail on the face of the bluff. Buck waited until he was certain Matthew and Adam were on their way up, before he started up the face of the bluff.

The four men arrived at the top at nearly the same time. Harding and Stirling were both shocked at the intense looks directed their way. Their faces registered total surprise.

"What's going on here?" Buck asked, authority ringing out in his voice. "What are you two up to?"

Reuben Stirling looked totally taken aback. Harding looked surprised but seemed to take a deep breath of relief.

"Reckon the jig's up," he said.

"And what jig would that be?" Buck asked, his voice heavy with sarcasm. "You boys kill the Chandlers?" he asked bluntly.

Shock now registered on Theo Harding's face.

"You think I had anything to do with that? No and no! Neither one of us had anything to do with that hellacious crime! How could you even think it?" Theo spoke in high dudgeon, clearly furious that Buck could think he had anything to do with killing Eldon and Camilla Chandler.

"What are you two up to?" Buck asked. "Look at you, Theo. You've lost weight in the last couple weeks, and by the looks of you, it seems to me you're not sleeping either. We know the two of you have met before, and we can't seem to come up with anything other than involvement with the crime. Whoever shot me did it from this bluff. You both seem suspect, to my way of thinking," Buck said curtly.

Stirling remained silent, but Theo took a deep breath and said, "We've had our reasons for meeting." He reached into his pocket and took out a huge bundle of greenbacks, handing them over to Stirling.

"There will be no more. I'll most likely tell Francis tonight and let the chips fall as they may." He turned to face the four men. "I first need to apologize to you, Matthew. As you must know by now, Reuben knows nothing about bookkeeping. Reuben Stirling is my son. I never married his mother, and although I knew it to be wrong, I gave her a bit of money and left her when she was expecting him. I didn't even know if she had a girl or a boy.

"When I met Francis, several years had gone by, and I thought the past would never catch up to me, but it did in the form of Reuben. He's threatened to tell Francis and anyone else in Napa who cares to hear. I've given him money and asked that he move on. There is nothing more here for him. Now that you all know, I'm sure he'll realize that."

Buck said, "I'm sorry, Theo, but we didn't know what to think." He turned toward Reuben. "Theo is right. You need to move on. If you ever show your face around these parts again, and I mean ever, I'll jail you for blackmail and throw away the key. Now get out!"

Reuben said, his voice full of sarcasm, "Thanks for the money, *Pops.* I'm sure it will see me living easy for a while. I won't be back. I actually didn't care about the money either. I simply wanted to know what kind of man my father was. Now I know. Good day," he said, tipped his hat, and rode down the side of the bluff.

"Whether you tell Francis or not is up to you, Theo. I just wish we'd have known it wasn't you before we wasted a lot of time and manpower waiting for you and Reuben to meet again. It also means we're back to square one."

Matthew said, "Perhaps we should start keeping an eye on Terrence Kerrigan."

"Well, they do seem to be the next best bet. I'll go around and tell the people they don't need to guard the main road anymore." He smacked the pommel of his saddle. "I thought we were going to solve this. Maybe we'll never know."

CHAPTER XXVIII

But I am poor and sorrowful: let thy salvation,
O God, set me up on high.

PSALM 69:29

THE SKY WAS SEAMLESS, not a cloud to be seen. No hint of a breeze raised a leaf or gave relief from the heat. The sun beat down merciless in its intensity. No one, not even the old-timers in the valley, could remember it being so hot. The road was dry, and dust lay heavy on the leaves of trees.

Dr. John rode to Sonoma. Being the hottest time of the day, he felt miserably hot. Sweat ran in runnels down his face, and he could feel it trickle down his chest. His shirt was stuck to his back. His inner thighs felt stuck to the leather of his saddle. He stopped and took another long drink from his canteen, brushing his sleeve across his forehead to remove the sweat.

Before he left Napa, he'd gotten Joe Woitt's brother, Keith, to go out to the McHaneys' to collect Hester's body. He'd told him she'd begun to really smell and to take a coffin and put her into it. Keith, although not a mortician, made a side business of making pine boxes. He'd been willing to help and rode out before Dr. John even left town.

Pulling into McCaully's, Dr. John knew it'd be late before he got home this day. He dismounted, and instead of tying up at the hitching post, he led his mount over to the side of the barn and let her drink from the trough. Leading her into the barn, which was a bit cooler, and into a stall, he removed her saddle and bridle. It was too hot to leave her saddled. Once his horse was taken care of, he made his way over to the house, knowing that most likely, Kirk and Caleb were out working somewhere on the ranch.

He knocked, and the housekeeper, Mrs. McDuffy, answered with hospitality. "Why Dr. John Meeks! It's been ages since I've seen you. Please, come on in. We've kept everything closed up, and it's much cooler in here than out there. Do come in." She closed the door hurriedly after he entered. "What brings you out to McCaully's? Er, McCaully-Bannister's?" She looked a bit flustered. "I'm sorry. We've been a bit off our regular schedule today." She raised a finger to her lips and whispered, "Miss Caitlin found out she's expecting a baby this morning." Her eyes sparkled with tears. "It seems no time at all that I helped deliver Miss Cait, and now here she is expecting a baby herself. We've all been surprised and ecstatic by the news."

"Well, I'll be sure to congratulate her if I see her."

"Before you say anything else, let me tell Duney to get you a drink of her ice-cold blackberry juice. Come on into the parlor." She bustled off to the kitchen and returned immediately. "Now, Dr. John, tell me why you're here." She gestured to a chair.

"I've been sitting for quite a spell, and if you don't mind, I'd rather stand. I came to find Caleb McHaney. Is he here at McCaully-Bannister's?" He pulled his handkerchief, which was beginning to look quite wilted, out of his pocket and dabbed at his head.

"Why, yes he is. Nice young man, isn't he? He arrived about four days ago. Mr. Kirk hired him on the spot, said he was a hard worker, and Ewen, who is foreman of the ranch, confirmed it."

"I've come with some really bad news for him. His mother passed away from a heart attack a few days ago, but she wasn't found until this morning when I rode out to check on her."

"Oh my, that's such a sad thing. She couldn't have been all that old. Caleb is quite young."

"Not yet forty, but she had a dicky heart."

Mrs. McDuffy said, "I'll see if I can round someone up to ride out and get him. Kirk will most likely ride back with you. I don't know though. He's been really busy. Please excuse me."

She went out the front door and walked over to the chow hall to talk to Gus, the man who cooked for the men.

When she entered, the two men talking at the table stopped in surprise. It was a rarity for a woman to be in the chow hall. Ewen stood, as did Rhys, a hired hand.

"What's the matter, Duffy? Something wrong?" Ewen's words were clipped. He was foreman of McCaully-Bannister Ranch, and by Duffy's presence, he knew something was wrong. He wondered if something might be the matter with Caitlin. She'd gone upstairs after lunch.

"Dr. John Meeks is here from Napa," she said succinctly. "He's here about the new hire, Caleb McHaney. His mother died of a heart attack, and Dr. John rode in to tell him. Do you think one of you could ride out and get him?"

"I can ride out there, Boss. I know where he's working," Rhys volunteered.

"Go," Ewen said, "but I wouldn't say anything to him. Just let him know he's wanted in the house. We'll let the doc break the news to him."

Rhys rose with alacrity, nodded his head to Mrs. McDuffy, and made his way out the door. He'd been with Caleb most of the morning and had taken a real shine to him. And it was true—he knew exactly where Caleb was working.

"Is Dr. John in the parlor?"

"Yes. He seems to be suffering with this heat," Duffy replied.

"Girl, we all are. It's just too blamed hot." He stood and stretched. "Reckon I'll go in with you and talk to Dr. John."

Caitlin had gone up to take a nap after lunch. She stretched hugely, and the realization that she was expecting a baby hit her afresh. *I am so excited! I can't wait until I tell Liberty. Won't she be surprised? Our babies won't be all that far apart.* Because it was so hot, she'd left her bedroom door open, and she heard voices.

She got up and straightened her blouse, checked her hair, and decided she still looked presentable. She made her way downstairs, surprised to see Dr. John there. Her first thought was that something might have happened to Liberty.

"Dr. John! How nice to see you. Is everything all right?"

"No, not really," he replied. "I'm waiting for Caleb McHaney to ride in. His mother passed away, and he needs to know." He stood in the middle of the parlor, looking out the front window, a glass of blackberry juice in his hand.

"Oh, how sad. I'm so sorry to hear that," Caitlin said and reached out a hand to shake Dr. John's. Nearly as tall as him, she looked him straight in the eyes.

He said, "I hear you have some very good news. Congratulations to you and, of course, Kirk. You know, we are expecting a baby too. Sally Ann is due next month. It'll be her second but my first. It is strange how many babies I've delivered, but having one's own is a different kettle of fish altogether. I fuss over Sally Ann as if there were no other women expecting a baby the world over." He smiled a little ruefully.

"Well, congratulations are in order for you too. I'm so excited, but I know I have a long wait."

Mrs. McDuffy came back in with Ewen, and the four talked together, waiting for Caleb to show up.

Rhys didn't ride out at a fast pace. It was far too hot. It took him a good half hour to get to the spot where Kirk, Caleb, and several other cowboys were cutting some of the early calves from their mamas. They were putting the weaned ones in a field far from the bunkhouse because they wanted to sleep at night, and for the first few nights it would be unbearably noisy.

Kirk saw Rhys first and paused to let him ride up.

Caleb had just thrown a lasso and snared the calf he was after. He was quite proud of his ability with a rope. He couldn't remember having so much fun.

Rhys rode up to Kirk and told him about Caleb's mother. Kirk's eyes flew to Caleb, and sorrow gripped his heart for the younger man. Caleb hadn't said much about leaving home, and Kirk knew better than to press him. Kirk knew Hester, not all that well, but he knew she could be a formidable woman when crossed. He'd seen it at a community potluck once.

Rhys said, "Ewen said not ta say anything to 'im and let the doc do it when he gets to the big house."

Kirk nodded in agreement. "I think this is going to take him pretty hard. I'll probably ride to Napa with him and be gone a few days for the funeral. I can stay at my brother's. I'll get Katie to go with me. She'll love seeing Liberty." He spoke his thoughts aloud to Rhys.

Rhys nodded. "It's always specially hard on a man to lose his mother." Kirk looked at him, a question in his eyes, but Rhys didn't volunteer any more information.

Kirk said, "I lost my mother to a boating accident when I was seventeen. They were on vacation, and the boiler blew. It was a shock and a real blow to me. Well, I reckon I'd better go tell him he's wanted in the house by Ewen."

He rode Fire over to where Caleb was.

Caleb saw him coming and stopped roping and waited.

"Rhys told me you're wanted up at the house. Ewen would like to talk with you."

Caleb's gut began to churn. *Either mother has taken a turn for the worse, or she's hunted me down and wants me to come home*, he thought. He nodded his head in acknowledgment and began wrapping his rope up.

"I'll ride in with you," Kirk said, his eyes friendly, as he too began to gather his rope up. He hung it over the pommel, same as Caleb, and the two men headed for the house. Rhys joined them. They rode in at a leisurely pace, and Kirk grieved for the younger man, sorry for the news he'd soon hear.

Rhys parted ways at the bunkhouse and said his good-byes to the other two.

Kirk and Caleb tied up their mounts, Kirk a bit surprised he didn't see Dr. John's horse tied up there.

They went into the house, and when Caleb saw Dr. John, his heart sank.

"Bad news?" he asked Dr. John.

"She passed away, Caleb, three or four days ago. I'm so sorry to have to tell you."

Caleb took a deep shuddering breath, and it was all he could do to hold the tears back. "I know you said she was bad off, but I didn't know she was that close to dying. I would'a stayed home and taken care of things. I reckon I'd seen her like that for some time, so when you told me she was dying, it was something I already knew, but I..." His voice quavered and trailed off.

"I'm sorry, son," Ewen said. "It's never an easy thing to have someone you love, die. My heart still grieves for Mac McCaully. You'll be needing to pack up a few things and get yourself back to Napa. Do you think you'll go back to farming, or will you come back?"

"I'll be back here, if you'll have me. I don't reckon I want to be a farmer. I'll probably sell the place up, which will take time. I'll get someone to do that for me. I'll plan to come back after the funeral, as soon as I get things straightened out," he said. He could feel the guilt beginning to press on him for not being there when she died. He looked over at Kirk, misery in his eyes.

Caitlin saw the look, and trying to divert his thoughts, she said, "Before you go, let me get you a drink, and we'll have a word of prayer, if that's all right with you?"

"Thank you. I'd appreciate it, in that order," he said.

Mrs. McDuffy went to the kitchen to tell Duney to get some more juice. Caitlin went to find Sweeney, her maid, to tell her to pack a few things. She knew Kirk would want to go with Caleb, and she wanted to see Liberty. She took the stairs two at a time and told Sweeney what she needed. "And pack at least one nice thing, please. I'm most likely going to the funeral."

The men sat down, and Caleb, his emotions raw, told the men why he'd left home. He told them about Hester pushing him to marry Eden Chandler and how she'd locked him out of the house, and for him it had been the last straw. "I feel so guilty knowing I left her when she must have needed me most. I...I..." He began to cry silently, the tears trailing down his browned face.

Dr. John said, "I knew your mother was a strong woman, but her heart just wasn't. It's not your fault, Caleb, for leaving. I didn't know her time was so near, either, and I'm a doctor. She could have lived a few more years. None of us know when our time is up. With a dicky heart, who really knows but the good Lord Himself? I'm serious, Caleb, when I say she could have lasted for a long time. Please don't blame yourself. You've done what you could, and at twenty-one, it's definitely time for you to make your own way, if that's what you wanted to do."

"Thanks, Dr. John. Reckon I needed to hear that." He wiped the tears with his shirtsleeve. Duney entered with a glass of juice for him, and he took it gratefully. He felt parched, and the tears clogged his throat. He drank half the glass without pause.

Caitlin came back down the stairs, and after patting Caleb on the back, she went to stand next to Kirk, who bowed his head.

"Let's pray," he said. "Lord, we don't understand the miracle of life's beginning, nor do we understand why death comes before we feel it's due. We do acknowledge Your wisdom and pray for strength for Caleb in the coming days. Grant him wisdom in the decisions he must make, grant peace to his heart, Lord, and please help him not to agonize over the what ifs that come to his mind. We know Your ways are higher than our ways, and Your thoughts than our thoughts. Help Caleb during this time of loss to focus on the good times and let the bad memories go. We ask this in Your peerless name. Amen."

"Thank you, Kirk," Caleb said gratefully. "I need to go get a few things from the bunkhouse, and I'll be ready shortly." He finished his glass of juice, and Caitlin held out her hand for the empty glass. Caleb strode to the door with mixed emotions but glad for the prayer Kirk had offered up. He went out, closing the door gently behind him.

Kirk said, "I need to get a few things together too." He headed up the stairs with Caitlin following him up to help Sweeney pack.

"I need to change out of my denims into something a bit more circumspect, don't you think, Mr. Bannister?"

He turned, and pulling his wife to himself, planted a kiss on her mouth. "We'll ride straight to the Rancho, so if you don't want to change, don't. No one there will be offended by your attire, and I like it." He grinned, and she grinned back at him.

"All right, I'll wear what I have on."

While everyone packed, Dr. John went out and saddled up his mare. By the time he was finished, all were ready to ride out.

They rode at a steady pace and talked as they traveled to Napa.

Dr. John informed them about Adam Brown and how Eldon and Camilla Chandler had written him into his will. They were shocked that he would do such a thing.

Caitlin voiced her opinion. "If my da had done such a thing, I'd be angry at him for all eternity, I think!"

Dr. John told them about the murders, but they knew about that, of course. Everyone for miles around had heard about the owners of Chandler Olives being gunned down.

"Has Buck gotten any leads? Does he have any suspects or any idea who did it?" Kirk asked.

"No, we have no idea, but Buck was shot and—"

"Buck was shot?" Kirk could scarcely believe it.

"Yes. If he hadn't turned in his saddle when he did, he'd be dead. As it was, he was shot right above his lung, and it went clean through. He's also engaged to marry Adam Brown's aunt, who came out west to be with her nephew. Love at first sight. I'd never credit such a thing if it hadn't happened to me personally. One look at Sally Ann, and all my previous thoughts of love flew out the window."

"You have all kinds of news, Dr. John!" Kirk exclaimed.

"You must keep this bit of information to yourself, but Theo Harding is one of Buck's suspects, as well as a man your brother hired a few weeks back, Reuben Stirling."

"Theo Harding? I don't believe it. He and Eldon were really close."

Dr. John then filled them in on how Buck had set up a system for guarding the road and seeing if they could catch whoever had been shooting off Eagles Bluff.

"I left when one Joe Woitt came riding into Sunrise and said Stirling had ridden to the top of Eagles Bluff and Harding looked to be meeting him there."

"Napa never seemed so interesting when I lived there," Kirk said with a grin. He sobered quickly as he glanced over at Caleb, who had listened to all the happenings.

Dr. John turned a bit in his saddle and said to Caleb, "I'll take care of the funeral arrangements if you like. I had Keith Woitt go out and get her body before I left to come here. You don't have to worry about that."

Caleb nodded. "Thanks, Dr. John. I'll probably ride to Sunrise and see if I can stay there for tonight. Don't think I feel up to going home right now. I'd appreciate it, too, if none of you say anything to Eden about my mother wanting me to marry her. She doesn't need any more stress, and the two of us are really good friends, but not romantically, that's for sure."

CHAPTER XXIX

Behold, how good and how pleasant it is
for brethren to dwell together in unity!

PSALM 133:1

THE EVENING WAS BEGINNING TO COOL OFF, and Adam and Gio stood on the porch of Sunrise Ranch, watching the sun go down. They'd enjoyed a delicious roast beef dinner and would have dessert a little later.

The western sky was streaked with red. The sun set the hills afire with its glow and was going down over the horizon. The beautiful sight signaled that the next day would most likely be as hot as this one.

"Thanks for filling me in on all the happenings on Eagles Bluff. Strange, isn't it? I'll bet Eldon never even knew about Theo having a son. Wonder if he'll tell his wife about it? I think I wouldn't," Gio said. "What was done in the past doesn't always predict the way a man will act in the future. I believe Theo Harding to be an honorable man today. Many times we don't allow for change in someone else, do we?"

"No, we don't, not even Christians. We categorize people and never allow for the work of the Holy Ghost in their lives. Many times we don't really know what forgiveness, salvation, and restoration look like, do we? We put someone in a box and don't allow for the power of God to get them out of that box, to change them from a heart of rebellion to a heart saved by grace. I reckon sometimes we put God in that box too, and think He only acts in the way we think He should."

Adam rambled on some more because he didn't know how to broach to Gio what was on his heart. Finally, he just came out and said it.

"Giovanni, I don't know exactly how to go about saying this, but how would you feel if I began to court Eden? What I mean to say is, I have come to have strong feelings for her, but she, I know, needs to mourn. I wouldn't be overt about it, not just yet, but…" Words failed Adam, and he simply looked openly at Giovanni.

Gio was having a difficult time trying to keep his face free from a smile or a grin, although his insides strummed a melody.

"I understand what you are saying, Adam. Do you feel her feelings for you have changed?"

"With no reservations I can say a resounding yes. Her feelings for me have changed drastically since Aunt Hattie came here. I can't say she has any romantic feelings for me, but she doesn't hate me anymore, and several times I've seen a look of admiration in her eyes. I reckon I'd like to have your stamp of approval on this, to court her, I mean."

"You not only have my stamp of approval, Adam Morgan Brown, you have Eldon and Camilla Chandler's stamp of approval too."

Adam looked at him quizzically. "What do you mean by that?"

"What I mean by that is the whole reason half of Sunrise Ranch was deeded over to you was that Eldon picked you out to have as a son-in-law. Had either of you married before his death, he would have changed his will and you would have been cut out of it."

Adam was stunned. "You're telling me that Eldon wanted me to marry Eden?"

"Yes, so much so he deeded half his estate to make sure you two met if something untoward happened to him."

"Well, now that is a mystery cleared up for me. I can see why you never said anything, and most likely that's still a good way to proceed where Eden is concerned. She's fragile, and I wouldn't want her to feel any pressure or feel she has to ward me off. We'll just keep this our secret, shall we?"

"Certainly, Adam. After all, you are the boss," Gio said with a wide grin.

The two men continued to talk, Adam becoming more and more aware that Giovanni was a wise man. Adam was grateful that God put him here at Sunrise Ranch. It'd been a long time since he'd enjoyed the companionship of another man. He'd not had a father since he was eleven years old, and Gio had every characteristic that Adam could admire in a man.

It was starting to get dark, but the deepness of it hadn't settled down yet. The two men on the porch could see a lone rider coming down the lane. Only the darker silhouette against the lighter color of the hills behind him alerted them to his presence.

Gio recognized him first. "Hello, Caleb, welcome to Sunrise Ranch," he called out.

Caleb raised his hand in greeting, and when he got closer, he asked, "Got a place where a body could sleep tonight? I could go on home, but emotionally I don't feel up to it tonight."

"Certainly, we have plenty of room," Adam said. Both he and Gio walked down the steps and greeted the bereft young man.

"Let me take your horse. Pepe's in the barn and will put her to bed for you." He took the reins, and Caleb lifted his satchel off the pommel.

"Thank you, Mr. Coletti. I appreciate it."

Gio nodded at him and led the horse into the barn.

Adam said, "I'm so sorry about your mother, Caleb. She was too young to have such a bad heart. Do you have any relatives that need to be notified?"

"Mother has a sister in Montana. I'll get a cable off to her tomorrow. I thank you for your hospitality. Dr. John told me Keith Woitt was to collect my mother's body. He is also watering and feeding the horse, the cow, and our chickens. I simply didn't feel like facing the empty house tonight. Thanks for letting me stay here."

"You're welcome to stay here until you decide what you want to do. I don't suppose you've had anything to eat. I'll get Berry to heat you up some leftover dinner. Come on in, Caleb, and consider us family."

Caleb followed Adam up the steps, and the bright lights of the lamps in the front entry seemed strange after the darkness outside.

Eden walked up to Caleb and hugged him. "Oh, Caleb, what sorrow you must have in your heart. I am so sorry. If there's anything I can do, please let me know." She held his face in her hands and stared into his heartbroken eyes. "Come into the kitchen, and we'll get you something to eat."

Adam and Caleb followed Eden into the kitchen, and Gio came in to join them. Caleb related to them all the joy working on McCaully-Bannister Ranch brought to his heart.

"I can't remember when I've felt so content," he said. "Except for worrying that I may have caused my mother heartache by leaving home, I have loved every minute I've been working at McCaully-Bannister's. Kirk is a good boss and lets you know exactly what is expected of you. You would think his foreman, Ewen Carr, was his father, the way he cares about Kirk. I like being with the other men in the bunkhouse, although one is a loud snorer and kept me awake half the night, until I took my bedroll and pillow and went over to the chow hall to sleep." He smiled tiredly. "Thanks for letting me stay here tonight. I just may take you up on sleeping here until I go back to Sonoma. I'll work around the house and get things in order, get rid of the chickens and the cow. I'll take the paint horse with me back to Sonoma. She's a real good horse and a pleasure to ride."

Dr. John, Kirk, and Caitlin waved a good-bye to Caleb as he turned into the wide lane to Sunrise Ranch. They rode on toward Rancho Bonito and town.

"I had no idea Hester was so difficult," Dr. John said. "I suppose there are a lot of people who live in misery, and no one else knows because everything looks good on the surface. I remember a few years back, this couple I saw in church every Sunday. Found out later the man beat his wife on a regular basis, but you'd never know, the way they smiled and talked on Sunday. There's a lot of evil in this world, isn't there?"

"Yes," Kirk said, "there is. What we need to remember as Christians is that no matter how bad it gets, Jesus wins in the end. He is Lord and in control. Liberty's stepfather and first husband were so evil it would beggar belief. She said she simply lived one day at a time and God gave her the grace to do so. God's grace is an amazing thing."

Caitlin said, "Looks like we're here. It was nice seeing you, Dr. John, and I'm sure we'll be seeing you at the funeral."

They said their farewells, and Dr. John Meeks rode for home at a faster clip, a very tired man.

In total darkness Kirk and Caitlin started up the long lane to Matthew and Liberty's Rancho Bonito. Both were excited. They wanted to support Caleb, but they enjoyed visiting with Matthew and Liberty.

"There's nothing quite like family when the relationships are what they're supposed to be, is there?" Kirk asked.

"No, I don't reckon there is. I don't take my sisters for granted anymore, that's for sure," Caitlin replied. "I went too long with a broken relationship with Aidan, and I'm so thankful we have made up and are the best of friends."

The house was lit up as if a party were in progress, and Kirk's eyes stung a bit with the memories of living here. Kirk had never met Donny, who walked up as they pulled up in front of the barn.

"Hello, I'm Donny Miller. Welcome to Rancho Bo— Well, I'll be jiggered!" he said. "You must be Matthew's brother, Kirk. My, you do look like him, don't you?"

Kirk grinned and Caitlin said, "Kirk looks a lot like Matthew. Thank you for your welcome." She stuck out her hand to shake his. "I must caution you—don't get too close to the stallion. He doesn't take to strangers much."

Kirk came around the stallion, Fire, and shook Donny's hand. "I'll just take him to the far stall and get him ready for bed," he said. Turning to Caitlin, he said, "Honey, go ahead in. I know you're excited to see Liberty to give her our news."

Donny took Queenie's reins, but Kirk walked ahead of him, leading Fire down to the far stall to brush him down, but more to keep him away from other horses or from being disturbed.

Caitlin headed up the flagstone walkway and didn't even knock. She opened the door and yelled, "Yoo-hoo! You've got company!"

Liberty jumped up from a deep leather chair and strode swiftly to Caitlin. "Oh, Cait, oh I'm so glad you're here! Where's Kirk?"

Matthew joined Liberty, and after giving his sister-in-law a hug, he strode out to the stable to welcome his brother.

Caitlin, after hugging Liberty, said, "You'll never guess! Kirk and I are expecting! I'm so excited! Oh, Liberty, our little ones will be close in age."

Liberty hugged Caitlin again and said, "Congratulations, Mrs. Bannister!" The two women grinned, and Liberty led Caitlin to the kitchen, where Conchita was heating up some chicken enchiladas for Kirk and Caitlin.

"You welcome, Mees Caitlin. I am happy to see you." Conchita hugged Caitlin, the top of Conchita's head breast high.

Liberty smiled, looking on. She was always happy to have company, but family was special.

It was early but already warm, having never cooled off much during the night, which was unusual for Napa. Windows were closed and drapes drawn by Dolly and Dorothy as soon as the occupants of the bedrooms were up.

Caleb awoke slowly and felt disoriented for a few seconds, wondering why he didn't hear the sounds of other men sleeping around him. He came fully awake as reality crashed in. He lay thinking about his mother, assessing his feelings. He could not remember a time when she'd been affectionate to him, never a hug or kiss on the cheek. She'd never pushed him about Eden until his father died. That's when their relationship had begun to deteriorate. *Truth to tell, I feel guilty because I feel free. I'm glad Dr. John will be taking care of the arrangements for the funeral. I wouldn't even know how to go about it.* He stretched and decided to get up.

He'd been surprised the night before to see one of the new flush toilets installed inside a little room that ran the length of the dressing room.

Dressing quickly, he stuffed his personal items back into the satchel just in case he didn't spend the night here again. He thought he would though. Just the thought of going home right now, for some reason, made his stomach churn. He was so sorry to recall the last words his mother had spoken to him: *After all I've done for you, Caleb, you could at least set my mind to rest and marry Eden Chandler. Children are supposed to obey their parents, so what kind of Christian does that make you, son?* She had sneered at him, shooed him out the door, and locked it. *Well, crying over spilt milk isn't going to make it any better. I'm just thankful I didn't say anything to her that I regret.* He took a deep breath, trying to calm the mixed feelings about his mother, and with satchel in hand, he went down to breakfast.

Eden was already there, fully dressed and waiting for him.

"Good morning, Caleb. I thought I'd ride to your house with you. I could help with whatever you need to do. We can bring your paint horse over here, and the cow even. You have quite a few chickens, but I'm sure they can be easily taken off your hands. There's a lot of people always wanting chickens."

Caleb, with tears in his eyes, said, "Thank you, Eden, I appreciate it. For some reason my stomach starts hurting just thinking of going home by myself. It won't be so bad with my best friend with me." He smiled affectionately at her.

"Well, we've both been through a bad patch and can only hope things will get better from now on."

Adam had been out in one of the sheds, as Gio was teaching him the rudiments of growing olives. He hadn't had breakfast and stopped at the great room door, seeing Caleb and Eden talking.

"Sorry," he said. "I hope I'm not interrupting anything. I can come back later, if need be."

Caleb replied, "No, not at all. Eden surprised me by volunteering to come help me pack up the house. You're welcome to come too, if you'd like."

Adam glanced at Eden and saw a flush starting up her neck as she gazed back at him. "What do you think, Eden? Do you want some time alone with your friend, or is it all right if I tag along?"

"You're more than welcome. You can drag his cow to Sunrise Ranch." She laughed, and the two men joined in.

"Have you two eaten yet?"

"I have. Caleb has not. Help yourselves, and I'll get you men some coffee." She headed over to the stove, where Berry handed her two steaming mugs of coffee.

"Thanks, Berry."

Adam and Caleb dished themselves up from a long sideboard ladened with breakfast food. Adam poured a glass of orange juice and went over to sit, and Eden sat beside him.

"I know you are just beginning to work a bit with Gio, but I think it's a good idea for you to come with us. Caleb...ah...Caleb and his mother didn't always see eye to eye, and his tummy's in a bit of a turmoil, going to their house. You would be a stabilizing presence." Her face was bland, but the blood had begun to climb up and into her cheeks at Adam's continued perusal of her face.

All the sudden, Caleb realized the quietness that had ensued, and as he went back to the table, his glance happened upon Eden.

Ah...she's finally found her man. He grinned inwardly at the look he'd seen exchanged between the two of them, who seemed totally oblivious to anything going on around them. *Well, mother wouldn't have been happy with that, would she? I am, though. I am very happy to see Eden fall in love with a man who will take care of her the way she deserves. Wonder if I'll ever find someone. As I said to mother, I'm far too young to marry yet. I've got things I want to do before I settle down.*

The moment was broken, but Eden knew where her heart now lay. There was great satisfaction in the knowing—relief even. She wasn't sure how Adam felt, but if the look he'd just given her was anything to go on, she had a pretty good idea. She was learning how to pray, to have her inner thoughts always shared with God. She thanked God for His love. She thanked Him for setting things in place. What was amazing was she could say with her whole heart, "Thank you, Father, for Adam."

She stared down at her coffee, no outward signs that her heart was singing a melody that sounded like a full orchestra. Eden was in love, with all the excitement of this new knowledge within her.

It wasn't long before the two men finished eating. They headed over to the McHaneys' house at a canter. The thought crossed Adam's mind that they'd make a good target for the shooter, but he shrugged his shoulders, knowing he was in God's hands. It wasn't long before the three arrived safely at the McHaneys'.

They first went to the barn, taking care of the horse and cow. Caleb milked it while Adam and Eden put a saddle and other things that Caleb could use or sell into a wagon bed.

Finally the three went into the house.

Everything appeared in order, and there wasn't much that Caleb wanted. There was a daguerreotype of his father and one of Hester and another of the two together. He carefully wrapped them up, placing them in a satchel. He was surprised that there was so little that he wanted. He went to his room to get a couple blankets and saw the letter on his dresser in his mother's hand, although it looked jittery. He picked it up but handed it to Eden.

Eden started to break the seal, but instead she handed it to Adam.

He opened the envelope and asked if Caleb wanted him to read it aloud, but Caleb shook his head.

"Just tell me if there's anything I need to know," he said.

Adam quickly perused the letter, and clearing his throat, he said, "Not much. She knew she was dying and, uh, she wanted you to sell the house and anything you can't use. She ends it saying she is sorry."

Caleb sighed and said, "Thanks, Adam."

"Do you want this?" Adam asked.

"No, you can throw it away. I wouldn't keep it anyway. I'm just glad she apologized. It makes me feel a bit better," Caleb replied.

Adam turned and went back to the living room to give Caleb and Eden time to talk, but they both followed him out.

Caleb said, "There isn't a thing here I want. I got the deed out of the buffet, and I'm thinking I'm just going to deed the property over to Keith Woitt. His brother, Joseph, owns the mercantile store in Napa. He's been helping Keith out, but Keith lives in a very small house, and his family is growing. I don't need any more money than what I'm earning right now at McCaully-Bannister's. I'll be glad to be done with this and move on with my life." He turned the chickens loose, knowing they could fend for themselves.

They rode back to Sunrise with the cow and horse both tied to the wagon and Caleb's mare pulling it. It was slow going and felt slower because of the heat beating down. When they arrived at Sunrise Ranch, Dr. John and Buck were there.

"The funeral is tomorrow," Dr. John said, "and Bertha said she'll have a small luncheon afterwards. I've notified everyone I've seen, and Bertha will send her man out to tell people. Perhaps someone here could let the Bannisters and others know."

Eden said, "I'll get one of the boys on it right away. Exactly what time is the funeral?"

"Eleven tomorrow morning. In this heat…well, it's a closed casket," he said a little ruefully.

"That's fine by me," Caleb said. "When I die, I want a closed casket too, and I don't want a wake either. Just let me die in peace, and put me in a pine box."

EPILOGUE

*Then shall the virgin rejoice in the dance, both young men
and old together: for I will turn their mourning into joy,
and will comfort them, and make them rejoice from their sorrow.*

JEREMIAH 31:13

ADAM GESTURED TO BUCK, who was sitting close to Hattie. He
got up and followed Adam up to his room. Adam closed the door quietly
after them.

"What's up, Adam? Why all the secrecy?"

"Take a look at this, Buck." He pulled the letter out of his breast
pocket. "Caleb didn't want to read this letter from his mother. He told
me just to tell him what it said. I told him she said she knew she was
dying, and she wanted him to sell the house and anything he couldn't
use, and that she ended it saying she was sorry." He handed the sheet
of vellum to Buck, who sat down in an easy chair to read the missive
that was Caleb's.

Caleb,

I know I'm not going to be able to talk to you again, thus this letter. I'm dying.

First of all, I wasn't your real mother. Your father had been married before. His first wife died, and I married him about six months later. One of the conditions was that he never was to tell you I wasn't your real mother. I thought to have children, but never did. I tried to do right by you, but I don't reckon with my temperament I was the best mother to you. I want you to sell the house and anything else you don't want.

I don't believe you will marry Eden Chandler now. When I yelled at you, after all the things I'd done for you, I meant it. I did a lot of things for you, Caleb. I was tired of being a pinchpenny and so I devised a plan. I killed the Chandlers and tried for the sheriff and Taylor Kerrigan. Eldon and Camilla never liked me, and I knew they'd thwart my plans for you with their hoity-toity ways. You wouldn't have a chance to marry Eden with them alive. The sheriff was a mistake. I didn't like him snooping around. He never did find anything that would lead to me. I tried for Taylor Kerrigan because that Eden kept seeing him. He's quite a good-looking man. I wanted you to marry Eden Chandler—we'd never have to worry about money again. You are the reason I failed. You are the reason nothing has worked out for me, and you are the reason I'm dying before my time. You've been nothing but a noose around my neck and a rebellious young man since your pa died. I'm right sorry I ever knew you.

Hester McHaney

"Whew! Unbelievable, isn't it?" Buck sat drumming his fingers on the arm of the chair. "You did some fast thinking, Adam. I'm proud of the way you handled this. Not telling Caleb the real gist of the letter is, I believe, better. He would end up having a strained relationship with Eden, knowing Hester killed her parents. They've always been good friends, and I'd hate to see that change. I think the fewer people who know about this, the better. I think it's only fair that Eden is told since it was her parents and would close the chapter, so to speak, in a book that needs an end." He sighed. "What a wicked, wicked woman."

"When I read it, I was stunned. I prayed quickly and decided to tell Caleb what I told you. As far as I am concerned, he doesn't ever need to know the rest of it."

"All right," Buck said heavily. "Do you want to tell Eden, or shall I?"

"You tell her, Buck. You're the sheriff. In fact, I think you should probably tell the Bannisters and Bertha. Anyone else is up to you. I'll tell Elijah Humphries the next time I see him."

"I'll tell Dr. John too," Buck said. "He deserves to know the truth, and I'll probably tell Theo and set his mind at rest. I have a feeling he thinks Stirling may have done it."

People milled around Bertha's backyard, plates loaded with food. Good conversation interspersed with laughter signaled happy guests.

Hester's funeral, two days before, had been sparsely attended. It surprised Caleb that she had so few friends. Eden had stuck close by his side throughout the ordeal, and they'd had a luncheon in the dining room at Bertha's, but very few people stayed for it. He was thankful for Eden and her friendship. Caleb planned to leave for McCaully-Bannister along with Caitlin and Kirk within the hour.

The atmosphere today was so different from the other day. Joy permeated the air. People from miles around had come to see their beloved sheriff marry. Chairs dotted the lawn under a canopy of tree leaves or canvas. It had cooled a bit but was still warm for early July.

Buck had talked to Eden right after his conversation, three days before, with Adam. She had cried but had been thankful to know who had killed her parents and why.

Eden determined never to tell Caleb about it. She agreed with Buck that it would destroy Caleb and his relationship with her. Buck told her he would swallow his pride as a sheriff and never let on that the case had been solved.

Hattie glowed with contentment and joy. Liberty stood talking to her along with Phoebe, Caitlin, and Abigail Humphries. Hattie regaled her listeners with anecdotes of happenings at Sunrise Ranch, and much laughter ensued.

Buck and Hattie were leaving for San Francisco for their honeymoon. Single women gathered, waiting for her to toss her bouquet. She had planned to forego this custom since it originally was a bouquet of garlic and herbs to ward off evil spirits, and she didn't go for that kind of folderol. Bertha had convinced her that the modern attitude was just fun. It symbolized that the girl who caught it would be the next bride. Several girls were waiting for the toss, and Hattie, her back turned to them, threw it over her head as hard as she could.

It flew over the heads of the waiting girls and thumped Eden on her ear. She was talking to Adam. She picked it up in surprise, looked back at Hattie, whose hand was covering her laugh, and saw shock among the girls who didn't have a chance to catch it. Several people clapped.

Adam, with laughter in his eyes, asked, "Will you marry me, Eden?"

"Yes! Oh, Adam, must we wait a whole year for mourning?"

"No, but we'll wait six months. How does that sound?"

Eden leaned in for a quick kiss to seal the pledge. Amid some gasps at her behavior and clapping and laughter from others, Adam pulled her to him and deepened the kiss.

CADY'S RESOLVE

(PREVIEW AND PROLOGUE)

Many will be purged, purified and refined,
but the wicked will act wickedly;
and none of the wicked will understand,
but those who have insight will understand.

DANIEL 12:10

RAIN BEAT HEAVILY ON THE TIN roof of the small cabin. It was little more than a shack. The wind cavorted, and the torrent slashed at every side of the one-room house. It poured off the eaves, making a rill of water surrounding the small structure. The noise inside was deafening as the deluge pounded at the tin. It was bone cold, and Cadence shivered under the thin, ragged quilt. When the wind suddenly abated, she heard drops of water hitting the buckets. The roof leaked, and the dampness seemed to cling to her. Her feet felt like blocks of ice.

What a misery, she thought as tears slipped in silent rivulets down her cheeks. She shivered and lay there in a ball, trying to get warm but knowing she wouldn't.

The cabin was cold and dank, the wood soaked from days of unending rain. She'd tried again and again to get the fire started, but she couldn't get the wet wood to burn. Shivering uncontrollably, her teeth chattered as nervousness added to the shivering. Pa should be back anytime now, she thought as she huddled under the blanket, wondering if she should leave or wait until the rain stopped. *I've been beaten before. Reckon I can stand it again. I don't think it's going to stop raining. I may as well head out now while it's dark.* The cold crawled up her spine and into her heart.

Her younger brother had died a week and a half before while she lay tired and worn by the fever that raged within her own body. Her mother had cropped her hair short as a boy's in an effort to cool her down as the fever mounted. While she lay recovering, her mother had taken sick as well. Not able to fight off the hot fever, her ma had succumbed to it before a week was gone, her life snuffed out. Cadence sobbed as she thought of her mother. *Maybe she hadn't wanted to get better. I know how much she loved Timmy, always trying to protect him from Pa's fists.*

She uncurled her body and sat up, wiping her face on the tattered quilt. She spoke aloud, "My satchel's ready. Think I'd better get out now before Pa gets back."

No sooner had the idea been formulated and spoken, when she heard him outside the door. She shivered violently and curled up again, trying to relax and act as though she were asleep.

Cadence peeked from under the thin quilt as he burst through the front door, kicking it shut behind him. He stood there listing a bit, nearly dropping a satchel he held in his hand. Thoroughly soaked from his ride home from the tavern, he looked toward the hearth. He stood swaying as he surveyed the one-room shanty. Cadence could smell him reeking of alcohol and garlic, but she stopped peeking when she saw him stomp toward her bed in the corner.

He started to grab Cadence by her hair, but it was shorn too short. He dropped the satchel and yanked her out of the small bed, dragging her onto the cold floor.

"Where's my fire, Cadence Cassidy? Why ha'ent you got a fire goin', huh?" he yelled as he looked down at her. "You lazy girl!" He drew back his leg and kicked her hard, but she rolled as his boot hit, and it wasn't as severe as it could have been. She grunted from pain and started to get up, but enraged, he kicked her again. She wasn't prepared for it. Her head snapped back, and she lay perfectly still, not wishing to incite him further.

Pulling her off the bed had removed the threadbare quilt that had covered her small satchel. He swayed as he saw it. He opened it, and Cadence drew in a painful breath as he noted aloud her meager belongings—"Clothes, a couple rags, and a hairbrush." He threw it across the room.

"Ah," he said, "gonna light out on me, huh? I'll show you!" In a rage, he kicked the dropped satchel under the bed, tied her ankle to the bedpost, and then fell onto the bed himself, leaving Cadence on the cold floor as he sank into a drunken stupor.

Cadence lay shivering and freezing cold. She felt carefully down her side, deciding no ribs were broken, although her side was painful to touch. *Maybe that one's cracked*, she thought. She was thankful she'd rolled with his kick. Her jaw was another matter. It was stiff, swollen, and very sore. She sat up with a groan before recalling that her pa had tied her to the bed. She knew in his state of drunkenness he wouldn't awaken for hours.

I've been seventeen for two months. I've put up with this for seventeen long years, but no more. With Mama and Timmy gone, there's no reason to stay.

Sidling closer to the bed, she felt under it for her small keepsakes case. Her hand felt nothing, and a small panic ensued before she remembered she'd moved it up behind the leg of the bed so her pa wouldn't find it. As she slid her hand further up, she connected with something else. *What's this?*

Cadence pulled out a beautifully tooled red leather satchel that was folded in half. Surprise filled her as she opened it and drew out some banknotes and a thickly folded bunch of papers. She unfolded it but realized it was too dark to see what the papers said. She couldn't read very well anyway. She didn't have time to waste, so she jammed the notes and papers back into the satchel. Breathing a sigh of relief, she felt her case right where she'd put it. She pulled it out from under the bed. Opening it, she drew out a small piece of broken mirror. With a diligence born of fear, she sawed at the rope that tied her fast to the bed.

Learn more about *Cady's Resolve* at:
www.maryannkerr.com

My books can be purchased on Amazon
My website: www.maryannkerr.com (signed copy)
Inklings Bookshop, Yakima, WA
Songs of Praise in Yakima, WA
Or by writing me at:
Mary Ann Kerr
10502 Estes Road
Yakima, WA (I charge no tax, sign the book, and the cost of
shipping priority mail is $6.49) (Media rate is ($4.00)

My public e-mail is: hello@maryannkerr.com where you can also
order a book.
You may message me on Facebook page: Mary Ann Kerr
(comments are welcome!)
When readers take the time to write or e-mail me their experience
reading my stories, I sometimes put their comments on my blog if
they don't mind.

Liberty's Inheritance	(sale price. . . . . $14.99)
Liberty's Land	(sale price. . . . . $14.99)
Liberty's Heritage	(sale price. . . . .$14.99)
Caitlin's Fire	(sale price. . . . . $14.99)
Tory's Father	(full price. . . . . $14.99)
Eden's Portion	(full price. . . . . $14.99)

Books by Peter A. Kerr (my author son)

Adam Meets Eve (nonfiction)—$10.00 + 5.65 shipping and handling
The Ark of Time (science fiction)—$12.00 + $5.65 shipping and handling

Book by Andrew Kerr (my author son and my cover and design guy)

Ants on Pirate Pond (children's black-and-white chapter book with darling
illustrations)—12.95 + $5.65 shipping and handling